Praise for J.

The Casual Vacancy

"*The Casual Vacancy* is a complete joy to read.... A stunning, brilliant, outrageously gripping and entertaining evocation of British society today."
—Henry Sutton, *Mirror* (UK)

"Rowling is most definitely a masterful storyteller.... *The Casual Vacancy* evolves into a scorching satire.... A page-turner." —Laura Miller, *Salon*

"A big, ambitious, brilliant, profane, funny, deeply upsetting, and magnificently eloquent novel of contemporary England, rich with literary intelligence.... This is a deeply moving book by somebody who understands both human beings and novels very, very deeply." —Lev Grossman, *Time*

"*The Casual Vacancy* is sometimes funny, often startlingly well observed.... Jane Austen herself would admire the way Rowling shows the news of Barry's death spreading like a virus around Pagford."
—Allison Pearson, *The Telegraph* (UK)

"A vivid read with great, memorable characters and a truly emotional payoff.... Rowling captures the humanity in everyone, even if that humanity is not always a pretty sight." —Elizabeth Gleick, *People*

"A study of provincial life with a large cast and multiple interlocking plots, drawing inspiration from Elizabeth Gaskell and George Eliot.... *The Casual Vacancy* immerses the reader in a richly peopled, densely imagined world."
—Theo Tait, *The Guardian* (UK)

"Rowling does a nice job laying out her twenty-plus characters' endless pretensions and weaknesses, which she punctures with gleeful flicks of a surprisingly sharp comic blade." —Rob Brunner, *Entertainment Weekly*

"An insanely compelling page-turner.... *The Casual Vacancy* is a comedy, but a comedy of the blackest sort, etched with acid and drawn with pitch....Rowling proves ever dexterous at launching multiple plot lines that roar along simultaneously, never entangling them except when she means to. She did not become the world's bestselling author by accident. She knows down in her bones how to make you keep turning the pages."   —Malcolm Jones, *Daily Beast*

"Rowling remains one of the funniest writers in the English language."
                                                        —Dan Kois, *Slate*

"This book represents a truckload of shrewdness....There were sentences I underlined for the sheer purpose of figuring out how English words could be combined so delightfully....Genuinely moving."   —Monica Hesse, *Washington Post*

"There are plenty of pleasures to be had in *The Casual Vacancy*....Parts of the story would be tonally of a piece with any Richard Price or Dennis Lehane novel, or an episode of *The Wire*."   —Steve Daly, *Parade*

"Rowling takes a near-Victorian pleasure in sketching out the novel's enormous cast of characters and showing how their very different lives intersect....Rowling's real skills lie in quick, cutting portraits of grown-up hypocrites and eccentrics, and in making the troubles and worries of adolescents feel as grave and important as those of their parents."
                                              —Nathan Whitlock, *Toronto Star*

"J.K. Rowling's contribution to literature has always been to remind us why we love reading in the first place, and *The Casual Vacancy* continues the cause....An old-fashioned novel in the tradition of Dickens or his modern-day counterpart Jonathan Franzen....When you finish, there's no denying that you have been told a story by someone who knows just what she's doing."   —Christine Pivovar, *Kansas City Star*

"In *The Casual Vacancy,* Rowling transports us to a dark contemporary version of George Eliot's village of Middlemarch, an outwardly pretty place with cobblestones and flower pots and a populace that slowly reveals itself to be seething with folly and ambition, marital and class tensions....A positively propulsive read."   —Meghan Cox Gurdon, *Wall Street Journal*

J.K. ROWLING

The Casual Vacancy

BACK BAY BOOKS

LITTLE, BROWN AND COMPANY

NEW YORK BOSTON LONDON

Back Bay Books / Little, Brown and Company
Hachette Book Group
1290 Avenue of the Americas, New York, NY 10104
littlebrown.com

Originally published in hardcover by Little, Brown and Company, September 2012
Published simultaneously in Great Britain by Little, Brown Book Group, September 2012
First Back Bay paperback edition, July 2013

Back Bay Books is an imprint of Little, Brown and Company. The Back Bay Books name and logo are trademarks of Hachette Book Group, Inc.

The publisher is not responsible for websites (or their content) that are not owned by the publisher.

The Hachette Speakers Bureau provides a wide range of authors for speaking events. To find out more, go to hachettespeakersbureau.com or call (866) 376-6591

ISBN 978-0-316-22853-4 (hc) / 978-0-316-22858-9 (pb) / 978-0-316-26561-4 (media tie-in pb) / 978-0-316-22854-1 (large print)
Library of Congress Control Number 2012943788

10 9 8 7 6 5 4 3 2 1

RRD-C

Printed in the United States of America

To Neil

Part One

6.11 A casual vacancy is deemed to have occurred:

(a) when a local councillor fails to make his declaration of acceptance of office within the proper time; or

(b) when his notice of resignation is received; or

(c) on the day of his death...

Charles Arnold-Baker
Local Council Administration,
Seventh Edition

Sunday

Barry Fairbrother did not want to go out to dinner. He had endured a thumping headache for most of the weekend and was struggling to make a deadline for the local newspaper.

However, his wife had been a little stiff and uncommunicative over lunch, and Barry deduced that his anniversary card had not mitigated the crime of shutting himself away in the study all morning. It did not help that he had been writing about Krystal, whom Mary disliked, although she pretended otherwise.

"Mary, I want to take you out to dinner," he had lied, to break the frost. "Nineteen years, kids! Nineteen years, and your mother's never looked lovelier."

Mary had softened and smiled, so Barry had telephoned the golf club, because it was nearby and they were sure of getting a table. He tried to give his wife pleasure in little ways, because he had come to realize, after nearly two decades together, how often he disappointed her in the big things. It was never intentional. They simply had very different notions of what ought to take up most space in life.

Barry and Mary's four children were past the age of needing a babysitter. They were watching television when he said good-bye to them for the last time, and only Declan, the youngest, turned to look at him, and raised his hand in farewell.

Barry's headache continued to thump behind his ear as he reversed out of the drive and set off through the pretty little town of Pagford, where they had lived as long as they had been married. They drove down Church Row, the steeply sloping street where the most expensive houses stood in all their Victorian extravagance

3

and solidity, around the corner by the mock-Gothic church, where he had once watched his twin girls perform *Joseph and the Amazing Technicolor Dreamcoat*, and across the Square, where they had a clear view of the dark skeleton of the ruined abbey that dominated the town's skyline, set high on a hill, melding with the violet sky.

All Barry could think of as he twiddled the steering wheel, navigating the familiar turns, were the mistakes he was sure he had made, rushing to finish the article he had just emailed to the *Yarvil and District Gazette*. Garrulous and engaging in person, he found it difficult to carry his personality onto paper.

The golf club lay a mere four minutes away from the Square, a little beyond the point where the town petered out in a final wheeze of old cottages. Barry parked the people carrier outside the club restaurant, the Birdie, and stood for a moment beside the car, while Mary reapplied her lipstick. The cool evening air was pleasant on his face. As he watched the contours of the golf course disintegrating into the dusk, Barry wondered why he kept up his membership. He was a bad golfer: his swing was erratic and his handicap was high. He had so many other calls on his time. His head throbbed worse than ever.

Mary switched off the mirror light and closed the passenger side door. Barry pressed the auto lock on the key ring in his hand; his wife's high heels clacked on the tarmac, the car's locking system beeped, and Barry wondered whether his nausea might abate once he had eaten.

Then pain such as he had never experienced sliced through his brain like a demolition ball. He barely noticed the smarting of his knees as they smacked onto the cold tarmac; his skull was awash with fire and blood; the agony was excruciating beyond endurance, except that endure it he must, for oblivion was still a minute away.

Mary screamed—and kept screaming. Several men came running from the bar. One of them sprinted back inside the building to see whether either of the club's retired doctors was present. A married couple, acquaintances of Barry and Mary's, heard the commotion from the restaurant, abandoned their starters and hurried outside to see what they could do. The husband called 999 on his mobile.

4

The ambulance had to come from the neighboring city of Yarvil, and it took twenty-five minutes to reach them. By the time the pulsing blue light slid over the scene, Barry was lying motionless and unresponsive on the ground in a pool of his own vomit; Mary was crouching beside him, the knees of her tights ripped, clutching his hand, sobbing and whispering his name.

Monday

I

"Brace yourself," said Miles Mollison, standing in the kitchen of one of the big houses in Church Row.

He had waited until half past six in the morning to make the call. It had been a bad night, full of long stretches of wakefulness punctuated by snatches of restless sleep. At four in the morning, he had realized that his wife was awake too, and they had talked quietly for a while in the darkness. Even as they discussed what they had been forced to witness, each trying to drive out vague feelings of fright and shock, feathery little ripples of excitement had tickled Miles' insides at the thought of delivering the news to his father. He had intended to wait until seven, but fear that somebody else might beat him to it had propelled him to the telephone early.

"What's happened?" boomed Howard's voice, with a slightly tinny edge; Miles had put him on speakerphone for Samantha's benefit. Mahogany brown in her pale pink dressing gown, she had taken advantage of their early waking to apply another handful of Self-Sun to her fading natural tan. The kitchen was full of the mingled smells of instant coffee and synthetic coconut.

"Fairbrother's dead. Collapsed at the golf club last night. Sam and I were having dinner at the Birdie."

"Fairbrother's *dead?*" roared Howard.

7

The inflection implied that he had been expecting some dramatic change in the status of Barry Fairbrother, but that even he had not anticipated actual death.

"Collapsed in the car park," repeated Miles.

"Good God," said Howard. "He wasn't much past forty, was he? Good God."

Miles and Samantha listened to Howard breathing like a blown horse. He was always short of breath in the mornings.

"What was it? Heart?"

"Something in his brain, they think. We went with Mary to the hospital and—"

But Howard was not paying attention. Miles and Samantha heard him speaking away from his mouthpiece.

"Barry Fairbrother! Dead! It's Miles!"

Miles and Samantha sipped their coffee, waiting for Howard to come back. Samantha's dressing gown gaped open as she sat at the kitchen table, revealing the contours of her big breasts as they rested on her forearms. Upwards pressure made them appear fuller and smoother than they were when they hung unsupported. The leathery skin of her upper cleavage radiated little cracks that no longer vanished when decompressed. She had been a great user of sunbeds when younger.

"What?" said Howard, back on the line. "What did you say about hospital?"

"Sam and I went in the ambulance," Miles enunciated clearly. "With Mary and the body."

Samantha noticed how Miles' second version emphasized what you might call the more commercial aspect of the story. Samantha did not blame him. Their reward for enduring the awful experience was the right to tell people about it. She did not think she would ever forget it: Mary wailing; Barry's eyes still half open above the muzzle-like mask; she and Miles trying to read the paramedic's expression; the cramped jolting; the dark windows; the terror.

"Good God," said Howard for the third time, ignoring Shirley's soft background questioning, his attention all Miles'. "He just popped down dead in the car park?"

8

"Yep," said Miles. "Moment I saw him it was pretty obvious there was nothing to be done."

It was his first lie, and he turned his eyes away from his wife as he told it. She remembered his big protective arm around Mary's shaking shoulders: *He'll be OK…he'll be OK…*

But after all, thought Samantha, giving Miles his due, *how were you supposed to know one way or the other, when they were strapping on masks and shoving in needles?* It had seemed as though they were trying to save Barry, and none of them had known for certain that it was no good until the young doctor had walked towards Mary at the hospital. Samantha could still see, with awful clarity, Mary's naked, petrified face, and the expression of the bespectacled, sleek-haired young woman in the white coat: composed, yet a little wary…they showed that sort of thing on television dramas all the time, but when it actually happened…

"Not at all," Miles was saying. "Gavin was only playing squash with him on Thursday."

"And he seemed all right then?"

"Oh yeah. Thrashed Gavin."

"Good God. Just goes to show you, doesn't it? Just goes to show. Hang on, Mum wants a word."

A clunk and a clatter, and Shirley's soft voice came on the line.

"What a dreadful shock, Miles," she said. "Are you all right?"

Samantha took a clumsy mouthful of coffee; it trickled from the corners of her mouth down the sides of her chin, and she mopped her face and chest with her sleeve. Miles had adopted the voice he often used when speaking to his mother: deeper than usual, a take-command nothing-fazes-me voice, punchy and no-nonsense. Sometimes, especially when drunk, Samantha would imitate Miles and Shirley's conversations. "Not to worry, Mummy. Miles here. Your little soldier." "Darling, you are wonderful: so big and brave and clever." Once or twice, lately, Samantha had done this in front of other people, leaving Miles cross and defensive, though pretending to laugh. There had been a row, last time, in the car going home.

"You went all the way to the hospital with her?" Shirley was saying from the speakerphone.

9

No, thought Samantha, *we got bored halfway there and asked to be let out.*

"Least we could do. Wish we could have done more."

Samantha got up and walked over to the toaster.

"I'm sure Mary was very grateful," said Shirley. Samantha crashed the lid of the bread bin and rammed four pieces of bread into the slots. Miles' voice became more natural.

"Yeah, well, once the doctors had told—confirmed that he was dead, Mary wanted Colin and Tessa Wall. Sam phoned them, we waited until they arrived and then we left."

"Well, it was very lucky for Mary that you were there," said Shirley. "Dad wants another word, Miles, I'll put him on. Speak later."

"'Speak later,'" Samantha mouthed at the kettle, waggling her head. Her distorted reflection was puffy after their sleepless night, her chestnut-brown eyes bloodshot. In her haste to witness the telling of Howard, Samantha had carelessly rubbed fake tanning lotion into the rims.

"Why don't you and Sam come over this evening?" Howard was booming. "No, hang on—Mum's reminded me we're playing bridge with the Bulgens. Come over tomorrow. For dinner. 'Bout seven."

"Maybe," said Miles, glancing at Samantha. "I'll have to see what Sam's got on."

She did not indicate whether or not she wanted to go. A strange sense of anticlimax filled the kitchen as Miles hung up.

"They can't believe it," he said, as if she hadn't heard everything.

They ate their toast and drank fresh mugs of coffee in silence. Some of Samantha's irritability lifted as she chewed. She remembered how she had woken with a jerk in their dark bedroom in the early hours, and had been absurdly relieved and grateful to feel Miles beside her, big and paunchy, smelling of vetiver and old sweat. Then she imagined telling customers at the shop about how a man had dropped dead in front of her, and about the mercy dash to hospital. She thought of ways to describe various aspects of the journey, and of the climactic scene with the doctor. The youth of that self-possessed woman had made the whole thing seem worse. They ought to give the job of breaking the news to someone older.

Then, with a further lift of her spirits, she recollected that she had an appointment with the Champêtre sales rep tomorrow; he had been pleasantly flirty on the telephone.

"I'd better get moving," said Miles, and he drained his coffee mug, his eyes on the brightening sky beyond the window. He heaved a deep sigh and patted his wife on her shoulder as he passed on the way to the dishwasher with his empty plate and mug.

"Christ, it puts everything in perspective, though, doesn't it, eh?"

Shaking his close-cropped, graying head, he left the kitchen.

Samantha sometimes found Miles absurd and, increasingly, dull. Every now and then, though, she enjoyed his pomposity in precisely the same spirit as she liked, on formal occasions, to wear a hat. It was appropriate, after all, to be solemn and a little worthy this morning. She finished her toast and cleared away her breakfast things, mentally refining the story she planned to tell her assistant.

II

"Barry Fairbrother's dead," panted Ruth Price.

She had almost run up the chilly garden path so as to have a few more minutes with her husband before he left for work. She didn't stop in the porch to take off her coat but, still muffled and gloved, burst into the kitchen where Simon and their teenage sons were eating breakfast.

Her husband froze, a piece of toast halfway to his lips, then lowered it with theatrical slowness. The two boys, both in school uniform, looked from one parent to the other, mildly interested.

"An aneurysm, they think," said Ruth, still a little breathless as she tweaked off her gloves finger by finger, unwinding her scarf and unbuttoning her coat. A thin dark woman with heavy, mournful eyes, the stark blue nurse's uniform suited her. "He collapsed at the golf club—Sam and Miles Mollison brought him in—and then Colin and Tessa Wall came…"

She darted out to the porch to hang up her things, and was back in time to answer Simon's shouted question.

"What's ananeurysm?"

"*An. Aneurysm.* A burst artery in the brain."

She flitted over to the kettle, switched it on, then began to sweep crumbs from the work surface around the toaster, talking all the while.

"He'll have had a massive cerebral hemorrhage. His poor, poor wife…she's absolutely devastated…"

Momentarily stricken, Ruth gazed out of her kitchen window over the crisp whiteness of her frost-crusted lawn, at the abbey across the valley, stark and skeletal against the pale pink and gray sky, and the panoramic view that was the glory of Hilltop House. Pagford, which by night was no more than a cluster of twinkling lights in a dark hollow far below, was emerging into chilly sunlight. Ruth saw none of it: her mind was still at the hospital, watching Mary emerge from the room where Barry lay, all futile aids to life removed. Ruth Price's pity flowed most freely and sincerely for those whom she believed to be like herself. "No, no, no, no," Mary had moaned, and that instinctive denial had reverberated inside Ruth, because she had been afforded a glimpse of herself in an identical situation…

Hardly able to bear the thought, she turned to look at Simon. His light-brown hair was still thick, his frame was almost as wiry as it had been in his twenties and the crinkles at the corners of his eyes were merely attractive, but Ruth's return to nursing after a long break had confronted her anew with the million and one ways the human body could malfunction. She had had more detachment when she was young; now she realized how lucky they all were to be alive.

"Couldn't they do anything for him?" asked Simon. "Couldn't they plug it up?"

He sounded frustrated, as though the medical profession had, yet again, bungled the business by refusing to do the simple and obvious thing.

Andrew thrilled with savage pleasure. He had noticed lately that his father had developed a habit of countering his mother's use of medical terms with crude, ignorant suggestions. *Cerebral hemorrhage. Plug it up.* His mother didn't realize what his father was up to. She never did. Andrew ate his Weetabix and burned with hatred.

"It was too late to do anything by the time they got him out to us," said Ruth, dropping teabags into the pot. "He died in the ambulance, right before they arrived."

"Bloody hell," said Simon. "What was he, forty?"

But Ruth was distracted.

"Paul, your hair's completely matted at the back. Have you brushed it at all?"

She pulled a hairbrush from her handbag and pushed it into her younger son's hand.

"No warning signs or anything?" asked Simon, as Paul dragged the brush through the thick mop of his hair.

"He'd had a bad headache for a couple of days, apparently."

"Ah," said Simon, chewing toast. "And he ignored it?"

"Oh, yes, he didn't think anything of it."

Simon swallowed.

"Goes to show, doesn't it?" he said portentously. "Got to watch yourself."

That's wise, thought Andrew, with furious contempt; *that's profound.* So it was Barry Fairbrother's own fault his brain had burst open. *You self-satisfied fucker,* Andrew told his father, loudly, inside his own head.

Simon pointed his knife at his elder son and said, "Oh, and by the way. *He's* going to be getting a job. Old Pizza Face there."

Startled, Ruth turned from her husband to her son. Andrew's acne stood out, livid and shiny, from his empurpling cheek, as he stared down into his bowl of beige mush.

"Yeah," said Simon. "Lazy little shit's going to start earning some money. If he wants to smoke, he can pay for it out of his own wages. No more pocket money."

"Andrew!" wailed Ruth. "You haven't been —?"

"Oh, yes, he has. I caught him in the woodshed," said Simon, his expression a distillation of spite.

"Andrew!"

"No more money from us. You want fags, you buy 'em," said Simon.

"But we said," whimpered Ruth, "we said, with his exams coming—"

"Judging by the way he fucked up his mocks, we'll be lucky if he gets any qualifications. He can get himself out to McDonald's early, get some experience," said Simon, standing up and pushing in his chair, relishing the sight of Andrew's hanging head, the dark pimpled edge of his face. "Because we're not supporting you through any resits, pal. It's now or never."

"Oh, Simon," said Ruth reproachfully.

"What?"

Simon took two stamping steps toward his wife. Ruth shrank back against the sink. The pink plastic brush fell out of Paul's hand.

"I'm not going to fund the little fucker's filthy habit! Fucking cheek of him, puffing away in *my* fucking shed!"

Simon hit himself on the chest on the word "my"; the dull thunk made Ruth wince.

"I was bringing home a salary when I was that spotty little shit's age. If he wants fags, he can pay for them himself, all right? *All right?*"

He had thrust his face to within six inches of Ruth's.

"Yes, Simon," she said very quietly.

Andrew's bowels seemed to have become liquid. He had made a vow to himself not ten days previously: had the moment arrived so soon? But his father stepped away from his mother and marched out of the kitchen toward the porch. Ruth, Andrew and Paul remained quite still; they might have promised not to move in his absence.

"Did you fill up the tank?" Simon shouted, as he always did when she had been working a night shift.

"Yes," Ruth called back, striving for brightness, for normality.

The front door rattled and slammed.

Ruth busied herself with the teapot, waiting for the billowing atmosphere to shrink back to its usual proportions. Only when Andrew was about to leave the room to clean his teeth did she speak.

"He worries about you, Andrew. About your health."

Like fuck he does, the cunt.

Inside his head, Andrew matched Simon obscenity for obscenity. Inside his head, he could take Simon in a fair fight.

Aloud, to his mother, he said, "Yeah. Right."

III

Evertree Crescent was a sickle moon of 1930s bungalows, which lay two minutes from Pagford's main square. In number thirty-six, a house tenanted longer than any other in the street, Shirley Mollison sat, propped up against her pillows, sipping the tea that her husband had brought her. The reflection facing her in the mirrored doors of the built-in wardrobe had a misty quality, due partly to the fact that she was not wearing glasses, and partly to the soft glow cast over the room by her rose-patterned curtains. In this flattering, hazy light, the dimpled pink and white face beneath the short silver hair was cherubic.

The bedroom was just large enough to accommodate Shirley's single bed and Howard's double, crammed together, nonidentical twins. Howard's mattress, which still bore his prodigious imprint, was empty. The soft purr and hiss of the shower was audible from where Shirley and her rosy reflection sat facing each other, savoring the news that seemed still to effervesce in the atmosphere, like bubbling champagne.

Barry Fairbrother was dead. Snuffed out. Cut down. No event of national importance, no war, no stock-market collapse, no terrorist attack, could have sparked in Shirley the awe, the avid interest and feverish speculation that currently consumed her.

She had hated Barry Fairbrother. Shirley and her husband, usually as one in all their friendships and enmities, had been a little out of step in this. Howard had sometimes confessed himself entertained by the bearded little man who opposed him so relentlessly across the long scratched tables in Pagford Church Hall; but Shirley made no distinction between the political and the personal. Barry had opposed Howard in the central quest of his life, and this made Barry Fairbrother her bitter enemy.

Loyalty to her husband was the main, but not the only, reason for Shirley's passionate dislike. Her instincts about people were finely honed in one direction only, like a dog that has been trained to sniff out narcotics. She was perennially aquiver to detect condescension, and had long detected its reek in the attitudes of Barry Fairbrother and his cronies on the Parish Council. The Fairbrothers of the world assumed that their university education made them better than people like her and Howard, that their views counted for more. Well, their arrogance had received a nasty blow today. Fairbrother's sudden death bolstered Shirley in the long-held belief that, whatever he and his followers might have thought, he had been of a lower and weaker order than her husband, who, in addition to all his other virtues, had managed to survive a heart attack seven years previously.

(Never for an instant had Shirley believed that her Howard would die, even while he was in the operating theater. Howard's presence on earth was, to Shirley, a given, like sunlight and oxygen. She had said as much afterwards, when friends and neighbors had spoken of miraculous escapes and how lucky that they had the cardiac unit so nearby in Yarvil, and how dreadfully worried she must have been.

"I always knew he'd pull through," Shirley had said, unruffled and serene. "I never doubted it."

And here he was, as good as ever; and there was Fairbrother in the morgue. It only went to show.)

In the elation of this early morning, Shirley was reminded of the day after her son Miles had been born. She had sat up in bed all those years ago, exactly like this, with sunlight streaming through the ward window, a cup of tea that somebody else had made her in her hands, waiting for them to bring in her beautiful new baby boy for feeding. Birth and death: there was the same consciousness of heightened existence and of her own elevated importance.

The news of Barry Fairbrother's sudden demise lay in her lap like a fat new baby to be gloated over by all her acquaintances; and she would be the fount, the source, for she was first, or nearly so, to receive the news.

None of the delight frothing and fizzing inside Shirley had been apparent while Howard had been in the room. They had merely exchanged the comments proper to sudden death before he had taken himself off to the shower. Naturally Shirley had known, as they slid stock words and phrases back and forth between them like beads on an abacus, that Howard must be as brimful of ecstasy as she was; but to express these feelings out loud, when the news of the death was still fresh in the air, would have been tantamount to dancing naked and shrieking obscenities, and Howard and Shirley were clothed, always, in an invisible layer of decorum that they never laid aside.

Another happy thought came to Shirley. She set down her cup and saucer on the bedside table, slipped out of bed, pulled on her candlewick dressing gown and her glasses, and padded down the hall to tap on the bathroom door.

"Howard?"

An interrogative noise answered over the steady patter of the shower.

"Do you think I should put something on the website? About Fairbrother?"

"Good idea," he called through the door, after a moment's consideration. "Excellent idea."

So she bustled along to the study. It had previously been the smallest bedroom in the bungalow, long since vacated by their daughter Patricia who had gone to London and was rarely mentioned.

Shirley was immensely proud of her skill on the Internet. She had been to evening classes in Yarvil ten years previously, where she had been one of the oldest students and the slowest. Nevertheless, she had persevered, determined to be the administrator of Pagford Parish Council's exciting new website. She logged herself in and brought up the Parish Council's homepage.

The brief statement flowed so easily that it was as if her fingers themselves were composing it.

Councillor Barry Fairbrother
It is with great regret that we announce the death of
Councillor Barry Fairbrother. Our thoughts are with his family
at this difficult time.

She read this through carefully, hit return and watched the message appear on the message board.

The Queen had lowered the flag on Buckingham Palace when Princess Diana had died. Her Majesty occupied a very special position in Shirley's interior life. Contemplating the message on the website, she was satisfied and happy that she had done the right thing. Learning from the best…

She navigated away from the Parish Council message board and dropped into her favorite medical website, where she painstakingly entered the words "brain" and "death" in the search box.

The suggestions were endless. Shirley scrolled through the possibilities, her mild eyes rolling up and down, wondering to which of these deadly conditions, some of them unpronounceable, she owed her present happiness. Shirley was a hospital volunteer; she had developed quite a little interest in matters medical since starting work at South West General, and occasionally offered diagnoses to her friends.

But there was no concentrating on long words and symptoms this morning: her thoughts skittered away to the further dissemination of the news; already she was mentally assembling and reshuffling a list of telephone numbers. She wondered whether Aubrey and Julia knew, and what they would say; and whether Howard would let her tell Maureen or reserve that pleasure for himself.

It was all *immensely* exciting.

IV

Andrew Price closed the front door of the small white house and followed his younger brother down the steep garden path, crunchy with frost, that led to the icy metal gate in the hedge and the lane beyond. Neither boy spared a glance for the familiar view spread out below them: the tiny town of Pagford cupped in a hollow between three hills, one of which was crested with the remains of the twelfth-century abbey. A thin river snaked around the edge of the hill and through town, straddled by a toy stone bridge. The scene was dull as a flat-painted backdrop to the brothers; Andrew despised the way that, on the rare occasions when the family had guests, his father seemed to take credit for it, as though he had designed and built the whole thing. Andrew had lately decided that he would prefer an outlook of asphalt, broken windows and graffiti; he dreamed of London and of a life that mattered.

The brothers marched to the end of the lane, ambling to a halt on the corner where they met the wider road. Andrew reached into the hedge, groped around for a while, then drew out a half-full packet of Benson & Hedges and a slightly damp box of matches. After several false starts, the heads of the matches crumbling against the strike, he succeeded in lighting up. Two or three deep drags, and then the grumbling engine of the school bus broke the stillness. Andrew carefully knocked out the glowing head of his cigarette and stowed the rest back in the packet.

The bus was always two-thirds full by the time it reached the turning for Hilltop House, because it had already skirted outlying farms and houses. The brothers sat apart as usual, each of them taking a double seat and turning to stare out of the window as the bus rumbled and lurched on down into Pagford.

At the foot of their hill was a house that stood in a wedge-shaped garden. The four Fairbrother children usually waited outside the front gate, but there was nobody there today. The curtains were all closed. Andrew wondered whether you usually sat in the dark when somebody died.

A few weeks previously, Andrew had got off with Niamh Fairbrother, one of Barry's twin daughters, at a disco in the school drama hall. She had shown a distasteful tendency to shadow his movements for a while afterwards. Andrew's parents were barely acquainted with the Fairbrothers; Simon and Ruth had hardly any friends, but they seemed to have had a tepid liking for Barry, who had managed the minuscule branch of the only bank still present in Pagford. Fairbrother's name had cropped up a lot in connection with such things as the Parish Council, town hall theatricals, and the Church Fun Run. These were things in which Andrew had no interest and from which his parents held themselves aloof, excepting the occasional sponsorship form or raffle ticket.

As the bus turned left and trundled down Church Row, past the spacious Victorian houses ranged in descending tiers, Andrew indulged in a little fantasy in which his father dropped dead, gunned down by an invisible sniper. Andrew visualized himself patting his sobbing mother on the back while he telephoned the undertaker. He had a cigarette in his mouth as he ordered the cheapest coffin.

The three Jawandas, Jaswant, Sukhvinder and Rajpal, got on the bus at the bottom of Church Row. Andrew had carefully chosen a seat with an empty place in front of it, and he willed Sukhvinder to sit in front of him, not for her own sake (Andrew's best friend Fats referred to her as TNT, short for "Tits 'N' Tash"), but because She so often chose to sit beside Sukhvinder. And whether because his telepathic promptings were particularly powerful this morning or not, Sukhvinder did indeed choose the seat in front. Jubilant, Andrew stared, unseeing, at the grimy window, and clutched his schoolbag more closely to him, to conceal the erection brought on by the heavy vibration of the bus.

Anticipation mounted with every fresh pitch and heave, as the cumbersome vehicle edged its way through the narrow streets, around the tight corner into the village square and toward the corner of Her road.

Andrew had never experienced this intensity of interest in any girl. She was newly arrived; an odd time to change schools, the spring term of the GCSE year. Her name was Gaia, and that was fitting, because he had never heard it before, and she was something entirely new. She had walked onto the bus one morning like a simple statement of the sublime heights to which nature could reach and sat herself down two seats in front of him, while he sat transfixed by the perfection of her shoulders and the back of her head.

Her hair was a coppery brown, and it fell in long loose waves to just below her shoulder blades; her nose was perfectly straight, narrow, foreshortened, emphasizing the provocative fullness of her pale mouth; her eyes were set wide apart, thick-lashed, of a heavily flecked greenish hazel, like a russet apple. Andrew had never seen her wear makeup, and no spot or blemish marred her skin. Her face was a synthesis of perfect symmetry and unusual proportion; he could have gazed at it for hours, trying to locate the source of its fascination. Only last week, he had returned home after a double lesson of biology in which, due to a divine random arrangement of tables and heads, he had been able to watch her almost constantly. Safe in his bedroom afterwards, he had written (following half an hour's staring at the wall, which succeeded a bout of masturbation) "beauty is geometry." He had torn the paper up immediately, and felt foolish every time he remembered it, but still, there was something in it. Her gorgeousness was a matter of minor adjustments to a pattern, so that a breathtaking harmony resulted.

She would be here any minute, and if she sat beside square and sulky Sukhvinder, as she so often did, she would be close enough to smell the nicotine on him. He liked to see inanimate objects react to her body; liked to see the bus seat give a little as she dropped her weight into it, and that copper-gold mass of hair curve against the steel bar at the top.

The bus driver slowed, and Andrew turned his face away from the door, pretending to be lost in contemplation; he would look around when she got on, as if he had only just realized that they had stopped; he would make eye contact, possibly nod. He waited to hear the doors open, but the soft throb of the engine was not interrupted by the familiar grind and thump.

Andrew glanced around and saw nothing but short, shabby little Hope Street: two lines of small terraced houses. The bus driver was leaning over to make sure she was not coming. Andrew wanted to tell him to wait, because only the previous week she had burst from one of those little houses and come running up the pavement (it had been acceptable to watch, because everyone had been watching), and the sight of her running had been enough to occupy his thoughts for hours, but the driver hauled at the big wheel and the bus set off again. Andrew returned to his contemplation of the dirty window with an ache in his heart and in his balls.

V

The small terraces in Hope Street had once been laborers' houses. Gavin Hughes was shaving slowly and with unnecessary care in the bathroom of number ten. He was so fair, and his beard so sparse, that the job really only needed to be done twice weekly; but the chilly, slightly grubby bathroom was the only place of sanctuary. If he dawdled in here until eight, he could plausibly say he needed to leave for work immediately. He dreaded having to talk to Kay.

He had only managed to head off discussion the previous evening by initiating the most prolonged and inventive coupling they had enjoyed since the very earliest days of their relationship. Kay had responded immediately and with unnerving enthusiasm: flicking herself from position to position; drawing up her strong, stocky legs for him; contorting like the Slavic acrobat she so closely resembled, with her olive skin and very short dark hair. Too late, he had realized that she was taking this uncharacteristic act of assertion as a tacit confession of those things he was determined to avoid saying. She had kissed him greedily; he had found her wet intrusive kisses erotic when the affair began, now he found them vaguely repellent. He took a long time to climax, his horror at what he had started constantly threatening to deflate his erection. Even this worked against him: she seemed to take his unusual stamina as a display of virtuosity.

When at last it was over, she had cuddled close to him in the darkness and stroked his hair for a while. Miserably he stared into the void, aware that after all his vague plans for loosening the ties, he had involuntarily tightened them. After she had fallen asleep, he had lain with one arm trapped underneath her, the damp sheet adhering unpleasantly to his thigh, on a mattress lumpy with old springs, and wished for the courage to be a bastard, to slip away and never return.

Kay's bathroom smelled of mold and damp sponges. A number of hairs were stuck to the side of the small bath. Paint was peeling off the walls.

"It needs some work," Kay had said.

Gavin had been careful not to volunteer any help. The things he had not said to her were his talisman and safeguard; he strung them together in his mind and checked them off like beads on a rosary. He had never said "love." He had never talked about marriage. He had never asked her to move to Pagford. And yet, here she was, and somehow, she made him feel responsible.

His face stared back at him from out of the tarnished mirror. There were purple shadows under his eyes, and his thinning blond hair was wispy and dry. The naked bulb overhead lit the weak, goaty face with forensic cruelty.

Thirty-four, he thought, *and I look at least forty.*

He lifted the razor and delicately strafed off those two thick blond hairs that grew either side of his prominent Adam's apple.

Fists pummeled the bathroom door. Gavin's hand slipped and blood dripped from his thin neck to speckle his clean white shirt.

"Your boyfriend," came a furious female scream, "is still in the bathroom and I am going to be late!"

"I've finished!" he shouted.

The gash stung, but what did that matter? Here was his excuse, ready-made: *Look what your daughter made me do. I'll have to go home and change my shirt before work.* With an almost light heart he grabbed the tie and jacket he had hung over the hook on the back of the door, and unlocked it.

Gaia pushed past, slammed the door behind her and rammed the lock home. Out on the tiny landing, which was thick with an unpleasant smell of burned rubber, Gavin remembered the headboard banging against the wall last night, the creaking of the cheap pine bed, Kay's groans and yelps. It was easy to forget, sometimes, that her daughter was in the house.

He jogged down the carpetless stairs. Kay had told him of her plans to sand and polish them, but he doubted that she would ever do it; her flat in London had been shabby and in poor repair. In any case, he was convinced that she was expecting to move in with him quite soon, but he would not allow it; that was the final bastion, and there, if forced, he would make his stand.

"What have you done to yourself?" Kay squealed, catching sight of the blood on his shirt. She was wearing the cheap scarlet kimono that he did not like, but which suited her so well.

"Gaia banged on the door and made me jump. I'm going to have to go home and change."

"Oh, but I've made you breakfast!" she said quickly.

He realized that the smell of burning rubber was actually scrambled eggs. They looked anemic and overcooked.

"I can't, Kay, I've got to change this shirt, I've got an early—"

She was already spooning the congealed mass onto plates.

"Five minutes, surely you can stay five—?"

The mobile phone in his jacket pocket buzzed loudly and he pulled it out, wondering whether he would have the nerve to pretend that it was an urgent summons.

"Jesus Christ," he said, in unfeigned horror.

"What's the matter?"

"Barry. Barry Fairbrother! He's…fuck, he's…he's dead! It's from Miles. Jesus Christ. Jesus fucking Christ!"

She laid down the wooden spoon.

"Who's Barry Fairbrother?"

"I play squash with him. He's only forty-four! Jesus Christ!"

He read the text message again. Kay watched him, confused.

She knew that Miles was Gavin's partner at the solicitor's, but had never been introduced to him. Barry Fairbrother was no more than a name to her.

There came a thunderous banging from the stairs: Gaia was stamping as she ran.

"Eggs," she stated, at the kitchen door. "Like you make me every morning. *Not.* And thanks to *him,*" with a venomous look at the back of Gavin's head, "I've probably missed the bloody bus."

"Well, if you hadn't spent so long doing your hair," Kay shouted at the figure of her retreating daughter, who did not respond, but stormed down the hall, her bag bouncing off the walls, and slammed the front door behind her.

"Kay, I've got to go," said Gavin.

"But look, I've got it all ready, you could have it before—"

"I've got to change my shirt. And, shit, I did Barry's will for him, I'll need to look it out. No, I'm sorry, I've got to go. I can't believe it," he added, rereading Miles' text. "I can't believe it. We only played squash on Thursday. I can't—Jesus."

A man had died; there was nothing she could say, not without putting herself in the wrong. He kissed her briefly on her unresponsive mouth, and then walked away, up the dark narrow hall.

"Will I see you—?"

"I'll call you later," he shouted over her, pretending not to hear.

Gavin hurried across the road to his car, gulping the crisp, cold air, holding the fact of Barry's death in his mind like a vial of volatile liquid that he dare not agitate. As he turned the key in the ignition, he imagined Barry's twin daughters crying, facedown in their bunk beds. He had seen them lying like that, one above the other, each playing on a Nintendo DS, when he passed the door of their bedroom the very last time he had gone round for dinner.

The Fairbrothers had been the most devoted couple he knew. He would never eat at their house again. He used to tell Barry how lucky he was. Not so lucky after all.

Someone was coming down the pavement towards him; in a panic that it was Gaia, coming to shout at him or to demand a lift, he reversed too hard and hit the car behind him: Kay's old

Vauxhall Corsa. The passerby drew level with his window, and was revealed to be an emaciated, hobbling old woman in carpet slippers. Sweating, Gavin swung his steering wheel around and squeezed out of the space. As he accelerated, he glanced in the rearview mirror and saw Gaia letting herself back into Kay's house.

He was having difficulty getting enough air into his lungs. There was a tight knot in his chest. Only now did he realize that Barry Fairbrother had been his best friend.

VI

The school bus had reached the Fields, the sprawling estate that lay on the outskirts of the city of Yarvil. Dirty gray houses, some of them spray-painted with initials and obscenities; the occasional boarded window; satellite dishes and overgrown grass—none of it was any more worthy of Andrew's sustained attention than the ruined abbey of Pagford, glittering with frost. Andrew had once been intrigued and intimidated by the Fields, but familiarity had long since rendered it all commonplace.

The pavements swarmed with children and teenagers walking towards school, many of them in T-shirts, despite the cold. Andrew spotted Krystal Weedon, byword and dirty joke. She was bouncing along, laughing uproariously, in the middle of a mixed group of teenagers. Multiple earrings swung from each ear, and the string of her thong was clearly visible above her low-slung tracksuit bottoms. Andrew had known her since primary school, and she featured in many of the most highly colored memories of his extreme youth. They had jeered at her name, but instead of crying, as most of the little girls would have done, five-year-old Krystal had caught on, cackled and shrieked, "Weed-on! Krystal weed-on!" And she had pulled down her pants in the middle of class and pretended to do it.

He retained a vivid memory of her bare pink vulva; it was as though Father Christmas had popped up in their midst; and he remembered Miss Oates, bright red in the face, marching Krystal from the room.

By the age of twelve, transposed to the comprehensive, Krystal had become the most well-developed girl in their year and had lingered at the back of the class, where they were supposed to take their maths worksheets when they had finished and swap them for the next in the series. How it had been initiated, Andrew (among the last to finish his maths, as ever) had no idea, but he had reached the plastic boxes of worksheets, neatly lined up on top of the cupboards at the back, to find Rob Calder and Mark Richards taking it in turns to cup and squeeze Krystal's breasts. Most of the other boys were looking on, electrified, their faces hidden from the teacher by their upstanding textbooks, while the girls, many of them flushed scarlet, were pretending not to have seen. Andrew had realized that half the boys had already had their turn, and that he was expected to take his. He had both wanted and not wanted to. It was not her breasts he feared, but the bold challenging look on her face; he had been frightened of doing it wrong. When the oblivious and ineffectual Mr. Simmonds had looked up at last and said, "You've been up there forever, Krystal, get a worksheet and sit down," Andrew had been almost entirely relieved.

Though they had long since been separated into different sets, they were still in the same registration class, so Andrew knew that Krystal was sometimes present, often not, and that she was in almost constant trouble. She knew no fear, like the boys who came to school with tattoos they had inked themselves, with split lips and cigarettes, and stories of clashes with the police, of drug taking and easy sex.

Winterdown Comprehensive lay just inside Yarvil, a large, ugly triple-storied building whose outer shell consisted of windows interspersed with turquoise-painted panels. When the bus doors creaked open, Andrew joined the swelling masses, black-blazered and sweatered, that were milling across the car park towards the school's two front entrances. As he was about to join the bottle-neck cramming itself through the double doors, he noticed a Nissan Micra pulling up, and detached himself to wait for his best friend.

Tubby, Tubs, Tubster, Flubber, Wally, Wallah, Fatboy, Fats: Stuart Wall was the most nicknamed boy in school. His loping walk, his skinniness, his thin sallow face, overlarge ears and permanently pained expression were distinctive enough, but it was his trenchant humor, his detachment and poise that set him apart. Somehow he managed to disassociate himself from everything that might have defined a less resilient character, shrugging off the embarrassment of being the son of a ridiculed and unpopular deputy head; of having a frumpy, overweight guidance teacher as a mother. He was preeminently and uniquely himself: Fats, school notable and landmark, and even the Fielders laughed at his jokes, and rarely bothered—so coolly and cruelly did he return jibes—to laugh at his unfortunate connections.

Fats' self-possession remained total this morning when, in full view of the parent-free hordes streaming past, he had to struggle out of the Nissan alongside not only his mother but his father too, who usually traveled to school separately. Andrew thought again of Krystal Weedon and her exposed thong, as Fats loped toward him.

"All right, Arf?" said Fats.

"Fats."

They moved together into the crowd, their schoolbags slung over their shoulders, buffeting the shorter kids in the face, creating a small space in their slipstream.

"Cubby's been crying," said Fats, as they walked up the teeming stairs.

"Say what?"

"Barry Fairbrother dropped dead last night."

"Oh yeah, I heard," said Andrew.

Fats gave Andrew the sly, quizzical look he used when others overreached themselves, pretended to know more than they did, pretended to be more than they were.

"My mum was at the hospital when they brought him in," said Andrew, nettled. "She works there, remember?"

"Oh, yeah," said Fats, and the slyness was gone. "Well, you know how him and Cubby were bum chums. And Cubby's going to announce it. Not good, Arf."

28

They parted at the top of the stairs for their respective registration rooms. Most of Andrew's class was already in their room, sitting on desks, swinging their legs, leaning up against the cupboards at the sides. Bags lay under chairs. Talk was always louder and freer than usual on Monday mornings, because assembly meant an open-air walk to the sports hall. Their registration teacher sat at her desk, marking people present as they came in. She never bothered to call the register formally; it was one of the many small ways in which she attempted to ingratiate herself with them, and the class despised her for it.

Krystal arrived as the bell rang for assembly. She shouted, "I'm here, miss!" from the doorway, and swung herself back out again. Everyone else followed her, still talking. Andrew and Fats were reunited at the top of the stairs and were borne by the general flow out of the back doors and across the wide gray tarmacked yard.

The sports hall smelled of sweat and trainers; the din of twelve hundred voraciously talking teenagers echoed off its bleak, whitewashed walls. A hard industrial-gray and much-stained carpet covered the floor, inset with different colored lines marking out badminton and tennis courts, hockey and football pitches; the stuff gave vicious burns if you fell on it bare-legged, but was easier on the backside than bare wood for those who had to sit on it for the duration of whole-school assembly. Andrew and Fats had attained the dignity of tubular-legged, plastic-backed chairs, ranged at the rear of the hall for the fifth and sixth years.

An old wooden lectern stood at the front, facing the pupils, and beside it sat the headmistress, Mrs. Shawcross. Fats' father, Colin "Cubby" Wall, walked over to take his place beside her. Very tall, he had a high, balding forehead, and an immensely imitable walk, his arms held rigid by his side, bobbing up and down more than was necessary for forward locomotion. Everyone called him Cubby, because of his infamous obsession with keeping the cubbyholes on the wall outside his school office in good order. The registers went into some of them after they had been marked, while others were assigned to specific departments. "Be sure and put it in the right cubbyhole, Ailsa!" "Don't leave it hanging out like that, it'll fall out

29

of the cubbyhole, Kevin!" "Don't walk over it, girl! Pick it up, give it here, it's meant to be in a cubbyhole!"

All the other teachers called them pigeonholes. It was widely assumed that they did this to set themselves apart from Cubby.

"Move along, move along," said Mr. Meacher, the woodwork teacher, to Andrew and Fats, who had left an empty seat between themselves and Kevin Cooper.

Cubby took his place behind the lectern. The pupils did not settle as quickly as they would have done for the headmistress. At the precise moment that the last voice died away, one of the double doors in the middle of the right-hand wall opened and Gaia walked in.

She glanced around the hall (Andrew permitted himself to watch, because half the hall was watching her; she was late, and unfamiliar, and beautiful, and it was only Cubby talking) and walked quickly, but not unduly so (because she had Fats' gift of self-possession) around the back of the students. Andrew's head could not revolve to keep watching her, but it struck him with a force that made his ears ring, that in moving along with Fats he had left an empty seat beside him.

He heard light, rapid footsteps coming closer, and then she was there; she had sat down right next to him. She nudged his chair, her body moving his. His nostrils caught a whisper of perfume. The whole of the left side of his body was burning with awareness of her, and he was grateful that the cheek nearest her was much less acne-ridden than the right. He had never been this close to her and wondered whether he dared look at her, make some sign of recognition; but immediately decided he had been paralyzed too long, and that it was too late to do so naturally.

Scratching his left temple to screen his face, he swiveled his eyeballs to glance down at her hands, clasped loosely on her lap. The nails were short, clean and unvarnished. There was a plain silver ring on one little finger.

Fats moved his elbow discreetly to put pressure on Andrew's side.

"Lastly," Cubby said, and Andrew realized that he had already heard Cubby say the word twice, and that the quietness in the hall had solidified into silence, as all fidgeting ceased and the air became stiff with curiosity, glee and unease.

"Lastly," said Cubby again, and his voice wobbled out of control, "I have a very…I have a very sad announcement to make. Mr. Barry Fairbrother, who has coached our extremely socksess… success…successful girls' rowing team for the past two years, has…"

He choked and passed a hand in front of his eyes.

"…died…"

Cubby Wall was crying in front of everybody; his knobbly bald head drooped onto his chest. A simultaneous gasp and giggle rolled across the watching crowd, and many faces turned toward Fats, who sat looking sublimely unconcerned; a little quizzical, but otherwise unmoved.

"…died…" sobbed Cubby, and the headmistress stood up, looking cross.

"…died…last night."

A loud squawk rose from somewhere in the middle of the lines of chairs at the back of the hall.

"Who laughed?" roared Cubby, and the air crackled with delicious tension. "HOW DARE YOU! What girl laughed, who was it?"

Mr. Meacher was already on his feet, gesticulating furiously at somebody in the middle of the row just behind Andrew and Fats; Andrew's chair was buffeted again, because Gaia had twisted in her seat to watch, like everyone else. Andrew's entire body seemed to have become super-sensory; he could feel the way Gaia's body was arched towards his. If he turned in the opposite direction, they would be breast to chest.

"*Who laughed?*" repeated Cubby, raising himself absurdly on tiptoe, as if he might be able to make out the culprit from where he was standing. Meacher was mouthing and beckoning feverishly at the person he had singled out for blame.

"Who is it, Mr. Meacher?" shouted Cubby.

Meacher appeared unwilling to say; he was still having difficulty in persuading the guilty party to leave her seat, but as Cubby began to show alarming signs of leaving the lectern to investigate personally, Krystal Weedon shot to her feet, scarlet in the face, and started pushing her way along the row.

"You will see me in my office immediately after assembly!" shouted Cubby. "Absolutely disgraceful—total lack of respect! Get out of my sight!"

But Krystal stopped at the end of the row, stuck up her middle finger at Cubby and screamed, "I DI'N' DO NOTHIN', YOU PRICK!"

There was an eruption of excited chatter and laughter; the teachers made ineffectual attempts to quell the noise, and one or two left their chairs to try and intimidate their own registration classes back into order.

The double doors swung shut behind Krystal and Mr. Meacher.

"Settle down!" shouted the headmistress, and a precarious quiet, rife with fidgeting and whispers, spread over the hall again. Fats was staring straight ahead, and there was for once a forced air to his indifference and a darker tinge to his skin.

Andrew felt Gaia fall back into her chair. He screwed up his courage, glanced left and grinned. She smiled right back.

VII

Though Pagford's delicatessen would not open until nine thirty, Howard Mollison had arrived early. He was an extravagantly obese man of sixty-four. A great apron of stomach fell so far down in front of his thighs that most people thought instantly of his penis when they first clapped eyes on him, wondering when he had last seen it, how he washed it, how he managed to perform any of the acts for which a penis is designed. Partly because his physique set off these trains of thought, and partly because of his fine line in banter, Howard managed to discomfort and disarm in almost equal measure, so that customers almost always bought more than they meant to on a first visit to the shop. He kept up the patter while he worked, one short-fingered hand sliding the meat slicer smoothly backwards and forwards, silky-fine slices of ham rippling onto the cellophane held below, a wink ever ready in his round blue eyes, his chins wobbling with easy laughter.

Howard had devised a costume to wear to work: white shirt-sleeves, a stiff dark-green canvas apron, corduroy trousers and a deerstalker into which he had inserted a number of fisherman's flies. If the deerstalker had ever been a joke, it had long since ceased to be. Every workday morning he positioned it, with unsmiling exactitude, on his dense gray curls, aided by a small mirror in the staff lavatory.

It was Howard's constant pleasure to open up in the mornings. He loved moving around the shop while the only sound was that of the softly humming chill cabinets, relished bringing it all back to life — flicking on the lights, pulling up the blinds, lifting lids to uncover the treasures of the chilled counter: the pale gray-green artichokes, the onyx-black olives, the dried tomatoes curled like ruby seahorses in their herb-flecked oil.

This morning, however, his enjoyment was laced with impatience. His business partner Maureen was already late, and, like Miles earlier, Howard was afraid that somebody might beat him to the telling of the sensational news, because she did not have a mobile phone.

He paused beside the newly hewn archway in the wall between the delicatessen and the old shoe shop, soon to become Pagford's newest café, and checked the industrial-strength clear plastic that prevented dust from settling in the delicatessen. They were planning to have the café open before Easter, in time to pull in the tourists to the West Country for whom Howard filled the windows annually with local cider, cheese and corn dollies.

The bell tinkled behind him, and he turned, his patched and reinforced heart pumping fast from excitement.

Maureen was a slight, round-shouldered woman of sixty-two, and the widow of Howard's original partner. Her stooping posture made her look much older than she was, though she strove, in so many ways, to keep a claw-grip on youth: dying her hair jet black, dressing in bright colors and wobbling on injudiciously high heels, which she changed for Dr. Scholl's sandals in the shop.

"Morning, Mo," said Howard.

He had been determined not to waste the announcement by rushing it, but customers would soon be upon them and he had a lot to say.

"Heard the news?"

She frowned at him interrogatively.

"Barry Fairbrother's dead."

Her mouth fell open.

"*No!* How?"

Howard tapped the side of his head.

"Something went. Up here. Miles was there, saw it all happen. Golf club car park."

"*No!*" she said again.

"Stone dead," said Howard, as though there were degrees of deadness, and the kind that Barry Fairbrother had contracted was particularly sordid.

Maureen's brightly lipsticked mouth hung slackly as she crossed herself. Her Catholicism always added a picturesque touch to such moments.

"Miles was there?" she croaked. He heard the yearning for every detail in her deep, ex-smoker's voice.

"D'you want to put on the kettle, Mo?"

He could at least prolong her agony for a few minutes. She slopped boiling tea over her hand in her haste to return to him. They sat together behind the counter, on the high wooden stools Howard had placed there for slack periods, and Maureen cooled her burned hand on a fistful of ice scraped from around the olives. Together they rattled through the conventional aspects of the tragedy: the widow ("she'll be lost, she lived for Barry"); the children ("four teenagers; what a burden without a father"); the relative youth of the dead man ("he wasn't much older than Miles, was he?"); and then, at last, they reached the real point of departure, beside which all else was aimless meandering.

"What'll happen?" Maureen asked Howard greedily.

"Ah," said Howard. "Well, now. That's the question, isn't it? We've got ourselves a casual vacancy, Mo, and it could make all the difference."

"We've got a...?" asked Maureen, frightened that she might have missed something crucial.

"Casual vacancy," repeated Howard. "What you call it when a council seat becomes vacant through a death. Proper term," he said pedagogically.

Howard was the Chair of the Parish Council, and First Citizen of Pagford. The position came with a gilt and enamel chain of office, now reposing in the tiny safe that he and Shirley had had installed at the bottom of their fitted wardrobes. If only Pagford District had been granted borough status, he would have been able to call himself Mayor; but even so, to all intents and purposes, that was what he was. Shirley had made this perfectly clear on the homepage of the council website, where, beneath a beaming and florid photograph of Howard in his First Citizen's chain, it was stated that he welcomed invitations to attend local civic and business functions. Just a few weeks previously, he had handed out the cycling proficiency certificates at the local primary school.

Howard sipped his tea and said with a smile to take off the sting, "Fairbrother was a bugger, mind, Mo. He could be a real bugger."

"Oh, I know," she said. "I know."

"I'd have had to have it out with him, if he'd lived. Ask Shirley. He could be an underhand bugger."

"Oh, I know."

"Well, we'll see. We'll see. This should be the end of it. Mind, I certainly didn't want to win like this," he added, with a deep sigh, "but speaking for the sake of Pagford...for the community...it's not all bad..."

Howard checked his watch.

"That's nearly half-past, Mo."

They were never late opening up, never early closing; the business was run with the ritual and regularity of a temple.

Maureen teetered over to unlock the door and pull up the

blinds. The Square was revealed in jerky increments as the blinds went up: picturesque and well kept, due in large part to the co-ordinated efforts of those proprietors whose properties faced onto it. Window boxes, hanging baskets and flower tubs were dotted about, planted in mutually agreed colors each year. The Black Canon (one of the oldest pubs in England) faced Mollison and Lowe across the Square.

Howard strode in and out of the back room, fetching long rec-tangular dishes containing fresh pâtés, and laying them, with their jewel-bright adornments of glistening citrus segments and berries, neatly beneath the glass counter. Puffing a little from exertion coming on top of so much early morning conversation, Howard set the last of the pâtés down and stood for a little while, looking out at the war memorial in the middle of the Square.

Pagford was as lovely as ever this morning, and Howard knew a sublime moment of exultation in the existence, both of himself, and of the town to which he belonged, as he saw it, like a pulsing heart. He was here to drink it all in—the glossy black benches, the red and purple flowers, the sunlight gilding the top of the stone cross—and Barry Fairbrother was gone. It was difficult not to sense a greater design in this sudden rearrangement of what Howard saw as the battlefield across which he and Barry had faced each other for so long.

"Howard," said Maureen sharply. *"Howard."*

A woman was striding across the Square; a thin, black-haired, brown-skinned woman in a trench coat, who was scowling at her booted feet as she walked.

"D'you think she…? Has she heard?" whispered Maureen.

"I don't know," said Howard.

Maureen, who had still not found time to change into her Dr. Scholl's, nearly turned an ankle as she backed away from the win-dows in haste, and hurried behind the counter. Howard walked slowly, majestically, to occupy the space behind the till, like a gunner moving to his post.

The bell tinkled, and Dr. Parminder Jawanda pushed open the door of the delicatessen, still frowning. She did not acknowledge Howard or Maureen, but made her way directly to the shelf of oils.

Maureen's eyes followed her with the rapt and unblinking attention of a hawk watching a field mouse.

"Morning," said Howard, when Parminder approached the counter with a bottle in her hand.

"Morning."

Dr. Jawanda rarely looked him in the eye, either at Parish Council meetings, or when they met outside the church hall. Howard was always amused by her inability to dissemble her dislike; it made him jovial, extravagantly gallant and courteous.

"Not at work today?"

"No," said Parminder, rummaging in her purse.

Maureen could not contain herself.

"Dreadful news," she said, in her hoarse, cracked voice. "About Barry Fairbrother."

"Mm," said Parminder, but then, "What?"

"About Barry Fairbrother," repeated Maureen.

"What about him?"

Parminder's Birmingham accent was still strong after sixteen years in Pagford. A deep vertical groove between her eyebrows gave her a perennially intense look, sometimes of crossness, sometimes of concentration.

"He died," said Maureen, gazing hungrily into the scowling face. "Last night. Howard's just been telling me."

Parminder remained quite still, with her hand in her purse. Then her eyes slid sideways to Howard.

"Collapsed and died in the golf club car park," Howard said. "Miles was there, saw it happen."

More seconds passed.

"Is this a joke?" demanded Parminder, her voice hard and high-pitched.

"Of course it's not a joke," said Maureen, savoring her own outrage. "Who'd make a joke like that?"

Parminder set down the oil with a bang on the glass-topped counter and walked out of the shop.

"Well!" said Maureen, in an ecstasy of disapproval. "'Is this a joke?' Charming!"

"Shock," said Howard wisely, watching Parminder hurrying back across the Square, her trench coat flapping behind her. "She'll be as upset as the widow, that one. Mind you, it'll be interesting," he added, scratching idly at the overfold of his belly, which was often itchy, "To see what she…"

He left the sentence unfinished, but it did not matter: Maureen knew exactly what he meant. Both, as they watched Councillor Jawanda disappear around a corner, were contemplating the casual vacancy: and they saw it, not as an empty space but as a magician's pocket, full of possibilities.

VIII

The Old Vicarage was the last and grandest of the Victorian houses in Church Row. It stood at the very bottom, in a big corner garden, facing St. Michael and All Saints across the road.

Parminder, who had run the last few yards down the street, fumbled with the stiff lock on the front door and let herself inside. She would not believe it until she heard it from somebody else, anybody else; but the telephone was already ringing ominously in the kitchen.

"Yes?"

"It's Vikram."

Parminder's husband was a cardiac surgeon. He worked at the South West General Hospital in Yarvil and he never usually called from work. Parminder gripped the receiver so tightly that her fingers hurt.

"I only heard by accident. It sounds like an aneurysm. I've asked Huw Jeffries to move the PM up the list. Better for Mary to know what it was. They could be doing him now."

"Right," whispered Parminder.

"Tessa Wall was there," he told her. "Call Tessa."

"Yes," said Parminder. "All right."

But when she had hung up, she sank down into one of the kitchen chairs and stared out of the window into the back garden without seeing it, her fingers pressed to her mouth.

Everything had shattered. The fact that it was all still there—the walls and the chairs and the children's pictures on the walls—meant nothing. Every atom of it had been blasted apart and reconstituted in an instant, and its appearance of permanence and solidity was laughable; it would dissolve at a touch, for everything was suddenly tissue-thin and friable.

She had no control over her thoughts; they had broken apart too, and random fragments of memory surfaced and spun out of sight again: dancing with Barry at the Walls' New Year's party, and the silly conversation they had had walking back from the last meeting of the Parish Council.

"You've got a cow-faced house," she had told him.

"*Cow*-faced? What does that mean?"

"It's narrower at the front than at the back. It's lucky. But you overlook a T-junction. That's unlucky."

"So we're luck neutral," Barry had said.

The artery in his head must have been bulging dangerously even then, and neither of them had known it.

Parminder walked blindly from the kitchen into the gloomy sitting room, which was in perpetual shade, no matter the weather, because of the towering Scots pine in the front garden. She hated that tree, but it lived on because of the fuss she and Vikram knew the neighbors would make if they felled it.

She couldn't settle. Through the hall, then back into the kitchen, where she seized the telephone and called Tessa Wall, who did not pick up. She must be at work. Parminder returned, trembling, to the kitchen chair.

Her grief was so big and wild it terrified her, like an evil beast that had erupted from under the floorboards. Barry, little, bearded Barry, her friend, her ally.

It was exactly the way her father had died. She had been fifteen, and they had come back from town to find him lying facedown on the lawn with the mower beside him, the sun hot on the back of his head. Parminder hated sudden death. The long wasting away that so many people feared was a comforting prospect to her; time to arrange and organize, time to say good-bye…

Her hands were still pressed tightly over her mouth. She stared at the grave, sweet visage of Guru Nanak pinned to the cork board.

(Vikram did not like the picture.

"What's that doing there?"

"I like it," she had said defiantly.)

Barry, dead.

She tamped down the awful urge to cry with a fierceness that her mother had always deplored, especially in the wake of her father's death, when her other daughters, and the aunts and cousins, were all wailing and beating their breasts. "And you were his favorite too!" But Parminder kept her unwept tears locked tightly inside where they seemed to undergo an alchemical transformation, returning to the outer world as lava slides of rage, disgorged periodically at her children and the receptionists at work.

She could still see Howard and Maureen behind the counter, the one immense, the other scrawny, and in her mind's eye they were looking down at her from a height as they told her that her friend was dead. With an almost welcome gush of fury and hatred she thought, *They're glad. They think they'll win now.*

She jumped up again, strode back into the sitting room and took down, from the top shelf, one volume of the *Sainchis,* her brand-new holy book. Opening it at random, she read, with no surprise, but rather a sense of looking at her own devastated face in a mirror:

O mind, the world is a deep, dark pit. On every side, Death casts forward his net.

IX

The room set aside for the guidance department at Winterdown Comprehensive opened off the school library. It had no windows and was lit by a single strip light.

Tessa Wall, head of guidance and wife of the deputy headmaster, entered the room at half-past ten, numb with fatigue and carrying a cup of strong instant coffee that she had brought up from the staff room. She was a short stout woman with a plain wide face, who cut her own graying hair—the blunt fringe was often a little lopsided—wore clothes of a homespun, crafty variety, and liked jewelry of beads and wood. Today's long skirt might have been made of hessian, and she had teamed it with a thick lumpy cardigan in pea green. Tessa hardly ever looked at herself in full-length mirrors, and boycotted shops where this was unavoidable.

She had attempted to soften the guidance room's resemblance to a cell by pinning up a Nepalese hanging she had owned since her student days: a rainbow sheet with a bright yellow sun and moon that emitted stylized, wavy rays. The rest of the bare painted surfaces were covered with a variety of posters that either gave helpful tips on boosting self-esteem or telephone numbers to call for anonymous help on a variety of health and emotional issues. The headmistress had made a slightly sarcastic remark about these the last time she had visited the guidance room.

"And if all else fails, they call ChildLine, I see," she had said, pointing to the most prominent poster.

Tessa sank into her chair with a low groan, took off her wristwatch, which pinched, and placed it on the desk beside various printed sheets and notes. She doubted that progress along the prearranged lines would be possible today; she doubted even whether Krystal Weedon would turn up. Krystal frequently walked out of school when upset, angry or bored. She was sometimes apprehended before she reached the gates and frog-marched back inside, swearing and shouting; at other times, she successfully evaded capture and escaped into days of truancy. Ten forty arrived, the bell sounded, and Tessa waited.

Krystal burst in through the door at ten fifty-one and slammed it behind her. She slumped down in front of Tessa with her arms folded across her ample bosom, her cheap earrings swinging.

"You can tell your 'usband," she said, her voice trembling, "that I never fuckin' laughed, all right?"

"Don't swear at me, please, Krystal," said Tessa.

"*I never laughed—all right?*" screamed Krystal.

A group of sixth-formers carrying folders had arrived in the library. They glanced through the glass pane in the door; one of them grinned at the sight of the back of Krystal's head. Tessa got up and let down the roller-blind over the window, then returned to her seat in front of the moon and sun.

"All right, Krystal. Why don't you tell me what happened?"

"Your *'usband* said sumthin' abou' Mister Fairbrother, right, an' I couldn't hear what he was saying, right, so Nikki tole me, and I couldn't fucking—"

"Krystal!—"

"—couldn't believe it, right, an' I shouted but I never laughed! I never fuck—"

"—Krystal—"

"*I never laughed, all right?*" shouted Krystal, arms tight across her chest, legs twisted together.

"All right, Krystal."

Tessa was used to the anger of students she saw most often in guidance. Many of them were devoid of workaday morals; they lied, misbehaved and cheated routinely, and yet their fury when wrongly accused was limitless and genuine. Tessa thought she recognized this as authentic outrage, as opposed to the synthetic kind that Krystal was adept at producing. In any case, the squawk Tessa had heard during assembly had struck her at the time as one of shock and dismay rather than amusement; Tessa had been filled with dread when Colin had publicly identified it as laughter.

"I seen Cubby—"

"Krystal!—"

"I tole your fuckin' 'usband—"

"Krystal, for the last time, please do not swear at me—"

"I told 'im I never laughed, I told 'im! An' he's still gave me fucking detention!"

Tears of fury gleamed in the girl's heavily penciled eyes. Blood had flowed into her face; peony pink, she glared at Tessa, poised to run, to swear, to give Tessa the finger too. Nearly two years of gossamer-fine trust, laboriously spun between them, was stretching, on the point of tearing.

"I believe you, Krystal. I believe you didn't laugh, but please do not swear at me."

Suddenly, stubby fingers were rubbing the smeary eyes. Tessa pulled a wad of tissues from out of her desk drawer and handed them across to Krystal, who grabbed them without thanks, pressed them to each eye and blew her nose. Krystal's hands were the most touching part of her: the fingernails were short and broad, untidily painted, and all her hand movements were as naive and direct as a small child's.

Tessa waited until Krystal's snorting breaths had slowed down. Then she said, "I can tell you're upset that Mr. Fairbrother has died—"

"Yer, I am," said Krystal, with considerable aggression. "So?"

Tessa had a sudden mental image of Barry listening in to this conversation. She could see his rueful smile; she heard him, quite clearly, saying "bless her heart." Tessa closed her stinging eyes, unable to speak. She heard Krystal fidget, counted slowly to ten, and opened her eyes again. Krystal was staring at her, arms still folded, flushed and defiant-looking.

"I'm very sorry about Mr. Fairbrother too," said Tessa. "He was an old friend of ours, actually. That's the reason Mr. Wall is a bit—"

"I told 'im I never—"

"Krystal, please let me finish. Mr. Wall is very upset today, and that's probably why he…why he misinterpreted what you did. I'll speak to him."

"He won't change his fuck—"

"*Krystal!*"

"Well, he won'."

Krystal banged the leg of Tessa's desk with her foot, beating out a rapid rhythm. Tessa removed her elbows from the desk, so as not to feel the vibration, and said, "I'll speak to Mr. Wall."

She adopted what she believed was a neutral expression and waited patiently for Krystal to come to her. Krystal sat in truculent silence, kicking the table leg, swallowing regularly.

"What was wrong with Mr. Fairbrother?" she said at last.

"They think an artery burst in his brain," said Tessa.

"Why did it?"

"He was born with a weakness he didn't know about," said Tessa.

Tessa knew that Krystal's familiarity with sudden death was greater than her own. People in Krystal's mother's circle died prematurely with such frequency that they might have been involved in some secret war of which the rest of the world knew nothing. Krystal had told Tessa how, when she was six years old, she had found the corpse of an unknown young man in her mother's bathroom. It had been the catalyst for one of her many removals into the care of her Nana Cath. Nana Cath loomed large in many of Krystal's stories about her childhood; a strange mixture of savior and scourge.

"Our crew'll be fucked now," said Krystal.

"No, it won't," said Tessa. "And don't swear, Krystal, please."

"It will," said Krystal.

Tessa wanted to contradict her, but the impulse was squashed by exhaustion. Krystal was right, anyway, said a disconnected, rational part of Tessa's brain. The rowing eight *would* be finished. Nobody except Barry could have brought Krystal Weedon into any group and kept her there. She would leave, Tessa knew it; probably Krystal knew it herself. They sat for a while without speaking, and Tessa was too tired to find words that might have changed the atmosphere between them. She felt shivery, exposed, skinned to the bone. She had been awake for over twenty-four hours.

(Samantha Mollison had telephoned from the hospital at ten o'clock, just as Tessa was emerging from a long soak in the bath to watch the BBC news. She had scrambled back into her clothes while Colin made inarticulate noises and blundered into the furniture. They had called upstairs to tell their son where they were going, then run out to the car. Colin had driven far too fast into Yarvil, as though he might bring Barry back if he could do the journey in record time; outstrip reality and trick it into rearranging itself.)

"If you ain' gonna talk to me, I'll go," said Krystal.

"Don't be rude, please, Krystal," said Tessa. "I'm very tired this morning. Mr. Wall and I were at the hospital last night with Mr. Fairbrother's wife. They're good friends of ours."

(Mary had unraveled completely when she had seen Tessa, flinging her arms around her, burying her face in Tessa's neck with a dreadful wailing shriek. Even as Tessa's own tears began to splatter down Mary's narrow back, she thought quite distinctly that the noise Mary was making was called keening. The body that Tessa had so often envied, slim and petite, had quaked in her arms, barely able to contain the grief it was being asked to bear.

Tessa could not remember Miles and Samantha leaving. She did not know them very well. She supposed that they had been glad to go.)

"I seen 'is wife," said Krystal. "Blonde woman, she come to see us race."

"Yes," said Tessa.

Krystal was chewing on the tips of her fingers.

"He were gonna get me talkin' to the paper," she said abruptly.

"What's that?" asked Tessa, confused.

"Mr. Fairbrother wuz. He wuz gonna get me interviewed. On me own."

There had once been a piece in the local paper about the Winterdown rowing eight coming first in the regional finals. Krystal, whose reading was poor, had brought a copy of the paper in to show Tessa, and Tessa had read the article aloud, inserting exclamations of delight and admiration. It had been the happiest guidance session she had ever known.

"Were they going to interview you because of rowing?" asked Tessa. "The crew again?"

"No," said Krystal. "Other stuff." Then, "When's his funeral?"

"We don't know yet," said Tessa.

Krystal gnawed at her nails, and Tessa could not summon the energy to break the silence that solidified around them.

X

The announcement of Barry's death on the Parish Council website sank with barely a ripple, a tiny pebble into the teeming ocean. All the same, the telephone lines in Pagford were busier than usual this Monday, and little knots of pedestrians kept congregating on the narrow pavements to check, in shocked tones, the exactness of their information.

As the news traveled, an odd transmutation took place. It happened to the signature dotting the files in Barry's office and to the emails littering in-boxes of his enormous acquaintance, which began to take on the pathos of the crumb trail of a lost boy in a forest. These rapid scribbles, the pixels arranged by fingers henceforth forever still, acquired the macabre aspect of husks. Gavin was already a little repelled by the sight of his dead friend's texts on his phone, and one of the girls from the rowing eight, still crying as she walked back from assembly, found a form that Barry had signed in her schoolbag, and became almost hysterical.

The twenty-three-year-old journalist at the *Yarvil and District Gazette* had no idea that Barry's once busy brain was now a heavy handful of spongy tissue on a metal tray in South West General. She read through what he had emailed her an hour before his death, then called his mobile number, but nobody answered. Barry's phone, which he had turned off at Mary's request before they left for the golf club, was sitting silently beside the microwave in the kitchen, along with the rest of his personal effects that the hospital had given her to take home. Nobody had touched them. These familiar objects—his key fob, his phone, his worn old wallet—seemed like pieces of the dead man himself; they might have been his fingers, his lungs.

Onwards and outwards the news of Barry's death spread, radiating, halo-like, from those who had been at the hospital. Onwards and outwards as far as Yarvil, reaching those who knew Barry only by sight or reputation or by name. Gradually the facts lost form and focus; in some cases they became distorted. In places, Barry himself was lost behind the nature of his ending, and he became no more than an eruption of vomit and piss, a twitching pile of catastrophe, and it seemed incongruous, even grotesquely comical, that a man should have died so messily at the smug little golf club.

So it was that Simon Price, who had been one of the first to hear about Barry's death, in his house on top of the hill overlooking Pagford, met a rebounding version at the Harcourt-Walsh print-works in Yarvil where he had worked ever since leaving school. It was borne to him on the lips of a young, gum-chewing forklift driver, whom Simon found skulking beside his office door, after a late-afternoon return from the bathroom.

The boy had not come, in the first place, to discuss Barry at all.

"That thing you said you migh' be int'rested in," he mumbled, when he had followed Simon into the office, and Simon had closed the door, "I cud do it for yeh Wednesday, if yeh still fancied it."

"Yeah?" said Simon, sitting himself down at his desk. "I thought you said it was all ready to go?"

"'Tis, but I can't fix up collection till Wednesday."

"How much did you say again?"

"Eighty notes, fer cash."

The boy chewed vigorously; Simon could hear his saliva working. Gum-chewing was one of Simon's many pet hates.

"It's the proper thing, though, is it?" Simon demanded. "Not some knockoff piece of crap?"

"Come straight from the warehouse," said the boy, shifting his feet and his shoulders. "Real thing, still boxed up."

"All right, then," said Simon. "Bring it in Wednesday."

"What, here?" The boy rolled his eyes. "Nah, not to work, mate...Where d'you live?"

"Pagford," said Simon.

"Where'bouts in Pagford?"

Simon's aversion to naming his home bordered on the supersti-tious. He not only disliked visitors—invaders of his privacy and possible despoilers of his property—but he saw Hilltop House as inviolate, immaculate, a world apart from Yarvil and the crashing, grinding printworks.

"I'll come and pick it up after work," said Simon, ignoring the question. "Where are you keeping it?"

The boy did not look happy. Simon glared at him.

"Well, I'd need the cash up front," the forklift driver temporized.

"You get the money when I've got the goods."

"Dun' work like that, mate."

Simon thought he might be developing a headache. He could not dislodge the horrible idea, implanted by his careless wife that morning, that a tiny bomb might tick undetected for ages inside a man's brain. The steady clatter and rumble of the printing press beyond the door was surely not good for him; its relentless battery might have been thinning his artery walls for years.

"All right," he grunted, and rolled over in his chair to extract his wallet from his back pocket. The boy stepped up to the desk, his hand out.

"D'yeh live anywhere near Pagford golf course?" he asked, as Simon counted out tenners into his palm. "Mate o' mine was up there las' night, an' saw a bloke drop dead. Jus' fuckin' puked an' keeled over an' died in the car park."

"Yeah, I heard," said Simon, massaging the last note between his fingers before he passed it over, to make sure there were not two stuck together.

"Bent councillor, he was. The bloke who died. He was takin' backhanders. Grays was paying him to keep them on as contractors."

"Yeah?" said Simon, but he was immensely interested.

Barry Fairbrother, who'd have thought it?

"I'll get back ter yeh, then," said the boy, shoving the eighty pounds deep into his back pocket. "And we'll go an' get it, Wednesday."

The office door closed. Simon forgot his headache, which was really no more than a twinge, in his fascination at the revelation of Barry Fairbrother's crookedness. Barry Fairbrother, so busy and sociable, so popular and cheerful: and all the time, trousering bribes from Grays.

The news did not rock Simon as it would have done nearly everybody else who had known Barry, nor did it diminish Barry in his eyes; on the contrary, he felt an increased respect for the dead man. Anyone with any brains was working, constantly and covertly, to grab as much as they could; Simon knew that. He gazed unseeingly at the spreadsheet on his computer screen, deaf once more to the grinding of the printworks beyond his dusty window.

There was no choice but to work from nine to five if you had a family, but Simon had always known that there were other, better ways; that a life of ease and plenty dangled over his head like a great bulging piñata, which he might smash open if only he had a stick big enough, and the knowledge of when to strike. Simon had the child's belief that the rest of the world exists as staging for their personal drama; that destiny hung over him, casting clues and signs in his path, and he could not help feeling that he had been vouchsafed a sign, a celestial wink.

Supernatural tip-offs had accounted for several apparently quixotic decisions in Simon's past. Years previously, when still a lowly apprentice at the printworks, with a mortgage he could barely afford and a newly pregnant wife, he had bet one hundred pounds on a well-favored Grand National runner called Ruthie's Baby, which had fallen at the second last. Shortly after they had bought Hilltop House, Simon had sunk twelve hundred pounds, which Ruth had been hoping to use for curtains and carpets, into a time-share scheme run by a flash, fiddling old acquaintance from Yarvil. Simon's investment had vanished with the company director, but although he had raged and sworn and kicked his younger son halfway down the stairs for getting in his way, he had not contacted the police. He had known about certain irregularities in the way the company operated before he put his money there, and he foresaw awkward questions.

Set against these calamities, though, were strokes of luck, dodges that worked, hunches that paid off, and Simon gave great weight to these when totaling his score; they were the reason that he kept faith with his stars, that reinforced him in his belief that the universe had more in store for him than the mug's game of working for a modest salary until he retired or died. Scams and shortcuts; leg-ups and back-scratches; everyone was at it, even, as it turned out, little Barry Fairbrother.

There, in his poky office, Simon Price gazed covetously on a vacancy among the ranks of insiders to a place where cash was now trickling down onto an empty chair with no lap waiting to catch it.

(Olden Days)

Trespassers

12.43 As against trespassers (who, in principle, must take other people's premises and their occupiers as they find them)…

Charles Arnold-Baker
Local Council Administration,
Seventh Edition

I

Pagford Parish Council was, for its size, an impressive force. It met once a month in a pretty Victorian church hall, and attempts to cut its budget, annex any of its powers or absorb it into some newfangled unitary authority had been strenuously and successfully resisted for decades. Of all the local councils under the higher authority of Yarvil District Council, Pagford prided itself on being the most obstreperous, the most vocal and the most independent.

Until Sunday evening, it had comprised sixteen local men and women. As the town's electorate tended to assume that a wish to serve on the Parish Council implied competence to do so, all sixteen councillors had gained their seats unopposed.

Yet this amicably appointed body was currently in a state of civil war. An issue that had been causing fury and resentment in Pagford for sixty-odd years had reached a definitive phase, and factions had rallied behind two charismatic leaders.

To grasp fully the cause of the dispute it was necessary to comprehend the precise depth of Pagford's dislike and mistrust of the city of Yarvil, which lay to its north.

Yarvil's shops, businesses, factories, and the South West General Hospital, provided the bulk of the employment in Pagford. The small town's youths generally spent their Saturday nights in Yarvil's cinemas and nightclubs. The city had a cathedral, several parks and two enormous shopping centers, and these things were pleasant enough to visit if you had sated yourself on Pagford's superior charms. Even so, to true Pagfordians, Yarvil was little more than a necessary evil. Their attitude was symbolized by the high hill, topped by Pargetter Abbey, which blocked Yarvil from Pagford's sight, and allowed the townspeople the happy illusion that the city was many miles further away than it truly was.

II

It so happened that Pargetter Hill also obscured from the town's view another place, but one that Pagford had always considered particularly its own. This was Sweetlove House, an exquisite, honey-colored Queen Anne manor, set in many acres of park and farmland. It lay within Pagford Parish, halfway between the town and Yarvil.

For nearly two hundred years the house had passed smoothly from generation to generation of aristocratic Sweetloves, until finally, in the early 1900s, the family had died out. All that remained these days of the Sweetloves' long association with Pagford, was the grandest tomb in the churchyard of St. Michael and All Saints, and a smattering of crests and initials over local records and buildings, like the footprints and coprolites of extinct creatures.

After the death of the last of the Sweetloves, the manor house had changed hands with alarming rapidity. There were constant fears in Pagford that some developer would buy and mutilate the beloved landmark. Then, in the 1950s, a man called Aubrey Fawley purchased the place. Fawley was soon known to be possessed of substantial private wealth, which he supplemented in mysterious ways in the City. He had four children, and a desire to settle permanently. Pagford's approval was raised to still giddier heights by the swiftly circulated intelligence that Fawley was descended, through a collateral line, from the Sweetloves. He was clearly half a local already, a man whose natural allegiance would be to Pagford and not to Yarvil. Old Pagford believed that the advent of Aubrey

Fawley meant the return of a charmed era. He would be a fairy godfather to the town, like his ancestors before him, showering grace and glamour over their cobbled streets.

Howard Mollison could still remember his mother bursting into their tiny kitchen in Hope Street with the news that Aubrey had been invited to judge the local flower show. Her runner beans had taken the vegetable prize three years in a row, and she yearned to accept the silver-plated rose bowl from a man who was already, to her, a figure of old-world romance.

III

But then, so local legend told, came the sudden darkness that attends the appearance of the wicked fairy.

Even as Pagford was rejoicing that Sweetlove House had fallen into such safe hands, Yarvil was busily constructing a swath of council houses to its south. The new streets, Pagford learned with unease, were consuming some of the land that lay between the city and the town.

Everybody knew that there had been an increasing demand for cheap housing since the war, but the little town, momentarily distracted by Aubrey Fawley's arrival, began to buzz with mistrust of Yarvil's intentions. The natural barriers of river and hill that had once been guarantors of Pagford's sovereignty seemed diminished by the speed with which the red-brick houses multiplied. Yarvil filled every inch of the land at its disposal, and stopped at the northern border of Pagford Parish.

The town sighed with a relief that was soon revealed to be premature. The Cantermill Estate was immediately judged insufficient to meet the population's needs, and the city cast about for more land to colonize.

It was then that Aubrey Fawley (still more myth than man to the people of Pagford) made the decision that triggered a festering sixty-year grudge.

Having no use for the few scrubby fields that lay beyond the new development, he sold the land to Yarvil Council for a good price, and used the cash to restore the warped paneling in the hall of Sweetlove House.

Pagford's fury was unconfined. The Sweetlove fields had been an important part of its buttress against the encroaching city; now the ancient border of the parish was to be compromised by an overspill of needy Yarvilians. Rowdy town hall meetings, seething letters to the newspaper and Yarvil Council, personal remonstrance with those in charge—nothing succeeded in reversing the tide.

The council houses began to advance again, but with one difference. In the brief hiatus following completion of the first estate, the council had realized that it could build more cheaply. The fresh eruption was not of red brick but of concrete in steel frames. This second estate was known locally as the Fields, after the land on which it had been built, and was marked as distinct from the Cantermill Estate by its inferior materials and design.

It was in one of the Fields' concrete and steel houses, already cracking and warping by the late 1960s, that Barry Fairbrother was born.

IV

In spite of Yarvil Council's bland assurances that maintenance of the new estate would be its own responsibility, Pagford—as the furious townsfolk had predicted from the first—was soon landed with new bills. While the provision of most services to the Fields, and the upkeep of its houses, fell to Yarvil Council, there remained matters that the city, in its lofty way, delegated to the parish: the maintenance of public footpaths, of lighting and public seating, of bus shelters and common land.

Graffiti blossomed on the bridges spanning the Pagford to Yarvil road; Fields bus shelters were vandalized; Fields teenagers strewed the play park with beer bottles and threw rocks at the street lamps. A local footpath, much favored by tourists and ramblers, became a popular spot for Fields youths to congregate, "and worse," as Howard Mollison's mother put it darkly. It fell to Pagford Parish Council to clean, to repair and to replace, and the funds dispersed by Yarvil were felt from the first to be inadequate for the time and expense required.

No part of Pagford's unwanted burden caused more fury or bitterness than the fact that Fields children now fell inside the catchment area of St. Thomas's Church of England Primary School. Young Fielders had the right to don the coveted blue and white uniform, to play in the yard beside the foundation stone laid by Lady Charlotte Sweetlove and to deafen the tiny classrooms with their strident Yarvil accents.

It swiftly became common lore in Pagford that houses in the Fields had become the prize and goal of every benefit-supported Yarvil family with school-age children; that there was a great ongoing scramble across the boundary line from the Cantermill Estate, much as Mexicans streamed into Texas. Their beautiful St. Thomas's—a magnet for professional commuters to Yarvil, who were attracted by the tiny classes, the rolltop desks, the aged stone building and the lush green playing field—would be overrun and swamped by the offspring of scroungers, addicts and mothers whose children had all been fathered by different men.

This nightmarish scenario had never been fully realized, because while there were undoubtedly advantages to St. Thomas's there were also drawbacks: the need to buy the uniform, or else to fill in all the forms required to qualify for assistance for the same; the necessity of attaining bus passes, and of getting up earlier to insure that the children arrived at school on time. Some households in the Fields found these onerous obstacles, and their children were absorbed instead by the large plain-clothes primary school that had been built to serve the Cantermill Estate. Most of the Fields pupils who came to St. Thomas's blended in well with their peers in Pagford; some, indeed, were admitted to be perfectly nice children. Thus Barry Fairbrother had moved up through the school, a popular and clever class clown, only occasionally noticing that the smile of a Pagford parent stiffened when he mentioned the place where he lived.

Nevertheless, St. Thomas's was sometimes forced to take in a Fields pupil of undeniably disruptive nature. Krystal Weedon had been living with her great-grandmother in Hope Street when the time came for her to start school, so that there was really no way of stopping her coming, even though, when she moved back to the Fields with her mother at the age of eight, there were high hopes locally that she would leave St. Thomas's for good.

Krystal's slow passage up the school had resembled the passage of a goat through the body of a boa constrictor, being highly visible and uncomfortable for both parties concerned. Not that Krystal was always in class: for much of her career at St. Thomas's she had been taught one-on-one by a special teacher.

By a malign stroke of fate, Krystal had been in the same class as Howard and Shirley's eldest granddaughter, Lexie. Krystal had once hit Lexie Mollison so hard in the face that she had knocked out two of her teeth. That they had already been wobbly was not felt, by Lexie's parents and grandparents, to be much of an extenuation.

It was the conviction that whole classes of Krystals would be waiting for their daughters at Winterdown Comprehensive that finally decided Miles and Samantha Mollison on removing both their daughters to St. Anne's, the private girls' school in Yarvil, where they had become weekly boarders. The fact that his granddaughters had been driven out of their rightful places by Krystal Weedon, swiftly became one of Howard's favorite conversational examples of the estate's nefarious influence on Pagford life.

V

The first effusion of Pagford's outrage had annealed into a quieter, but no less powerful, sense of grievance. The Fields polluted and corrupted a place of peace and beauty, and the smoldering townsfolk remained determined to cut the estate adrift. Yet boundary reviews had come and gone, and reforms in local government had swept the area without effecting any change: the Fields remained part of Pagford. Newcomers to the town learned quickly that abhorrence of the estate was a necessary passport to the goodwill of that hard core of Pagfordians who ran everything.

But now, at long last—over sixty years after Old Aubrey Fawley had handed Yarvil that fatal parcel of land—after decades of patient work, of strategizing and petitioning, of collating information and haranguing subcommittees—the anti-Fielders of Pagford found themselves, at last, on the trembling threshold of victory.

The recession was forcing local authorities to streamline, cut and reorganize. There were those on the higher body of Yarvil District Council who foresaw an advantage to their electoral fortunes if the crumbling little estate, likely to fare poorly under the austerity measures imposed by the national government, were to be scooped up, and its disgruntled inhabitants joined to their own voters.

Pagford had its own representative in Yarvil: District Councillor Aubrey Fawley. This was not the man who had enabled the construction of the Fields, but his son, "Young Aubrey," who had inherited Sweetlove House and who worked through the week as a merchant banker in London. There was a whiff of penance in Aubrey's involvement in local affairs, a sense that he ought to make right the wrong that his father had so carelessly done to the little town. He and his wife Julia donated and gave out prizes at the agricultural show, sat on any number of local committees, and threw an annual Christmas party to which invitations were much coveted.

It was Howard's pride and delight to think that he and Aubrey were such close allies in the continuing quest to reassign the Fields to Yarvil, because Aubrey moved in a higher sphere of commerce that commanded Howard's fascinated respect. Every evening, after the delicatessen closed, Howard removed the tray of his old-fashioned till, and counted up coins and dirty notes before placing them in a safe. Aubrey, on the other hand, never touched money during his office hours, and yet he caused it to move in unimaginable quantities across continents. He managed it and multiplied it and, when the portents were less propitious, he watched magisterially as it vanished. To Howard, Aubrey had a mystique that not even a worldwide financial crash could dent; the delicatessen owner was impatient of anyone who blamed the likes of Aubrey for the mess in which the country found itself. Nobody had complained when things were going well, was Howard's oft-repeated view, and he accorded Aubrey the respect due to a general injured in an unpopular war.

Meanwhile, as a district councillor, Aubrey was privy to all kinds of interesting statistics, and in a position to share a good deal of information with Howard about Pagford's troublesome satellite. The two men knew exactly how much of the district's resources were poured, without return or apparent improvement, into the Fields' dilapidated streets; that nobody owned their own house in the Fields (whereas the red-brick houses of the Cantermill Estate were almost all in private hands these days; they had been prettified almost beyond recognition, with window boxes and porches and neat front lawns); that nearly two-thirds of Fields dwellers lived entirely off the state; and that a sizable proportion passed through the doors of the Bellchapel Addiction Clinic.

VI

Howard carried the mental image of the Fields with him always, like a memory of a nightmare: boarded windows daubed with obscenities; smoking teenagers loitering in the perennially defaced bus shelters;

satellite dishes everywhere, turned to the skies like the denuded ovules of grim metal flowers. He often asked rhetorically why they could not have organized and made the place over—what was stopping the residents from pooling their meager resources and buying a lawnmower between the lot of them? But it never happened: the Fields waited for the councils, District and Parish, to clean, to repair, to maintain; to give and give and give again.

Howard would then recall the Hope Street of his boyhood, with its tiny back gardens, each hardly more than tablecloth-sized squares of earth, but most, including his mother's, bristling with runner beans and potatoes. There was nothing, as far as Howard could see, to stop the Fielders growing fresh vegetables; nothing to stop them disciplining their sinister, hooded, spray-painting offspring; nothing to stop them pulling themselves together as a community and tackling the dirt and the shabbiness; nothing to stop them cleaning themselves up and taking jobs; nothing at all. So Howard was forced to draw the conclusion that they were choosing, of their own free will, to live the way they lived, and that the estate's air of slightly threatening degradation was nothing more than a physical manifestation of ignorance and indolence.

Pagford, by contrast, shone with a kind of moral radiance in Howard's mind, as though the collective soul of the community was made manifest in its cobbled streets, its hills, its picturesque houses. To Howard, his birthplace was much more than a collection of old buildings, and a fast-flowing, tree-fringed river, the majestic silhouette of the abbey above or the hanging baskets in the Square. For him, the town was an ideal, a way of being; a micro-civilization that stood firmly against a national decline.

"I'm a Pagford man," he would tell summertime tourists, "born and bred." In so saying, he was giving himself a profound compliment disguised as a commonplace. He had been born in Pagford and he would die there, and he had never dreamed of leaving, nor itched for more change of scene than could be had from watching the seasons transform the surrounding woods and river; from watching the Square blossom in spring or sparkle at Christmas.

Barry Fairbrother had known all this; indeed, he had said it. He had laughed right across the table in the church hall, laughed right in Howard's face. "You know, Howard, you *are* Pagford to me." And Howard, not discomposed in the slightest (for he had always met Barry joke for joke), had said, "I'll take that as a great compliment, Barry, however it was intended."

He could afford to laugh. The one remaining ambition of Howard's life was within touching distance: the return of the Fields to Yarvil seemed imminent and certain.

Then, two days before Barry Fairbrother had dropped dead in a car park, Howard had learned from an unimpeachable source that his opponent had broken all known rules of engagement, and had gone to the local paper with a story about the blessing it had been for Krystal Weedon to be educated at St. Thomas's.

The idea of Krystal Weedon being paraded in front of the reading public as an example of the successful integration of the Fields and Pagford might (so Howard said) have been funny, had it not been so serious. Doubtless Fairbrother would have coached the girl, and the truth about her foul mouth, the endlessly interrupted classes, the other children in tears, the constant removals and reintegrations, would be lost in lies.

Howard trusted the good sense of his fellow townsfolk, but he feared journalistic spin and the interference of ignorant do-gooders. His objection was both principled and personal: he had not yet forgotten how his granddaughter had sobbed in his arms, with bloody sockets where her teeth had been, while he tried to soothe her with a promise of triple prizes from the tooth fairy.

Tuesday

I

Two mornings after her husband's death, Mary Fairbrother woke at five o'clock. She had slept in the marital bed with her twelve-year-old, Declan, who had crawled in, sobbing, shortly after midnight. He was sound asleep now, so Mary crept out of the room and went down into the kitchen to cry more freely. Every hour that passed added to her grief, because it bore her further away from the living man, and because it was a tiny foretaste of the eternity she would have to spend without him. Again and again she found herself forgetting, for the space of a heartbeat, that he was gone forever and that she could not turn to him for comfort.

When her sister and brother-in-law came through to make breakfast, Mary took Barry's phone and withdrew into the study, where she started looking for the numbers of some of Barry's huge acquaintance. She had only been at it a matter of minutes when the mobile in her hands rang.

"Yes?" she murmured.

"Oh, hello! I'm looking for Barry Fairbrother. Alison Jenkins from the *Yarvil and District Gazette*."

The young woman's jaunty voice was as loud and horrible in Mary's ear as a triumphal fanfare; the blast of it obliterated the sense of the words.

"Sorry?"

"Alison Jenkins from the *Yarvil and District Gazette*. I want to speak to Barry Fairbrother? It's about his article on the Fields."

"Oh?" said Mary.

"Yes, he hasn't attached details of this girl he talks about. We're supposed to interview her. Krystal Weedon?"

Each word felt to Mary like a slap. Perversely, she sat still and silent in Barry's old swivel chair and let the blows rain upon her.

"Can you hear me?"

"Yes," said Mary, her voice cracking. "I can hear you."

"I know Mr. Fairbrother was very keen to be present when we interview Krystal, but time's running—"

"He won't be able to be present," said Mary, her voice eliding into a screech. "He won't be able to talk about the *bloody* Fields any more, or about anything, ever again!"

"What?" said the girl on the end of the line.

"My husband is *dead,* all right. He's *dead,* so *the Fields* will have to get on without him, won't they?"

Mary's hands were shaking so much that the mobile slipped through her fingers, and for the few moments before she managed to cut the call, she knew that the journalist heard her ragged sobs. Then she remembered that most of Barry's last day on earth and their wedding anniversary had been given over to his obsession with the Fields and Krystal Weedon; fury erupted, and she threw the mobile so hard across the room that it hit a framed picture of their four children, knocking it to the floor. She began to scream and cry at once, and her sister and brother-in-law both came running upstairs and burst into the room.

All they could get out of her at first was, "The Fields, the bloody, *bloody* Fields..."

"It's where me and Barry grew up," her brother-in-law muttered, but he explained no further, for fear of inflaming Mary's hysteria.

II

Social worker Kay Bawden and her daughter Gaia had moved from London only four weeks previously, and were Pagford's very newest inhabitants. Kay was unfamiliar with the contentious history of the Fields; it was simply the estate where many of her clients lived. All she knew about Barry Fairbrother was that his death had precipitated the miserable scene in her kitchen, when her lover Gavin had fled from her and her scrambled eggs, and so dashed all the hopes his lovemaking had roused in her.

Kay spent Tuesday lunchtime in a layby between Pagford and Yarvil, eating a sandwich in her car, and reading a large stack of notes. One of her colleagues had been signed off work due to stress, with the immediate result that Kay had been lumbered with a third of her cases. Shortly before one o'clock, she set off for the Fields.

She had already visited the estate several times, but she was not yet familiar with the warrenlike streets. At last she found Foley Road, and identified from a distance the house that she thought must belong to the Weedons. The file had made it clear what she was likely to meet, and her first glimpse of the house met her expectations.

A pile of refuse was heaped against the front wall: carrier bags bulging with filth, jumbled together with old clothes and unbagged, soiled nappies. Bits of the rubbish had tumbled or been scattered over the scrubby patch of lawn, but the bulk of it remained piled beneath one of the two downstairs windows. A bald old tire sat in the middle of the lawn; it had been shifted sometime recently, because a foot away there was a flattened yellowish-brown circle of dead grass. After ringing the doorbell, Kay noticed a used condom glistening in the grass beside her feet, like the gossamer cocoon of some huge grub.

She was experiencing that slight apprehension that she had never quite overcome, although it was nothing compared to the nerves with which she had faced unknown doors in the early days. Then, in spite of all her training, in spite of the fact that a colleague usually accompanied her, she had, on occasion, been truly afraid.

Dangerous dogs; men brandishing knives; children with grotesque injuries; she had found them all, and worse, in her years of entering strangers' houses.

Nobody came in answer to the bell, but she could hear a small child grizzling through the ground-floor window on her left, which was ajar. She tried rapping on the door instead and a tiny flake of peeling cream paint fell off and landed on the toe of her shoe. It reminded her of the state of her own new home. It would have been nice if Gavin had offered to help with some of her redecorating, but he had said not a word. Sometimes Kay counted over the things that he had not said or done, like a miser looking through IOUs, and felt bitter and angry, and determined to extract repayment.

She knocked again, sooner than she would have done if she had not wanted to distract herself from her own thoughts, and this time, a distant voice said, "I'm fuckin' *comin'*."

The door swung open to reveal a woman who appeared simultaneously childlike and ancient, dressed in a dirty pale-blue T-shirt and a pair of men's pajama bottoms. She was the same height as Kay, but shrunken; the bones of her face and sternum showed sharply through the thin white skin. Her hair, which was home-dyed, coarse and very red, looked like a wig on top of a skull, her pupils were minuscule and her chest virtually breastless.

"Hello, are you Terri? I'm Kay Bawden, from Social Services. I'm covering for Mattie Knox."

There were silvery pockmarks all over the woman's fragile gray-white arms, and an angry red, open sore on the inside of one forearm. A wide area of scar tissue on her right arm and lower neck gave the skin a shiny plastic appearance. Kay had known an addict in London who had accidentally set fire to her house, and realized too late what was happening.

"Yeah, righ'," said Terri, after an overlong pause. When she spoke, she seemed much older; several of her teeth were missing. She turned her back on Kay and took a few unsteady steps down the dark hallway. Kay followed. The house smelled of stale food, of sweat, of unshifted filth. Terri led Kay through the first door on the left, into a tiny sitting room.

66

There were no books, no pictures, no photographs, no television; nothing except a pair of filthy old armchairs and a broken set of shelves. Debris littered the floor. A pile of brand-new cardboard boxes piled against the wall struck an incongruous note.

A bare-legged little boy was standing in the middle of the floor, dressed in a T-shirt and a bulging pull-up nappy. Kay knew from the file that he was three and a half. His whining seemed unconscious and unmotivated, a sort of engine noise to signal that he was there. He was clutching a miniature cereal packet.

"So this must be Robbie?" said Kay.

The boy looked at her when she said his name, but kept grizzling.

Terri shoved aside a scratched old biscuit tin, which had been sitting on one of the dirty frayed armchairs, and curled herself into the seat, watching Kay from beneath drooping eyelids. Kay took the other chair, on the arm of which was perched an overflowing ashtray. Cigarette ends had fallen into the seat of Kay's chair; she could feel them beneath her thighs.

"Hello, Robbie," said Kay, opening Terri's file.

The little boy continued to whine, shaking the cereal packet; something inside it rattled.

"What have you got in there?" Kay asked.

He did not answer, but shook the packet more vigorously. A small plastic figure flew out of it, soared in an arc and fell down behind the cardboard boxes. Robbie began to wail. Kay watched Terri, who was staring at her son, blank-faced. Eventually, Terri murmured, "S'up, Robbie?"

"Shall we see if we can get it out?" said Kay, quite glad of a reason to stand up and brush down the back of her legs. "Let's have a look."

She put her head close to the wall to look into the gap behind the boxes. The little figure was wedged near the top. She forced her hand into the gap. The boxes were heavy and difficult to move. Kay managed to grasp the model, which, once she had it in her hand, she saw to be a squat, fat Buddha-like man, bright purple all over.

"Here you are," she said.

Robbie's wailing ceased; he took the figure and put it back inside the cereal packet, which he started to shake again.

Kay glanced around. Two small toy cars lay upside down under the broken shelves.

"Do you like cars?" Kay asked Robbie, pointing at them.

He did not follow the direction of her finger, but squinted at her with a mixture of calculation and curiosity. Then he trotted off and picked up a car and held it up for her to see.

"Broom," he said. "Ca."

"That's right," said Kay. "Very good. Car. Broom broom."

She sat back down and took her notepad out of her bag.

"So, Terri. How have things been going?"

There was a pause before Terri said, "All righ'."

"Just to explain: Mattie has been signed off sick, so I'm covering for her. I'll need to go over some of the information she's left me, to check that nothing's changed since she saw you last week, all right?

"So, let's see: Robbie is in nursery now, isn't he? Four mornings a week and two afternoons?"

Kay's voice seemed to reach Terri only distantly. It was like talking to somebody sitting at the bottom of a well.

"Yeah," she said, after a pause.

"How's that going? Is he enjoying it?"

Robbie crammed the matchbox car into the cereal box. He picked up one of the cigarette butts that had fallen off Kay's trousers, and squashed it on top of the car and the purple Buddha.

"Yeah," said Terri drowsily.

But Kay was poring over the last of the untidy notes Mattie had left before she had been signed off.

"Shouldn't he be there today, Terri? Isn't Tuesday one of the days he goes?"

Terri seemed to be fighting a desire to sleep. Once or twice her head rocked a little on her shoulders. Finally she said, "Krystal was s'posed to drop him and she never."

"Krystal is your daughter, isn't she? How old is she?"

"Fourteen," said Terri dreamily, "'n'a half."

Kay could see from her notes that Krystal was sixteen. There was a long pause.

Two chipped mugs stood at the foot of Terri's armchair. The dirty liquid in one of them had a bloody look. Terri's arms were folded across her flat breast.

"I had him dressed," said Terri, dragging the words from deep in her consciousness.

"Sorry, Terri, but I've got to ask," said Kay. "Have you used this morning?"

Terri passed a bird's-claw hand over her mouth.

"Nah."

"Wantashit," said Robbie, and he scurried toward the door.

"Does he need help?" Kay asked, as Robbie vanished from sight, and they heard him scampering upstairs.

"Nah, 'e can doot alone," slurred Terri. She propped her drooping head on her fist, her elbow on the armchair. Robbie let out a shout from the landing.

"Door! Door!"

They heard him thumping wood. Terri did not move.

"Shall I help him?" Kay suggested.

"Yeah," said Terri.

Kay climbed the stairs and operated the stiff handle on the door for Robbie. The room smelled rank. The bath was gray, with successive brown tidemarks around it, and the toilet had not been flushed. Kay did this before allowing Robbie to scramble onto the seat. He screwed up his face and strained loudly, indifferent to her presence. There was a loud splash, and a noisome new note was added to the already putrid air. He got down and pulled up his bulging nappy without wiping; Kay made him come back, and tried to persuade him to do it for himself, but the action seemed quite foreign to him. In the end she did it for him. His bottom was sore: crusty, red and irritated. The nappy stank of ammonia. She tried to remove it, but he yelped, lashed out at her, then pulled away, scampering back down to the sitting room with his nappy sagging. Kay wanted to wash her hands, but there was no soap. Trying not to inhale, she closed the bathroom door behind her.

She glanced into the bedrooms before returning downstairs. The contents of all three spilled out onto the cluttered landing. They were all sleeping on mattresses. Robbie seemed to be sharing a room with his mother. A couple of toys lay among the dirty clothes strewn all over the floor: cheap, plastic and too young for him. To Kay's surprise, the duvet and pillows both had covers on them.

Back in the sitting room, Robbie was whining again, banging his fist against the stack of cardboard boxes. Terri was watching from beneath half-closed eyelids. Kay brushed off the seat of her chair before sitting back down.

"Terri, you're on the methadone program at the Bellchapel Clinic, isn't that right?"

"Mm," said Terri drowsily.

"And how's that going, Terri?"

Pen poised, Kay waited, pretending that the answer was not sitting in front of her.

"Are you still going to the clinic, Terri?"

"Las' week. Friday, I goes."

Robbie pounded the boxes with his fists.

"Can you tell me how much methadone you're on?"

"Hundred and fifteen mils," said Terri.

It did not surprise Kay that Terri could remember this, but not the age of her daughter.

"Mattie says here that your mother has been helping with Robbie and Krystal; is that still the case?"

Robbie flung his hard, compact little body against the pile of boxes, which swayed.

"Be careful, Robbie," said Kay, and Terri said, "Leave 'em," with the closest thing to alertness Kay had heard in her dead voice.

Robbie returned to beating the boxes with his fists, for the pleasure, apparently, of listening to the hollow drumbeat.

"Terri, is your mother still helping to look after Robbie?"

"Not m'mother, gran."

"Robbie's gran?"

"*My* gran, innit. She dun...she ain't well."

Kay glanced over at Robbie again, her pen at the ready. He was not underweight; she knew that from the feel and look of him, half-naked, as she had wiped his backside. His T-shirt was dirty, but

70

his hair, when she had bent over him, had smelled surprisingly of shampoo. There were no bruises on his milk-white arms and legs, but there was the sodden, bagging nappy; he was three and a half.

"M'ungry," he shouted, giving the box a final, futile whack. "M'ungry."

"You c'n'ave a biscuit," slurred Terri, but not moving. Robbie's yells turned to noisy sobs and screams. Terri made no attempt to leave her chair. It was impossible to talk over the din.

"Shall I get him one?" shouted Kay.

"Yeah."

Robbie ran past Kay into the kitchen. It was almost as dirty as the bathroom. Other than the fridge, cooker and washing machine, there were no gadgets; the counters carried only dirty plates, another overflowing ashtray, carrier bags, moldy bread. The lino was tacky and stuck to the soles of Kay's shoes. Rubbish had overflowed the bin, on top of which sat a pizza box, precariously balanced.

"'N there," said Robbie, jabbing a finger at the wall unit without looking at Kay. "'N there."

More food than Kay had expected was stacked in the cupboard: tins, a packet of biscuits, a jar of instant coffee. She took two biscuits from the packet and handed them to him; he snatched them and ran away again, back to his mother.

"So, do you like going to the nursery, Robbie?" she asked him, as he sat scoffing the biscuits on the floor.

He did not answer.

"Yeah, 'e likes it," said Terri, slightly more awake. "Don' you, Robbie? 'E likes it."

"When was he last there, Terri?"

"Las' time. Yesterday."

"Yesterday was Monday, he couldn't have been there then," said Kay, making notes. "That isn't one of the days he goes."

"Wha'?"

"I'm asking about nursery. Robbie's supposed to be there today. I need to know when he was last there."

"I told you, din' I? Las' time."

Her eyes were more fully open than Kay had yet seen them. The timbre of her voice was still flat, but antagonism was struggling to the surface.

"Are you a dyke?" she asked.

"No," said Kay, still writing.

"You look like a dyke," said Terri.

Kay continued to write.

"Juice," Robbie shouted, chocolate smeared over his chin.

This time Kay did not move. After another long pause, Terri lurched out of her chair and wove her way into the hall. Kay leaned forward and shifted the loose lid of the biscuit tin Terri had displaced when she sat down. Inside was a syringe, a bit of grubby cotton wool, a rusty-looking spoon and a dusty polythene bag. Kay snapped the lid back on firmly, while Robbie watched her. Terri returned, after some distant clattering, carrying a cup of juice, which she shoved at the little boy.

"There," she said, more to Kay than to her son, and she sat back down again. She missed the seat and collided with the arm of the chair on her first attempt; Kay heard the bone collide with wood, but Terri seemed to feel no pain. She settled herself back into the sagging cushions and surveyed the social worker with bleary indifference.

Kay had read the file from cover to cover. She knew that nearly everything of value in Terri Weedon's life had been sucked into the black hole of her addiction; that it had cost her two children; that she barely clung to two more; that she prostituted herself to pay for heroin; that she had been involved in every sort of petty crime; and that she was currently attempting rehab for the umpteenth time.

But not to feel, not to care...*Right now,* Kay thought, *she's happier than I am.*

III

At the start of the second post-lunch period, Stuart "Fats" Wall walked out of school. His experiment in truancy was undertaken in no rash spirit; he had decided the previous night that he would miss the double period of computing that finished the afternoon. He might have chosen to skip any lesson, but it so happened that his best friend Andrew Price (known to Fats as Arf) was in a different set in computing, and Fats, in spite of his best efforts, had not succeeded in being demoted to join him.

Fats and Andrew were perhaps equally aware that the admiration in their relationship flowed mostly from Andrew to Fats; but Fats alone suspected that he needed Andrew more than Andrew needed him. Lately, Fats had started to regard this dependency in the light of a weakness, but he reasoned that, while his liking for Andrew's company lingered, he might as well miss a double period where he had to do without it anyway.

Fats had been told by a reliable informant that the one fail-safe way of quitting the Winterdown grounds without being spotted from a window was to climb over the side wall by the bike shed. This, therefore, he did, dropping down by his fingertips into the narrow lane on the other side. He landed without mishap, strode off along the narrow path and turned left, onto the busy dirty main road.

Safely on his way, he lit a cigarette and proceeded past the run-down little shops. Five blocks along, Fats turned left again, into the first of the streets that made up the Fields. He loosened his school tie with one hand as he walked, but did not remove it. He did not care that he was, conspicuously, a schoolboy. Fats had never even attempted to customize his uniform in any way; to pin badges on his lapels or adjust his tie knot to suit fashion; he wore his school clothes with the disdain of a convict.

The mistake ninety-nine percent of humanity made, as far as Fats could see, was being ashamed of what they were; lying about it, trying to be somebody else. Honesty was Fats' currency, his weapon and defense. It frightened people when you were honest; it shocked them. Other people, Fats had discovered, were mired in embarrassment and pretense, terrified that their truths might leak out, but Fats was attracted by rawness, by everything that was ugly but honest, by the dirty things about which the likes of his father felt humiliated and disgusted. Fats thought a lot about messiahs and pariahs; about men labeled mad or criminal; noble misfits shunned by the sleepy masses.

The difficult thing, the glorious thing, was to be who you really were, even if that person was cruel or dangerous, *particularly* if cruel and dangerous. There was courage in not disguising the animal you happened to be. On the other hand, you had to avoid pretending to be more of an animal than you were: take that path, start exaggerating or faking and you became just another Cubby, just as much of a liar, a hypocrite. *Authentic* and *inauthentic* were words that Fats used often, inside his own head; they had laser-precise meaning for him, in the way he applied them to himself and others.

He had decided that he possessed traits that were authentic, which ought therefore to be encouraged and cultivated; but also that some of his habits of thought were the unnatural product of his unfortunate upbringing, and consequently inauthentic and to be purged. Lately, he had been experimenting with acting on what he thought were his authentic impulses, and ignoring or suppressing the guilt and fear (inauthentic) that such actions seemed to engender. Undoubtedly, this was becoming easier with practice. He wanted to toughen up inside, to become invulnerable, to be free of the fear of consequences: to rid himself of spurious notions of goodness and badness.

One of the things that had begun to irritate him about his own dependence on Andrew was that the latter's presence sometimes curbed and limited the full expression of Fats' authentic self. Somewhere in Andrew was a self-drawn map of what constituted fair play, and lately Fats had caught looks of displeasure, confusion and disappointment poorly disguised on his old friend's face. Andrew pulled up short at extremes of baiting and derision. Fats did not hold this against Andrew; it would have been inauthentic for Andrew to join in, unless that was what he really, truly wanted. The trouble was that Andrew was displaying an attachment to the kind of morality against which Fats was waging an increasingly determined war. Fats suspected that the right thing to do, the correctly unsentimental act in pursuit of full authenticity, would have been to cut Andrew adrift; and yet he still preferred Andrew's company to anybody else's.

Fats was convinced that he knew himself particularly well; he explored the nooks and crevices of his own psyche with an attention he had recently ceased to give to anything else. He spent hours interrogating himself about his own impulses, desires and fears, attempting to discriminate between those that were truly his and those that he had been taught to feel. He examined his own attachments (nobody else he knew, he was sure, was ever this honest with themselves; they drifted, half asleep, through life): and his conclusion had been that Andrew, whom he had known since he was five, was the person for whom he felt the most straightforward affection; that, even though he was now old enough to see through her, he retained an attachment to his mother that was not his own fault; and that he actively despised Cubby, who represented the acme and pinnacle of inauthenticity.

On the Facebook page that Fats curated with a care he devoted to almost nothing else, he had highlighted a quotation he had found on his parents' bookshelves:

> I do not want believers, I think I am too malicious to believe in myself ... I have a terrible fear I shall one day be pronounced holy ... I do not want to be a saint, rather even a buffoon ... perhaps I am a buffoon ...

Andrew liked it very much, and Fats liked how impressed he was.

In the time it took him to pass the bookmaker's—mere seconds—Fats' thoughts lit on his father's dead friend, Barry Fairbrother. Three long loping strides past the racehorses printed on posters behind the grubby glass, and Fats saw Barry's joking, bearded face, and heard Cubby's booming excuse of a laugh, which had often rung out almost before Barry had made one of his feeble jokes, in the mere excitement of his presence. Fats did not wish to examine these memories any further; he did not interrogate himself on the reasons for his instinctive inner flinch; he did not ask himself whether the dead man had been authentic or inauthentic; he dismissed the idea of Barry Fairbrother, and his father's ludicrous distress, and pressed on.

Fats was curiously joyless these days, even though he made everybody else laugh as much as ever. His quest to rid himself of restrictive morality was an attempt to regain something he was sure had been stifled in him, something that he had lost as he had left childhood. What Fats wanted to recover was a kind of innocence, and the route he had chosen back to it was through all the things that were supposed to be bad for you, but which, paradoxically, seemed to Fats to be the one true way to authenticity; to a kind of purity. It was curious how often everything was back to front, the inverse of what they told you; Fats was starting to think that if you flipped every bit of received wisdom on its head you would have the truth. He wanted to journey through dark labyrinths and wrestle with the strangeness that lurked within; he wanted to crack open piety and expose hypocrisy; he wanted to break taboos and squeeze wisdom from their bloody hearts; he wanted to achieve a state of amoral grace, and be baptized backwards into ignorance and simplicity.

And so he decided to break one of the few school rules he had not yet contravened, and walked away, into the Fields. It was not merely that the crude pulse of reality seemed nearer here than in any other place he knew; he also had a vague hope of stumbling across certain notorious people about whom he was curious, and, though he barely acknowledged it to himself, because it was one of the few yearnings for which he did not have words, he sought an open door, and a dawning recognition, and a welcome to a home he did not know he had.

Moving past the putty-colored houses on foot, rather than in his mother's car, he noticed that many of them were free of graffiti and debris, and that some imitated (as he saw it) the gentility of Pagford, with net curtains and ornaments on the windowsills. These details were less readily apparent from a moving vehicle, where Fats' eye was irresistibly drawn from boarded window to debris-strewn lawn. The neater houses held no interest for Fats. What drew him on were the places where chaos or lawlessness was in evidence, even if only of the puerile spray-canned variety.

Somewhere near here (he did not know exactly where) lived Dane Tully. Tully's family was infamous. His two older brothers and his father spent a lot of time in prison. There was a rumor that the last time Dane had had a fight (with a nineteen-year-old, so the story went, from the Cantermill Estate), his father had escorted him to the rendezvous, and had stayed to fight Dane's opponent's older brothers. Tully had turned up at school with his face cut, his lip swollen and his eye blacked. Everyone agreed that he had put in one of his infrequent appearances simply to show off his injuries.

Fats was quite sure that he would have played it differently. To care what anyone else thought of your smashed face was inauthentic. Fats would have liked to fight, and then to go about his normal life, and if anyone knew it would be because they had glimpsed him by chance.

Fats had never been hit, despite offering increasing provocation. He thought, often these days, about how it would feel to get into a fight. He suspected that the state of authenticity he sought would include violence; or, at least, would not *preclude* violence. To be prepared to hit, and to take a hit, seemed to him to be a form of courage to which he ought to aspire. He had never needed his fists: his tongue had sufficed; but the emergent Fats was starting to despise his own articulacy and to admire authentic brutality. The matter of knives, Fats debated with himself more gingerly. To buy a blade now, and let it be known he was carrying it, would be an act of crashing inauthenticity, a pitiful aping of the likes of Dane Tully; Fats' insides crawled at the thought of it. If ever the time came when he *needed* to carry a knife, that would be different. Fats did not rule out the possibility that such a time would come, though he admitted to himself that the idea was frightening. Fats was scared of things that pierced flesh, of needles and blades. He had been the only one to faint when they had had their meningitis vaccinations back at St. Thomas's. One of the few ways that Andrew had found to discompose Fats was to unsheath his EpiPen around him; the Adrenalin-filled needle that Andrew was supposed to carry with him at all times because of his dangerous nut allergy. It made Fats feel sick when Andrew brandished it at him or pretended to jab him with it.

Wandering without any particular destination, Fats caught sight of the sign to Foley Road. That was where Krystal Weedon lived. He was unsure whether she was in school today, and it was not his intention to make her think that he had come looking for her.

They had an agreement to meet on Friday evening. Fats had told his parents that he was going to Andrew's because they were collaborating on an English project. Krystal seemed to understand what they were going to do; she seemed up for it. She had so far allowed him to insert two fingers inside her, hot and firm and slippery; he had unhooked her bra and been permitted to place his hands on her warm, heavy breasts. He had sought her out deliberately at the Christmas disco; led her out of the hall under Andrew's and the others' incredulous gazes, round the back of the drama hall. She had seemed quite as surprised as anybody else, but had offered, as he had hoped and expected, virtually no resistance. His targeting of Krystal had been a deliberate act; and he had had his cool and brazen retort ready, when it had come to facing down his mates' jeers and taunts.

"If you want chips, you don't go to a fucking salad bar."

He had thought out that analogy in advance, but he had still had to spell it out for them.

"You boys keep wanking. I want a shag."

That had wiped the smiles off their faces. He could tell that all of them, Andrew included, were forced to choke down their jeers at his choice, in admiration of his unabashed pursuit of the one, the only true goal. Fats had undoubtedly chosen the most direct route to get there; none of them could argue with his commonsense practicality, and Fats could tell that every single one of them was asking himself why he had not had the guts to consider this means to a most satisfactory end.

"Do me a favor, and don't mention this to my mother, all right?" Fats had muttered to Krystal, coming up for air in between long, wet explorations of each other's mouths, while his thumbs had rubbed backwards and forwards over her nipples.

She had half sniggered, then kissed him with more aggression. She had not asked him why he had picked her, had not asked him anything really; she seemed, like him, to be pleased by the reactions of their entirely separate tribes, to glory in the watchers' confusion; even in his friends' pantomime of disgust. He and Krystal had barely spoken to each other during three further bouts of carnal exploration and experimentation. Fats had engineered all of them, but she had made herself more readily available than usual, choosing to hang about in places he might find her easily. Friday night was the first time they would meet by prearrangement. He had bought condoms.

The prospect of finally going all the way had something to do with him truanting today and coming to the Fields, although he had not thought of Krystal herself (as opposed to her splendid breasts and that miraculously unguarded vagina) until he saw the name of her street.

Fats doubled back, lighting another cigarette. Something about seeing the name of Foley Road had given him a strange sense that his timing was wrong. The Fields today were banal and inscrutable, and that which he sought, the thing he hoped to recognize when he found it, was curled up somewhere, out of sight. And so he walked back to school.

IV

Nobody was answering their telephone. Back in the Child Protection team's room, Kay had been punching in numbers on and off for nearly two hours, leaving messages, asking everyone to call her back: the Weedons' health visitor, their family doctor, the Cantermill

Nursery and the Bellchapel Addiction Clinic. Terri Weedon's file lay open on the desk in front of her, bulging and battered.

"Using again, is she?" said Alex, one of the women with whom Kay shared an office. "Bellchapel'll kick her out for good this time. She claims she's terrified Robbie'll be taken off her, but she can't keep off the smack."

"It's the third time she's been through Bellchapel," said Una.

On the basis of what she had seen that afternoon, Kay thought the time was right for a case review, to pull together those professionals who shared responsibility for individual fragments of Terri Weedon's life. She continued to press redial between dealing with other work, while in the corner of the office their own telephone rang repeatedly and clicked immediately onto the answering machine. The Child Protection team's room was cramped and cluttered, and it smelled of spoiled milk, because Alex and Una had a habit of emptying the dregs of their coffee cups into the pot of a depressed-looking yucca plant in the corner.

Mattie's most recent notes were untidy and chaotic, peppered with crossings out, misdated and partial. Several key documents were missing from the file, including a letter sent by the addiction clinic a fortnight previously. It was quicker to ask Alex and Una for information.

"Last case review woulda been..." said Alex, frowning at the yucca plant, "over a year ago, I reckon."

"And they thought Robbie was OK to stay with her then, obviously," said Kay, the receiver pressed between ear and shoulder as she tried and failed to find the notes of the review in the bulging folder.

"It wasn't a case of him staying with her; it was whether he was going to go back to her or not. He was put out to a foster mother, because Terri was beaten up by a client and ended up in hospital. She got clean, got out, and was mad to get Robbie back. She went back on the Bellchapel program, she was off the game and makin' a proper effort. Her mother was saying she'd help. So she got him home and a few months later she'd started shooting up again."

"It's not Terri's mother who helps, though, is it?" said Kay, whose head was starting to ache, as she tried to decipher Mattie's big, untidy writing. "It's her grandmother, the kids' greatgrandmother. So she must be knocking on, and Terri said something about her being ill, this morning. If Terri's the only carer now…"

"The daughter's sixteen," said Una. "She mostly takes care of Robbie."

"Well, she's not doing a great job," said Kay. "He was in a pretty bad state when I got there this morning."

But she had seen far worse: welts and sores, gashes and burns, tar-black bruises; scabies and nits; babies lying on carpets covered in dog shit; kids crawling on broken bones; and once (she dreamed of it, still), a child who had been locked in a cupboard for five days by his psychotic stepfather. That one had made the national news. The most immediate danger to Robbie Weedon's safety had been the pile of heavy boxes in his mother's sitting room, which he had attempted to climb when he realized that it attracted Kay's full attention. Kay had carefully restacked them into two lower piles before leaving. Terri had not liked her touching the boxes; nor had she liked Kay telling her that she ought to take off Robbie's sodden nappy. Terri had been roused, in fact, to foulmouthed, though still slightly hazy, fury, and had told Kay to fuck off and stay away.

Kay's mobile rang and she picked it up. It was Terri's key drug worker.

"I've been trying to get you for days," said the woman crossly. It took several minutes for Kay to explain that she was not Mattie, but this did not much reduce the woman's antagonism.

"Yeah, we're still seeing her, but she tested positive last week. If she uses again, she's out. We've got twenty people right now who could take her place on the program and maybe get some benefit from it. This is the third time she's been through."

Kay did not say she knew that Terri had used that morning.

"Have either of you got any paracetamol?" Kay asked Alex and Una, once the drug worker had given her full details of Terri's attendance and lack of progress at the clinic, and rung off.

Kay took her painkillers with tepid tea, lacking the energy to get up and go to the water cooler in the corridor. The office was stuffy, the radiator cranked up high. As the daylight faded from the sky outside, the strip lighting over her desk intensified: it turned her multitude of papers a bright yellow-white; buzzing black words marched in endless lines.

"They're going to close down Bellchapel Clinic, you watch," said Una, who was working at her PC with her back to Kay. "Got to make cuts. Council funds one of the drug workers. Pagford Parish owns the building. I heard they're planning to tart it up and try and rent to a better-paying client. They've had it in for that clinic for years."

Kay's temple throbbed. The name of her new hometown made her feel sad. Without pausing to think, she did the thing that she had vowed not to do after he had failed to call the previous evening: she picked up her mobile and keyed in Gavin's office number.

"Edward Collins and Co," said a woman's voice, after the third ring. They answered your calls immediately out in the private sector, when money might depend on it.

"Could I speak to Gavin Hughes, please?" said Kay, staring down at Terri's file.

"Who's speaking, please?"

"Kay Bawden," said Kay.

She did not look up; she did not want to catch either Alex's or Una's eyes. The pause seemed interminable.

(They had met in London at Gavin's brother's birthday party. Kay had not known anyone there, except for the friend who had dragged her along for support. Gavin had just split up with Lisa; he had been a little drunk, but had seemed decent, reliable and conventional, not at all the kind of man that Kay usually went for. He had poured out the story of his broken relationship, and then gone home with her to the flat in Hackney. He had been keen while the affair remained long-distance, visiting at weekends and telephoning her regularly; but when, by a miracle, she had got the job in Yarvil, for less money, and put her flat in Hackney on the market, he had seemed to take fright...)

"His line's still busy, would you like to hold?"

"Yes, please," said Kay miserably.

(If she and Gavin did not work out...but they *had* to work out. She had moved for him, changed jobs for him, uprooted her daughter for him. He would never have let that happen, surely, unless his intentions were serious? He must have thought through the consequences if they split up: how awful and awkward it would be, running across each other constantly in a tiny town like Pagford?)

"Putting you through," said the secretary, and Kay's hopes soared.

"Hi," said Gavin. "How are you?"

"Fine," lied Kay, because Alex and Una were listening. "Are you having a good day?"

"Busy," said Gavin. "You?"

"Yes."

She waited, the phoned pressed tightly against her ear, pretending that he was speaking to her, listening to the silence.

"I wondered whether you wanted to meet up tonight," she asked finally, feeling sick.

"Er...I don't think I can," he said.

How can you not know? What have you got on?

"I might have to do something...it's Mary. Barry's wife. She wants me to be a pallbearer. So I might have to...I think I've got to find out what that involves and everything."

Sometimes, if she simply remained quiet, and let the inadequacy of his excuses reverberate on the air, he became ashamed and back-tracked.

"I don't suppose that'll take all evening, though," he said. "We could meet up later, if you wanted."

"All right, then. Do you want to come over to mine, as it's a school night?"

"Er...yeah, OK."

"What time?" she asked, wanting him to make one decision.

"I dunno...nine-ish?"

After he had rung off, Kay kept the phone pressed tightly to her ear for a few moments, then said, for the benefit of Alex and Una, "I do, too. See you later, babe."

V

As guidance teacher, Tessa's hours varied more than her husband's. She usually waited until the end of the school day to take their son home in her Nissan, leaving Colin (whom Tessa—although she knew what the rest of the world called him, including nearly all the parents who had caught the habit from their children—never addressed as Cubby) to follow them, an hour or two later, in his Toyota. Today, though, Colin met Tessa in the car park at twenty past four, while the schoolchildren were still swarming out of the front gates into parental cars, or onto their free buses.

The sky was a cold iron-gray, like the underside of a shield. A sharp breeze lifted the hems of skirts and rattled the leaves on the immature trees; a spiteful, chill wind that sought out your weakest places, the nape of your neck and your knees, and which denied you the comfort of dreaming, of retreating a little from reality. Even after she had closed the car door on it, Tessa felt ruffled and put out, as she would have been by somebody crashing into her without apology.

Beside her in the passenger seat, his knees absurdly high in the cramped confines of her car, Colin told Tessa what the computing teacher had come to his office to tell him, twenty minutes previously.

"...not there. Didn't turn up for the whole double period. Said he thought he'd better come straight and tell me. So that'll be all over the staff room, tomorrow. Exactly what he wants," said Colin furiously, and Tessa knew that they were not talking about the computing teacher anymore. "He's just sticking two fingers up at me, as usual."

Her husband was pale with exhaustion, with shadows beneath his reddened eyes, and his hands were twitching slightly on the handle of his briefcase. Fine hands, with big knuckles and long slender fingers, they were not altogether dissimilar from their son's. Tessa had pointed this out to her husband and son recently; neither had evinced the smallest pleasure at the thought that there was some faint physical resemblance between them.

"I don't think he's—" began Tessa, but Colin was talking again.

"—So, he'll get detention like everyone else and I'll damn well

84

punish him at home too. We'll see how he likes that, shall we? We'll see whether that's a laughing matter. We can start by grounding him for a week, we'll see how funny that is."

Biting back her response, Tessa scanned the sea of black-clad students, walking with heads down, shivering, drawing their thin coats close, their hair blown into their mouths. A chubby-cheeked and slightly bewildered-looking first year was looking all around for a lift that had not arrived. The crowd parted and there was Fats, loping along with Arf Price as usual, the wind blowing his hair off his gaunt face. Sometimes, at certain angles, in certain lights, it was easy to see what Fats would look like as an old man. For an instant, from the depths of her tiredness, he seemed a complete stranger, and Tessa thought how extraordinary it was that he was turning away to walk toward her car, and that she would have to go back out into that horrible hyperreal breeze to let him in. But when he reached them, and gave her his small grimace of a smile, he reconstituted himself immediately into the boy she loved in spite of it all, and she got out again, and stood stoically in the knife-sharp wind while he folded himself into the car with his father, who had not offered to move.

They pulled out of the car park, ahead of the free buses, and set off through Yarvil, past the ugly, broken-down houses of the Fields, toward the bypass that would speed them back to Pagford. Tessa watched Fats in the rearview mirror. He was slumped in the back, gazing out of the window, as though his parents were two people who had picked him up hitchhiking, connected to him merely by chance and proximity.

Colin waited until they reached the bypass; then he asked, "Where were you when you should have been in computing this afternoon?"

Tessa glanced irresistibly into the mirror again. She saw her son yawn. Sometimes, even though she denied it endlessly to Colin, Tessa wondered whether Fats really was waging a dirty, personal war on his father with the whole school as audience. She knew things about her son she would not have known if she had not worked in guidance; students told her things, sometimes innocently, sometimes slyly.

Miss, do you mind Fats smoking? D'you let him do it at home?

She locked away this small repository of illicit booty, obtained unintentionally, and brought it to neither her husband's nor her son's attention, even though it dragged at her, weighed on her.

"Went for a walk," Fats said calmly. "Thought I'd stretch the old legs."

Colin twisted in his seat to look at Fats, straining against his seat belt as he shouted, his gestures further restricted and hampered by his overcoat and briefcase. When he lost control, Colin's voice rose higher and higher, so that he was shouting almost in falsetto. Through it all, Fats sat in silence, an insolent half-smile curving his thin mouth, until his father was screaming insults at him, insults that were blunted by Colin's innate dislike of swearing, his self-consciousness when he did it.

"You cocky, self-centered little…little *shit,*" he screamed, and Tessa, whose eyes were so full of tears that she could barely see the road, was sure that Fats would be duplicating Colin's timid, falsetto swearing for the benefit of Andrew Price tomorrow morning.

Fats does a great imitation of Cubby's walk, miss, have you seen it?

"How dare you talk to me like that? How *dare* you skip classes?"

Colin screamed and raged, and Tessa had to blink the tears out of her eyes as she took the turning to Pagford and drove through the Square, past Mollison and Lowe, the war memorial and the Black Canon; she turned left at St. Michael and All Saints into Church Row, and, at last, into the driveway of their house, by which time Colin had shouted himself into squeaky hoarseness and Tessa's cheeks were glazed and salty. When they all got out, Fats, whose expression had not altered a whit during his father's long diatribe, let himself in through the front door with his own key, and proceeded upstairs at a leisurely pace without looking back.

Colin threw his briefcase down in the dark hall and rounded on Tessa. The only illumination came from the stained-glass panel over the front door, which cast strange colors over his agitated, domed and balding head, half bloody, half ghostly blue.

"D'you see?" he cried, waving his long arms, "D'you see what I'm dealing with?"

"Yes," she said, taking a handful of tissues from the box on the hall table and mopping her face, blowing her nose. "Yes, I do."

"Not a thought in his head for what we're going through!" said Colin, and he started to sob, big whooping dry sobs, like a child with croup. Tessa hurried forward and put her arms around Colin's chest, a little above his waist, for, short and stout as she was, that was the highest bit she could reach. He stooped, clinging to her; she could feel his trembling, and the heaving of his rib cage under his coat.

After a few minutes, she gently disengaged herself, led him into the kitchen and made him a pot of tea.

"I'm going to take a casserole up to Mary's," said Tessa, after she had sat for a while, stroking his hand. "She's got half the family there. We'll get an early night, once I'm back."

He nodded and sniffed, and she kissed him on the side of his head before heading out to the freezer. When she came back, carrying the heavy, icy dish, he was sitting at the table, cradling his mug in his big hands, his eyes closed.

Tessa set down the casserole, wrapped in a polythene bag, on the tiles beside the front door. She pulled on the lumpy green cardigan she often wore instead of a jacket, but did not put on her shoes. Instead, she tiptoed upstairs to the landing and then, taking less trouble to be quiet, up the second flight to the loft conversion.

A swift burst of ratlike activity greeted her approach to the door. She knocked, giving Fats time to hide whatever it was he had been looking at online, or, perhaps, the cigarettes he did not know she knew about.

"Yeah?"

She pushed open the door. Her son was crouching stagily over his schoolbag.

"Did you have to play truant today, of all days?"

Fats straightened up, long and stringy; he towered over his mother.

"I was there. I came in late. Bennett didn't notice. He's useless."

"Stuart, please. *Please*."

She wanted to shout at the kids at work, sometimes, too. She wanted to scream, *You must accept the reality of other people. You think that reality is up for negotiation, that we think it's whatever you say it is. You must accept that we are as real as you are; you must accept that you are not God.*

"Your father's very upset, Stu. Because of Barry. Can't you understand that?"

"Yes," said Fats.

"I mean, it's like Arf dying would be to you."

He did not respond, nor did his expression alter much, yet she sensed his disdain, his amusement.

"I know you think you and Arf are very different orders of being to the likes of your father and Barry—"

"No," said Fats, but only, she knew, in the hope of ending the conversation.

"I'm going to take some food over to Mary's house. I am begging you, Stuart, not to do anything else to upset your father while I'm gone. Please, Stu."

"Fine," he said, with half a laugh, half a shrug. She felt his attention swooping, swallowlike, back to his own concerns, even before she had closed the door.

VI

The spiteful wind blew away the low-hanging cloud of late afternoon and, at sunset, died out. Three houses along from the Walls', Samantha Mollison sat facing her lamp-lit reflection in the dressing-table mirror, and found the silence and the stillness depressing.

It had been a disappointing couple of days. She had sold virtually nothing. The sales rep from Champêtre had turned out to be a jowly man with an abrasive manner and a holdall full of ugly bras. Apparently he reserved his charm for the preliminaries, for in person he was all business, patronizing her, criticizing her stock, pushing for an order. She had been imagining somebody younger, taller and sexier; she had wanted to get him and his garish under-wear out of her little shop as quickly as possible.

She had bought a "with deepest sympathy" card for Mary Fairbrother that lunchtime, but could not think what to write in it, because, after their nightmare journey to the hospital together, a simple signature did not seem enough. Their relationship had never been close. You bumped up against each other all the time in a place as small as Pagford, but she and Miles had not really *known* Barry and Mary. If anything, it might have been said that they were in opposing camps, what with Howard and Barry's endless clashes about the Fields...not that she, Samantha, gave a damn one way or another. She held herself above the smallness of local politics.

Tired, out of sorts and bloated after a day of indiscriminate snacking, she wished that she and Miles were not going to dinner at her parents-in-law's. Watching herself in the mirror, she put her hands flat against the sides of her face and pulled the skin gently back towards her ears. A younger Samantha emerged by millim-eters. Turning her face slowly from side to side, she examined this taut mask. Better, much better. She wondered what it would cost; how much it would hurt; whether she would dare. She tried to imagine what her mother-in-law would say if she appeared with a firm new face. Shirley and Howard were, as Shirley frequently reminded them, helping to pay for their granddaughters' education.

Miles entered the bedroom; Samantha released her skin and picked up her under-eye concealer, tilting her head back, as she always did when applying makeup: it pulled the slightly sagging skin at her jaw taut and minimized the pouches under her eyes. There were short, needle-deep lines at the edges of her lips. These could be filled, she had read, with a synthetic, injectable compound. She wondered how much difference that would make; it would surely be cheaper than a facelift, and perhaps Shirley would not notice. In the mirror over her shoulder, she saw Miles pulling off his tie and shirt, his big belly spilling over his work trousers.

"Weren't you meeting someone today? Some rep?" he asked. Idly he scratched his hairy navel, staring into the wardrobe.

"Yes, but it wasn't any good," said Samantha. "Crappy stuff."

Miles enjoyed what she did; he had grown up in a home where retail was the only business that mattered, and he had never lost the respect for commerce that Howard had instilled in him. Then there were all the opportunities for jokes, and for other less subtly disguised forms of self-congratulation that her line of trade afforded. Miles never seemed to tire of making the same old quips or the same sly allusions.

"Bad fit?" he inquired knowledgeably.

"Bad design. Horrible colors."

Samantha brushed and tied back her thick dry brown hair, watching Miles in the mirror as he changed into chinos and a polo shirt. She was on edge, feeling that she might snap or cry at the smallest provocation.

Evertree Crescent was only a few minutes away, but Church Row was steep, so they drove. Darkness was falling properly, and at the top of the road they passed a shadowy man with Barry Fairbrother's silhouette and gait; it gave Samantha a shock and she glanced back at him, wondering who he could be. Miles' car turned left at the top of the road, then, barely a minute later, right, into the half-moon of 1930s bungalows.

Howard and Shirley's house, a low, wide-windowed building of red brick, boasted generous sweeps of green lawn at the front and back, which were mown into stripes during the summer by Miles. During the long years of their occupancy, Howard and Shirley had added carriage lamps, a white wrought-iron gate and terracotta pots full of geraniums on either side of the front door. They had also put up a sign beside the doorbell, a round, polished piece of wood on which was written, in old Gothic black lettering complete with quotation marks, "Ambleside."

Samantha was sometimes cruelly witty at the expense of her parents-in-law's house. Miles tolerated her jibes, accepting the implication that he and Samantha, with their stripped-back floors and doors, their rugs on bare boards, their framed art prints and their stylish, uncomfortable sofa, had the better taste; but in his secret soul he preferred the bungalow in which he had grown up. Nearly every surface was covered with something plushy and soft; there were no drafts and the reclining chairs were deliciously comfortable. After he mowed the lawn in the summer, Shirley would bring him a cool beer while he lay back in one of them, watching the cricket on the wide-screen TV. Sometimes one of his daughters would come with him and sit beside him, eating ice cream with chocolate sauce especially made for her granddaughters by Shirley.

"Hello, darling," said Shirley, when she opened the door. Her short, compact shape suggested a neat little pepper pot, in its sprigged apron. She stood on tiptoe for her tall son to kiss her, then said, "Hello, Sam," and turned away immediately. "Dinner's nearly ready. Howard! Miles and Sam are here!"

The house smelled of furniture polish and good food. Howard emerged from the kitchen, a bottle of wine in one hand, a corkscrew in the other. In a practiced move, Shirley backed smoothly into the dining room, enabling Howard, who took up almost the entire width of the hall, to pass, before she trotted into the kitchen.

"Here they are, the good Samaritans," boomed Howard. "And how's the brassiere business, Sammy? Breasting the recession all right?"

"Business is surprisingly bouncy, actually, Howard," said Samantha.

Howard roared with laughter, and Samantha was sure that he would have patted her on the bottom if he had not been holding the corkscrew and bottle. She tolerated all of her father-in-law's little squeezes and slaps as the harmless exhibitionism of a man grown too fat and old to do anything more; in any case, it annoyed Shirley, which always pleased Samantha. Shirley never showed her displeasure openly; her smile did not flicker, nor did her tone of sweet reasonableness falter, but within a short time of any of Howard's mild lewdnesses, she always tossed a dart, hidden in a feathery flourish, at her daughter-in-law. Mention of the girls' escalating school fees, solicitous inquiries about Samantha's diet, asking Miles whether he did not think Mary Fairbrother had an awfully pretty figure; Samantha endured it all, smiling, and punished Miles for it later.

"Hello, Mo!" said Miles, preceding Samantha into what Howard and Shirley called the lounge. "Didn't know you were going to be here!"

"Hello, handsome," said Maureen, in her deep, gravelly voice. "Give me a kiss."

Howard's business partner was sitting in a corner of the sofa, clutching a tiny glass of sherry. She was wearing a fuchsia pink dress with dark stockings and high patent-leather heels. Her jet-black hair was heavily lacquered into a bouffant, beneath which her face was pale and monkeyish, with a thick smear of shocking pink lipstick that puckered as Miles bent low to kiss her cheek.

"Been talking business. Plans for the new café. Hello, Sam, sweetheart," Maureen added, patting the sofa beside her. "Oh, you are lovely and tanned, is that still from Ibiza? Come sit down by me. What a shock for you at the golf club. It must have been ghastly."

"Yes, it was," said Samantha.

And for the first time she found herself telling somebody the story of Barry's death, while Miles hovered, looking for a chance to interrupt. Howard handed out large glasses of Pinot Grigio, paying close attention to Samantha's account. Gradually, in the glow of Howard's and Maureen's interest, with the alcohol kindling a comforting fire inside her, the tension Samantha had carried with her for two days seemed to drain away and a fragile sense of well-being blossomed.

The room was warm and spotless. Shelving units on either side of the gas fire displayed an array of ornamental china, nearly all of it commemorating some royal landmark or anniversary of the reign of Elizabeth II. A small bookcase in the corner contained a mixture of royal biographies and the glossy cookbooks that had overrun the kitchen. Photographs adorned the shelves and walls: Miles and his younger sister Patricia beamed from a twin frame in matching school uniforms; Miles and Samantha's two daughters, Lexie and Libby, were represented over and again from babyhood to teens. Samantha figured only once in the family gallery, though in one of the largest and most prominent pictures. It showed her and Miles' wedding day sixteen years before. Miles was young and handsome, piercing blue eyes crinkled at the photographer, whereas

Samantha's eyes were closed in a half blink, her face was turned sideways, her chin was doubled by her smile at a different lens. The white satin of her dress strained across breasts already swollen with her early pregnancy, making her look huge.

One of Maureen's thin clawlike hands was playing with the chain she always wore around her neck, on which hung a crucifix and her late husband's wedding ring. When Samantha reached the point in her story where the doctor told Mary that there was nothing they could do, Maureen put her free hand on Samantha's knee and squeezed.

"Dishing up!" called Shirley. Though she had not wanted to come, Samantha felt better than she had in two days. Maureen and Howard were treating her like a mixture of heroine and invalid, and both of them patted her gently on the back as she passed them on her way into the dining room.

Shirley had turned down the dimmer switch, and lit long pink candles to match the wallpaper and the best napkins. The steam rising from their soup plates in the gloom made even Howard's wide, florid face look otherworldly. Having drunk almost to the bottom of her big wineglass, Samantha thought how funny it would be if Howard announced that they were about to hold a séance, to ask Barry for his own account of the events at the golf club.

"Well," said Howard, in a deep voice, "I think we ought to raise our glasses to Barry Fairbrother."

Samantha tipped back her glass quickly, to stop Shirley seeing that she had already downed most of its contents.

"It was almost certainly an aneurysm," announced Miles, the instant the glasses had landed back on the tablecloth. He had withheld this information even from Samantha, and he was glad, because she might have squandered it just now, while talking to Maureen and Howard. "Gavin phoned Mary to give the firm's condolences and touch base about the will, and Mary confirmed it. Basically, an artery in his head swelled up and burst" (he had looked up the term on the Internet, once he had found out how to spell it, back in his office after speaking to Gavin). "Could have happened at any time. Some sort of inborn weakness."

"Ghastly," said Howard; but then he noticed that Samantha's glass was empty, and heaved himself out of his chair to top it up. Shirley drank soup for a while with her eyebrows hovering near her hairline. Samantha slugged down more wine in defiance.

"D'you know what?" she said, her tongue slightly unwieldy. "I thought I saw him on the way here. In the dark. Barry."

"I expect it was one of his brothers," said Shirley dismissively. "They're all alike."

But Maureen croaked over Shirley, drowning her out.

"I thought I saw Ken, the evening after he died. Clear as day, standing in the garden, looking up at me through the kitchen window. In the middle of his roses."

Nobody responded; they had heard the story before. A minute passed, full of nothing but soft slurps, then Maureen spoke again with her raven's caw.

"Gavin's quite friendly with the Fairbrothers, isn't he, Miles? Doesn't he play squash with Barry? *Didn't* he, I should say."

"Yeah, Barry thrashed him once a week. Gavin must be a lousy player; Barry had ten years on him."

Near identical expressions of complacent amusement touched the candlelit faces of the three women around the table. If nothing else, they had in common a slightly perverse interest in Miles' stringy young business partner. In Maureen's case, this was merely a manifestation of her inexhaustible appetite for all the gossip of Pagford, and the goings-on of a young bachelor were prime meat. Shirley took a particular pleasure in hearing all about Gavin's inferiorities and insecurities, because these threw into delicious contrast the achievements and self-assertion of the twin gods of her life, Howard and Miles. But in the case of Samantha, Gavin's passivity and caution awoke a feline cruelty; she had a powerful desire to see him slapped awake, pulled into line or otherwise mauled by a feminine surrogate. She bullied him a little in person whenever they met, taking pleasure in the conviction that he found her overwhelming, hard to handle.

"So how are things going, these days," asked Maureen, "with his lady friend from London?"

"She's not in London anymore, Mo. She's moved into Hope

Street," said Miles. "And if you ask me, he's regretting he ever went near her. You know Gavin. Born with cold feet."

Miles had been a few years above Gavin at school, and there was forever a trace of the sixth-form prefect in the way he spoke about his business partner.

"Dark girl? Very short hair?"

"That's her," said Miles. "Social worker. Flat shoes."

"Then we've had her in the deli, haven't we, How?" said Maureen excitedly. "I wouldn't have had her down as much of a cook, though, not by the look of her."

Roast loin of pork followed the soup. With the connivance of Howard, Samantha was sliding gently toward contented drunkenness, but something in her was making forlorn protests, like a man swept out to sea. She attempted to drown it in more wine.

A pause rolled out across the table like a fresh tablecloth, pristine and expectant, and this time everybody seemed to know that it was for Howard to set out the new topic. He ate for a while, big mouthfuls washed down with wine, apparently oblivious to their eyes upon him. Finally, having cleared half his plate, he dabbed at his mouth with his napkin and spoke.

"Yes, it will be interesting to see what happens on council now." He was forced to pause to suppress a powerful burp; for a moment he looked as if he might be sick. He thumped his chest. "Pardon me. Yes. It'll be very interesting indeed. With Fairbrother gone"—businesslike, Howard reverted to the form of the name he habitually used—"I can't see his article for the paper coming off. Unless Bends-Your-Ear takes it on, obviously," he added.

Howard had dubbed Parminder Jawanda "Bends-Your-Ear Bhutto" after her first attendance as a parish councillor. It was a popular joke among the anti-Fielders.

"The look on her face," said Maureen, addressing Shirley. "The look on her face, when we told her. Well...I always thought...*you* know..."

Samantha pricked up her ears, but Maureen's insinuation was surely laughable. Parminder was married to the most gorgeous man in Pagford: Vikram, tall and well made, with an aquiline nose, eyes fringed with thick black lashes, and a lazy, knowing smile. For years, Samantha had tossed back her hair and laughed more often than necessary whenever she paused in the street to pass the time of day with Vikram, who had the same kind of body Miles had had before he had given up rugby and become soft and paunchy.

Samantha had heard somewhere, not long after they had become her neighbors, that Vikram and Parminder had had an arranged marriage. She had found this idea unspeakably erotic. Imagine being *ordered* to marry Vikram, *having* to do it; she had wrought a little fantasy in which she was veiled and shown into a room, a virgin condemned to her fate…Imagine looking up, and knowing you were getting *that*…Not to mention the additional frisson of his job: that much responsibility would have given a much uglier man sex appeal…

(Vikram had performed Howard's quadruple bypass, seven years previously. In consequence, Vikram could not enter Mollison and Lowe without being subjected to a barrage of jocular banter.

"To the head of the queue, please, Mr. Jawanda! Move aside, please, ladies — no, Mr. Jawanda, I insist — this man saved my life, patched up the old ticker — what will it be, Mr. Jawanda, sir?"

Howard always insisted that Vikram take free samples and a little extra of everything he bought. In consequence, Samantha suspected, of these antics, Vikram almost never entered the delicatessen anymore.)

She had lost the thread of the conversation, but it did not matter. The others were still droning on about something that Barry Fairbrother had written to the local paper.

"…was going to have to talk to him about it," boomed Howard. "It was a very underhand way of doing things. Well, well, that's water under the bridge now.

"What we should be thinking about is who's going to replace Fairbrother. We shouldn't underestimate Bends-Your-Ear, however upset she might be. That would be a great mistake. She's probably trying to rustle up somebody already, so we ought to be thinking about a decent replacement ourselves. Sooner rather than later. Simple matter of good governance."

"What will that mean, exactly?" Miles asked. "An election?"

"Possibly," said Howard, with a judicious air, "but I doubt it. It's only a casual vacancy. If there isn't enough interest in an election—though, as I say, we must not underestimate Bends-Your-Ear—but if she can't raise nine people to propose a public vote, it'll be a simple question of co-opting a new councillor. In that case, we'd need nine members' votes to get the co-option ratified. Nine's the quorum. Three years of Fairbrother's term of office left to run. Worth it. Could swing the whole thing, putting one of our side in, instead of Fairbrother."

Howard drummed his thick fingers against the bowl of his wineglass, looking at his son across the table. Both Shirley and Maureen were watching Miles too, and Miles, Samantha thought, was looking back at his father like a big fat Labrador, quivering in expectation of a treat.

A beat later than she would have done if she had been sober, Samantha realized what this was all about, and why a strangely celebratory air hung over the table. Her intoxication had been liberating, but all of a sudden it was restrictive, for she was not sure that her tongue would be wholly biddable after more than a bottle of wine and a long stretch of silence. She therefore thought the words, rather than speaking them aloud.

You'd better bloody well tell them you'll need to discuss it with me first, Miles.

VII

Tessa Wall had not meant to stay long at Mary's—she was never comfortable about leaving her husband and Fats alone in the house together—but somehow her visit had stretched to a couple of hours. The Fairbrothers' house was overflowing with camp beds and sleeping bags; their extended family had closed in around the gaping vacuum left by death, but no amount of noise and activity could mask the chasm into which Barry had vanished.

Alone with her thoughts for the first time since their friend had died, Tessa retraced her steps down Church Row in the darkness, her feet aching, her cardigan inadequate protection against the cold. The only noise was the clicking of the wooden beads around her neck, and the dim sounds of television sets in the houses she was passing.

Quite suddenly, Tessa thought: *I wonder whether Barry knew.*

It had never occurred to her before that her husband might have told Barry the great secret of her life, the rotten thing that lay buried at the heart of her marriage. She and Colin never even discussed it (though a whiff of it tainted many a conversation, particularly lately...).

Tonight, though, Tessa had thought she caught half a glance from Mary, at the mention of Fats...

You're exhausted, and you're imagining things, Tessa told herself firmly. Colin's habits of secrecy were so strong, so deeply entrenched, that he would never have told; not even Barry, whom he idolized. Tessa hated to think that Barry might have known... that his kindness toward Colin had been actuated by pity for what she, Tessa, had done...

When she entered the sitting room, she found her husband sitting in front of the television, wearing his glasses, the news on in the background. He had a sheaf of printed papers in his lap and a pen in his hand. To Tessa's relief, there was no sign of Fats.

"How is she?" Colin asked.

"Well, you know...not great," said Tessa. She sank into one of the old armchairs with a little moan of relief, and pulled off her worn-down shoes. "But Barry's brother's being marvelous."

"In what way?"

"Well...you know...helping."

She closed her eyes and massaged the bridge of her nose and her eyelids with her thumb and forefinger.

"I always thought he seemed a bit unreliable," said Colin's voice.

"Really?" said Tessa, from the depths of her voluntary darkness.

"Yes. Remember when he said he'd come and referee for that game against Paxton High? And he canceled with about half an hour's notice and Bateman had to do it instead?"

Tessa fought down an impulse to snap. Colin had a habit of making sweeping judgments based on first impressions, on single actions. He never seemed to grasp the immense mutability of human nature, nor to appreciate that behind every nondescript face lay a wild and unique hinterland like his own.

"Well, he's being lovely with the kids," said Tessa carefully. "I've got to go to bed."

She did not move, but sat concentrating on the separate aches in different parts of her body: in her feet, her lower back, her shoulders.

"Tess, I've been thinking."

"Hmm?"

Glasses shrank Colin's eyes to molelike proportions, so that the high, balding knobbly forehead seemed even more pronounced.

"Everything Barry was trying to do on the Parish Council. Everything he was fighting for. The Fields. The addiction clinic. I've been thinking about it all day." He drew a deep inward breath. "I've pretty much decided that I'm going to take over for him."

Misgivings crashed over Tessa, pinning her to her chair, rendering her momentarily speechless. She struggled to keep her expression professionally neutral.

"I'm sure it's what Barry would have wanted," said Colin. His strange excitement was tinged with defensiveness.

Never, said Tessa's most honest self, *never for a second would Barry have wanted you to do this. He would have known you are the very last person who ought to do it.*

"Gosh," she said. "Well. I know Barry was very…but it would be a huge commitment, Colin. And it's not as though Parminder's gone. She's still there, and she'll still be trying to do everything Barry wanted."

I should have phoned Parminder, thought Tessa as she said it, with a guilty bump in her stomach. *Oh, God, why didn't I think to call Parminder?*

"But she'll need support; she'll never be able to stand up to them all on her own," said Colin. "And I guarantee Howard Mollison will be lining up some puppet to replace Barry right now. He's probably already—"

"Oh, Colin—"

"I bet he has! You know what he's like!"

The papers in Colin's lap fell, disregarded, in a smooth white waterfall onto the floor.

"I want to do this for Barry. I'll take over where he left off. I'll make sure everything he worked for doesn't go up in smoke. I know the arguments. He always said he got opportunities he'd never have had otherwise, and look how much he gave back to the community. I'm definitely going to stand. I'm going to look into what I've got to do, tomorrow."

"All right," said Tessa. Years of experience had taught her that Colin ought not to be opposed in the first throes of his enthusiasm, or it would simply entrench him in his determination to proceed. Those same years had taught Colin that Tessa often pretended to agree before raising objections. These kinds of exchanges were always infused with their mutual, unexpressed remembrance of that long-buried secret. Tessa felt that she owed him. He felt that he was owed.

"This is something I really want to do, Tessa."

"I understand that, Colin."

She pulled herself out of the chair, wondering whether she would have the energy to get upstairs.

"Are you coming to bed?"

"In a minute. I want to finish looking through these first."

He was gathering up the printed sheets he had let fall; his reckless new project seemed to be giving him a feverish energy.

Tessa undressed slowly in their bedroom. Gravity seemed to have become more powerful; it was such an effort to lift her limbs, to force her recalcitrant zip to do as she wished. She pulled on her dressing gown and went into the bathroom, where she could hear Fats moving around overhead. She often felt lonely and drained these days, shuttling between her husband and son, who seemed to exist entirely independently, as alien to each other as landlord and lodger.

Tessa went to take off her wristwatch, then realized that she had mislaid it yesterday. So tired...she kept losing things...and how could she have forgotten to call Parminder? Tearful, worried and tense, she shuffled off to bed.

Wednesday

I

Krystal Weedon had spent Monday and Tuesday nights on her friend Nikki's bedroom floor after an especially bad fight with her mother. This had started when Krystal arrived home from hanging out with her mates at the precinct and found Terri talking to Obbo on the doorstep. Everyone in the Fields knew Obbo, with his bland puffy face and his gap-toothed grin, his bottle-bottom glasses and his filthy old leather jacket.

"Jus' keep 'em 'ere fer us, Ter, fer a coupla days? Few quid in it for yeh?"

"Wha's she keepin'?" Krystal had demanded. Robbie scrambled out from between Terri's legs to cling tightly to Krystal's knees. Robbie did not like men coming to the house. He had good reason.

"Nuthin'. Compu'ers."

"Don'," Krystal had said to Terri.

She did not want her mother to have spare cash. She would not have put it past Obbo to cut out the middle step and pay her for the favor with a bag of smack.

"Don' take 'em."

But Terri had said yes. All Krystal's life, her mother had said yes to everything and everyone: agreeing, accepting, forever acquiescing: *yeah, all righ', go on then, 'ere yeh go, no problem.*

Krystal had gone to hang out at the swings under a darkening sky with her friends. She felt strained and irritable. She could not seem to grasp the fact of Mr. Fairbrother's death, but kept experiencing punches to the stomach that made her want to lash out at some-body. She was also unsettled and guilty about having stolen Tessa Wall's watch. But why had the silly bitch put it there in front of Krystal and closed her eyes? What did she expect?

Being with the others did not help. Jemma kept needling her about Fats Wall; finally Krystal exploded and lunged at her; Nikki and Leanne had to hold Krystal back. So Krystal stormed home, to find that Obbo's computers had arrived. Robbie was trying to climb the stacked boxes in the front room, while Terri sat there in dazed oblivion, her works lying out on the floor. As Krystal had feared, Obbo had paid Terri with a bag of heroin.

"You stupid fuckin' junkie bitch, they'll kick yer ou' the fuckin' clinic again!"

But heroin took Krystal's mother where she was beyond reach. Though she responded by calling Krystal a little bitch and a whore, it was with vacant detachment. Krystal slapped Terri across the face. Terri told her to fuck off and die.

"You fuckin' look after him fer a fuckin' change then, you useless fuckin' smackhead cow!" Krystal screamed. Robbie ran howling up the hall after her, but she slammed the front door on him.

Krystal liked Nikki's house better than any other. It was not as tidy as her Nana Cath's, but it was friendlier, comfortingly loud and busy. Nikki had two brothers and a sister, so Krystal slept on a folded-up duvet between the sisters' beds. The walls were covered with pictures cut out of magazines, arranged as a collage of desirable boys and beautiful girls. It had never occurred to Krystal to embel-lish her own bedroom walls.

But guilt was clawing at her insides; she kept remembering Robbie's terrified face as she slammed the door on him, so on Wednesday morning she came home. In any case, Nikki's family was not keen on her staying more than two nights in a row. Nikki had once told her, with characteristic forthrightness, that it was all right with her mum if it didn't happen too often, but that Krystal was to stop using them as a hostel, and especially to stop turning up past midnight.

Terri seemed as glad as she ever was to see Krystal back. She talked about the new social worker's visit, and Krystal wondered nervously what the stranger had thought of the house, which lately had sunk even further below its usual filthy tidemark. Krystal was especially worried that Kay had found Robbie at home when he ought to have been at nursery, because Terri's commitment to keeping Robbie in preschool, which he had begun while with his foster mother, had been a key condition of his negotiated return to the family home the previous year. She was also furious that the social worker had caught Robbie wearing a nappy, after all the work Krystal had put in to persuade him to use the toilet.

"So whaddid she say?" Krystal demanded of Terri.

"Tole me she wuz gonna come back," said Terri.

Krystal had a bad feeling about this. Their usual social worker seemed content to let the Weedon family get along without much interference. Vague and haphazard, often getting their names wrong, and confusing their circumstances with those of other clients, she turned up every two weeks with no apparent aim except to check that Robbie was still alive.

The new menace worsened Krystal's mood. When straight, Terri was cowed by her daughter's anger and let Krystal boss her around. Making the most of her temporary authority, Krystal ordered Terri to put on some proper clothes, forced Robbie back into clean pants, reminded him he couldn't piss in this kind, and marched him off to nursery. He bawled when she made to leave; at first she got ratty with him, but finally she crouched down and promised him that she would come back and pick him up at one, and he let her go.

Then Krystal truanted, even though Wednesday was the day she liked best at school, because she had both PE and guidance, and set to work to clean up the house a bit, sloshing pine-scented disinfectant over the kitchen, scraping all the old food and cigarette butts into bin liners. She hid the biscuit tin holding Terri's works, and heaved remaining computers (three had already been collected) into the hall cupboard.

All the time she was chiseling food off the plates, Krystal's thoughts kept returning to the rowing team. She would have had training the following night, if Mr. Fairbrother had still been alive. He usually gave her a lift both ways in the people carrier, because she had no other means of getting over to the canal in Yarvil. His twin daughters, Niamh and Siobhan, and Sukhvinder Jawanda came in the car too. Krystal had no regular contact with these three girls during school hours, but since becoming a team, they had always said "all right?" when they passed each other in the corridors. Krystal had expected them to look down their noses at her, but they were OK once you got to know them. They laughed at her jokes. They had adopted some of her favorite phrases. She was, in some sense, the crew's leader.

Nobody in Krystal's family had ever owned a car. If she concentrated, she could smell the interior of the people carrier, even over the stink of Terri's kitchen. She loved its warm, plasticky scent. She would never be in that car again. There had been trips on a hired minibus too, with Mr. Fairbrother driving the whole team, and sometimes they had stayed overnight when they competed against far-flung schools. The team had sung Rihanna's "Umbrella" in the back of the bus: it had become their lucky ritual, their theme tune, with Krystal doing Jay-Z's rap, solo, at the start. Mr. Fairbrother had nearly pissed himself the first time he heard her do it:

> *Uh huh uh huh, Rihanna…*
> *Good girl gone bad —*
> *Take three —*
> *Action.*
> *No clouds in my storms…*
> *Let it rain, I hydroplane into fame*
> *Comin' down with the Dow Jones…*

Krystal had never understood the words.

Cubby Wall had sent round a letter to them all, saying that the team would not be meeting until they could find a new coach, but they would never find a new coach, so that was a pile of shit; they all knew that.

It had been Mr. Fairbrother's team, his pet project. Krystal had taken a load of abuse from Nikki and the others for joining. Their sneering had hidden incredulity and, later on, admiration, because the team had won medals (Krystal kept hers in a box she had stolen from Nikki's house. Krystal was much given to sneaking things into her pockets that belonged to people she liked. This box was plastic and decorated with roses: a child's jewelry box, really. Tessa's watch was curled up inside it now).

The best time of all had been when they'd beaten those snotty little bitches from St. Anne's; that day had been the very best of Krystal's life. The headmistress had called the team up in front of the whole school at the next assembly (Krystal had been a bit mortified: Nikki and Leanne had been laughing at her) but then everyone had applauded them...it had meant something, that Winterdown had hammered St. Anne's.

But it was all finished, all over, the trips in the car and the rowing and the talking to the local newspaper. She had liked the idea of being in the newspaper again. Mr. Fairbrother had said he was going to be there with her when it happened. Just the two of them.

"What will they wanna talk to me abou', like?"

"Your life. They're interested in your life."

Like a celebrity. Krystal had no money for magazines, but she saw them in Nikki's house and at the doctor's, if she took Robbie. This would have been even better than being in the paper with the team. She had burst with excitement at the prospect, but somehow she had managed to keep her mouth shut and had not even boasted about it to Nikki or Leanne. She had wanted to surprise them. It was as well she had not said anything. She would never be in the paper again.

There was a hollowness in Krystal's stomach. She tried not to think anymore about Mr. Fairbrother as she moved around the house, cleaning inexpertly but doggedly, while her mother sat in the kitchen, smoking and staring out of the back window.

Shortly before midday, a woman pulled up outside the house in an old blue Vauxhall. Krystal caught sight of her from Robbie's bedroom window. The visitor had very short dark hair and was wearing black trousers, a beaded, ethnic sort of necklace, and carrying a large tote bag over her shoulder that seemed to be full of files.

Krystal ran downstairs.

"I think it's 'er," she called to Terri, who was in the kitchen. "The social."

The woman knocked and Krystal opened the door.

"Hello, I'm Kay; I'm covering for Mattie? You must be Krystal."

"Yeah," said Krystal, not bothering to return Kay's smile. She showed her into the sitting room and saw her take in its new, ramshackle tidiness: the emptied ashtray, and most of the stuff that had been lying around was crammed onto the broken shelves. The carpet was still filthy, because the Hoover did not work, and the towel and the zinc ointment were lying on the floor, with one of Robbie's matchbox cars perched on top of the plastic tub. Krystal had tried to distract Robbie with the car while she scraped his bottom clean.

"Robbie's at nursery," Krystal told Kay. "I've took 'im. I've put 'im back in pants. She keeps puttin' 'im back in pull-ups. I've told 'er not to. I put cream on his bum. It'll be all right, it's on'y nappy rash."

Kay smiled at her again. Krystal peered around the doorway and shouted, "*Mum!*"

Terri joined them from the kitchen. She was wearing a dirty old sweatshirt and jeans, and looked better for being more covered up.

"Hello, Terri," said Kay.

"All righ'?" said Terri, taking a deep drag from her cigarette.

"Siddown," Krystal instructed her mother, who obeyed, curling up in the same chair as before. "D'yer wanna cup of tea or summat?" Krystal asked Kay.

"That'd be great," said Kay, sitting down and opening her folder. "Thanks."

Krystal hurried out of the room. She was listening carefully, trying to make out what Kay was saying to her mother.

"You probably weren't expecting to see me again this soon, Terri," she heard Kay say (she had a strange accent: it sounded like a London one, like the posh new bitch at school half the boys had stiffies for), "but I was quite concerned about Robbie yesterday. He's back at nursery today, Krystal says?"

"Yeah," said Terri. "She took 'im. She come back this morning."

"She's come back? Where has she been?"

"I jus' bin at a—jus' slep' over at a friend's," said Krystal, hurrying back to the sitting room to speak for herself.

"Yeah, bu' she come back this morning," said Terri.

Krystal went back to the kettle. It made such a racket as it came to the boil that she could not make out any of what her mother and the social worker were saying to each other. She sloshed milk into the mugs with the tea bags, trying to be as quick as possible, then carried the three red-hot mugs through to the sitting room in time to hear Kay say, "...spoke to Mrs. Harper at the nursery yesterday—"

"Tha' bitch," said Terri.

"There y'are," Krystal told Kay, setting the teas on the floor and turning one of the mugs so that its handle faced her.

"Thanks very much," Kay said. "Terri, Mrs. Harper told me that Robbie has been absent a lot over the last three months. He hasn't had a full week for a while, has he?"

"Wha'?" said Terri. "No, 'e ain'. Yeah, 'e 'as. 'E only jus' mist yesterday. An' when 'e had his sore throat."

"When was that?"

"Wha'? Monf 'go...monf 'na 'alf...'bout."

Krystal sat down on the arm of her mother's chair. She glared down at Kay from her position of height, energetically chewing gum, her arms folded like her mother's. Kay had a thick open folder on her lap. Krystal hated folders. All the stuff they wrote about you, and kept, and used against you afterwards.

"I takes Robbie to the nurs'ry," she said. "On my way to school."

"Well, according to Mrs. Harper, Robbie's attendance has fallen off quite a bit," said Kay, looking down the notes she had made of her conversation with the nursery manager. "The thing is, Terri, you did commit to keeping Robbie in preschool when he was returned to you last year."

"I ain' fuckin'—" Terri began.

"No, shurrup, righ'?" Krystal said loudly to her mother. She addressed Kay. "He were ill, righ', his tonsils were all up, I got 'im antibiotics off the doctor."

"And when was that?"

"Tha' was 'bout free weeks—anyway, righ'—"

"When I was here yesterday," Kay said, addressing Robbie's mother again (Krystal was chewing vigorously, her arms making a double barrier around her ribs), "you seemed to be finding it very difficult to respond to Robbie's needs, Terri."

Krystal glanced down at her mother. Her spreading thigh was twice as thick as Terri's.

"I di'n'—I never…" Terri changed her mind. "'E's fine."

A suspicion darkened Krystal's mind like the shadow of some circling vulture.

"Terri, you'd used when I arrived yesterday, hadn't you?"

"No, I fuckin' hadn'! Tha's a fuckin'—you're fuckin'—I ain' used, all righ'?"

A weight was pressing on Krystal's lungs and her ears were ringing. Obbo must have given her mother, not a single bag, but a bundle. The social worker had seen her blasted. Terri would test positive at Bellchapel next time, and they would chuck her out again…

(…and without methadone, they would return again to that nightmare place where Terri became feral, when she would again start opening her broken-toothed mouth for strangers' dicks, so she could feed her veins. And Robbie would be taken away again, and this time he might not come back. In a little red plastic heart hanging from the key ring in Krystal's pocket was a picture of Robbie, aged one. Krystal's real heart had started pounding the way it did when she rowed full stretch, pulling, pulling through the water, her muscles singing, watching the other crew slide backwards…)

"You fuckin'," she shouted, but nobody heard her, because Terri was still bawling at Kay, who sat with her mug held in her hands, looking unmoved.

"I ain' fuckin' used, you ain' go' no proof—"

"You fuckin' stupid," said Krystal, louder.

"I ain' fuckin' used, tha's a fuckin' lie," screamed Terri; an animal snared in a net, thrashing around, tangling herself tighter. "I never fuckin' did, righ', I never—"

"They'll kick you out the fuckin' clinic again, you stupid fuckin' bitch!"

"Don' you dare fuckin' talk ter me like tha'!"

"All right," said Kay loudly over the din, putting her mug back on the floor and standing up, scared at what she had unleashed; then she shouted "Terri!" in real alarm, as Terri hoisted herself up in the chair to half crouch on its other arm, facing her daughter; like two gargoyles they were almost nose to nose, screaming.

"*Krystal!*" cried Kay, as Krystal raised her fist.

Krystal flung herself violently off the chair, away from her mother. She was surprised to feel warm liquid flowing down her cheeks, and thought confusedly of blood, but it was tears, only tears, clear and shining on her fingertips when she wiped them away.

"All right," said Kay, unnerved. "Let's calm down, please."

"*You* fuckin' calm down," Krystal said. Shaking, she wiped her face with her forearm, then marched back over to her mother's chair. Terri flinched, but Krystal merely snatched up the cigarette packet, slid out the last cigarette and a lighter, and lit up. Puffing on the cigarette, she walked away from her mother to the window and turned her back, trying to press away more tears before they fell.

"OK," said Kay, still standing, "if we can talk about this calmly—"

"Oh, fuck off," said Terri dully.

"This is about Robbie," Kay said. She was still on her feet, scared to relax. "That's what I'm here for. To make sure that Robbie is all right."

"So 'e missed fuckin' nursery," said Krystal, from the window. "Tha's norra fuckin' crime."

"…norra fuckin' crime," agreed Terri, in a dim echo.

"This isn't only about nursery," said Kay. "Robbie was uncomfortable and sore when I saw him yesterday. He's much too old to be wearing a nappy."

"I took 'im outta the fuckin' nappy, 'e's in pants now, I toldja!" said Krystal furiously.

"I'm sorry, Terri," said Kay, "but you weren't in any fit condition to have sole charge of a small child."

"I never—"

"You can keep telling me you haven't used," Kay said; and Krystal heard something real and human in Kay's voice for the first time: exasperation, irritation. "But you're going to be tested at the clinic. We both know you're going to test positive. They're saying it's your last chance, that they'll throw you out again."

Terri wiped her mouth with the back of her hand.

"Look, I can see neither of you wants to lose Robbie—"

"Don' fuckin' take him away, then!" shouted Krystal.

"It's not as simple as that," said Kay. She sat down again and lifted the heavy folder back onto her lap from the floor where it had fallen. "When Robbie came back to you last year, Terri, you were off the heroin. You made a big commitment to staying clean and going through the program, and you agreed to certain other things, like keeping Robbie in nursery—"

"Yeh, an' I took 'im—"

"—for a bit," said Kay. "For a bit you did, but, Terri, a token effort isn't enough. After what I found when I called here yesterday, and after talking to your key drug worker and to Mrs. Harper, I'm afraid I think we need to have another look at how things are working."

"What's that mean?" said Krystal. "Another fuckin' case review, is it? Why'djer need one, though? Why'djer need one? He's all righ', I'm lookin' after—*fuckin' shurrup!*" she screamed at Terri, who was trying to shout along from her chair. "She ain'—I'm lookin' after 'im, all righ'?" she bellowed at Kay, pink in the face, her heavily kohled eyes brimming with tears of anger, jabbing a finger at her own chest.

Krystal had visited Robbie regularly at his foster parents during the month he had been away from them. He had clung to her, wanted her to stay for tea, cried when she left. It had been like having half your guts cut out of you and held hostage. Krystal had wanted Robbie to go to Nana Cath's, the way she had gone all those times in her childhood, whenever Terri had fallen apart. But Nana Cath was old and frail now, and she had no time for Robbie.

"I understand that you love your brother and that you're doing your best for him, Krystal," Kay said, "but you're not Robbie's legal—"

"Why ain' I? I'm his fuckin' sister, ain' I?"

"All right," said Kay firmly. "Terri, I think we need to face facts here. Bellchapel will definitely throw you off the program if you turn up, claim you haven't used and then test positive. Your drug worker made that perfectly clear to me on the phone."

Shrunken in the armchair, a strange hybrid of old lady and child with her missing teeth, Terri's gaze was vacant and inconsolable.

"I think the only way you can possibly avoid being thrown out," Kay went on, "is to admit, up front, that you've used, take responsibility for the lapse and show your commitment to turning over a new leaf."

Terri simply stared. Lying was the only way Terri knew to meet her many accusers. *Yeah, all righ', go on, then, give it 'ere,* and then, *No, I never, no I ain', I never fuckin' did…*

"Was there any particular reason you used heroin this week, when you're already on a big dose of methadone?" Kay asked.

"Yeah," said Krystal. "Yeah, because Obbo turned up, an' she never fuckin' says no to 'im!"

"Shurrup," said Terri, but without heat. She seemed to be trying to take in what Kay had said to her: this bizarre, dangerous advice about telling the truth.

"Obbo," repeated Kay. "Who's Obbo?"

"Fuckin' tosser," said Krystal.

"Your dealer?" asked Kay.

"Shurrup," Terri advised Krystal again.

"Why didn' yeh jus' tell 'im fuckin' no?" Krystal shouted at her mother.

"All right," said Kay, again. "Terri, I'm going to call your drug worker back. I'm going to try and persuade her that I think there would be a benefit to the family from your staying on the program."

"Will yeh?" asked Krystal, astonished. She had been thinking of Kay as a huge bitch, a bigger bitch even than that foster mother, with her spotless kitchen and the way she had of speaking kindly to Krystal, which made Krystal feel like a piece of shit.

"Yes," said Kay, "I will. But, Terri, as far as we're concerned, I mean the Child Protection team, this is serious. We are going to have to monitor Robbie's home situation closely. We need to see a change, Terri."

"All righ', yeah," said Terri; agreeing as she agreed to everything, to everyone.

But Krystal said, "You will, yeah. She will. I'll help 'er. She will."

II

Shirley Mollison spent Wednesdays at South West General in Yarvil. Here, she and a dozen fellow volunteers performed non-medical jobs, such as pushing the library trolley around the beds, looking after patients' flowers and making trips to the shop in the lobby for those who were bedridden and without visitors. Shirley's favorite activity was going from bed to bed, taking orders for meals. Once, carrying her clipboard and wearing her laminated pass, she had been mistaken by a passing doctor for a hospital administrator.

The idea of volunteering had come to Shirley during her longest-ever conversation with Julia Fawley, during one of the wonderful Christmas parties at Sweetlove House. Here, she had learned that Julia was involved in fund-raising for the pediatric wing of the local hospital.

"What we really need is a royal visit," Julia had said, her eyes straying to the door over Shirley's shoulder. "I'm going to get Aubrey to have a quiet word with Norman Bailey. Excuse me, I must say hello to Lawrence..."

Shirley was left standing there beside the grand piano, saying, "Oh, of course, of course," to thin air. She had no idea who Norman Bailey was, but she felt quite light-headed. The very next day, without even telling Howard what she was up to, she telephoned South West General and asked about volunteer work. Ascertaining that nothing was required but a blameless character, a sound mind and strong legs, she had demanded an application form.

Volunteer work had opened a whole new, glorious world to Shirley. This was the dream that Julia Fawley had inadvertently handed her beside the grand piano: that of herself, standing with her hands clasped demurely in front of her, her laminated pass around her neck, while the Queen moved slowly down a line of beaming helpers. She saw herself dropping a perfect curtsy; the Queen's attention caught, she stopped to chat; she congratulated Shirley on generously giving her free time…a flash and a photograph, and the newspapers next day…*"The Queen chats to hospital volunteer Mrs. Shirley Mollison…"* Sometimes, when Shirley really concentrated on this imaginary scene, an almost holy feeling came over her.

Volunteering at the hospital had given Shirley a glittering new weapon with which to whittle down Maureen's pretentions. When Ken's widow had been transformed, Cinderella-like, from shopgirl to business partner, she had taken on airs that Shirley (though enduring it all with a pussycat smile) found infuriating. But Shirley had retaken the higher ground; she worked, not for profit but out of the goodness of her heart. It was classy to volunteer; it was what women did who had no need of extra cash; women like herself and Julia Fawley. What was more, the hospital gave Shirley access to a vast mine of gossip to drown out Maureen's tedious prattling about the new café.

This morning, Shirley stated her preference for ward twenty-eight in a firm voice to the volunteer supervisor, and was duly sent off to the oncology department. She had made her only friend among the nursing staff on ward twenty-eight; some of the young nurses could be curt and patronizing to the volunteers, but Ruth Price, who had recently returned to nursing after a break of sixteen years, had been charming from the first. They were both, as Shirley put it, Pagford women, which made a bond.

(Though, as it happened, Shirley was not Pagford-born. She and her younger sister had grown up with their mother in a cramped and untidy flat in Yarvil. Shirley's mother had drunk a lot; she had never divorced the girls' father, whom they did not see. Local men had all seemed to know Shirley's mother's name, and smirked when they said it…but that was a long time ago, and Shirley took the view that the past disintegrated if you never mentioned it. She refused to remember.)

Shirley and Ruth greeted each other with delight, but it was a busy morning and there was no time for anything but the most rudimentary exchange about Barry Fairbrother's sudden death. They agreed to meet for lunch at half past twelve, and Shirley strode off to fetch the library trolley.

She was in a wonderful mood. She could see the future as clearly as if it had already happened. Howard, Miles and Aubrey Fawley were going to unite to cut the Fields adrift forever, and this would be the occasion for a celebratory dinner at Sweetlove House…

Shirley found the place dazzling: the enormous garden with its sundial, its topiary hedges and its ponds; the wide paneled hallway; the silver-framed photograph on the grand piano, showing the owner sharing a joke with the Princess Royal. She detected no condescension whatsoever in the Fawleys' attitude towards her or her husband; but then there were so many distracting scents competing for her attention whenever she came within the Fawleys' orbit. She could just imagine the five of them sitting down to a private dinner in one of those delicious little side rooms, Howard sitting next to Julia, she on Aubrey's right hand, and Miles in between them. (In Shirley's fantasy, Samantha was unavoidably detained elsewhere.)

Shirley and Ruth found each other by the yogurts at half-past twelve. The clattering hospital canteen was not yet as crowded as it would be by one, and the nurse and the volunteer found, without too much difficulty, a sticky, crumb-strewn table for two against the wall.

"How's Simon? How are the boys?" asked Shirley, when Ruth had wiped down the table, and they had decanted the contents of their trays and sat facing each other, ready for chat.

"Si's fine, thanks, fine. Bringing home our new computer today. The boys can't wait; you can imagine."

This was quite untrue. Andrew and Paul both possessed cheap laptops; the PC sat in the corner of the tiny sitting room and neither boy touched it, preferring to do nothing that took them within the vicinity of their father. Ruth often spoke of her sons to Shirley as though they were much younger than they were: portable, tractable, easily amused. Perhaps she sought to make herself younger, to emphasize the age difference between herself and Shirley—which stood at nearly two decades—to make them even more like mother and daughter. Ruth's mother had died ten years previously; she missed having an older woman in her life, and Shirley's relationship with her own daughter was, she had hinted to Ruth, not all it could have been.

"Miles and I have always been very close. Patricia, though, she was always rather a difficult character. She's up in London now."

Ruth longed to probe, but a quality that she and Shirley shared and admired in each other was a genteel reticence; a pride in presenting an unruffled surface to the world. Ruth laid her piqued curiosity aside, therefore, though not without a private hope that she would find out, in due course, what made Patricia so difficult.

Shirley and Ruth's instant liking for each other had been rooted in their mutual recognition that the other was a woman like herself, a woman whose deepest pride lay in having captured and retained the affection of her husband. Like Freemasons, they shared a fundamental code, and were therefore secure in each other's company in a way that they were not with other women. Their complicity was still more enjoyable for being spiced by a sense of superiority, because each secretly pitied the other for her choice of husband. To Ruth, Howard was physically grotesque, and she was puzzled to understand how her friend, who retained a plump yet delicate prettiness, could ever have agreed to marry him. To Shirley, who could not remember ever setting eyes on Simon, who had never heard him mentioned in connection with the higher workings of Pagford, and who understood Ruth to lack even a rudimentary social life, Ruth's husband sounded a reclusive inadequate.

"So I saw Miles and Samantha bringing Barry in," Ruth said, launching into the main subject without preamble. She had much less conversational finesse than Shirley, finding it difficult to disguise her greed for Pagford gossip, of which she was deprived, stuck high on the hill above town, isolated by Simon's unsociability. "Did they actually see it happen?"

"Oh yes," said Shirley. "They were having dinner at the golf club. Sunday night, you know; the girls were back at school, and Sam prefers eating out, she's not much of a cook…"

Bit by bit, over their shared coffee breaks, Ruth had learned some of the inside story of Miles and Samantha's marriage. Shirley had told her how her son had been obliged to marry Samantha, because Samantha had fallen pregnant with Lexie.

"They've made the best of it," Shirley sighed, brightly brave. "Miles did the right thing; I wouldn't have had it any other way. The girls are lovely. It's a pity Miles didn't have a son; he would have been wonderful with a boy. But Sam didn't want a third."

Ruth treasured up every veiled criticism Shirley made of her daughter-in-law. She had taken an immediate dislike to Samantha years before, when she had accompanied four-year-old Andrew to the nursery class at St. Thomas's, and there met Samantha and her daughter Lexie. With her loud laugh, and her boundless cleavage, and a fine line in risqué jokes for the schoolyard mothers, Samantha had struck Ruth as dangerously predatory. For years, Ruth had watched scornfully as Samantha stuck out her massive chest while talking to Vikram Jawanda at parents' evenings, and steered Simon around the edge of classrooms to avoid having to talk to her.

Shirley was still recounting the secondhand tale of Barry's final journey, giving all possible weight to Miles' quick thinking in calling the ambulance, to his support of Mary Fairbrother, to his insistence on remaining with her at the hospital until the Walls arrived. Ruth listened attentively, though with a slight impatience; Shirley was much more entertaining when she was enumerating the inadequacies of Samantha than when extolling the virtues of Miles. What was more, Ruth was bursting with something thrilling that she wished to tell Shirley.

"So there's an empty seat on the Parish Council," Ruth said, the moment that Shirley reached the point in the story where Miles and Samantha ceded the stage to Colin and Tessa Wall.

"We call it a casual vacancy," said Shirley kindly.

Ruth took a deep breath.

"Simon," she said, excited at the mere telling of it, "is thinking of standing!"

Shirley smiled automatically, raised her eyebrows in polite surprise, and took a sip of tea to hide her face. Ruth was completely unaware that she had said anything to discompose her friend. She had assumed that Shirley would be delighted to think of their husbands sitting on the Parish Council together, and had a vague notion that Shirley might be helpful in bringing this about.

"He told me last night," Ruth went on, importantly. "He's been thinking about it for a while."

Certain other things that Simon had said, about the possibility of taking over bribes from Grays to keep them on as council contractors, Ruth had pushed out of her mind, as she pushed out all of Simon's little dodges, his petty criminalities.

"I had no idea Simon was interested in getting involved in local government," said Shirley, her tone light and pleasant.

"Oh yes," said Ruth, who had had no idea either, "he's very keen."

"Has he been talking to Dr. Jawanda?" asked Shirley, sipping her tea again. "Did she suggest standing to him?"

Ruth was thrown by this, and her genuine puzzlement showed.

"No, I…Simon hasn't been to the doctor in ages. I mean, he's very healthy."

Shirley smiled. If he was acting alone, without the support of the Jawanda faction, then the threat posed by Simon was surely negligible. She even pitied Ruth, who was in for a nasty surprise. She, Shirley, who knew everybody who counted in Pagford, would have been hard-pressed to recognize Ruth's husband if he came into the delicatessen: who on earth did poor Ruth think would vote for him? On the other hand, Shirley knew that there was one question that Howard and Aubrey would want her to ask as a matter of routine.

"Simon's always lived in Pagford, hasn't he?"

"No, he was born in the Fields," said Ruth.

"Ah," said Shirley.

She peeled back the foil lid of her yogurt, picked up her spoon and took a thoughtful mouthful. The fact that Simon was likely to have a pro-Fields bias was, whatever his electoral prospects, worth knowing.

"Will it be on the website, how you put your name forward?" Ruth asked, still hoping for a late gush of helpfulness and enthusiasm.

"Oh yes," said Shirley vaguely. "I expect so."

III

Andrew, Fats and twenty-seven others spent the last period on Wednesday afternoon in what Fats called "spazmatics." This was the second-from-bottom maths set, taken by the department's most incompetent teacher: a blotchy-faced young woman fresh from teacher training, who was incapable of keeping good order, and who often seemed to be on the verge of tears. Fats, who had set himself on a course of determined underachievement over the previous year, had been demoted to spazmatics from the top set. Andrew, who had struggled with numbers all his life, lived in fear that he would be relegated to the very bottom set, along with Krystal Weedon and her cousin, Dane Tully.

Andrew and Fats sat at the back of the room together. Occasionally, when he had tired of entertaining the class or whipping it into further disruption, Fats would show Andrew how to do a sum. The level of noise was deafening. Miss Harvey shouted over the top of them all, begging for quiet. Worksheets were defaced by obscenities; people got up constantly to visit each other's desks, scraping their chair legs across the floor; small missiles flew across the room whenever Miss Harvey looked away. Sometimes Fats made excuses to walk up and down the room, imitating Cubby's bouncy up-and-down stiff-armed walk. Fats' humor was at its broadest here; in English, where he and Andrew were both in the top set, he did not bother to use Cubby for material.

Sukhvinder Jawanda was sitting directly in front of Andrew.

Long ago, in primary school, Andrew, Fats and the other boys had pulled Sukhvinder's long, blue-black plait; it was the easiest thing to catch hold of when playing tag, and it had once presented an irresistible temptation when dangling, like now, down her back, hidden from the teacher. But Andrew no longer had any desire to tug it, nor to touch any part of Sukhvinder; she was one of the few girls over whom his eyes glided without the slightest interest. Since Fats had pointed it out, he had noticed the soft dark down on her upper lip. Sukhvinder's older sister, Jaswant, had a lithe curvy figure, a tiny waist and a face that, prior to the advent of Gaia, had seemed beautiful to Andrew, with its high cheekbones, smooth golden skin and almond-shaped liquid-brown eyes. Naturally, Jaswant had always been completely beyond his reach: two years older and the cleverest girl in the sixth form, with an aura of being aware, to the last hard-on, of her own attractions.

Sukhvinder was the only person in the room who was making absolutely no noise. With her back hunched and her head bent low over her work, she appeared to be cocooned in concentration. She had pulled the left sleeve of her jumper down so that it completely covered her hand, enclosing the cuff to make a woolly fist. Her total stillness was almost ostentatious.

"The great hermaphrodite sits quiet and still," murmured Fats, his eyes fixed on the back of Sukhvinder's head. "Mustachioed, yet large-mammaried, scientists remain baffled by the contradictions of the hairy man-woman."

Andrew sniggered, yet he was not entirely at his ease. He would have enjoyed himself more if he knew that Sukhvinder could not hear what Fats was saying. The last time that he had been over at Fats' house, Fats had shown him the messages he was sending regularly to Sukhvinder's Facebook page. He had been scouring the Internet for information and pictures about hirsutism, and was sending a quotation or an image a day.

It was sort of funny, but it made Andrew uncomfortable. Strictly speaking, Sukhvinder was not asking for it: she seemed a very easy target. Andrew liked it best when Fats directed his savage tongue towards figures of authority, the pretentious or the self-satisfied.

"Separated from its bearded, bra-wearing herd," said Fats, "it sits, lost in thought, wondering whether it would suit a goatee."

Andrew laughed, then felt guilty, but Fats lost interest, and turned his attention to transforming every zero on his worksheet into a puckered anus. Andrew reverted to trying to guess where the decimal point should go, and contemplating the prospect of the school bus home, and Gaia. It was always much more difficult to find a seat where he might keep her in his eyeline on the school-to-home trip, because she was frequently boxed in before he got there, or too far away. Their shared amusement in Monday morning's assembly had led nowhere. She had not made eye contact with him on the bus either morning since, nor in any other way demonstrated that she knew he existed. In the four weeks of his infatuation, Andrew had never actually spoken to Gaia. He attempted to formulate opening lines while the din of spazmatics crashed around him. *"That was funny, Monday, in assembly…"*

"Sukhvinder, are you all right?"

Miss Harvey, who had bent down over Sukhvinder's work to mark it, was gawping into the girl's face. Andrew watched Sukhvinder nod and draw in her hands, obscuring her face, still hunched up over her work.

"Wallah!" stage-whispered Kevin Cooper, from two rows in front. "Wallah! Peanut!"

He was trying to draw their attention to what they already knew: that Sukhvinder, judging by the gentle quivering of her shoulders, was crying, and that Miss Harvey was making hopeless, harried attempts to find out what was wrong. The class, detecting a further lapse in their teacher's vigilance, raged louder than ever.

"Peanut! Wallah!"

Andrew could never decide whether Kevin Cooper irritated intentionally or accidentally, but he had an infallible knack for grating on people. The nickname "Peanut" was a very old one, which had clung to Andrew in primary school; he had always hated it. Fats had forced the name out of fashion by never using it; Fats had always been the final arbiter in such matters. Cooper was even getting Fats' name wrong: "Wallah" had enjoyed only a brief popularity, last year.

"Peanut! Wallah!"

"Fuck off, Cooper, you glans-headed moron," said Fats under his breath. Cooper was hanging over the back of his seat, staring at Sukhvinder, who had curled over, her face almost touching the desk, while Miss Harvey crouched beside her, her hands fluttering comically, forbidden to touch her, and unable to elicit any explanation for her distress. A few more people had noticed this unusual disturbance and were staring; but at the front of the room, several boys continued to rampage, oblivious to everything but their own amusement. One of them seized the wood-backed board rubber from Miss Harvey's vacated desk. He threw it.

The rubber soared right across the room and crashed into the clock on the back wall, which plummeted to the ground and shattered: shards of plastic and metal innards flew everywhere, and several girls, including Miss Harvey, shrieked in shock.

The door of the classroom flew open and bounced, with a bang, off the wall. The class fell quiet. Cubby was standing there, flushed and furious.

"What is going on in this room? What is all this noise?"

Miss Harvey shot up like a jack-in-a-box beside Sukhvinder's desk, looking guilty and frightened.

"Miss Harvey! Your class is making an almighty racket. What's going on?"

Miss Harvey seemed struck dumb. Kevin Cooper hung over the back of his chair, grinning, looking from Miss Harvey to Cubby to Fats and back again.

Fats spoke.

"Well, to be perfectly frank, Father, we've been running rings around this poor woman."

Laughter exploded. Miss Harvey's neck was disfigured by a rising maroon rash. Fats balanced himself nonchalantly on the rear legs of his chair, his face perfectly straight, looking at Cubby with challenging detachment.

"That's enough," said Cubby. "If I hear any more noise like that from this class, I'll put the whole lot of you in detention. Do you understand? All of you."

He shut the door on their laughter.

"You heard the deputy headmaster!" cried Miss Harvey, scurrying to the front of the room. "Be quiet! I want quiet! You—Andrew—and you, Stuart—you can clear up that mess! Pick up all those bits of clock!"

They set up a routine cry of injustice at this, supported shrilly by a couple of the girls. The actual perpetrators of the destruction, of whom everybody knew Miss Harvey was afraid, sat smirking at their desks. As there were only five minutes remaining until the end of the school day, Andrew and Fats set about stringing out the clearing up until they would be able to abandon it unfinished. While Fats garnered further laughs by bouncing hither and thither, stiff-armed, doing the Cubby walk, Sukhvinder wiped her eyes surreptitiously with her wool-covered hand and sank back into obscurity.

When the bell rang, Miss Harvey made no attempt to control or contain the thunderous clamor or rush for the door. Andrew and Fats kicked various bits of clock under the cupboards at the back of the room, and swung their schoolbags over their shoulders again.

"Wallah! Wallah!" called Kevin Cooper, hurrying to catch up with Andrew and Fats as they headed down the corridor. "Do you call Cubby 'Father' at home? Seriously? Do you?"

He thought he had something on Fats; he thought he had got him.

"You're a dickhead, Cooper," said Fats wearily, and Andrew laughed.

IV

"Dr. Jawanda's running about fifteen minutes late," the receptionist told Tessa.

"Oh, that's fine," said Tessa. "I'm in no hurry."

It was early evening, and the waiting-room windows made patches of clear royal blue against the walls. There were only two other people there: a misshapen, wheezing old woman wearing carpet slippers, and a young mother who was reading a magazine while her toddler rummaged in the toy box in the corner. Tessa took a battered old *Heat* magazine from the table in the middle, sat down and flicked through the pages, looking at the pictures. The delay gave her more time to think about what she was going to say to Parminder.

They had spoken, briefly, on the telephone this morning. Tessa had been full of contrition that she had not called at once to let Parminder know about Barry. Parminder had said it was fine, for Tessa not to be silly, that she was not upset at all; but Tessa, with her lengthy experience of the thin-skinned and fragile, could tell that Parminder, beneath her prickly carapace, was wounded. She had tried to explain that she had been utterly exhausted the last couple of days, and that she had had to deal with Mary, Colin, Fats, Krystal Weedon; that she had felt overwhelmed, lost and incapable of thinking of more than the immediate problems that had been thrown at her. But Parminder had cut her off in the middle of her rambling excuses and said calmly that she would see her later at the surgery.

Dr. Crawford emerged, white-haired and bearlike, from his room, gave Tessa a cheery wave, and said, "Maisie Lawford?" The young mother had some difficulty in persuading her daughter to abandon the old toy telephone on wheels that the latter had found in the toy box. While being pulled gently by the hand after Dr. Crawford, the little girl gazed longingly over her shoulder at the telephone, whose secrets she would never now discover.

When the door closed on them, Tessa realized that she was smiling fatuously, and hastily rearranged her own features. She was going to become one of those awful old ladies who cooed indiscriminately over small children and frightened them. She would have loved a chubby little blond daughter to go with her skinny, dark boy. How awful it was, thought Tessa, remembering Fats the toddler, the way tiny ghosts of your living children haunted your heart; they could never know, and would hate it if they did, how their growing was a constant bereavement.

Parminder's door opened; Tessa looked up.

"Mrs. Weedon," said Parminder. Her eyes met Tessa's, and she gave a smile that was no smile at all, but a mere tightening of the mouth. The little old lady in carpet slippers got up with difficulty and hobbled away around the partition wall after Parminder. Tessa heard Parminder's surgery door snap shut.

She read the captions to a series of photographs showing a footballer's wife in all the different outfits she had worn over the previous five days. Studying the young woman's long thin legs, Tessa wondered how different her life would have been if she had had legs like that. She could not help but suspect that it would have been almost entirely different. Tessa's legs were thick, shapeless and short; she would have hidden them perpetually in boots, only it was difficult to find many that would zip up over her calves. She remembered telling a sturdy little girl in guidance that looks did not matter, that personality was much more important. *What rubbish we tell children,* thought Tessa, turning the page of her magazine.

An out-of-sight door opened with a bang. Somebody was shouting in a cracked voice.

"You're makin' me bloody worse. This in't right. I've come to you for help. It's your job — it's your — "

Tessa and the receptionist locked eyes, then turned towards the sound of the shouting. Tessa heard Parminder's voice, its Brummie accent still discernible after all these years in Pagford.

"Mrs. Weedon, you're still smoking, which affects the dose I have to prescribe you. If you'd give up your cigarettes — smokers metabolize Theophylline more quickly, so the cigarettes are not only worsening your emphysema, but actually affecting the ability of the drug to — "

"Don' you shout at me! I've 'ad enough of you! I'll report you! You've gave me the wrong fuckin' pills! I wanna see someone else! I wanna see Dr. Crawford!"

The old lady appeared around the wall, wobbling, wheezing, her face scarlet.

"She'll be the death of me, that Paki cow! Don' you go near 'er!" she shouted at Tessa. "She'll fuckin' kill yer with her drugs, the Paki bitch!"

She tottered toward the exit, spindle-shanked, unsteady on her slippered feet, her breath rattling, swearing as loudly as her beleaguered lungs would permit. The door swung shut behind her. The receptionist exchanged another look with Tessa. They heard Parminder's surgery door close again.

It was five minutes before Parminder reappeared. The receptionist stared ostentatiously at her screen.

"Mrs. Wall," said Parminder, with another tight non-smile.

"What was that about?" Tessa asked, when she had taken a seat at the end of Parminder's desk.

"Mrs. Weedon's new pills are upsetting her stomach," said Parminder calmly. "So we're doing your bloods today, aren't we?"

"Yes," said Tessa, both intimidated and hurt by Parminder's cold professional demeanor. "How are you doing, Minda?"

"Me?" said Parminder. "I'm fine. Why?"

"Well...Barry...I know what he meant to you and what you meant to him."

Tears welled in Parminder's eyes and she tried to blink them away, but too late; Tessa had seen them.

"Minda," she said, laying her plump hand on Parminder's thin one, but Parminder whipped it away as if Tessa had stung her; then, betrayed by her own reflex, she began to cry in earnest, unable to hide in the tiny room, though she had turned her back as nearly as she could in her swivel chair.

"I felt sick when I realized I hadn't phoned you," Tessa said, over Parminder's furious attempts to quell her own sobs. "I wanted to curl up and die. I meant to call," she lied, "but we hadn't slept, we spent almost the whole night at the hospital, then we had to go straight out to work. Colin broke down at assembly when he announced it, then he caused a bloody awful scene with Krystal Weedon in front of everyone. And then Stuart decided to play truant. And Mary's falling apart...but I'm so sorry, Minda, I should've called."

"...iculous," said Parminder thickly, her face hidden behind a tissue she had pulled out from her sleeve. "...Mary...most important..."

"You would have been one of the very first people Barry called," said Tessa sadly, and, to her horror, she burst into tears too.

"Minda, I'm so sorry," she sobbed, "but I was having to deal with Colin and all the rest of them."

"Don't be silly," said Parminder, gulping as she dabbed at her thin face. "We're being silly."

No, we're not. Oh, let go for once, Parminder…

But the doctor squared her thin shoulders, blew her nose and sat up straight again.

"Did Vikram tell you?" asked Tessa timidly, tweaking a handful of tissues from the box on Parminder's desk.

"No," said Parminder. "Howard Mollison. In the deli."

"Oh God, Minda, I'm so sorry."

"Don't be silly. It's fine."

Crying had made Parminder feel slightly better; friendlier towards Tessa, who was wiping her own plain, kind face. This was a relief, for now that Barry was gone, Tessa was Parminder's only real friend in Pagford. (She always said "in Pagford" to herself, pretending that somewhere beyond the little town she had a hundred loyal friends. She never quite admitted to herself that these consisted only of the memories of her gang of schoolmates back in Birmingham, from whom the tide of life had long since separated her; and the medical colleagues with whom she had studied and trained, who still sent Christmas cards, but who never came to see her, and whom she never visited.)

"How's Colin?"

Tessa moaned.

"Oh, Minda…Oh God. He says he's going to run for Barry's seat on the Parish Council."

The pronounced vertical furrow between Parminder's thick, dark brows deepened.

"Can you imagine Colin running for election?" Tessa asked, her sodden tissues crumpled tightly in her fist. "Coping with the likes of Aubrey Fawley and Howard Mollison? Trying to fill Barry's shoes, telling himself he's got to win the battle for Barry—all the responsibility—"

"Colin copes with a lot of responsibility at work," said Parminder.

"Barely," said Tessa, without thinking. She felt instantly disloyal and started to cry again. It was so strange; she had entered the surgery thinking that she would offer comfort to Parminder, but instead here she was, pouring out her own troubles instead. "You know what Colin's like, he takes everything to heart so much, he takes everything so *personally*…"

"He copes very well, you know, all things considered," said Parminder.

"Oh, I know he does," said Tessa wearily. The fight seemed to go out of her. "I know."

Colin was almost the only person towards whom stern, self-contained Parminder showed ready compassion. In return, Colin would never hear a word against her; he was her dogged champion in Pagford; "An excellent GP," he would snap at anyone who dared to criticize her in his hearing. "Best I've ever had." Parminder did not have many defenders; she was unpopular with the Pagford old guard, having a reputation for being grudging with antibiotics and repeat prescriptions.

"If Howard Mollison gets his way, there won't be an election at all," said Parminder.

"What d'you mean?"

"He's sent round an email. It came in half an hour ago."

Parminder turned to her computer monitor, typed in a password, and brought up her inbox. She angled the monitor so that Tessa could read Howard's message. The first paragraph expressed regret at Barry's death. The next suggested that, in view of the fact that a year of Barry's term had already expired, co-opting a replacement might be preferable to going through the onerous process of a full election.

"He's lined someone up already," said Parminder. "He's trying to crowbar in some crony before anyone can stop him. I wouldn't be surprised if it was Miles."

"Oh, surely not," said Tessa instantly. "Miles was at the hospital with Barry…no, he was very upset by it—"

"You're so damn naive, Tessa," said Parminder, and Tessa was shocked by the savagery in her friend's voice. "You don't understand what Howard Mollison's like. He's a vile man, vile. You didn't hear him when he found out that Barry had written to the paper about the Fields. You don't know what he's trying to do with the methadone clinic. You wait. You'll see."

Her hand was trembling so much that it took her a few attempts to close down Mollison's email.

"You'll see," she repeated. "All right, we'd better get on, Laura needs to go in a minute. I'll check your blood pressure first."

Parminder was doing Tessa a favor, seeing her late like this, after school. The practice nurse, who lived in Yarvil, was going to drop off Tessa's blood sample to the hospital lab on her way home. Feeling nervous and oddly vulnerable, Tessa rolled up the sleeve of the old green cardigan. The doctor wound the Velcro cuff around her upper arm. At close quarters, Parminder's strong resemblance to her second daughter was revealed, for their different builds (Parminder being wiry, and Sukhvinder buxom) became indiscernible, and the similarity of their facial features emerged: the hawkish nose, the wide mouth with its full lower lip, and the large, round, dark eyes. The cuff tightened painfully around Tessa's flabby upper arm, while Parminder watched the gauge.

"One sixty-five over eighty-eight," said Parminder, frowning. "That's high, Tessa; too high."

Deft and skillful in all her movements, she stripped the wrapping from a sterile syringe, straightened out Tessa's pale, mole-strewn arm and slid the needle into the crook.

"I'm taking Stuart into Yarvil tomorrow night," Tessa said, looking up at the ceiling. "To get him a suit for the funeral. I can't stand the scene there'll be, if he tries to go in jeans. Colin'll go berserk."

She was trying to divert her own thoughts from the dark, mysterious liquid flowing up into the little plastic tube. She was afraid that it would betray her; that she had not been as good as she should have been; that all the chocolate bars and muffins she had eaten would show up as traitorous glucose.

Then she thought bitterly that it would be much easier to resist chocolate if her life were less stressful. Given that she spent nearly all her time trying to help other people, it was hard to see muffins as so very naughty. As she watched Parminder labeling vials of her blood, she found herself hoping, though her husband and friend might think it heresy, that Howard Mollison would triumph, and prevent an election happening at all.

V

Simon Price left the printworks on the stroke of five every day without fail. He had put in his hours, and that was that; home was waiting, clean and cool, high on the hill, a world away from the perpetual clank and whir of the Yarvil plant. To linger in the factory after clocking-off time (though now a manager, Simon had never ceased to think in the terms of his apprenticeship) would constitute a fatal admission that your home life was lacking or, worse, that you were trying to brownnose senior management.

Today, though, Simon needed to make a detour before going home. He met up with the gum-chewing forklift driver in the car park, and together they drove through the darkening streets, with the boy giving directions, into the Fields, actually passing the house in which Simon had grown up. He had not been past the place for years; his mother was dead, and he had not seen his father since he was fourteen and did not know where he was. It unsettled and depressed Simon to see his old home with one window boarded over and the grass ankle-deep. His late mother had been house proud.

The youth told Simon to park at the end of Foley Road, then got out, leaving Simon behind, and headed toward a house of particularly squalid appearance. From what Simon could see by the light of the nearest street lamp, it seemed to have a pile of filth heaped beneath a downstairs window. It was only now that Simon asked himself how sensible it had been to come and pick up the stolen computer in his own car. These days, surely, they would have CCTV on the estate, to keep an eye on all the little thugs and hoodies. He glanced around, but he could not see any cameras; nobody seemed to be looking at him except a fat woman who was openly staring through one of the small, square institutional-looking windows. Simon scowled at her, but she continued to watch him as she smoked her cigarette, so he screened his face with his hand, glaring through the windscreen.

His passenger was already emerging from the house, straddling a little as he walked back towards the car, carrying the boxed computer. Behind him, in the doorway of the house he had left, Simon saw an adolescent girl with a small boy at her feet, who stepped out of sight as he watched, dragging the child with her.

Simon turned the key in the ignition, revving the engine as the gum chewer came nearer.

"Careful," said Simon, leaning across to unlock the passenger door. "Just put it down here."

The boy set the box down on the still-warm passenger seat. Simon had intended to open it and check that it was what he had paid for, but a growing sense of his own imprudence overrode the desire. He contented himself with giving the box a shove: it was too heavy to move easily; he wanted to get going.

"You all right if I leave you here?" he called loudly to the boy, as if he was already speeding away from him in the car.

"Can you give us a lift up to the Crannock Hotel?

"Sorry, mate, I'm going the other way," said Simon. "Cheers."

Simon accelerated. In his rearview mirror he saw the boy standing there, looking outraged; saw his lips form the words "fuck you!" But Simon didn't care. If he cleared out quickly, he might avoid his number plate being captured on one of those grainy black and white films they played back on the news.

He reached the bypass ten minutes later, but even after he had left Yarvil behind, quitted the dual carriageway and driven up the hill toward the ruined abbey, he was ruffled and tense, and experienced none of the satisfaction that was usually his when he crested the peak in the evenings and caught the first glimpse of his own house, far across the hollow where Pagford lay, a tiny white hand-kerchief on the opposite hillside.

Though she had been home barely ten minutes, Ruth already had dinner on and was laying the table when Simon carried the computer inside; they kept early hours in Hilltop House, as was Simon's preference. Ruth's exclamations of excitement at the sight of the box irritated her husband. She did not understand what he had been through; she never understood that there were risks involved in getting stuff cheap. For her part, Ruth sensed at once that Simon was in one of the tightly wound moods that often presaged an explosion, and coped the only way she knew how: by jabbering brightly about her day, in the hope that the mood would dissolve once he had food inside him, and as long as nothing else happened to irritate him.

Promptly at six o'clock, by which time Simon had unboxed the computer and discovered that there was no instruction manual, the family sat down to eat.

Andrew could tell that his mother was on edge, because she was making random conversation with a familiar, artificially cheery note in her voice. She seemed to think, despite years of contrary experience, that if she made the atmosphere polite enough, his father would not dare shatter it. Andrew helped himself to shepherd's pie (made by Ruth, and defrosted on work nights) and avoided eye contact with Simon. He had more interesting things to think about than his parents. Gaia Bawden had said "hi" to him when he had come face-to-face with her outside the biology lab; said it automatically and casually, but had not looked at him once all lesson.

Andrew wished he knew more about girls; he had never got to know one well enough to fathom how their minds worked. The yawning gap in his knowledge had not mattered much until Gaia had walked onto the school bus for the first time, and provoked in him a laser-sharp interest focused on her as an individual; a quite different feeling to the wide and impersonal fascination that had been intensifying in him over several years, concerned with the sprouting of breasts and the appearance of bra straps through white school shirts, and his slightly squeamish interest in what menstruation actually entailed.

Fats had girl cousins who sometimes came to visit. Once, going into the Walls' bathroom right after the prettiest of them had used it, Andrew had found a transparent Lil-Lets wrapper lying beside the bathroom bin. This actual, physical evidence that a girl in his vicinity was having a period there and then was, to thirteen-year-old Andrew, akin to the sighting of a rare comet. He had had enough sense not to tell Fats what he had seen or found or how exciting a discovery it had been. Instead he had picked up the wrapper between his fingernails, dropped it quickly into the bin, then washed his hands more vigorously than he had ever washed them in his life.

Andrew spent a lot of time staring at Gaia's Facebook page on his laptop. It was almost more intimidating than she was in person. He spent hours poring over photographs of the people that she had left behind in the capital. She came from a different world: she had black friends, Asian friends, friends with names he could never have pronounced. There was a photograph of her in a swimsuit that was burned into his brain, and another of her, leaning up against a filthily good-looking coffee-skinned boy. He had no spots, and actual stubble. By a process of careful examination of all her messages, Andrew had concluded that this was an eighteen-year-old called Marco de Luca. Andrew stared at Marco and Gaia's communications with the concentration of a code breaker, unable to decide whether they indicated a continuing relationship or not.

His Facebook browsing was often tinged with anxiety, because Simon, whose understanding of how the Internet worked was limited, and who instinctively mistrusted it as the only area of his sons' life where they were freer and more at ease than he, would sometimes erupt unexpectedly into their bedrooms to check what they were viewing. Simon claimed that he was making sure that they were not running up huge bills, but Andrew knew it to be one more manifestation of his father's need to exert control, and the cursor hovered constantly over the box that would shut the page whenever he was perusing Gaia's details online.

Ruth was still rattling from topic to topic, in a fruitless attempt to make Simon produce more than surly monosyllables.

"Ooooh," she said suddenly. "I forgot: I spoke to Shirley today, Simon, about you maybe standing for the Parish Council."

The words hit Andrew like a punch.

"You're standing for the council?" he blurted.

Simon slowly raised his eyebrows. One of the muscles in his jaw was twitching.

"Is that a problem?" he asked, in a voice that throbbed with aggression.

"No," lied Andrew.

You've got to be fucking joking. You? Standing for election? Oh fuck, no.

"It sounds like you've got a problem with it," said Simon, still staring straight into Andrew's eyes.

"No," said Andrew again, dropping his gaze to his shepherd's pie.

"What's wrong with me standing for the council?" Simon continued. He was not about to let it go. He wanted to vent his tension in a cathartic outburst of rage.

"Nothing's wrong. I was surprised, that's all."

"Should I have consulted you first?" said Simon.

"No."

"Oh, *thank you*," said Simon. His lower jaw was protruding, as it often did when he was working up to losing control. "Have you found a job yet, you skiving, sponging little shit?"

"No."

Simon glared at Andrew, not eating, but holding a cooling forkful of shepherd's pie in midair. Andrew switched his attention back to his food, determined not to offer further provocation. The air pressure within the kitchen seemed to have increased. Paul's knife rattled against his plate.

"Shirley says," Ruth piped up again, her voice high-pitched, determined to pretend all was well until this became impossible, "that it'll be on the council website, Simon. About how you put your name forward."

Simon did not respond.

Her last, best attempt thwarted, Ruth fell silent too. She was afraid that she might know what was at the root of Simon's bad mood. Anxiety gnawed at her; she was a worrier, she always had been; she couldn't help it. She knew that it drove Simon mad when she begged him for reassurance. She must not say anything.

"Si?"

"What?"

"It's all right, isn't it? About the computer?"

She was a dreadful actress. She tried to make her voice casual and calm, but it was brittle and high-pitched.

This was not the first time stolen goods had entered their home. Simon had found a way of fiddling the electricity meter too, and did small jobs on the side, at the printworks, for cash. All of it gave her little pains in the stomach, kept her awake at night; but Simon was contemptuous of people who did not dare take the shortcuts (and part of what she had loved about him, from the beginning, was that this rough and wild boy, who was contemptuous, rude and aggressive to nearly everyone, had taken the trouble to attract her; that he, who was so difficult to please, had selected her, alone, as worthy).

"What are you talking about?" Simon asked quietly. The full focus of his attention shifted from Andrew to Ruth, and was expressed by the same unblinking, venomous stare.

"Well, there won't be any...any trouble about it, will there?"

Simon was seized with a brutal urge to punish her for intuiting his own fears and for stoking them with her anxiety.

"Yeah, well, I wasn't going to say anything," he said, speaking slowly, giving himself time to make up a story; "but there was a bit of trouble when they were nicked, as it turns out." Andrew and Paul paused in their eating and stared. "Some security guard got beaten up. I didn't know anything about it till it was too late. I only hope there's no comeback."

Ruth could barely breathe. She could not believe the evenness of his tone, the calmness with which he spoke of violent robbery. This explained his mood when he had come home; this explained everything.

"That's why it's essential nobody mentions we've got it," said Simon.

He subjected each of them to a fierce glare, to impress the dangers on them by sheer force of personality.

"We won't," Ruth breathed.

Her rapid imagination was already showing her the police at the door; the computer examined; Simon arrested, wrongly accused of aggravated assault—jailed.

"Did you hear Dad?" she said to her sons, in a voice barely louder than a whisper. "You mustn't tell anybody we've got a new computer."

"It should be all right," said Simon. "It should be fine. As long as everyone keeps their traps shut."

He turned his attention back to his shepherd's pie. Ruth's eyes flittered from Simon to her sons and back again. Paul was pushing food around his plate, silent, frightened.

But Andrew had not believed a word his father said.

You're a lying fucking bastard. You just like scaring her.

When the meal was finished, Simon got up and said, "Well, let's see whether the bloody thing works, at least. You," he pointed at Paul, "go and get it out of the box and put it carefully—*carefully*—on the stand. You," he pointed at Andrew, "you do computing, don't you? You can tell me what to do."

Simon led the way into the sitting room. Andrew knew that he was trying to catch them out, that he wanted them to mess up: Paul, who was small and nervous, might drop the computer, and he, Andrew, was sure to blunder. Behind them in the kitchen, Ruth was clattering around, clearing away the dinner things. She, at least, was out of the immediate line of fire.

Andrew went to assist Paul as he lifted the hard drive.

"He can do it, he's not that much of a pussy!" snapped Simon.

By a miracle, Paul, his arms trembling, set it down on the stand without mishap, then waited with his arms dangling limply at his sides, blocking Simon's access to the machine.

"Get out of my way, you stupid little prick," Simon shouted. Paul scurried off to watch from behind the sofa. Simon picked up a lead at random and addressed Andrew.

"Where do I put this?"

Up your arse, you bastard.

"If you give it to me—"

"I'm asking where I fucking put it!" roared Simon. "You do computing—tell me where it goes!"

Andrew leaned around the back of the computer; he instructed Simon wrong at first, but then, by chance, got the right socket.

They had nearly finished by the time Ruth joined them in the sitting room. Andrew could tell, from one fleeting look at her, that she did not want the thing to work; that she wanted Simon to dump it somewhere, and never mind the eighty quid.

Simon sat down in front of the monitor. After several fruitless attempts, he realized that the cordless mouse had no batteries in it. Paul was sent sprinting from the room to fetch some from the kitchen. When he held them out to his father on his return, Simon snatched them out of his hand, as if Paul might try and whip them away.

His tongue down between his lower teeth and his lip, so that his chin bulged out stupidly, Simon made an exaggerated overfiddling business of inserting the batteries. He always pulled this mad, brutish face as a warning that he was reaching the end of his tether, descending into the place where he could not be held accountable for his actions. Andrew imagined walking out and leaving his father to it, depriving him of the audience he preferred when working himself up; he could almost feel the mouse hitting him behind the ear as, in his imagination, he turned his back.

"Get—fucking—IN!"

Simon began to emit the low, animal noise, unique to him, that matched his aggressively wadded face.

"Uhhlll…uhhlll…CUNTING THING! You fucking do it! *You!* You've got pissy little girl's fingers!"

Simon slammed the control and the batteries into Paul's chest. Paul's hands shook as he fitted the little metal tubes into place; he snapped the plastic cover shut and held the controls back out to his father.

"Thank you, *Pauline.*"

Simon's chin was still jutting like a Neanderthal's. He habitually acted as though inanimate objects were conspiring to irritate him. Once again he placed the mouse on the mat.

Let it work.

A small white arrow appeared on screen and swooped cheerily around at Simon's command.

A tourniquet of fear was released; relief gushed through three of the watchers; Simon stopped pulling his Neanderthal face. Andrew visualized a line of Japanese men and woman in white coats: the people who had assembled this flawless machine, all of them with delicate, dextrous fingers like Paul's; they were bowing to him, sweetly civilized and gentle. Silently, Andrew blessed them and their families. They would never know how much had hung on this particular machine working.

Ruth, Andrew and Paul waited attentively while Simon put the computer through its paces. He brought up menus, had difficulty getting rid of them, clicked icons whose functions he did not understand, and was confused by the outcomes, but he had descended from the plateau of dangerous rage. Having blundered his way back to the desktop, he said, looking up at Ruth, "Seems all right, doesn't it?"

"It's great!" she said at once, forcing a smile, as though the last half hour had not happened, he had bought the machine at Dixons, and connected it without the threat of violence. "It's faster, Simon. Much faster than the last one."

He hasn't opened the Internet yet, you silly woman.

"Yeah, I thought that too."

He glared at his two sons.

"This is brand new and expensive, so you two treat it with respect, you understand? And don't tell anyone we've got it," Simon added, and a gust of renewed malice chilled the room. "All right? Do you understand me?"

They nodded again. Paul's face was tight and pinched. Unseen by his father, he traced a figure of eight on the outside of his leg with his slender forefinger.

"And one of you draw the bloody curtains. Why are they still open?"

Because we've all been standing here, watching you behave like a prick.

Andrew pulled the curtains shut and left the room.

Even after he had reached his bedroom and lain back down on his bed, Andrew was unable to resume his pleasurable meditations on the person of Gaia Bawden. The prospect of his father standing for the council had loomed out of nowhere like some gigantic iceberg, casting its shadow over everything, even Gaia.

For all of Andrew's life, Simon had been a contented prisoner of his own contempt for other people, making his house a fortress against the world where his will was law, and where his mood constituted the family's daily weather. As he had grown older, Andrew had become aware that his family's almost total isolation was not typical, and become slightly embarrassed by it. Friends' parents would ask him where he lived, unable to place his family; they would ask casual questions about whether his mother or father intended to come to social events or fund-raisers. Sometimes they remembered Ruth from the primary school years, when mothers mixed in the playground. She was much more sociable than Simon. Perhaps, if she had not married such an antisocial man, she would have been more like Fats' mother, meeting friends for lunch or dinner, busily connected to the town.

On the very rare occasions that Simon came face-to-face with a person whom he felt it worth courting, he adopted a salt-of-the-earth bluff persona that made Andrew cringe. Simon would talk over them, crack clumsy jokes and often stepped, unwittingly, on all kinds of sensitivities, because he neither knew anything, nor cared much, about the people with whom he was forced to converse. Lately, Andrew had asked himself whether Simon even saw other humans as real.

Why his father had been seized with the aspiration to perform on a wider stage, Andrew could not fathom, but calamity was surely inevitable. Andrew knew other parents, the sort who did sponsored cycle rides to raise money for the Square's new Christmas lights, or ran the Brownies, or set up book clubs. Simon did nothing that required collaboration, and had never evinced the smallest interest in anything that did not benefit him directly.

Awful visions surged in Andrew's churning mind: Simon making a speech larded with the transparent lies that his wife swallowed whole; Simon pulling his Neanderthal face in an attempt to intimidate an opponent; Simon losing control and starting to spew all his favorite swearwords into a microphone: *cunting, fucking, pissy, shit...*

Andrew pulled his laptop toward him, but pushed it away again almost at once. He made no move to touch the mobile on his desk. This magnitude of anxiety and shame could not be contained in an instant message or a text; he was alone with it, and even Fats would not understand, and he did not know what to do.

Friday

Barry Fairbrother's body had been moved to the undertaker's. The deep black cuts in the white scalp, like the grooves of skates on ice, were hidden by his forest of thick hair. Cold, waxen and empty, the body lay, re-dressed in Barry's anniversary dinner shirt and trousers, in a dimly lit viewing room where soft music played. Touches of discreet makeup had returned a life-like glow to his skin. It was almost as though he slept; but not quite.

Barry's two brothers, his widow and his four children went to bid the body good-bye on the eve of the burial. Mary had been undecided, almost until the minute of departure, as to whether she should allow all of the children to see their father's remains. Declan was a sensitive boy, prone to nightmares. It was while she was still in a fever pitch of indecision on Friday afternoon that there was an upset.

Colin "Cubby" Wall had decided that he wanted to go and say good-bye to Barry's body too. Mary, usually compliant and agreeable, had found this excessive. Her voice had grown shrill on the telephone to Tessa; then she had begun to cry again, and said that it was just that she had not planned a large procession past Barry, that this was really a family affair…Dreadfully apologetic, Tessa said that she quite understood, and was then left to explain to Colin, who retreated into a mortified, wounded silence.

He had simply wanted to stand alone beside Barry's body and pay silent homage to a man who had occupied a unique place in his life. Colin had poured truths and secrets he had confided to no other friend into Barry's ears, and Barry's small brown eyes, robin bright, had never ceased to regard him with warmth and kindness. Barry had been Colin's closest-ever friend, giving him an experience of male comradeship he had never known before moving to Pagford, and was sure he would never have again. That he, Colin, who felt himself to be perpetually the outsider and the oddball, for whom life was a matter of daily struggle, had managed to forge a friendship with the cheerful, popular and eternally optimistic Barry, had always seemed a small miracle. Colin clutched what was left of his dignity to him, resolved never to hold this against Mary, and spent the rest of the day meditating on how surprised and hurt Barry would have been, surely, at his widow's attitude.

Three miles outside Pagford, in an attractive cottage called the Smithy, Gavin Hughes was trying to fight off an intensifying gloom. Mary had called earlier. In a voice that trembled with the weight of tears, she had explained how the children had all contributed ideas for tomorrow's funeral service. Siobhan had grown a sunflower from seed, and was going to cut it and put it on top of the coffin. All four kids had written letters to put inside the casket with their father. Mary had composed one too, and was going to put it in Barry's shirt pocket, over his heart.

Gavin put down the receiver, sickened. He did not want to know about the children's letters, nor about the long-nurtured sunflower, yet his mind kept returning to these things as he ate lasagne alone at his kitchen table. Though he would have done anything to avoid reading it, he kept trying to imagine what Mary had written in her letter.

A black suit was hanging in dry cleaner's polythene in his bedroom, like an unwelcome guest. His appreciation of the honor Mary had done him, in publicly acknowledging him as one of those closest to the popular Barry, had long since been overwhelmed by dread. By the time he was washing up his plate and cutlery at the sink, Gavin would have gladly missed the funeral altogether. As for the idea of viewing his dead friend's body, it had not, and would never have occurred to him.

He and Kay had had a nasty row the previous evening, and had not spoken since. It had all been triggered by Kay asking Gavin if he would like her to go with him to the funeral.

"Christ, no," Gavin had said, before he could stop himself.

He had seen her expression, and knew instantly that she had heard. *Christ, no, people will think we're a couple. Christ, no, why would I want you?* And although these were precisely his feelings, he had attempted to bluff his way through.

"I mean, you didn't know him, did you? It'd be a bit weird, wouldn't it?"

But Kay had let rip; tried to corner him, to make him tell her what he really felt, what he wanted, what future he envisioned for the two of them. He had fought back with every weapon in his arsenal, being alternately obtuse, evasive and pedantic, for it was wonderful how you could obscure an emotional issue by appearing to seek precision. At last she had told him to get out of her house; he had obeyed, but he knew that it was not over. That would be way too much to hope for. Gavin's reflection in the kitchen window was drawn and miserable; Barry's stolen future seemed to hang over his own life like a looming cliff; he felt inadequate and guilty, but he still wished that Kay would move back to London.

Night drew in over Pagford, and in the Old Vicarage Parminder Jawanda perused her wardrobe, wondering what to wear to say good-bye to Barry. She had several dark dresses and suits, any one of which would be appropriate, and yet still she looked backwards and forwards along the rail of clothes, mired in indecision.

Wear a sari. It'll upset Shirley Mollison. Go on, wear a sari.

It was so stupid to think that—mad and wrong—and even worse to think it in Barry's voice. Barry was dead; she had endured nearly five days of deep grief for him, and tomorrow they would bury him in the earth. The prospect was unpleasant to Parminder. She had always hated the idea of interment, of a body lying whole under the ground, slowly rotting away, riddled with maggots and flies. The Sikh way was to cremate and to scatter the ashes in running water.

She let her eyes wander up and down the hanging garments, but her saris, worn to family weddings and get-togethers back in Birmingham, seemed to call to her. What was this strange urge to don one? It felt uncharacteristically exhibitionist. She reached out to touch the folds of her favorite, dark blue and gold. She had last worn it to the Fairbrothers' New Year's party, when Barry had attempted to teach her to jive. It had been a most unsuccessful experiment, mainly because he did not know what he was doing himself; but she could remember laughing as she almost never laughed, uncontrollably, madly, the way she had seen drunk women laugh.

The sari was elegant and feminine, forgiving of middle-aged spread: Parminder's mother, who was eighty-two, wore it daily. Parminder herself had no need of its camouflaging properties: she was as slim as she had been at twenty. Yet she pulled out the long, dark length of soft material and held it up against her dressing gown, letting it fall to caress her bare feet, looking down its length at its subtle embroidery. To wear it would feel like a private joke between herself and Barry, like the cow-faced house and all the funny things Barry had said about Howard, as they walked away from interminable, ill-humored council meetings.

There was a terrible weight on Parminder's chest, but did not the Guru Granth Sahib exhort friends and relatives of the dead not to show grief, but to celebrate their loved one's reunion with God? In an effort to keep traitorous tears at bay, Parminder silently intoned the nighttime prayer, the kirtan sohila.

My friend, I urge you that this is the opportune time to serve the saints.
Earn divine profit in this world and live in peace and comfort in the next.
Life is shortening day and night.
O mind, meet the Guru and set right your affairs...

Lying on her bed in her dark room, Sukhvinder could hear what every member of her family was doing. There was the distant murmur of the television directly below her, punctuated by the muffled laughter of her brother and her father, who were watching a Friday-night comedy show. She could make out her elder sister's voice across the landing, talking on her mobile to one of her many friends. Nearest of all was her mother, clunking and scraping in the built-in wardrobe on the other side of the wall.

Sukhvinder had drawn the curtains over her window and placed a draft excluder, shaped like a long sausage dog, along the bottom of her door. In the absence of a lock, the dog impeded the door's progress; it gave her warning. She was sure that nobody would come in, though. She was where she ought to be, doing what she ought to be doing. Or so they thought.

She had just performed one of her dreadful daily rituals: the opening of her Facebook page, and the removal of another post from a sender she did not know. As often as she blocked the person bombarding her with these messages, they changed their profile and sent more. She never knew when one would appear. Today's had been a black and white image, a copy of a nineteenth-century circus poster.

La Véritable Femme à Barbe, Miss Anne Jones Elliot.

It showed the photograph of a woman in a lacy dress, with long dark hair and a luxuriant beard and mustache.

She was convinced that it was Fats Wall who was sending them, although it might have been somebody else. Dane Tully and his friends, for instance, who made soft, grunting apelike noises whenever she spoke in English. They would have done it to anybody of her color; there were hardly any brown faces at Winterdown. It made her feel humiliated and stupid, especially as Mr. Garry never told them off. He affected not to hear them, or else to hear only background chatter. Perhaps he, too, thought that Sukhvinder Kaur Jawanda was an ape, a hairy ape.

Sukhvinder lay on her back on top of her covers and wished with all of her being that she was dead. If she could have achieved suicide, simply by willing it, she would have done it without hesitation. Death had come to Mr. Fairbrother; why could it not happen to her? Better yet, why could they not swap places? Niamh and Siobhan could have their father back, and she, Sukhvinder, could simply slip into nonbeing: wiped out, wiped clean.

Her self-disgust was like a nettle suit; every part of her prickled and burned with it. She had to will herself, moment by moment, to endure, to remain stationary; not to rush to do the one and only thing that helped. The whole family had to be in bed before she acted. But it was agony to lie like this, listening to her own breathing, conscious of the useless weight of her own ugly and disgusting body on the bed. She liked to think of drowning, of sinking down into cool green water, and feeling herself slowly pressed into nothingness...

The great hermaphrodite sits quiet and still...

Shame ran down her body like a burning rash as she lay in the darkness. She had never heard the word before Fats Wall spoke it in maths on Wednesday. She would not have been able to look it up: she was dyslexic. But he had been kind enough to explain what it meant, so there was no need.

The hairy man-woman...

He was worse than Dane Tully, whose taunts had no variety. Fats Wall's evil tongue fashioned a fresh, tailor-made torture every time he saw her, and she could not shut her ears. His every insult and jibe was branded on Sukhvinder's memory, sticking there as no useful fact had ever done. If she could have been examined on the things he had called her, she would have achieved the first A grade of her life. *Tash 'N' Tits. Hermaphrodite. The Bearded Dumbbell.*

Hairy, heavy and stupid. Plain and clumsy. Lazy, according to her mother, whose criticism and exasperation rained down upon her daily. A bit slow, according to her father, who said it with an affection that did not mitigate his lack of interest. He could afford to be nice about her bad grades. He had Jaswant and Rajpal, both top of every class they took.

"Poor old Jolly," Vikram would say carelessly, after glancing through her report.

But her father's indifference was preferable to her mother's anger. Parminder did not seem able to comprehend or accept that she had produced a child who was not gifted. If any of the subject teachers made the slightest hint that Sukhvinder might try harder, Parminder seized upon it in triumph.

"'Sukhvinder is easily discouraged and needs to have more faith in her abilities.' There! You see? Your teacher is saying you don't try hard enough, Sukhvinder."

Of the only class in which Sukhvinder had reached the second set, computing—Fats Wall was not there, so she sometimes dared put up her hand to answer questions—Parminder said dismissively, "The amount of time you children spend on the Internet, I'm surprised you're not in set one."

Never would it have occurred to Sukhvinder to tell either of her parents about the ape grunts or about Stuart Wall's endless stream of malice. It would mean confessing that people beyond the family also saw her as substandard and worthless. In any case, Parminder was friends with Stuart Wall's mother. Sukhvinder sometimes wondered why Stuart Wall did not worry about their mothers' connection, but concluded that he knew that she would not give him away. He saw through her. He saw her cowardice, as he knew her every worst thought about herself, and was able to articulate it for the amusement of Andrew Price. She had fancied Andrew Price once, before she realized that she was utterly unfit to fancy anyone; before she realized that she was laughable and strange.

Sukhvinder heard her father's voice and Rajpal's, growing louder as they came up the stairs. Rajpal's laughter reached a crescendo right outside her door.

"It's late," she heard her mother call from her bedroom. "Vikram, he should be in bed."

Vikram's voice came through Sukhvinder's door, close by, loud and warm.

"Are you asleep already, Jolly?"

It was her childhood nickname, bestowed in irony. Jaswant had been Jazzy, and Sukhvinder, a grizzling, unhappy baby, rarely smiling, had become Jolly.

"No," Sukhvinder called back. "I've only just gone to bed."

"Well, it might interest you to know that your brother, here—"

But what Rajpal had done was lost in his shouting protests, his laughter; she heard Vikram moving away, still teasing Rajpal.

Sukhvinder waited for the house to fall silent. She clung to the prospect of her only consolation, as she would have hugged a life belt, waiting, waiting, for them all to go to bed…

(And as she waited, she remembered that evening not long ago, at the end of rowing training, when they had been walking through the darkness toward the car park by the canal. You were so tired after rowing. Your arms and your stomach muscles ached, but it was a good clean pain. She always slept properly after rowing. And then Krystal, bringing up the rear of the group with Sukhvinder, had called her a silly Paki bitch.

It had come out of nowhere. They had all been messing around with Mr. Fairbrother. Krystal thought she was being funny. She used "fucking" interchangeably with "very," and seemed to see no difference between them. Now she said "Paki" as she would have said "dozy" or "dim." Sukhvinder was conscious of her face falling, and experienced the familiar sliding, scalding sensation in her stomach.

"*What* did you say?"

Mr. Fairbrother had wheeled around to face Krystal. None of them had ever heard him properly angry before.

"I di'n mean nuthin'," said Krystal, half taken aback, half defiant. "I was on'y jokin'. She knows I was jus' jokin'. Don' yeh?" she demanded of Sukhvinder, who muttered cravenly that she knew it was a joke.

"I never want to hear you use that word again."

They all knew how much he liked Krystal. They all knew he had paid for her to go on a couple of their trips out of his own pocket. Nobody laughed louder than Mr. Fairbrother at Krystal's jokes; she could be very funny.

They walked on, and everybody was embarrassed. Sukhvinder was afraid to look at Krystal; she felt guilty, as she always did.

They were approaching the people carrier when Krystal said, so quietly that even Mr. Fairbrother did not hear it: "I wuz jokin'."

And Sukhvinder said quickly, "I know."

"Yeah, well. S'ry."

It came out as a mangled monosyllable, and Sukhvinder thought it tactful not to acknowledge it. Nevertheless, it cleaned her out. It restored her dignity. On the way back to Pagford, she initiated, for the first time ever, the singing of the team's lucky song, asking Krystal to start with Jay-Z's rap.)

Slowly, very slowly, her family seemed to be putting themselves to bed at last. Jaswant spent a long time in the bathroom, clinking and crashing around. Sukhvinder waited until Jaz had finished primping herself, until her parents had stopped talking in their room, for the house to fall silent.

Then, at last, it was safe. She sat up and pulled the razor blade out from a hole in the ear of her old cuddly rabbit. She had stolen the blade from Vikram's store in the bathroom cabinet. She got off the bed and groped for the torch on her shelf, and a handful of tissues, then moved into the furthest part of her room, into the little round turret in the corner. Here, she knew, the torch's light would be confined, and would not show around the edges of the door. She sat down with her back against the wall, pushed up the sleeve of her nightshirt and examined by torchlight the marks left by her last session, still visible, crisscrossed and dark on her arm, but healing. With a slight shiver of fear that was a blessed relief in its narrow, immediate focus, she placed the blade halfway up her forearm and sliced into her own flesh.

Sharp, hot pain and the blood came at once; when she had cut herself right up to her elbow she pressed the wad of tissues onto the long wound, making sure nothing leaked onto her nightshirt or the carpet. After a minute or two, she cut again, horizontally, across the first incision, making a ladder, pausing to press and to mop as she went. The blade drew the pain away from her screaming thoughts and transmuted it into animal burning of nerves and skin: relief and release in every cut.

At last she wiped the blade clean and surveyed the mess she had made; the wounds intersecting, bleeding, hurting so much that tears were rolling down her face. She might sleep if the pain did not keep her awake; but she must wait for ten or twenty minutes, until the fresh cuts had clotted over. She sat with her knees drawn up, closed her wet eyes, and leaned against the wall beneath the window.

Some of her self-hatred had oozed out with the blood. Her mind drifted away to Gaia Bawden, the new girl, who had taken such an unaccountable fancy to her. Gaia could have hung out with anyone, with her looks and that London accent, yet she kept seeking out Sukhvinder at lunchtimes and on the bus. Sukhvinder did not understand it. She almost wanted to ask Gaia what she thought she was playing at; day by day she expected the new girl to realize that she, Sukhvinder, was hairy and apelike, slow and stupid, someone to be despised and grunted at and insulted. No doubt she would recognize her mistake soon, and Sukhvinder would be left, as usual, to the bored pity of her oldest friends, the Fairbrother twins.

Saturday

I

Every parking space in Church Row was taken by nine o'clock in the morning. Darkly clothed mourners moved, singly, in pairs and in groups, up and down the street, converging, like a stream of iron filings drawn to a magnet, on St. Michael and All Saints. The path leading to the church doors became crowded, then overflowed; those who were displaced fanned out among the graves, seeking safe spots to stand between the headstones, fearful of trampling on the dead, yet unwilling to move too far from the church entrance. It was clear to everyone that there would not be enough pews for all the people who had come to say good-bye to Barry Fairbrother.

His coworkers from the bank, who were grouped around the most extravagant of the Sweetlove tombs, wished that the august representative from head office would move on and take his inane small talk and his clumsy jokes with him. Lauren, Holly and Jennifer from the rowing team had separated from their parents to huddle together in the shade of a mossy-fingered yew. Parish councillors, a motley bunch, talked solemnly in the middle of the path: a clutch of balding heads and thick-lensed glasses; a smattering of black straw hats and cultured pearls. Men from the squash and golf clubs hailed each other in subdued fashion; old friends from university recognized each other from afar and edged together; and in between milled what seemed to be most of Pagford, in their smartest and most somber-hued clothes. The air droned with quiet conversations; faces flickered, watching and waiting.

Tessa Wall's best coat, which was of gray wool, was cut so tightly around the armholes that she could not raise her arms above chest height. Standing beside her son on one side of the church path, she was exchanging sad little smiles and waves with acquaintances, while continuing to argue with Fats through lips she was trying not to move too obviously.

"For God's sake, Stu. He was your father's best friend. Just this once, show some consideration."

"No one told me it was going to go on this bloody long. You told me it'd be over by half-past eleven."

"Don't swear. I said we'd leave St. Michael's at about half-past eleven—"

"— so I thought it'd be over, didn't I? So I arranged to meet Arf."

"But you've got to come to the burial, your father's a pallbearer! Ring Arf and tell him it'll have to be tomorrow instead."

"He can't do tomorrow. Anyway, I haven't got my mobile on me. Cubby told me not to bring it to church."

"Don't call your father Cubby! You can ring Arf on mine," said Tessa, burrowing in her pocket.

"I don't know his number by heart," lied Fats coldly.

She and Colin had eaten dinner without Fats the previous evening, because he had cycled up to Andrew's place, where they were working on their English project together. That, at any rate, was the story Fats had given his mother, and Tessa had pretended to believe it. It suited her too well to have Fats out of the way, incapable of upsetting Colin.

At least he was wearing the new suit that Tessa had bought for him in Yarvil. She had lost her temper at him in the third shop, because he had looked like a scarecrow in everything he had tried on, gawky and graceless, and she had thought angrily that he was doing it on purpose; that he could have inflated the suit with a sense of fitness if he chose.

"Shh!" said Tessa preemptively. Fats was not speaking, but Colin was approaching them, leading the Jawandas; he seemed, in his overwrought state, to be confusing the role of pallbearer with that of usher; hovering by the gates, welcoming people. Parminder looked grim and gaunt in her sari, with her children trailing behind her; Vikram, in his dark suit, looked like a film star.

A few yards from the church doors, Samantha Mollison was waiting beside her husband, looking up at the bright off-white sky and musing on all the wasted sunshine beating down on top of the high ceiling of cloud. She was refusing to be dislodged from the hard-surfaced path, no matter how many old ladies had to cool their ankles in the grass; her patent-leather high heels might sink into the soft earth, and become dirty and clogged.

When acquaintances hailed them, Miles and Samantha responded pleasantly, but they were not speaking to each other. They had had a row the previous evening. A few people had asked after Lexie and Libby, who usually came home at weekends, but both girls were staying over at friends' houses. Samantha knew that Miles regretted their absence; he loved playing paterfamilias in public. Perhaps, she thought, with a most pleasurable leap of fury, he would ask her and the girls to pose with him for a picture on his election leaflets. She would enjoy telling him what she thought of that idea.

She could tell that he was surprised by the turnout. No doubt he was regretting that he did not have a starring role in the forthcoming service; it would have been an ideal opportunity to begin a surreptitious campaign for Barry's seat on the council with this big audience of captive voters. Samantha made a mental note to drop a sarcastic allusion to the missed opportunity when a suitable occasion arose.

"Gavin!" called Miles, at the sight of a familiar, fair and narrow head.

"Oh, hi, Miles. Hi, Sam."

Gavin's new black tie shone against his white shirt. There were violet bags under his light eyes. Samantha leaned in on tiptoes, so that he could not decently avoid kissing her on the cheek and inhaling her musky perfume.

"Big turnout, isn't it?" Gavin said, gazing around.

"Gavin's a pallbearer," Miles told his wife, in precisely the way that he would have announced that a small and unpromising child had been awarded a book token for effort. In truth, he had been a little surprised when Gavin had told him he had been accorded this honor. Miles had vaguely imagined that he and Samantha would be privileged guests, surrounded by a certain aura of mystery and importance, having been at the deathbed. It might have been a nice gesture if Mary, or somebody close to Mary, had asked him, Miles, to read a lesson, or say a few words to acknowledge the important part he had played in Barry's final moments.

Samantha was deliberately unsurprised that Gavin had been singled out.

"You and Barry were quite close, weren't you, Gav?"

Gavin nodded. He felt jittery and a little sick. He had had a very bad night's sleep, waking in the early hours from horrible dreams in which, first, he had dropped the coffin, so that Barry's body spilled out onto the church floor; and, secondly, he had overslept, missed the funeral, and arrived at St. Michael and All Saints to find Mary alone in the graveyard, white-faced and furious, screaming at him that he had ruined the whole thing.

"I'm not sure where I ought to be," he said, looking around. "I've never done this before."

"Nothing to it, mate," said Miles. "There's only one requirement, really. Don't drop anything, hehehe."

Miles' girlish laugh contrasted oddly with his deep speaking voice. Neither Gavin nor Samantha smiled.

Colin Wall loomed out of the mass of bodies. Big and awkward-looking, with his high, knobbly forehead, he always made Samantha think of Frankenstein's monster.

"Gavin," he said. "There you are. I think we should probably stand out on the pavement, they'll be here in a few minutes."

"Right-ho," said Gavin, relieved to be ordered around.

"Colin," said Miles, with a nod.

"Yes, hello," said Colin, flustered, before turning away and forcing his way back through the mass of mourners.

Then came another small flurry of movement, and Samantha

154

heard Howard's loud voice: "Excuse me...so sorry...trying to join our family..." The crowd parted to avoid his belly, and Howard was revealed, immense in a velvet-faced overcoat. Shirley and Maureen bobbed in his wake, Shirley neat and composed in navy blue, Maureen scrawny as a carrion bird, in a hat with a small black veil.

"Hello, hello," said Howard, kissing Samantha firmly on both cheeks. "And how's Sammy?"

Her answer was swallowed up in a widespread, awkward shuffling, as everybody began retreating backwards off the path: there was a certain discreet jockeying for position; nobody wanted to relinquish their claim to a place near the church entrance. With this cleaving in two of the crowd, familiar individuals were revealed like separate pips along the break. Samantha spotted the Jawandas: coffee-brown faces among all the whey; Vikram, absurdly handsome in his dark suit; Parminder dressed in a sari (why did she do it? Didn't she know she was playing right into the likes of Howard and Shirley's hands?), and beside her, dumpy little Tessa Wall in a gray coat, which was straining at the buttons.

Mary Fairbrother and the children were walking slowly up the path to the church. Mary was terribly pale, and appeared pounds thinner. Could she have lost so much weight in six days? She was holding one of the twins' hands, with her other arm around the shoulders of her younger son, and the eldest, Fergus, marching behind. She walked with her eyes fixed straight ahead, her soft mouth pursed tight. Other family members followed Mary and the children; the procession moved over the threshold and was swallowed up in the dingy interior of the church.

Everyone else moved towards the doors at once, which resulted in an undignified jam. The Mollisons found themselves shunted together with the Jawandas.

"After you, Mr. Jawanda, sir, after you..." boomed Howard, holding out an arm to let the surgeon walk in first. But Howard made sure to use his bulk to prevent anybody else taking precedence over him, and followed Vikram immediately through the entrance, leaving their families to follow on.

A royal-blue carpet ran the length of the aisle of St. Michael and

All Saints. Golden stars glimmered on the vaulted ceiling; brass plaques reflected the glow of the hanging lamps. The stained-glass windows were elaborate and gorgeously hued. Halfway down the nave, on the epistle side, St. Michael himself stared down from the largest window, clad in silver armor. Sky-blue wings curved out of his shoulders; in one hand he held aloft a sword, in the other, a pair of golden scales. A sandaled foot rested on the back of a writhing bat-winged Satan, who was dark gray in color and attempting to raise himself. The saint's expression was serene.

Howard stopped level with St. Michael and indicated that his party should file into the pew on the left; Vikram turned right into the opposite one. While the remaining Mollisons, and Maureen, filed past him into the pew, Howard remained planted on the royal-blue carpet, and addressed Parminder as she passed him.

"Dreadful, this. Barry. Awful shock."

"Yes," she said, loathing him.

"I always think those frocks look comfy; are they?" he added, nodding at her sari.

She did not answer, but took her place beside Jaswant. Howard sat down too, making of himself a prodigious plug at the end of the pew that would seal it off to newcomers.

Shirley's eyes were fixed respectfully on her knees, and her hands were clasped, apparently in prayer, but she was really mulling over Howard and Parminder's little exchange about the sari. Shirley belonged to a section of Pagford that quietly lamented the fact that the Old Vicarage, which had been built long ago to house a High Church vicar with muttonchop whiskers and a starched-aproned staff, was now home to a family of Hindus (Shirley had never quite grasped what religion the Jawandas were). She thought that if she and Howard went to the temple, or the mosque, or wherever it was the Jawandas worshipped, they would doubtless be required to cover their heads and remove their shoes and who knew what else, otherwise there would be outcry. Yet it was acceptable for Parminder to flaunt her sari in church. It was not as though Parminder did not have normal clothes, for she wore them to work every day. The double standard of it all was what rankled; not a thought for the disrespect it showed to *their* religion, and, by extension, to Barry Fairbrother himself, of whom she was supposed to have been so fond.

Shirley unclasped her hands, raised her head, and gave her attention over to the outfits of people who were passing, and of the size and number of Barry's floral tributes. Some of these had been heaped up against the communion rail. Shirley spotted the offering from the council, for which she and Howard had organized the collection. It was a large, round traditional wreath of white and blue flowers, which were the colors of Pagford's arms. Their flowers and all the other wreaths were overshadowed by the life-sized oar, made of bronze chrysanthemums, which the girls' rowing team had given.

Sukhvinder turned in her pew to look for Lauren, whose florist mother had made the oar; she wanted to mime that she had seen it and liked it, but the crowd was dense and she could not spot Lauren anywhere. Sukhvinder was mournfully proud that they had done it, especially when she saw that people were pointing it out to each other as they settled themselves in their seats. Five of the eight girls on the team had stumped up money for the oar. Lauren had told Sukhvinder how she had tracked down Krystal Weedon at lunchtime, and exposed herself to the piss-taking of Krystal's friends, who were sitting smoking on a low wall by the newsagent's. Lauren had asked Krystal if she wanted to chip in. "Yeah, I will, all righ'," Krystal had said; but she had not, so her name was not on the card. Nor, as far as Sukhvinder could see, had Krystal come to the funeral.

Sukhvinder's insides were like lead, but the ache of her left forearm coupled with the sharp twinges of pain when she moved it was a counterirritant, and at least Fats Wall, glowering in his black suit, was nowhere near her. He had not made eye contact with her when their two families had met, briefly, in the churchyard; he was restrained by the presence of their parents, as he was sometimes restrained by the presence of Andrew Price.

Late the previous evening, her anonymous cyber-torturer had sent her a black and white picture of a naked Victorian child, covered in soft dark hair. She had seen it and deleted it while dressing for the funeral.

When had she last been happy? She knew that in a different life, long before anyone had grunted at her, she had sat in this church, and been quite content for years; she had sung hymns with gusto at Christmas, Easter and Harvest Festival. She had always liked St. Michael, with his pretty, feminine, Pre-Raphaelite face, his curly golden hair…but this morning, for the first time, she saw him differently, with his foot resting almost casually on that writhing dark devil; she found his untroubled expression sinister and arrogant.

The pews were packed. Muffled clunks, echoing footsteps and quiet rustlings animated the dusty air as the unlucky ones continued to file in at the back of the church and took up standing room along the left-hand wall. Some hopeful souls tiptoed down the aisle in case of an overlooked place in the crammed pews. Howard remained immovable and firm, until Shirley tapped his shoulder and whispered, *"Aubrey and Julia!"*

At which Howard turned massively, and waved the service sheet to attract the Fawleys' attention. They came briskly down the carpeted aisle: Aubrey, tall, thin and balding in his dark suit, Julia with her light-red hair pulled back into a chignon. They smiled their thanks as Howard moved along, shunting the others up, making sure that the Fawleys had plenty of room.

Samantha was jammed so tightly between Miles and Maureen that she could feel Maureen's sharp hip joint pressing into her flesh on one side and the keys in Miles' pocket on the other. Furious, she attempted to secure herself a centimeter or so more room, but neither Miles nor Maureen had anywhere else to go, so she stared straight ahead, and turned her thoughts vengefully to Vikram, who had lost none of his appeal in the month or so since she had last seen him. He was so conspicuously, irrefutably good-looking, it was silly; it made you want to laugh. With his long legs and his broad shoulders, and the flatness of his belly where his shirt tucked into his trousers, and those dark eyes with the thick black lashes, he looked like a god compared to other Pagford men, who were so slack and pallid and porky. As Miles leaned forward to exchange whispered pleasantries with Julia Fawley, his keys ground painfully into Samantha's upper thigh, and she imagined Vikram ripping open the navy wrap dress she was wearing, and in her fantasy she had omitted to put on the matching camisole that concealed her deep canyon of cleavage...

The organ stops creaked and silence fell, except for a soft persistent rustle. Heads turned: the coffin was coming up the aisle.

The pallbearers were almost comically mismatched: Barry's brothers were both five foot six, and Colin Wall, at the rear, six foot two, so that the back end of the coffin was considerably higher than the front. The coffin itself was not made of polished mahogany, but of wickerwork.

It's a bloody picnic basket! thought Howard, outraged.

Looks of surprise flitted across many faces as the willow box passed them, but some had known all about the coffin in advance. Mary had told Tessa (who had told Parminder) how the choice of material had been made by Fergus, Barry's eldest son, who wanted willow because it was a sustainable, quick-growing material and therefore environmentally friendly. Fergus was a passionate enthusiast for all things green and ecologically sound.

Parminder liked the willow coffin better, much better, than the stout wooden box in which most English disposed of their dead. Her grandmother had always had a superstitious fear of the soul being trapped inside something heavy and solid, deploring the way that British undertakers nailed down the lids. The pallbearers lowered the coffin onto the brocade-draped bier and retreated: Barry's son, brothers and brother-in-law edged into the front pews, and Colin walked jerkily back to join his family.

For two quaking seconds Gavin hesitated. Parminder could tell that he was unsure of where to go, his only option to walk back down the aisle under the eyes of three hundred people. But Mary must have made a sign to him, because he ducked, blushing furiously, into the front pew beside Barry's mother. Parminder had only ever spoken to Gavin when she had tested and treated him for chlamydia. He had never met her gaze again.

"I am the resurrection and the life, saith the Lord; he that believeth in me, though he were dead, yet shall he live: and whosoever liveth and believeth in me shall never die..."

The vicar did not sound as if he were thinking about the sense of the words issuing from his mouth, but only about his own delivery, which was singsong and rhythmic. Parminder was familiar with his style; she had attended carol services for years with all the other St. Thomas's parents. Long acquaintance had not reconciled her to the white-faced warrior saint staring down at her, nor all the dark wood, the hard pews, the alien altar with its jeweled golden cross, nor the dirgy hymns, which she found chilly and unsettling.

So she withdrew her attention from the self-conscious drone of the vicar and thought again of her father. She had seen him out of the kitchen window, flat on his face, while her radio continued to blare from on top of the rabbit hutch. He had been lying there for two hours while she, her mother and her sisters had been browsing in Topshop. She could still feel her father's shoulder beneath his hot shirt as she had shaken it. *"Dadiii. Dadiiiii."*

They had scattered Darshan's ashes in the sad little River Rea in Birmingham. Parminder could remember the dull clay look of its surface, on an overcast day in June, and the stream of tiny white and gray flakes floating away from her.

The organ clunked and wheezed into life, and she got to her feet with everybody else. She caught a glimpse of the backs of Niamh and Siobhan's red-gold heads; they were exactly the age she had been when Darshan had been taken from them. Parminder experienced a rush of tenderness, and an awful ache, and a confused desire to hold them and to tell them that she knew, she knew, she understood...

Morning has broken, like the first morning...

Gavin could hear a shrill treble from along the row: Barry's younger son's voice had not yet broken. He knew that Declan had chosen the hymn. That was another of the ghastly details of the service that Mary had chosen to share with him.

He was finding the funeral an even worse ordeal than he had expected. He thought it might have been better with a wooden coffin; he had had an awful, visceral awareness of Barry's body inside that light wickerwork case; the physical weight of him was shocking. All those complacently staring people, as he walked up the aisle; did they not understand what he was actually carrying?

Then had come the ghastly moment when he had realized that nobody had saved him a place, and that he would have to walk all the way back again while everybody stared, and hide among the standees at the back...but instead he had been forced to sit in the first pew, horribly exposed. It was like being in the front seat of a rollercoaster, bearing the brunt of every awful twist and lurch.

Sitting there, mere feet from Siobhan's sunflower, its head as big as a saucepan lid, in the middle of a big burst of yellow freesias and daylilies, he actually wished that Kay had come with him; he could not believe it, but there it was. He would have been consoled by the presence of somebody who was on his side; somebody simply to keep him a seat. He had not considered what a sad bastard he might look, turning up alone.

The hymn ended. Barry's older brother walked to the front to speak. Gavin did not know how he could bear to do it, with Barry's corpse lying right in front of him beneath the sunflower (grown from seed, over months); nor how Mary could sit so quietly, with her head bowed, apparently looking at the hands clasped in her lap. Gavin tried, actively, to provide his own interior interference, so as to dilute the impact of the eulogy.

He's going to tell the story about Barry meeting Mary, once he's got past this kid stuff...happy childhood, high jinks, yeah, yeah...Come on, move it along...

They would have to put Barry back in the car, and drive all the way to Yarvil to bury him in the cemetery there, because the tiny graveyard of St. Michael and All Saints had been declared full twenty years previously. Gavin imagined lowering the wickerwork coffin into the grave under the eyes of this crowd. Carrying it in and out of the church would be nothing compared to that...

One of the twins was crying. Out of the corner of his eye, Gavin saw Mary reach out a hand to hold her daughter's.

Let's get on with it, for fuck's sake. Please.

"I think it's fair to say that Barry always knew his own mind,"

Barry's brother was saying hoarsely. He had got a few laughs with tales of Barry's scrapes in childhood. The strain in his voice was palpable. "He was twenty-four when we went off on my stag weekend to Liverpool. First night there, we leave the campsite and go off to the pub, and there behind the bar is the landlord's student daughter, a beautiful blonde, helping out on a Saturday night. Barry spent the whole night propping up the bar, chatting her up, getting her into trouble with her dad and pretending he didn't know who the rowdy lot in the corner were."

A weak laugh. Mary's head was drooping; both hands were clutching those of the child on either side.

"He told me that night, back in the tent, that he was going to marry her. I thought, *Hang on, I'm the one who's supposed to be drunk.*" Another little titter. "Baz made us go back to the same pub the next night. When we got home, the first thing he did was buy her a postcard and send it to her, telling her he'd be back next weekend. They were married a year to the day after they met, and I think everyone who knew them would agree that Barry knew a good thing when he saw it. They went on to have four beautiful children, Fergus, Niamh, Siobhan and Declan…"

Gavin breathed carefully in and out, in and out, trying not to listen, and wondering what on earth his own brother would find to say about him under the same circumstances. He had not had Barry's luck; his romantic life did not make a pretty story. He had never walked into a pub and found the perfect wife standing there, blond, smiling and ready to serve him a pint. No, *he* had had Lisa, who had never seemed to think him up to scratch; seven years of escalating warfare had culminated in a dose of the clap; and then, with barely a break, there had been Kay, clinging to him like an aggressive and threatening barnacle…

But, all the same, he would ring her later, because he didn't think he would be able to stand going back to his empty cottage after this. He would be honest, and tell her how horrible and stressful the funeral had been, and that he wished she had come with him. That would surely deflect any lingering umbrage about their row. He did not want to be alone tonight.

Two pews back, Colin Wall was sobbing, with small but audible gasps, into a large, wet handkerchief. Tessa's hand rested on his thigh, exerting gentle pressure. She was thinking about Barry; about how she had relied upon him to help her with Colin; of the consolation of shared laughter; of Barry's boundless generosity of spirit. She could see him clearly, short and ruddy, jiving with Parminder at their last party; imitating Howard Mollison's strictures on the Fields; advising Colin tactfully, as only he could have done, to accept Fats' behavior as adolescent, rather than sociopathic.

Tessa was scared of what the loss of Barry Fairbrother would mean to the man beside her; scared of how they would manage to accommodate this huge ragged absence; scared that Colin had made a vow to the dead that he could not keep, and that he did not realize how little Mary, to whom he kept wanting to talk, liked him. And through all Tessa's anxiety and sorrow was threaded the usual worry, like an itchy little worm: Fats, and how she was going to avert an explosion, how she would make him come with them to the burial, or how she might hide from Colin that he had not come—which might, after all, be easier.

"We are going to finish today's service with a song chosen by Barry's daughters, Niamh and Siobhan, which meant a lot to them and their father," said the vicar. He managed, by his tone, to disassociate himself personally from what was about to happen.

The beat of the drum rang so loudly through hidden speakers that the congregation jumped. A loud American voice was saying "*uh huh, uh huh*" and Jay-Z rapped:

> *Good girl gone bad —*
> *Take three —*
> *Action.*
> *No clouds in my storms...*
> *Let it rain, I hydroplane into fame*
> *Comin' down with the Dow Jones...*

Some people thought that it was a mistake: Howard and Shirley threw outraged glances at each other, but nobody pressed stop, or ran up the aisle apologizing. Then a powerful, sexy female voice started to sing:

> *You had my heart*
> *And we'll never be worlds apart*
> *Maybe in magazines*
> *But you'll still be my star…*

The pallbearers were carrying the wicker coffin back down the aisle, and Mary and the children were following.

> *…Now that it's raining more than ever*
> *Know that we'll still have each other*
> *You can stand under my umbuh-rella*
> *You can stand under my umbuh-rella*

The congregation filed slowly out of the church, trying not to walk in time to the beat of the song.

II

Andrew Price took the handlebars of his father's racing bicycle and walked it carefully out of the garage, making sure that he did not scrape the car. Down the stone steps and through the metal gate he carried it; then, in the lane, he put his foot on one pedal, scooted a few yards and swung his other leg over the saddle. He soared left onto the vertiginously sloping hillside road and sped, without touching his brakes, down toward Pagford.

The hedgerows and sky blurred; he imagined himself in a velodrome as the wind whipped his clean hair and his stinging face, which he had just scrubbed clean. Level with the Fairbrothers' wedge-shaped garden he applied the brakes, because some months previously he had taken this sharp turn too fast and fallen off, and had had to return home immediately with his jeans ripped open and grazes all down one side of his face...

He freewheeled, with only one hand on the bars, into Church Row, and enjoyed a second, though lesser, downhill burst of speed, slightly checked when he saw that they were loading a coffin onto a hearse outside the church, and that a dark-clothed crowd was spilling out between the heavy wooden doors. Andrew pedaled furiously around the corner and out of sight. He did not want to see Fats emerging from church with a distraught Cubby, wearing the cheap suit and tie that he had described with comical disgust during yesterday's English lesson. It would have been like interrupting his friend having a crap.

As Andrew cycled slowly around the Square, he slicked his hair back off his face with one hand, wondering what the cold air had done to his purple-red acne and whether the antibacterial face wash had done anything to soothe the angry look of it. And he told himself the cover story: he had come from Fats' house (which he might have done, there was no reason why not), which meant that Hope Street was as obvious a route down to the river as cutting through the first side street. Therefore there was no need for Gaia Bawden (if she happened to be looking out of the window of her house, and happened to see him, and happened to recognize him) to think that he had come this way because of her. Andrew did not anticipate having to explain to her his reason for cycling up her street, but he still held the fake story in his mind, because he believed it gave him an air of cool detachment.

He simply wanted to know which was her house. Twice already, at weekends, he had cycled along the short terraced street, every nerve in his body tingling, but he had been unable, as yet, to discover which house harbored the Grail. All he knew, from his furtive glimpses through the dirty school-bus windows, was that she lived on the right-hand even-numbered side.

As he turned the corner, he tried to compose his features, acting the part of a man cycling slowly towards the river by the most

direct route, lost in his own serious thoughts, but ready to acknowledge a classmate, should they show themselves…

She was there. On the pavement. Andrew's legs continued to
pump, though he could not feel the pedals, and he was suddenly
aware how thin the tires were on which he balanced. She was
rummaging in her leather handbag, her copper-brown hair hanging around her face. Number ten on the door ajar behind her, and
a black T-shirt falling short of her waist; a band of bare skin, and a
heavy belt and tight jeans…when he was almost past her, she closed
the door and turned; her hair fell back from her beautiful face, and
she said, quite clearly, in her London voice, "Oh, hi."

"Hi," he said. His legs kept pedaling. Six feet away, twelve feet
away; why hadn't he stopped? Shock kept him moving, he dared
not look back; he was at the end of her street already; *for fuck's sake
don't fall off*; he turned the corner, too stunned to gauge whether
he was more relieved or disappointed that he had left her behind.

Holy shit.

He cycled on towards the wooded area at the base of Pargetter
Hill, where the river glinted intermittently through the trees, but
he could see nothing except Gaia burned onto his retina like neon.
The narrow road turned into an earthy footpath, and the gentle
breeze off the water caressed his face, which he did not think had
turned red, because it had all happened so quickly.

"Fucking hell!" he said aloud to the fresh air and the deserted path.

He raked excitedly through this magnificent, unexpected treasure
trove: her perfect body, revealed in tight denim and stretchy cotton;
number ten behind her, on a chipped, shabby blue door; "oh, hi,"
easily and naturally—so his features were definitely logged somewhere in the mind that lived behind the astonishing face.

The bike jolted on the newly pebbly and rough ground. Elated,
Andrew dismounted only when he began to overbalance. He
wheeled the bicycle on through the trees, emerging onto the
narrow riverbank, where he slung the bicycle down on the ground
among the wood anemones that had opened like tiny white stars
since his last visit.

His father had said, when he first started to borrow the bike:

"You chain it up if you're going in a shop. I'm warning you, if that gets nicked…"

But the chain was not long enough to go around any of the trees and, in any case, the further he rode from his father the less Andrew feared him. Still thinking about the inches of flat, bare midriff and Gaia's exquisite face, Andrew strode to the place where the bank met the eroded side of the hill, which hung like an earthy, rocky cliff in a sheer face above the fast-flowing green water.

The narrowest lip of slippery, crumbling bank ran along the bottom of the hillside. The only way of navigating it, if your feet had grown to be twice the length they had been when they had first made the trip, was to edge along sideways, pressed to the sheer face, holding tight to roots and bits of protruding rock.

The mulchy green smell of the river and of wet soil was deeply familiar to Andrew, as was the sensation of this narrow ledge of earth and grass under his feet, and the cracks and rocks he sought with his hands on the hillside. He and Fats had found the secret place when they were eleven years old. They had known that what they were doing was forbidden and dangerous; they had been warned about the river. Terrified, but determined not to tell each other so, they had sidled along this tricky ledge, grabbing at anything that protruded from the rocky wall and, at the very narrowest point, clutching fistfuls of each other's T-shirts.

Years of practice enabled Andrew, though his mind was barely on the job, to move crabwise along the solid wall of earth and rock with the water gushing three feet beneath his trainers; then with a deft duck and swing, he was inside the fissure in the hillside that they had found so long ago. Back then, it had seemed like a divine reward for their daring. He could no longer stand up in it; but, slightly larger than a two-man tent, it was big enough for two teenage boys to lie, side by side, with the river rushing past and the trees dappling their view of the sky, framed by the triangular entrance.

The first time they had been here, they had poked and dug at the back wall with sticks, but they had not found a secret passageway leading to the abbey above; so they gloried instead in the fact that they alone had discovered the hiding place, and swore that it would be their secret in perpetuity. Andrew had a vague memory of a solemn oath, spit and swearwords. They had called it the Cave when they had first discovered it, but it was now, and had been for some time past, the Cubby Hole.

The little recess smelled earthy, though the sloping ceiling was made of rock. A dark green tidemark showed that it had flooded in the past, not quite to the roof. The floor was covered in their cigarette butts and cardboard roaches. Andrew sat down, with his legs dangling over the sludge-green water, and pulled his cigarettes and lighter out of his jacket, bought with the last of his birthday money, now that his allowance had been stopped. He lit up, inhaled deeply, and relived the glorious encounter with Gaia Bawden in as much detail as he could ring out of it: narrow waist and curving hips; creamy skin between leather and T-shirt; full, wide mouth; "oh, hi." It was the first time he had seen her out of school uniform. Where was she going, alone with her leather handbag? What was there in Pagford for her to do on a Saturday morning? Was she perhaps catching the bus into Yarvil? What did she get up to when she was out of his sight; what feminine mysteries absorbed her?

And he asked himself for the umpteenth time whether it was conceivable that flesh and bone wrought like that could contain a banal personality. It was only Gaia who had ever made him wonder this: the idea of body and soul as separate entities had never once occurred to him until he had clapped eyes on her. Even while trying to imagine what her breasts would look and feel like, judged by the visual evidence he had managed to gather through a slightly translucent school shirt, and what he knew was a white bra, he could not believe that the allure she held for him was exclusively physical. She had a way of moving that moved him as much as music, which was what moved him most of all. Surely the spirit animating that peerless body must be unusual too? Why would nature make a vessel like that, if not to contain something still more valuable?

Andrew knew what naked women looked like, because there were no parental controls on the computer in Fats' conversion bedroom. Together they had explored as much online porn as they could access for free: shaven vulvas; pink labia pulled wide to show darkly gaping slits; spread buttocks revealing the puckered buttons of anuses; thickly lipsticked mouths, dripping semen. Andrew's excitement was underpinned, always, by the panicky awareness that you could only hear Mrs. Wall approaching the room when she reached the creaking halfway stair. Sometimes they found weirdness that made them roar with laughter, even when Andrew was unsure whether he was more excited or repulsed (whips and saddles, harnesses, ropes, hoses; and once, at which even Fats had not managed to laugh, close-ups of metal-bolted contraptions, and needles protruding from soft flesh, and women's faces frozen, screaming).

Together he and Fats had become connoisseurs of silicone-enhanced breasts, enormous, taut and round.

"Plastic," one of them would point out, matter-of-factly, as they sat in front of the monitor with the door wedged shut against Fats' parents. The on-screen blonde's arms were raised as she sat astride some hairy man, her big brown-nippled breasts hanging off her narrow rib cage like bowling balls, thin, shiny purple lines under each of them showing where the silicone had been inserted. You could almost tell how they would feel, looking at them: firm, as if there were a football underneath the skin. Andrew could imagine nothing more erotic than a natural breast; soft and spongy and perhaps a little springy, and the nipples (he hoped) contrastingly hard.

And all of these images blurred in his mind, late at night, with the possibilities offered by real girls, human girls, and the little you managed to feel through clothes if you managed to move in close enough. Niamh was the less pretty of the Fairbrother twins, but she had been the more willing, in the stuffy drama hall, during the Christmas disco. Half hidden by the musty stage curtain in a dark corner, they had pressed against each other, and Andrew had put his tongue into her mouth. His hands had inched as far as her bra strap and no further, because she kept pulling away. He had been driven, chiefly, by the knowledge that somewhere outside in the darkness, Fats was going further. And now his brain teemed and throbbed with Gaia. She was both the sexiest girl he had ever seen and the source of another, entirely inexplicable yearning. Certain chord changes, certain beats, made the very core of him shiver, and so did something about Gaia Bawden.

He lit a new cigarette from the end of the first and threw the butt into the water below. Then he heard a familiar scuffling, and leaned forward to see Fats, still wearing his funeral suit, spread-eagled on the hill wall, moving from handhold to handhold as he edged along the narrow lip of bank, towards the opening where Andrew sat.

"Fats."

"Arf."

Andrew pulled in his legs to give Fats room to climb into the Cubby Hole.

"Fucking hell," said Fats, when he had clambered inside. He was spiderlike in his awkwardness, with his long limbs, his skinniness emphasized by the black suit.

Andrew handed him a cigarette. Fats always lit up as though he were in a high wind, one hand cupped around the flame to shield it, scowling slightly. He inhaled, blew a smoke ring out of the Cubby Hole and loosened the dark gray tie around his neck. He appeared older and not, after all, so very foolish in the suit, which bore traces of earth on the knees and cuffs from the journey to the cave.

"You'd think they *were* bum chums," Fats said, after he had taken another powerful drag on his cigarette.

"Cubby upset, was he?"

"Upset? He's having fucking hysterics. He's given himself hiccups. He's worse than the fucking widow."

Andrew laughed. Fats blew another smoke ring and pulled at one of his overlarge ears.

"I bowed out early. They haven't even buried him yet."

They smoked in silence for a minute, both looking out at the sludgy river. As he smoked, Andrew contemplated the words "bowed out early," and the amount of autonomy Fats seemed to have, compared to himself. Simon and his fury stood between Andrew and too much freedom: in Hilltop House, you sometimes copped for punishment simply because you were present. Andrew's imagination had once been caught by a strange little module in their philosophy and religion class, in which primitive gods had been discussed in all their arbitrary wrath and violence, and the attempts of early civilizations to placate them. He had thought then of the nature of justice as he had come to know it: of his father as a pagan god, and of his mother as the high priestess of the cult, who attempted to interpret and intercede, usually failing, yet still insisting, in the face of all the evidence, that there was an underlying magnanimity and reasonableness to her deity.

Fats rested his head against the stone side of the Cubby Hole and blew smoke rings at the ceiling. He was thinking about what he wanted to tell Andrew. He had been mentally rehearsing the way he would start, all through the funeral service, while his father gulped and sobbed into his handkerchief. Fats was so excited by the prospect of telling, that he was having difficulty containing himself; but he was determined not to blurt it out. The telling of it was, to Fats, of almost equal importance to the doing of it. He did not want Andrew to think that he had hurried here to say it.

"You know how Fairbrother was on the Parish Council?" said Andrew.

"Yeah," said Fats, glad that Andrew had initiated a space-filler conversation.

"Si-Pie's saying he's going to stand for his seat."

"Si-Pie is?"

Fats frowned at Andrew.

"What the fuck's got into him?"

"He reckons Fairbrother was getting backhanders from some contractor." Andrew had heard Simon discussing it with Ruth in the kitchen that morning. It had explained everything. "He wants a bit of the action."

"That wasn't Barry Fairbrother," said Fats, laughing as he flicked ash onto the cave floor. "And that wasn't the Parish Council. That was What's-his-name Frierly, up in Yarvil. He was on the school board at Winterdown. Cubby had a fucking fit. Local press calling him for a comment and all that. Frierly got done for it. Doesn't Si-Pie read the *Yarvil and District Gazette*?"

Andrew stared at Fats.

"Fucking typical."

He ground out his cigarette on the earthy floor, embarrassed by his father's idiocy. Simon had got the wrong end of the stick yet again. He spurned the local community, sneered at their concerns, was proud of his isolation in his poxy little house on the hill; then he got a bit of misinformation and decided to expose his family to humiliation on the basis of it.

"Crooked as fuck, Si-Pie, isn't he?" said Fats.

They called him Si-Pie because that was Ruth's nickname for her husband. Fats had heard her use it once, when he had been over for his tea, and had never called Simon anything else since.

"Yeah, he is," said Andrew, wondering whether he would be able to dissuade his father from standing by telling him he had the wrong man and the wrong council.

"Bit of a coincidence," said Fats, "because Cubby's standing as well."

Fats exhaled through his nostrils, staring at the crevice wall over Andrew's head.

"So will voters go for the cunt," he said, "or the twat?"

Andrew laughed. There was little he enjoyed more than hearing his father called a cunt by Fats.

"Now have a shifty at this," said Fats, jamming his cigarette between his lips and patting his hips, even though he knew that the envelope was in the inside breast pocket. "Here you go," he said, pulling it out and opening it to show Andrew the contents: brown peppercorn-sized pods in a powdery mix of shriveled stalks and leaves.

"Sensimilla, that is."

"What is it?"

"Tips and shoots of your basic unfertilized marijuana plant," said Fats, "specially prepared for your smoking pleasure."

"What's the difference between that and the normal stuff?" asked Andrew, with whom Fats had split several lumps of waxy black cannabis resin in the Cubby Hole.

"Just a different smoke, isn't it?" said Fats, stubbing out his own cigarette. He took a packet of Rizlas from his pocket, drew out three of the fragile papers and gummed them together.

"Did you get it off Kirby?" asked Andrew, poking at and sniffing the contents of the envelope.

Everyone knew Skye Kirby was the go-to man for drugs. He was a year above them, in the lower sixth. His grandfather was an old hippie, who had been up in court several times for growing his own.

"Yeah. Mind, there's a bloke called Obbo," said Fats, slitting cigarettes and emptying the tobacco onto the papers, "in the Fields, who'll get you anything. Fucking smack, if you want it."

"You don't want smack, though," said Andrew, watching Fats' face.

"Nah," said Fats, taking the envelope back, and sprinkling the sensimilla onto the tobacco. He rolled the joint together, licking the end of the papers to seal it, poking the roach in more neatly, twisting the end into a point.

"Nice," he said happily.

He had planned to tell Andrew his news after introducing the sensimilla as a kind of warm-up act. He held out his hand for Andrew's lighter, inserted the cardboarded end between his own lips and lit up, taking a deep, contemplative drag, blowing out the smoke in a long blue jet, then repeating the process.

"Mmm," he said, holding the smoke in his lungs, and imitating Cubby, whom Tessa had given a wine course one Christmas. "Herby. A strong aftertaste. Overtones of...fuck..."

He experienced a massive headrush, even though he was sitting, and exhaled, laughing.

"...try that."

Andrew leaned across and took the joint, giggling in anticipation, and at the beatific smile on Fats' face, which was quite at odds with his usual constipated scowl.

Andrew inhaled and felt the power of the drug radiate out from his lungs, unwinding and loosening him. Another drag, and he thought that it was like having your mind shaken out like a duvet, so that it resettled without creases, so that everything became smooth and simple and easy and good.

"Nice," he echoed Fats, smiling at the sound of his own voice.

He passed the joint back into Fats' waiting fingers and savored this sense of well-being.

"So, you wanna hear something interesting?" said Fats, grinning uncontrollably.

"Go on."

"I fucked her last night."

Andrew nearly said "who?," before his befuddled brain remembered: Krystal Weedon, of course; Krystal Weedon, who else?

"Where?" he asked, stupidly. It was not what he wanted to know.

Fats stretched out on his back in his funeral suit, his feet toward the river. Wordlessly, Andrew stretched out beside him, in the opposite direction. They had slept like this, "top and tail," when they had stayed overnight at each other's houses as children. Andrew gazed up at the rocky ceiling, where the blue smoke hung, slowly furling, and waited to hear everything.

"I told Cubby and Tess I was at yours, so you know," said Fats. He passed the joint into Andrew's reaching fingers, then linked his long hands on his chest, and listened to himself telling. "Then I got the bus to the Fields. Met her outside Oddbins."

"By Tesco's?" asked Andrew. He did not know why he kept asking dumb questions.

"Yeah," said Fats. "We went to the rec. There's trees in the corner behind the public bogs. Nice and private. It was getting dark."

Fats shifted position and Andrew handed back the joint.

"Getting in's harder than I thought it would be," said Fats, and Andrew was mesmerized, half inclined to laugh, afraid of missing every unvarnished detail Fats could give him. "She was wetter when I was fingering her."

A giggle rose like trapped gas in Andrew's chest, but was stifled there.

"Lot of pushing to get in properly. It's tighter than I thought."

Andrew saw a jet of smoke rise from the place where Fats' head must be.

"I came in about ten seconds. It feels fucking great once you're in."

Andrew fought back laughter, in case there was more.

"I wore a johnny. It'd be better without."

He pushed the joint back into Andrew's hand. Andrew pulled on it, thinking. Harder to get in than you thought; over in ten seconds. It didn't sound much; yet what wouldn't he give? He imagined Gaia Bawden flat on her back for him and, without meaning to, let out a small groan, which Fats did not seem to hear. Lost in a fug of erotic images, pulling on the joint, Andrew lay with his erection on the patch of earth his body was warming and listened to the soft rush of the water a few feet from his head.

"What matters, Arf?" asked Fats, after a long, dreamy pause.

His head swimming pleasantly, Andrew answered, "Sex."

"Yeah," said Fats, delighted. "Fucking. That's what matters. Propogun…propogating the species. Throw away the johnnies. Multiply."

"Yeah," said Andrew, laughing.

"And death," said Fats. He had been taken aback by the reality of that coffin, and how little material lay between all the watching vultures and an actual corpse. He was not sorry that he had left before it disappeared into the ground. "Gotta be, hasn't it? Death."

"Yeah," said Andrew, thinking of war and car crashes, and dying in blazes of speed and glory.

"Yeah," said Fats. "Fucking and dying. That's it, innit? Fucking and dying. That's life."

"Trying to get a fuck and trying not to die."

"Or trying to die," said Fats. "Some people. Risking it."

"Yeah. Risking it."

There was more silence, and their hiding place was cool and hazy.

"And music," said Andrew quietly, watching the blue smoke hanging beneath the dark rock.

"Yeah," said Fats, in the distance. "And music."

The river rushed on past the Cubby Hole.

Part Two

Fair Comment

7.33   Fair comment on a matter of public interest is
not actionable.

Charles Arnold-Baker
Local Council Administration,
Seventh Edition

I

It rained on Barry Fairbrother's grave. The ink blurred on the cards. Siobhan's chunky sunflower head defied the pelting drops, but Mary's lilies and freesias crumpled, then fell apart. The chrysanthemum oar darkened as it decayed. Rain swelled the river, made streams in the gutters and turned the steep roads into Pagford glossy and treacherous. The windows of the school bus were opaque with condensation; the hanging baskets in the Square became bedraggled, and Samantha Mollison, windscreen wipers on full tilt, suffered a minor collision in the car on the way home from work in the city.

A copy of the *Yarvil and District Gazette* stuck out of Mrs. Catherine Weedon's door in Hope Street for three days, until it became sodden and illegible. Finally, social worker Kay Bawden tugged it out of the letterbox, peered in through the rusty flap and spotted the old lady spread-eagled at the foot of the stairs. A policeman helped break down the front door, and Mrs. Weedon was taken away in an ambulance to South West General.

Still the rain fell, forcing the sign painter who had been hired to rename the old shoe shop to postpone the job. It poured for days and into the nights, and the Square was full of hunchbacks in waterproofs, and umbrellas collided on the narrow pavements.

Howard Mollison found the gentle patter against the dark window soothing. He sat in the study that had once been his daughter Patricia's bedroom, and contemplated the email that he had received from the local newspaper. They had decided to run Councillor Fairbrother's article arguing that the Fields ought to remain with Pagford, but in the interests of balance, they hoped that another councillor might make the case for reassignment in the following issue.

Backfired on you, hasn't it, Fairbrother? thought Howard happily. *There you were, thinking you'd have it all your own way...*

He closed the email and turned instead to the small pile of papers beside him. These were the letters that had come trickling in, requesting an election to fill Barry's vacant seat. The constitution stated that it required nine applications to enforce a public vote, and he had received ten. He read them over, while his wife's and his business partner's voices rose and fell in the kitchen, stripping bare between them the meaty scandal of old Mrs. Weedon's collapse and belated discovery.

"...don't walk out on your doctor for nothing, do you? Screaming at the top of her voice, Karen said—"

"—saying she'd been given the wrong drugs, yes, I know," said Shirley, who considered that she had a monopoly on medical speculation, given that she was a hospital volunteer. "They'll run tests up at the General, I expect."

"I'd be feeling very worried if I were Dr. Jawanda."

"She's probably hoping the Weedons are too ignorant to sue, but that won't matter if the General finds out it was the wrong medication."

"She'll be struck off," said Maureen with relish.

"That's right," said Shirley, "and I'm afraid a lot of people will feel good riddance. *Good riddance.*"

Methodically Howard sorted letters into piles. Miles' completed application forms he set aside on their own. The remaining communications were from fellow Parish Councillors. There were no surprises here; as soon as Parminder had emailed him to tell him that she knew of somebody who was interested in standing for Barry's seat, he had expected these six to rally round her, demanding an election. Together with Bends-Your-Ear herself, they were the ones he dubbed "The Obstreperous Faction," whose leader had recently fallen. Onto this pile he placed the completed forms of Colin Wall, their chosen candidate.

Into a third pile he placed four more letters, which were, like-wise, from expected sources: professional complainers of Pagford, known to Howard as perennially dissatisfied and suspicious, all pro-lific correspondents to the *Yarvil and District Gazette*. Each had their own obsessive interest in some esoteric local issue, and considered themselves "independent minded"; they would be the ones most likely to scream "nepotism" if Miles had been co-opted; but they were among the most anti-Fields people in town.

Howard took the last two letters in each hand, weighing them up. One of them was from a woman whom he had never met, who claimed (Howard took nothing for granted) to work at the Bellchapel Addiction Clinic (the fact that she styled herself "Ms." inclined him to believe her). After some hesitation, he placed this on top of Cubby Wall's application forms.

The last letter, unsigned and typed on a word processor, demanded an election in intemperate terms. It had an air of haste and carelessness and was littered with typos. The letter extolled the virtues of Barry Fairbrother and named Miles specifically as "unfit to fill his sheos." Howard wondered whether Miles had a disgrun-tled client out there who might prove to be an embarrassment. It was good to be forewarned of such potential hazards. However, Howard doubted whether the letter, being anonymous, counted as a vote for an election. He therefore fed it into the little desktop shredder that Shirley had given him for Christmas.

II

Edward Collins & Co., the Pagford solicitors, occupied the upper floor of a terraced brick house, with an optician's on the ground floor. Edward Collins was deceased and his firm comprised two men: Gavin Hughes who was the salaried partner, with one window in his office, and Miles Mollison, who was the equity partner, with two windows. They shared a secretary who was twenty-eight, single, plain but with a good figure. Shona laughed too long at all Miles' jokes, and treated Gavin with a patronage that was almost offensive.

The Friday after Barry Fairbrother's funeral, Miles knocked on Gavin's door at one o'clock and entered without waiting for a summons. He found his partner looking up at the dark gray sky through the rain-speckled window.

"I'm going to nip up the road for lunch," said Miles. "If Lucy Bevan's early, will you tell her I'll be back at two? Shona's out."

"Yeah, fine," said Gavin.

"Everything all right?"

"Mary's called. There's a bit of a glitch with Barry's life insurance. She wants me to help her sort it."

"Right, well, you can handle that, can't you? I'll be back at two, anyway."

Miles slipped on his overcoat, jogged down the steep stairs and walked briskly up the rain-swept little street that led to the Square. A momentary break in the clouds caused sunlight to flood the glistening war memorial and the hanging baskets. Miles experienced a rush of atavistic pride as he hurried across the Square towards Mollison and Lowe, that Pagford institution, that classiest of emporia; a pride that familiarity had never blighted, but rather deepened and ripened.

The bell tinkled at the door as Miles pushed it open. There was something of a lunchtime rush on: a queue of eight waited at the counter and Howard, in his mercantile regalia, fisherman's flies glinting in his deerstalker, was in full tongue.

"...and a quarter of black olives, Rosemary, to *you*. Nothing else, now? Nothing else for Rosemary...that'll be eight pounds, sixty-two pence; we'll call it eight, my love, in light of our long and fruitful association..."

Giggles and gratitude; the rattle and crash of the till.

"And here's my lawyer, come to check up on me," boomed Howard, winking and chuckling over the heads of the queue at

Miles. "If you'll wait for me in the back, sir, I'll try not to say anything incriminating to Mrs. Howson..."

Miles smiled at the middle-aged ladies, who beamed back. Tall, with thick, close-cropped graying hair, big round blue eyes, his paunch disguised by his dark overcoat, Miles was a reasonably attractive addition to the hand-baked biscuits and local cheeses. He navigated his way carefully between the little tables piled high with delicacies and paused at the big arch hewn between delicatessen and the old shoe shop, which was denuded of its protective plastic curtain for the first time. Maureen (Miles recognized the handwriting) had put up a sign on a sandwich board in the middle of the arch: *No Entry. Coming Soon...The Copper Kettle*. Miles peered through into the clean, spare space that would soon be Pagford's newest and best café; it was plastered and painted, with freshly varnished black boards underfoot.

He sidled around the corner of the counter and edged past Maureen, who was operating the meat slicer, affording her the opportunity for a gruff and ribald laugh, then ducked through the door that led into the dingy little back room. Here was a Formica table, on which Maureen's *Daily Mail* lay folded; Howard's and Maureen's coats hanging on hooks, and a door leading to the lavatory, which exuded a scent of artificial lavender. Miles hung up his overcoat and drew up an old chair to the table.

Howard appeared a minute or two later, bearing two heaped plates of delicatessen fare.

"Definitely decided on the 'Copper Kettle' then?" asked Miles.

"Well, Mo likes it," said Howard, setting down a plate in front of his son.

He lumbered out, returned with two bottles of ale, and closed the door with his foot so that the room was enveloped in a windowless gloom relieved only by the dim pendant light. Howard sat down with a deep grunt. He had been conspiratorial on the telephone midmorning, and kept Miles waiting a few moments longer while he flipped off the lid of one bottle.

"Wall's sent his forms in," he said at last, handing over the beer.

"Ah," said Miles.

"I'm going to set a deadline. Two weeks from today for every-one to declare."

"Fair enough," said Miles.

"Mum reckons this Price bloke is still interested. Have you asked Sam if she knows who he is yet?"

"No," said Miles.

Howard scratched an underfold of the belly that rested close to his knees as he sat on the creaking chair.

"Everything all right with you and Sam?"

Miles admired, as always, his father's almost psychic intuition.

"Not great."

He would not have confessed it to his mother, because he tried not to fuel the constant cold war between Shirley and Samantha, in which he was both hostage and prize.

"She doesn't like the idea of me standing," Miles elaborated. Howard raised his fair eyebrows, his jowls wobbling as he chewed. "I don't bloody know what's got into her. She's on one of her anti-Pagford kicks."

Howard took his time swallowing. He dabbed at his mouth with a paper napkin and burped.

"She'll come round quickly enough once you're in," he said. "The social side of it. Plenty for the wives. Functions at Sweetlove House. She'll be in her element." He took another swig of ale and scratched his belly again.

"I can't picture this Price," said Miles, returning to the essential point, "but I've got a feeling he had a kid in Lexie's class at St. Thomas's."

"Fields-born, though, that's the thing," said Howard. "Fields-born, which could work to our advantage. Split the pro-Fields vote between him and Wall."

"Yeah," said Miles. "Makes sense."

This had not occurred to him. He marveled at the way his father's mind worked.

"Mum's already rung his wife and got her to download the forms for him. I might get Mum to call him back tonight, tell her he's got two weeks, try and force his hand."

"Three candidates then?" said Miles. "With Colin Wall."

"I haven't heard of anyone else. It's possible, once details hit the website, someone else'll come forward. But I'm confident about our chances. I'm confident. Aubrey called," Howard added. There was always a touch of additional portentousness in Howard's tone when he used Aubrey Fawley's Christian name. "Right behind you, goes without saying. He's back this evening. He's been in town."

Usually, when a Pagfordian said "in town," they meant "in Yarvil." Howard and Shirley used the phrase, in imitation of Aubrey Fawley, to mean "in London."

"He mentioned something about us all getting together for a chat. Maybe tomorrow. Might even invite us over to the house. Sam'd like that."

Miles had just taken a large bite of soda bread and liver pâté, but he conveyed his agreement with an emphatic nod. He liked the idea that Aubrey Fawley was "right behind" him. Samantha might jeer at his parents' thralldom to the Fawleys, but Miles noticed that on those rare occasions when Samantha came face-to-face with either Aubrey or Julia, her accent changed subtly and her demeanor became markedly more demure.

"Something else," said Howard, scratching his belly again. "Got an email from the *Yarvil and District Gazette* this morning. Asking for my views on the Fields. As chair of the Parish Council."

"You're kidding? I thought Fairbrother had stitched that one up—"

"Backfired, didn't it?" said Howard, with immense satisfaction. "They're going to run his article, and they want someone to argue against the following week. Give them the other side of the story. I'd appreciate a hand. Lawyer's turn of phrase, and all that."

"No problem," said Miles. "We could talk about that bloody addiction clinic. That'd make the point."

"Yes—very good idea—excellent."

In his enthusiasm, he had swallowed too much at once and Miles had to bang him on the back until his coughing had subsided. At last, dabbing his watering eyes with a napkin, Howard said breathlessly, "Aubrey's recommending the District cuts funding from their end, and I'm going to put it to our lot that it's time to terminate the lease on the building. It wouldn't hurt to make the case in the press. How much time and money's gone into that bloody place with nothing to show for it. I've got the figures." Howard burped sonorously. "Bloody disgraceful. Pardon me."

III

Gavin cooked for Kay at his house that evening, opening tins and crushing garlic with a sense of ill usage.

After a row, you had to say certain things to secure a truce: those were the rules, everyone knew that. Gavin had telephoned Kay from his car on the way back from Barry's burial and told her that he wished she had been there, that the whole day had been horrible and that he hoped he could see her that night. He considered these humble admissions no more or less than the price he had to pay for an evening of undemanding companionship.

But Kay seemed to consider them more in the light of a down payment on a renegotiated contract. *You missed me. You needed me when you were upset. You're sorry we didn't go as a couple. Well, let's not make that mistake again.* There had been a certain complacency about the way she had treated him since; a briskness, a sense of renewed expectation.

He was making spaghetti Bolognese tonight; he had deliberately omitted to buy a pudding or to lay the table in advance; he was at pains to show her that he had not made much of an effort. Kay seemed oblivious, even determined to take this casual attitude as a compliment. She sat at his small kitchen table, talking to him over the pitter-patter of rain on the skylight, her eyes wandering over the fixtures and fittings. She had not often been here.

"I suppose Lisa chose this yellow, did she?"

She was doing it again: breaking taboos, as though they had

recently passed to a deeper level of intimacy. Gavin preferred not to talk about Lisa if he could avoid it; surely she knew that by now? He shook oregano onto the mince in his frying pan and said, "No, this was all the previous owner. I haven't got round to changing it yet."

"Oh," she said, sipping wine. "Well, it's quite nice. A bit bland."

This rankled with Gavin, as, in his opinion, the interior of the Smithy was superior in every way to that of ten Hope Street. He watched the pasta bubbling, keeping his back to her.

"Guess what?" she said. "I met Samantha Mollison this afternoon."

Gavin wheeled around; how did Kay even know what Samantha Mollison looked like?

"Just outside the deli in the Square; I was on my way in to get this," said Kay, clinking the wine bottle beside her with a flick of her nail. "She asked me whether I was *Gavin's girlfriend.*"

Kay said it archly, but actually she had been heartened by Samantha's choice of words, relieved to think that this was how Gavin described her to his friends.

"And what did you say?"

"I said—I said yes."

Her expression was crestfallen. Gavin had not meant to ask the question quite so aggressively. He would have given a lot to prevent Kay and Samantha ever meeting.

"Anyway," Kay proceeded with a slight edge to her voice, "She's asked us for dinner next Friday. Week today."

"Oh, bloody hell," said Gavin crossly.

A lot of Kay's cheerfulness deserted her.

"What's the problem?"

"Nothing. It's—nothing," he said, prodding the bubbling spaghetti. "It's just that I see enough of Miles during work hours, to be honest."

It was what he had dreaded all along: that she would worm her way in and they would become Gavin-and-Kay, with a shared social circle, so that it would become progressively more difficult to excise her from his life. How had he let this happen? Why had he allowed her to move down here? Fury at himself mutated easily into anger with her. Why couldn't she realize how little he wanted her, and take herself off without forcing him to do the dirty? He drained the spaghetti in the sink, swearing under his breath as he speckled himself with boiling water.

"You'd better call Miles and Samantha and tell them 'no,' then," said Kay.

Her voice had hardened. As was Gavin's deeply ingrained habit, he sought to deflect an imminent conflict and hoped that the future would look after itself.

"No, no," he said, dabbing at his wet shirt with a tea towel. "We'll go. It's fine. We'll go."

But in his undisguised lack of enthusiasm, he sought to put down a marker to which he could refer, retrospectively. *You knew I didn't want to go. No, I didn't enjoy it. No, I don't want it to happen again.*

They ate for several minutes in silence. Gavin was afraid that there would be another row, and that Kay would force him to discuss underlying issues again. He cast around for something to say, and so started telling her about Mary Fairbrother and the life insurance company.

"They're being real bastards," he said. "He was heavily insured, but their lawyers are looking for a way not to pay out. They're trying to make out he didn't make a full disclosure."

"In what way?"

"Well, an uncle died of an aneurysm, too. Mary swears Barry told the insurance agent that when he signed the policy, but it's nowhere in the notes. Presumably the bloke didn't realize it can be a genetic thing. I don't know that Barry did, come to…"

Gavin's voice broke. Horrified and embarrassed, he bowed his flushing face over his plate. There was a hard chunk of grief in his throat and he couldn't shift it. Kay's chair legs scraped on the floor; he hoped that she was off to the bathroom, but then felt her arms around his shoulders, drawing him to her. Without thinking, he put a single arm around her, too.

It was so good to be held. If only their relationship could be distilled into simple, wordless gestures of comfort. Why had humans ever learned to talk?

He had dribbled snot onto the back of her top.

"Sorry," he said thickly, wiping it away with his napkin.

He withdrew from her and blew his nose. She dragged her chair to sit beside him and put a hand on his arm. He liked her so much better when she was silent, and her face was soft and concerned, as it was now.

"I still can't...he was a good bloke," he said. "Barry. He was a good bloke."

"Yes, everyone says that about him," said Kay.

She had never been allowed to meet this famous Barry Fairbrother, but she was intrigued by the show of emotion from Gavin, and by the person who had caused it.

"Was he funny?" she asked, because she could imagine Gavin in thrall to a comedian, to a rowdy ringleader, propping up the bar.

"Yeah, I s'pose. Well, not particularly. Normal. He liked a laugh but he was just such a...such a *nice* bloke. He liked people, you know?"

She waited, but Gavin did not seem able to elucidate further on the niceness of Barry.

"And the kids...and Mary...poor Mary...God, you've got no idea."

Kay continued to pat his arm gently, but her sympathy had chilled a little. No idea, she thought, what it was to be alone? No idea how hard it was to be left in sole charge of a family? Where was his pity for her, Kay?

"They were really happy," said Gavin, in a cracked voice. "She's in pieces."

Wordlessly, Kay stroked his arm, reflecting that she had never been able to afford to go to pieces.

"I'm all right," he said, wiping his nose on his napkin and picking up his fork. By the smallest of twitches, he indicated that she should remove her hand.

IV

Samantha's dinner invitation to Kay had been motivated by a mixture of vengefulness and boredom. She saw it as retaliation against Miles, who was always busy with schemes in which he gave her no say but with which he expected her to cooperate; she wanted to see how he liked it when she arranged things without consulting him. Then she would be stealing a march on Maureen and Shirley, those nosy old crones, who were so fascinated by Gavin's private affairs but knew next to nothing about the relationship between him and his London girlfriend. Finally, it would afford her another opportunity to sharpen her claws on Gavin for being pusillanimous and indecisive about his love life: she might talk about weddings in front of Kay or say how nice it was to see Gavin making a commitment at last.

However, her plans for the discomfiture of others gave Samantha less pleasure than she had hoped. When on Saturday morning she told Miles what she had done, he reacted with suspicious enthusiasm.

"Great, yeah, we haven't had Gavin round for ages. And nice for you to get to know Kay."

"Why?"

"Well, you always got on with Lisa, didn't you?"

"Miles, I hated Lisa."

"Well, OK…maybe you'll like Kay better!"

She glared at him, wondering where all this good humor was coming from. Lexie and Libby, home for the weekend and cooped up in the house because of the rain, were watching a music DVD in the sitting room; a guitar-laden ballad blared through to the kitchen where their parents stood talking.

"Listen," said Miles, brandishing his mobile, "Aubrey wants to have a talk with me about the council. I've just called Dad, and the Fawleys have invited us all to dinner tonight at Sweetlove—"

"No thanks," said Samantha, cutting him off. She was suddenly full of a fury she could barely explain, even to herself. She walked out of the room.

They argued in low voices all over the house through the day, trying not to spoil their daughters' weekend. Samantha refused to change her mind or to discuss her reasons. Miles, afraid of getting angry at her, was alternately conciliatory and cold.

"How do you think it's going to look if you don't come?" he said at ten to eight that evening, standing in the doorway of the sitting room, ready to leave, wearing a suit and tie.

"It's nothing to do with me, Miles," Samantha said. "You're the one running for office."

She liked watching him dither. She knew that he was terrified of being late, yet wondering whether he could still persuade her to go with him.

"You know they'll be expecting both of us."

"Really? Nobody sent me an invitation."

"Oh, come off it, Sam, you know they meant—they took it for granted—"

"More fool them, then. I've told you, I don't fancy it. You'd better hurry. You don't want to keep Mummy and Daddy waiting."

He left. She listened to the car reversing out of the drive, then went into the kitchen, opened a bottle of wine and brought it back into the sitting room with a glass. She kept picturing Howard, Shirley and Miles all having dinner together at Sweetlove House. It would surely be the first orgasm Shirley had had in years.

Her thoughts swerved irresistibly to what her accountant had said to her during the week. Profits were way down, whatever she had pretended to Howard. The accountant had actually suggested closing the shop and concentrating on the online side of the business. This would be an admission of failure that Samantha was not prepared to make. For one thing, Shirley would love it if the shop closed; she had been a bitch about it from the start. *I'm sorry, Sam, it's not really my taste…just a teeny bit over the top…*But Samantha loved her little red and black shop in Yarvil; loved getting away from Pagford every day, chatting to customers, gossiping with Carly, her assistant. Her world would be tiny without the shop she had nurtured for fourteen years; it would contract, in short, to Pagford.

(Pagford, bloody Pagford. Samantha had never meant to live here. She and Miles had planned a year out before starting work, a round-the-world trip. They had their itinerary mapped out, their visas ready. Samantha had dreamed about walking barefoot and hand in hand on long white Australian beaches. And then she had found out that she was pregnant.

She had come down to visit him at "Ambleside," a day after she had taken the pregnancy test, one week after their graduation. They were supposed to be leaving for Singapore in eight days' time.

Samantha had not wanted to tell Miles in his parents' house; she was afraid that they would overhear. Shirley seemed to be behind every door Samantha opened in the bungalow.

So she waited until they were sitting at a dark corner table in the Black Canon. She remembered the rigid line of Miles' jaw when she told him; he seemed, in some indefinable way, to become older as the news hit him.

He did not speak for several petrified seconds. Then he said, "Right. We'll get married."

He told her that he had already bought her a ring, that he had been planning to propose somewhere good, somewhere like the top of Ayers Rock. Sure enough, when they got back to the bungalow, he unearthed the little box from where he had already hidden it in his rucksack. It was a small solitaire diamond from a jeweler's in Yarvil; he had bought it with some of the money his grandmother had left him. Samantha had sat on the edge of Miles' bed and cried and cried. They had married three months later.)

Alone with her bottle of wine, Samantha turned on the television. It brought up the DVD Lexie and Libby had been watching: a frozen image of four young men singing to her in tight T-shirts; they looked barely out of their teens. She pressed play. After the boys finished their song, the DVD cut to an interview. Samantha slugged back her wine, watching the band joking with each other, then becoming earnest as they discussed how much they loved their fans. She thought that she would have known them as Americans even if the sound had been off. Their teeth were perfect.

It grew late; she paused the DVD, went upstairs and told the girls to leave the PlayStation and go to bed; then she returned to the sitting room, where she was three-quarters of the way down the bottle of wine. She had not turned on the lamps. She pressed play and kept drinking. When the DVD finished, she put it back to the beginning and watched the bit she had missed.

One of the boys appeared significantly more mature than the other three. He was broader across the shoulders; biceps bulged beneath the short sleeves of his T-shirt; he had a thick strong neck and a square jaw. Samantha watched him undulating, staring into the camera with a detached serious expression on his handsome face, which was all planes and angles and winged black eyebrows.

She thought of sex with Miles. It had last happened three weeks previously. His performance was as predictable as a Masonic handshake. One of his favorite sayings was "if it's not broke, don't fix it."

Samantha emptied the last of the bottle into her glass and imagined making love to the boy on the screen. Her breasts looked better in a bra these days; they spilled everywhere when she lay down; it made her feel flabby and awful. She pictured herself, forced back against a wall, one leg propped up, a dress pushed up to her waist and that strong dark boy with his jeans round his knees, thrusting in and out of her...

With a lurch in the pit of her stomach that was almost like happiness, she heard the car turning back into the drive and the beams of the headlights swung around the dark sitting room.

She fumbled with the controls to turn over to the news, which took her much longer than it ought to have done; she shoved the empty wine bottle under the sofa and clutched her almost empty glass as a prop. The front door opened and closed. Miles entered the room behind her.

"Why are you sitting here in the dark?"

He turned on a lamp and she glanced up at him. He was as well groomed as he had been when he left, except for the raindrops on the shoulders of his jacket.

"How was dinner?"

"Fine," he said. "You were missed. Aubrey and Julia were sorry you couldn't make it."

"Oh, I'm sure. And I'll bet your mother cried with disappointment."

He sat down in an armchair at right angles to her, staring at her. She pushed her hair out of her eyes.

"What's this all about, Sam?"

"If you don't know, Miles—"

But she was not sure herself; or at least, she did not know how to condense this sprawling sense of ill-usage into a coherent accusation.

"I can't see how me standing for the Parish Council—"

"Oh, for God's sake, Miles!" she shouted, and was then slightly taken aback by how loud her voice was.

"Explain to me, please," he said, "what possible difference it can make to you?"

She glared at him, struggling to articulate it for his pedantic legal mind, which was like a fiddling pair of tweezers in the way that it seized on poor choices of word, yet so often failed to grasp the bigger picture. What could she say that he would understand? That she found Howard and Shirley's endless talk about the council boring as hell? That he was quite tedious enough already, with his endlessly retold anecdotes about the good old days back at the rugby club and his self-congratulatory stories about work, without adding pontifications about the Fields?

"Well, I was under the impression," said Samantha, in their dimly lit sitting room, "That we had other plans."

"Like what?" said Miles. "What are you talking about?"

"We said," Samantha articulated carefully over the rim of her trembling glass, "that once the girls were out of school, we'd go traveling. We promised each other that, remember?"

The formless rage and misery that had consumed her since Miles announced his intention to stand for the council had not once led her to mourn the year's traveling she had missed, but at this moment it seemed to her that that was the real problem; or at least, that it came closest to expressing both the antagonism and the yearning inside her.

Miles seemed completely bewildered.

"What *are* you talking about?"

"When I got pregnant with Lexie," Samantha said loudly, "and we couldn't go traveling, and your bloody mother made us get married in double-quick time, and your father got you a job with Edward Collins, you said, *we agreed*, that we'd do it when the girls were grown up; we said we'd go away and do all the things we missed out on."

He shook his head slowly.

"This is news to me," he said. "Where the hell has this come from?"

"Miles, we were in the Black Canon. I told you I was pregnant, and you said—for Christ's sake, Miles—I told you I was pregnant, and you promised me, you *promised*—"

"You want a holiday?" said Miles. "Is that it? You want a holiday?"

"No, Miles, I don't want a bloody holiday, I want—don't you remember? We said we'd take a year out and do it later, when the kids were grown up!"

"Fine, then." He seemed unnerved, determined to brush her aside. "Fine. When Libby's eighteen; in four years' time, we'll talk about it again. I don't see how me becoming a councillor affects any of this."

"Well, apart from the bloody *boredom* of listening to you and your parents whining about the Fields for the rest of our natural lives—"

"Our *natural* lives?" he smirked. "As opposed to—?"

"Piss off," she spat. "Don't be such a bloody smartarse, Miles, it might impress your mother—"

"Well, frankly, I still don't see what the problem—"

"The *problem*," she shouted, "is that this is about our *future*, Miles. *Our* future. And I don't want to bloody talk about it in four years' time, I want to talk about it *now!*"

"I think you'd better eat something," said Miles. He got to his feet. "You've had enough to drink."

"Screw you, Miles!"

"Sorry, if you're going to be abusive…"

He turned and walked out of the room. She barely stopped herself throwing her wineglass after him.

The council: if he got on it, he would never get off; he would never renounce his seat, the chance to be a proper Pagford big shot, like Howard. He was committing himself anew to Pagford, retaking his vows to the town of his birth, to a future quite different from the one he had promised his distraught new fiancée as she sat sobbing on his bed.

When had they last talked about traveling the world? She was not sure. Years and years ago, perhaps, but tonight Samantha decided that she, at least, had never changed her mind. Yes, she had always expected that some day they would pack up and leave, in search of heat and freedom, half the globe away from Pagford, Shirley, Mollison and Lowe, the rain, the pettiness and the sameness. Perhaps she had not thought of the white sands of Australia and Singapore with longing for many years, but she would rather be there, even with her heavy thighs and her stretch marks, than here, trapped in Pagford, forced to watch as Miles turned slowly into Howard.

She slumped back down on the sofa, groped for the controls, and switched back to Libby's DVD. The band, now in black and white, was walking slowly along a long empty beach, singing. The broad-shouldered boy's shirt was flapping open in the breeze. A fine trail of hair led from his navel down into his jeans.

V

Alison Jenkins, the journalist from the *Yarvil and District Gazette*, had at last established which of the many Weedon households in Yarvil housed Krystal. It had been difficult: nobody was registered to vote at the address and no landline number was listed for the property. Alison visited Foley Road in person on Sunday, but Krystal was out, and Terri, suspicious and antagonistic, refused to say when she would be back or confirm that she lived there.

Krystal arrived home a mere twenty minutes after the journalist had departed in her car, and she and her mother had another row.

"Why din't ya tell her to wait? She was gonna interview me abou' the Fields an' stuff!"

"Interview *you?* Fuck off. Wha' the fuck for?"

The argument escalated and Krystal walked out again, off to

Nikki's, with Terri's mobile in her tracksuit bottoms. She frequently made off with this phone; many rows were triggered by her mother demanding it back and Krystal pretending that she didn't know where it was. Dimly, Krystal hoped that the journalist might know the number somehow and call her directly.

She was in a crowded, jangling café in the shopping center, telling Nikki and Leanne all about the journalist, when the mobile rang.

"'Oo? Are you the journalist, like?"

"…o's 'at…'erri?"

"It's Krystal. 'Oo's this?"

"…'m your…'nt…other…'ister."

"'Oo?" shouted Krystal. One finger in the ear not pressed against the phone, she wove her way between the densely packed tables to reach a quieter place.

"Danielle," said the woman, loud and clear on the other end of the telephone. "I'm yer mum's sister."

"Oh, yeah," said Krystal, disappointed.

Fuckin' snobby bitch, Terri always said when Danielle's name came up. Krystal was not sure that she had ever met Danielle.

"It's abou' your great gran."

"'O'o?"

"*Nana Cath,*" said Danielle impatiently. Krystal reached the balcony overlooking the shopping center forecourt; reception was strong here; she stopped.

"Wha's wrong with 'er?" said Krystal. It felt as though her stomach was flipping over, the way it had done as a little girl, turning somersaults on a railing like the one in front of her. Thirty feet below, the crowds surged, carrying plastic bags, pushing buggies and dragging toddlers.

"She's in South West General. She's been there a week. She's had a stroke."

"She's bin there a week?" said Krystal, her stomach still swooping. "Nobody told us."

"Yeah, well, she can't speak prop'ly, but she's said your name twice."

"Mine?" asked Krystal, clutching the mobile tightly.

"Yeah. I think she'd like to see yeh. It's serious. They're sayin' she migh' not recover."

"Wha' ward is it?" asked Krystal, her mind buzzing.

"Twelve. High-dependency. Visiting hours are twelve till four, six till eight. All righ'?"

"Is it—?"

"I gotta go. I only wanted to let you know, in case you want to see her. Bye."

The line went dead. Krystal lowered the mobile from her ear, staring at the screen. She pressed a button repeatedly with her thumb, until she saw the word "blocked." Her aunt had withheld her number.

Krystal walked back to Nikki and Leanne. They knew at once that something was wrong.

"Go an' see 'er," said Nikki, checking the time on her own mobile. "Yeh'll ge' there fer two. Ge' the bus."

"Yeah," said Krystal blankly.

She thought of fetching her mother, of taking her and Robbie to go and see Nana Cath too, but there had been a huge row a year before, and her mother and Nana Cath had had no contact since. Krystal was sure that Terri would take an immense amount of persuading to go to the hospital, and was not sure that Nana Cath would be happy to see her.

It's serious. They're saying she might not recover.

"'Ave yeh gor enough cash?" said Leanne, rummaging in her pockets as the three of them walked up the road toward the bus stop.

"Yeah," said Krystal, checking. "It's on'y a quid up the hospital, innit?"

They had time to share a cigarette before the number twenty-seven arrived. Nikki and Leanne waved her off as though she were going somewhere nice. At the very last moment, Krystal felt scared and wanted to shout "Come with me!" But then the bus pulled away from the curb, and Nikki and Leanne were already turning away, gossiping.

The seat was prickly, covered in some old smelly fabric. The bus trundled onto the road that ran by the precinct and turned right into one of the main thoroughfares that led through all the big-name shops.

Fear fluttered inside Krystal's belly like a fetus. She had known that Nana Cath was getting older and frailer, but somehow, vaguely, she had expected her to regenerate, to return to the heyday that had seemed to last so long; for her hair to turn black again, her spine to straighten and her memory to sharpen like her caustic tongue. She had never thought about Nana Cath dying, always associating her with toughness and invulnerability. If she had considered them at all, Krystal would have thought of the deformity to Nana Cath's chest, and the innumerable wrinkles crisscrossing her face, as honorable scars sustained during her successful battle to survive. Nobody close to Krystal had ever died of old age.

(Death came to the young in her mother's circle, sometimes even before their faces and bodies had become emaciated and ravaged. The body that Krystal had found in the bathroom when she was six had been of a handsome young man, as white and lovely as a statue, or that was how she remembered him. But sometimes she found that memory confusing and doubted it. It was hard to know what to believe. She had often heard things as a child that adults later contradicted and denied. She could have sworn that Terri had said, "It was yer dad." But then, much later, she had said, "Don' be so silly. Yer dad's not dead, 'e's in Bristol, innee?" So Krystal had had to try and reattach herself to the idea of Banger, which was what everybody called the man they said was her father.

But always, in the background, there had been Nana Cath. She had escaped foster care because of Nana Cath, ready and waiting in Pagford, a strong if uncomfortable safety net. Swearing and furious, she had swooped, equally aggressive to Terri and to the social workers, and taken her equally angry great-granddaughter home.

Krystal did not know whether she had loved or hated that little house in Hope Street. It was dingy and it smelled of bleach; it gave you a hemmed-in feeling. At the same time, it was safe, entirely safe. Nana Cath would only let approved individuals in through the door. There were old-fashioned bath cubes in a glass jar on the end of the bath.)

What if there were other people at Nana Cath's bedside, when she got there? She would not recognize half her own family, and the idea that she might come across strangers tied to her by blood scared her. Terri had several half sisters, products of her father's multiple liaisons, whom even Terri had never met; but Nana Cath tried to keep up with them all, doggedly maintaining contact with the large disconnected family her sons had produced. Occasionally, over the years, relatives Krystal did not recognize had turned up at Nana Cath's while she was there. Krystal thought that they eyed her askance and said things about her under their voices to Nana Cath; she pretended not to notice and waited for them to leave, so that she could have Nana Cath to herself again. She especially disliked the idea that there were any other children in Nana Cath's life.

("'Oo are *they?*" Krystal had asked Nana Cath when she was nine, pointing jealously at a framed photograph of two boys in Paxton High uniforms on Nana Cath's sideboard.

"Them's two o' my great-grandsons," said Nana Cath. "Tha's Dan and tha's Ricky. They're your cousins."

Krystal did not want them as cousins, and she did not want them on Nana Cath's sideboard.

"An' who's *tha'*?" she demanded, pointing at a little girl with curly golden hair.

"Tha's my Michael's little girl, Rhiannon, when she were five. Beau'iful, weren't she? Bu' she wen' an' married some wog," said Nana Cath.

There had never been a photograph of Robbie on Nana Cath's sideboard.

Yeh don't even know who the father is, do yeh, yer whore? I'm washin' my 'ands of yeh. I've 'ad enough, Terri, I've 'ad it: you can look after it yourself.)

The bus trundled on through town, past all the Sunday afternoon shoppers. When Krystal had been small, Terri had taken her into the center of Yarvil nearly every weekend, forcing her into a pushchair long past the age when Krystal needed it, because it was so much easier to hide nicked stuff with a pushchair, push it down under the kid's legs, hide it under the bags in the basket under the seat. Sometimes Terri would go on tandem shoplifting trips with the sister she spoke to, Cheryl, who was married to Shane Tully. Cheryl and Terri lived four streets away from each other in the Fields, and petrified the air with their language when they argued, which was frequently. Krystal never knew whether she and her Tully cousins were supposed to be on speaking terms or not, and no longer bothered keeping track, but she spoke to Dane whenever she ran across him. They had shagged, once, after splitting a bottle of cider out on the rec when they were fourteen. Neither of them had ever mentioned it afterwards. Krystal was hazy on whether or not it was legal, doing your cousin. Something Nikki had said had made her think that maybe it wasn't.

The bus rolled up the road that led to the main entrance of South West General, and stopped twenty yards from an enormous long rectangular gray and glass building. There were patches of neat grass, a few small trees and a forest of signposts.

Krystal followed two old ladies out of the bus and stood with her hands in her tracksuit pockets, looking around. She had already forgotten what kind of ward Danielle had told her Nana Cath was on; she recalled only the number twelve. She approached the nearest signpost with a casual air, squinting at it almost incidentally: it bore line upon line of impenetrable print, with words as long as Krystal's arm and arrows pointing left, right, diagonally. Krystal did not read well; being confronted with large quantities of words made her feel intimidated and aggressive. After several surreptitious glances at the arrows, she decided that there were no numbers there at all, so she followed the two old ladies towards the double glass doors at the front of the main building.

The foyer was crowded and more confusing than the signposts. There was a bustling shop, which was separated from the main hall by floor to ceiling windows; there were rows of plastic chairs, which seemed to be full of people eating sandwiches; there was a packed café in the corner; and a kind of hexagonal counter in the middle of the floor, where women were answering inquiries as they checked their computers. Krystal headed there, her hands still in her pockets.

"Where's ward twelve?" Krystal asked one of the women in a surly voice.

"Third floor," said the woman, matching her tone.

Krystal did not want to ask anything else out of pride, so she turned and walked away, until she spotted lifts at the far end of the foyer and entered one going up.

It took her nearly fifteen minutes to find the ward. Why didn't they put up numbers and arrows, not these stupid long words? But then, walking along a pale green corridor with her trainers squeaking on the linoleum floor, someone called her name.

"Krystal?"

It was her aunt Cheryl, big and broad in a denim skirt and tight white vest, with banana-yellow black-rooted hair. She was tattooed from her knuckles to the tops of her thick arms, and wore multiple gold hoops like curtain rings in each ear. There was a can of Coke in her hand.

"She ain' bothered, then?" said Cheryl. Her bare legs were planted firmly apart, like a sentry guard.

"'Oo?"

"Terri. She din' wanna come?"

"She don' know ye'. I on'y jus' 'eard. Danielle called an' tole me."

Cheryl ripped off the ring-pull and slurped Coke, her tiny eyes sunken in a wide, flat face that was mottled like corned beef, scrutinizing Krystal over the top of the can.

"I tole Danielle ter call yeh when it 'appened. Three days she were lyin' in the 'ouse, and no one fuckin' found 'er. The state of 'er. Fuckin' 'ell."

Krystal did not ask Cheryl why she herself had not walked the short distance to Foley Road to tell Terri the news. Evidently the sisters had fallen out again. It was impossible to keep up.

"Where is she?" asked Krystal.

Cheryl led the way, her flip-flops making a slapping noise on the floor.

"Hey," she said, as they walked. "I 'ad a call fr'm a journalist about you."

"Didja?"

"She give me a number."

Krystal would have asked more questions, but they had entered a very quiet ward, and she was suddenly frightened. She did not like the smell.

Nana Cath was almost unrecognizable. One side of her face was terribly twisted, as though the muscles had been pulled with a wire. Her mouth dragged to one side; even her eye seemed to droop. There were tubes taped to her, a needle in her arm. Lying down, the deformity in her chest was much more obvious. The sheet rose and fell in odd places, as if the grotesque head on its scrawny neck protruded from a barrel.

When Krystal sat down beside her, Nana Cath made no movement. She simply gazed. One little hand trembled slightly.

"She ain' talkin', bu' she said yer name, twice, las' nigh'," Cheryl told her, staring gloomily over the rim of her can.

There was a tightness in Krystal's chest. She did not know whether it would hurt Nana Cath to hold her hand. She edged her own fingers to within a few inches of Nana Cath's, but let them rest on the bedspread.

"Rhiannon's bin in," said Cheryl. "An' John an' Sue. Sue's tryin' ter get hold of Anne-Marie."

Krystal's spirits leaped.

"Where is she?" she asked Cheryl.

"Somewhere out Frenchay way. Y'know she's got a baby now?"

"Yeah, I 'eard," said Krystal. "Wha' was it?"

"Dunno," said Cheryl, swigging Coke.

Someone at school had told her: *Hey, Krystal, your sister's up the duff!* She had been excited by the news. She was going to be an auntie, even if she never saw the baby. All her life, she had been in love with the idea of Anne-Marie, who had been taken away before Krystal was born; spirited into another dimension, like a fairy-tale character, as beautiful and mysterious as the dead man in Terri's bathroom.

Nana Cath's lips moved.

"Wha'?" said Krystal, bending low, half scared, half elated.

"D'yeh wan' somethin', Nana Cath?" asked Cheryl, so loudly that whispering guests at other beds stared over.

Krystal could hear a wheezing, rattling noise, but Nana Cath seemed to be making a definite attempt to form a word. Cheryl was leaning over the other side, one hand gripping the metal bars at the head of the bed.

"...Oh...mm," said Nana Cath.

"Wha'?" said Krystal and Cheryl together.

The eyes had moved millimeters: rheumy, filmy eyes, looking at Krystal's smooth young face, her open mouth, as she leaned over her great-grandmother, puzzled, eager and fearful.

" ...*owin*..." said the cracked old voice.

"She dunno wha' she's sayin'," Cheryl shouted over her shoulder at the timid couple visiting at the next bed. "Three days lef' on the fuckin' floor, 's 'not surprisin', is it?"

But tears had blurred Krystal's eyes. The ward with its high windows dissolved into white light and shadow; she seemed to see a flash of bright sunlight on dark green water, fragmented into brilliant shards by the splashing rise and fall of oars.

"Yeah," she whispered to Nana Cath. "Yeah, I goes rowin', Nana."

But it was no longer true, because Mr. Fairbrother was dead.

VI

"The fuck have you done to your face? Come off the bike again?" asked Fats.

"No," said Andrew. "Si-Pie hit me. I was trying to tell the stupid cunt he'd got it wrong about Fairbrother."

He and his father had been in the woodshed, filling the baskets that sat on either side of the wood burner in the sitting room. Simon had hit Andrew around the head with a log, knocking him into the pile of wood, grazing his acne-covered cheek.

D'you think you know more about what goes on than I do, you spotty little shit? If I hear you've breathed a word of what goes on in this house—

I haven't—

I'll fucking skin you alive, d'you hear me? How do you know Fairbrother wasn't on the fiddle too, eh? And the other fucker was the only one dumb enough to get caught?

And then, whether out of pride or defiance, or because his fantasies of easy money had taken too strong a hold on his imagination to become dislodged by facts, Simon had sent in his application forms. Humiliation, for which the whole family would surely pay, was a certainty.

Sabotage. Andrew brooded on the word. He wanted to bring his father crashing down from the heights to which his dreams of easy money had raised him, and he wanted to do it, if at all possible (for he preferred glory without death), in such a way that Simon would never know whose maneuverings had brought his ambitions to rubble.

He confided in nobody, not even Fats. He told Fats nearly everything, but the few omissions were the vast topics, the ones that occupied nearly all his interior space. It was one thing to sit in Fats' room with hard-ons and look up "girl-on-girl action" on the Internet: quite another to confess how obsessively he pondered ways of engaging Gaia Bawden in conversation. Likewise, it was easy to sit in the Cubby Hole and call his father a cunt, but never would he have told how Simon's rages turned his hands cold and his stomach queasy.

But then came the hour that changed everything. It started with nothing more than a yearning for nicotine and beauty. The rain had passed off at last, and the pale spring sun shone brightly on the fish-scale dirt on the school-bus windows as it jerked and lurched through the narrow streets of Pagford. Andrew was sitting near the back, unable to see Gaia, who was hemmed in at the front by Sukhvinder and the fatherless Fairbrother girls, newly returned to school. He had barely seen Gaia all day and faced a barren evening with only stale Facebook pictures to console him.

As the bus approached Hope Street, it struck Andrew that neither of his parents was at home to notice his absence. Three cigarettes that Fats had given him resided in his inside pocket; and Gaia was getting up, holding tightly to the bar on the back of the seat, readying herself to descend, still talking to Sukhvinder Jawanda.

Why not? *Why not?*

So he got up too, swung his bag over his shoulder, and when the bus stopped walked briskly up the aisle after the two girls as they got out.

"See you at home," he threw out to a startled Paul as he passed.

He reached the sunny pavement and the bus rumbled away. Lighting up, he watched Gaia and Sukhvinder over the top of his cupped hands. They were not heading towards Gaia's house in Hope Street, but ambling up towards the Square. Smoking and scowling slightly in unconscious imitation of the most unselfconscious person he knew — Fats — Andrew followed them, his eyes feasting on Gaia's copper-brown hair as it bounced on her shoulder blades, the swing of her skirt as her hips swayed beneath it.

The two girls slowed down as they approached the Square, advancing towards Mollison and Lowe, which had the most impressive facade of them all: blue and gold lettering across the front and four hanging baskets. Andrew hung back. The girls paused to examine a small white sign pasted to the window of the new café, then disappeared into the delicatessen.

Andrew walked once around the Square, past the Black Canon and the George Hotel, and stopped at the sign. It was a hand-lettered advertisement for weekend staff.

Hyperconscious of his acne, which was particularly virulent at the moment, he knocked out the end of his cigarette, put the long stub back into his pocket and followed Gaia and Sukhvinder inside.

The girls were standing beside a little table piled high with boxed oatcakes and crackers, watching the enormous man in the deerstalker behind the counter talking to an elderly customer. Gaia looked around when the bell over the door tinkled.

"Hi," Andrew said, his mouth dry.

"Hi," she replied.

Blinded by his own daring, Andrew walked nearer, and the schoolbag over his shoulder bumped into the revolving stand of guides to Pagford and *Traditional West Country Cooking*. He seized the stand and steadied it, then hastily lowered his bag.

"You after a job?" Gaia asked him quietly, in her miraculous London accent.

"Yeah," he said. "You?"

She nodded.

"Flag it up on the suggestion page, Eddie," Howard was booming at the customer. "Post it on the website, and I'll get it on the agenda for you. Pagford Parish Council—all one word—dot co, dot UK, slash, Suggestion Page. Or follow the link. Pagford..." He reiterated slowly, as the man pulled out paper and a pen with a quivering hand, "...Parish..."

Howard's eyes flicked over the three teenagers waiting quietly beside the savory biscuits. They were wearing the halfhearted uniform of Winterdown, which permitted so much laxity and variation that it was barely a uniform at all (unlike that of St. Anne's, which comprised a neat tartan skirt and a blazer). For all that, the white girl was stunning; a precision-cut diamond set off by the plain Jawanda daughter, whose name Howard did not know, and a mouse-haired boy with violently erupted skin.

The customer creaked out of the shop, the bell tinkled.

"Can I help you?" Howard asked, his eyes on Gaia.

"Yeah," she said, moving forwards. "Um. About the jobs." She pointed at the small sign in the window.

"Ah, yes," said Howard, beaming. His new weekend waiter had let him down a few days previously; thrown over the café for Yarvil and a supermarket job. "Yes, yes. Fancy waitressing, do you? We're offering minimum wage—nine to half past five, Saturdays—twelve to half past five, Sundays. Opening two weeks from today; training provided. How old are you, my love?"

She was perfect, *perfect,* exactly what he had been imagining: fresh-faced and curvy; he could just imagine her in a figure-hugging black dress with a lace-edged white apron. He would teach her to use the till, and show her around the stockroom; there would be a bit of banter, and perhaps a little bonus on days when the takings were up.

Howard sidled out from behind the counter and, ignoring Sukhvinder and Andrew, took Gaia by the upper arm, and led her through the arch in the dividing wall. There were no tables and chairs there yet, but the counter had been installed and so had a tiled black and cream mural on the wall behind it, which showed the Square in Yesteryear. Crinolined women and men in top hats swarmed everywhere; a brougham carriage had drawn up outside a clearly marked Mollison and Lowe, and beside it was the little café, *The Copper Kettle*. The artist had improvised an ornamental pump instead of the war memorial.

Andrew and Sukhvinder were left behind, awkward and vaguely antagonistic to each other.

"Yes? Can I help you?"

A stooping woman with a jet-black bouffant had emerged from out of a back room. Andrew and Sukhvinder muttered that they were waiting, and then Howard and Gaia reappeared in the archway. When he saw Maureen, Howard dropped Gaia's arm, which he had been holding absentmindedly while he explained to her what a waitress's duties would be.

"I might have found us some more help for the Kettle, Mo," he said.

"Oh, yes?" said Maureen, switching her hungry gaze to Gaia. "Have you got experience?"

But Howard boomed over her, telling Gaia all about the delicatessen and how he liked to think it was a bit of a Pagford institution, a bit of a landmark.

"Thirty-five years, it's been," said Howard, with a majestic disdain of his own mural. "The young lady's new to town, Mo," he added.

"And you two are after jobs as well, are you?" Maureen asked Sukhvinder and Andrew.

Sukhvinder shook her head; Andrew made an equivocal movement with his shoulders; but Gaia said, with her eyes on the girl, "Go on. You said you might."

Howard considered Sukhvinder, who would most certainly not appear to advantage in a tight black dress and frilly apron; but his fertile and flexible mind was firing in all directions. A compliment to her father—something of a hold over her mother—an unasked favor granted; there were matters beyond the purely aesthetic that ought, perhaps, to be considered here.

"Well, if we get the business we're expecting, we could probably do with two," he said, scratching his chins with his eyes on Sukhvinder, who had blushed unattractively.

"I don't…" she said, but Gaia urged her.

"Go on. Together."

Sukhvinder was flushed, and her eyes were watering.

"I…"

"Go on," whispered Gaia.

"I…all right."

"We'll give you a trial, then, Miss Jawanda," said Howard.

Doused in fear, Sukhvinder could hardly breathe. What would her mother say?

"And I suppose you're wanting to be potboy, are you?" Howard boomed at Andrew.

Potboy?

"It's heavy lifting we need, my friend," said Howard, while Andrew blinked at him nonplussed: he had only read the large type at the top of the sign. "Pallets into the stockroom, crates of milk up from the cellar and rubbish bagged up at the back. Proper manual labor. Do you think you can handle that?"

"Yeah," said Andrew. Would he be there when Gaia was there? That was all that mattered.

"We'll need you early. Eight o'clock, probably. We'll say eight till three, and see how it goes. Trial period of two weeks."

"Yeah, fine," said Andrew.

"What's your name?"

When Howard heard it, he raised his eyebrows.

"Is your father Simon? Simon Price?"

"Yeah."

Andrew was unnerved. Nobody knew who his father was, usually.

Howard told the two girls to come back on Sunday afternoon, when the till was to be delivered, and he would be at liberty to instruct them; then, though he showed an inclination to keep Gaia in conversation, a customer entered, and the teenagers took their chance to slip outside.

Andrew could think of nothing to say once they found themselves on the other side of the tinkling glass door; but before he could marshal his thoughts, Gaia threw him a careless "bye," and walked away with Sukhvinder. Andrew lit up the second of Fats' three fags (this was no time for a half-smoked stub), which gave him an excuse to remain stationary while he watched her walk away into the lengthening shadows.

"Why do they call him 'Peanut,' that boy?" Gaia asked Sukhvinder, once they were out of earshot of Andrew.

"He's allergic," said Sukhvinder. She was horrified at the prospect of telling Parminder what she had done. Her voice sounded like somebody else's. "He nearly died at St. Thomas's; somebody gave him one hidden in a marshmallow."

"Oh," said Gaia. "I thought it might be because he had a tiny dick."

She laughed, and so did Sukhvinder, forcing herself, as though jokes about penises were all she heard, day in, day out.

Andrew saw them both glance back at him as they laughed, and knew that they were talking about him. The giggling might be a hopeful sign; he knew that much about girls, anyway. Grinning at nothing but the cooling air, he walked off, schoolbag over his shoulder, cigarette in his hand, across the Square towards Church Row, and thence to forty minutes of steep climbing up out of town to Hilltop House.

The hedgerows were ghostly pale with white blossom in the dusk, blackthorn blooming on either side of him, celandine fringing the lane with tiny, glossy heart-shaped leaves. The smell of the flowers, the deep pleasure of the cigarette and the promise of weekends with Gaia; everything blended together into a glorious symphony of elation and beauty as Andrew puffed up the hill. The next time Simon said "got a job, Pizza Face?" he would be able to say "yes." He was going to be Gaia Bawden's weekend workmate.

And, to cap it all, he knew at last exactly how he might plunge an anonymous dagger straight between his father's shoulder blades.

VII

Once the first impulse of spite had worn off, Samantha bitterly regretted inviting Gavin and Kay to dinner. She spent Friday morning joking with her assistant about the dreadful evening she was bound to have, but her mood plummeted once she had left Carly in charge of Over the Shoulder Boulder Holders (a name that had made Howard laugh so hard the first time he had heard it that it had brought on an asthma attack, and which made Shirley scowl whenever it was spoken in her presence). Driving back to Pagford ahead of the rush hour, so that she could shop for ingredients and start cooking, Samantha tried to cheer herself up by thinking of nasty questions to ask Gavin. Perhaps she might wonder aloud why Kay had not moved in with him: that would be a good one.

Walking home from the Square with bulging Mollison and Lowe carrier bags in each hand, she came across Mary Fairbrother beside the cash-point machine in the wall of Barry's bank.

"Mary, hi…how are you?"

Mary was thin and pale, with gray patches around her eyes. Their conversation was stilted and strange. They had not spoken since the journey in the ambulance, barring brief, awkward condolences at the funeral.

"I've been meaning to drop in," Mary said, "you were so kind—and I wanted to thank Miles—"

"No need," Samantha said awkwardly.

"Oh, but I'd like—"

"Oh, but then, please do—"

After Mary had walked away, Samantha had the awful feeling that she might have given the impression that that evening would be a perfect time for Mary to come round.

Once home, she dropped the bags in the hall and telephoned Miles at work to tell him what she had done, but he displayed an infuriating equanimity about the prospect of adding a newly widowed woman to their foursome.

"I can't see what the problem is, really," he said. "Nice for Mary to get out."

"But I didn't say we were having Gavin and Kay over—"

"Mary likes Gav," said Miles. "I wouldn't worry about it."

He was, Samantha thought, being deliberately obtuse, no doubt in retaliation for her refusal to go to Sweetlove House. After she had hung up, she wondered whether to call Mary to tell her not to come that evening, but she was afraid of sounding rude, and settled for hoping that Mary would find herself unequal to calling in after all.

Stalking into the sitting room, she put on Libby's boy band DVD at full volume so that she would be able to hear it in the kitchen, then carried the bags through and set to work preparing a casserole and her fall-back pudding, Mississippi mud pie. She would have liked to buy one of Mollison and Lowe's large gateaux, to save herself some work, but it would have got straight back to Shirley, who frequently intimated that Samantha was overreliant on frozen food and ready meals.

Samantha knew the boy band DVD so well by now that she was able to visualize the images matching the music blaring through to the kitchen. Several times that week, while Miles was upstairs in his home study or on the telephone to Howard, she had watched it again. When she heard the opening bars of the track where the muscular boy walked, with his shirt flapping open, along the beach, she went through to watch in her apron, absentmindedly sucking her chocolatey fingers.

She had planned on having a long shower while Miles laid the table, forgetting that he would be late home, because he had to drive into Yarvil to pick up the girls from St. Anne's. When Samantha realized why he had not returned, and that their daughters would be with him when he did, she had to fly around to organize the dining room herself, then find something to feed Lexie and Libby before the guests arrived. Miles found his wife in her work clothes at half past seven, sweaty, cross and inclined to blame him for what had been her own idea.

Fourteen-year-old Libby marched into the sitting room without greeting Samantha and removed the disc from the DVD player.

"Oh, good, I was wondering what I'd done with that," she said. "Why's the TV on? Have you been *playing* it?"

Sometimes, Samantha thought that her younger daughter had a look of Shirley about her.

"I was watching the news, Libby. I haven't got time to watch DVDs. Come through, your pizza's ready. We've got people coming round."

"Frozen pizza *again?*"

"Miles! I need to change. Can you mash the potatoes for me? Miles?"

But he had disappeared upstairs, so Samantha pounded the potatoes herself, while her daughters ate at the island in the middle of the kitchen. Libby had propped the DVD cover against her glass of Diet Pepsi, and was ogling it.

"Mikey's *so lush,*" she said, with a carnal groan that took Samantha aback; but the muscular boy was called Jake. Samantha was glad they did not like the same one.

Loud and confident Lexie was jabbering about school; a machine-gun torrent of information about girls whom Samantha did not know, with whose antics and feuds and regroupings she could not keep up.

"All right, you two, I've got to change. Clear away when you're done, all right?"

She turned down the heat under the casserole and hurried upstairs. Miles was buttoning up his shirt in the bedroom, watching himself in the wardrobe mirror. The whole room smelled of soap and aftershave.

"Everything under control, hon?"

"Yes, thanks. So glad you've had time to shower," spat Samantha, pulling out her favorite long skirt and top, slamming the wardrobe door.

"You could have one now."

"They'll be here in ten minutes; I won't have time to dry my hair and put on makeup." She kicked off her shoes; one of them hit the radiator with a loud clang. "When you've finished preening, could you please go downstairs and sort out drinks?"

After Miles had left the room, she tried to untangle her thick hair and repair her makeup. She looked awful. Only when she had changed did she realize that she was wearing the wrong bra for her clinging top. After a frantic search, she remembered that the right one was drying in the utility room; she hurried out onto the landing but the doorbell rang. Swearing, she scuttled back to the bedroom. The boy band's music was blaring out of Libby's room.

Gavin and Kay had arrived on the dot of eight because Gavin was afraid of what Samantha might say if they turned up late; he could imagine her suggesting that they had lost track of time because they were shagging or that they must have had a row. She seemed to think that one of the perks of marriage was that it gave you rights of comment and intrusion over single people's love lives. She also thought that her crass, uninhibited way of talking, especially when drunk, constituted trenchant humor.

"Hello-ello-ello," said Miles, moving back to let Gavin and Kay inside. "Come in, come in. Welcome to Casa Mollison."

He kissed Kay on both cheeks and relieved her of the chocolates she was holding.

"For us? Thanks very much. Lovely to meet you properly at last. Gav's been keeping you under wraps for far too long."

Miles shook the wine out of Gavin's hand, then clapped him on the back, which Gavin resented.

"Come on through, Sam'll be down in a mo. What'll you have to drink?"

Kay would ordinarily have found Miles rather smooth and over-familiar, but she was determined to suspend judgment. Couples had to mix with each other's circles, and manage to get along in them. This evening represented significant progress in her quest to infiltrate the layers of his life to which Gavin had never admitted her, and she wanted to show him that she was at home in the Mollisons' big, smug house, that there was no need to exclude her anymore. So she smiled at Miles, asked for a red wine, and admired the spacious room with its stripped pine floorboards, its over-cushioned sofa and its framed prints.

"Been here for, ooh, getting on for fourteen years," said Miles, busy with the corkscrew. "You're down in Hope Street, aren't you? Nice little houses, some great fixer-upper opportunities down there."

Samantha appeared, smiling without warmth. Kay, who had previously seen her only in an overcoat, noted the tightness of her orange top, beneath which every detail of her lacy bra was clearly visible. Her face was even darker than her leathery chest; her eye makeup was thick and unflattering and her jangling gold earrings and high-heeled golden mules were, in Kay's opinion, tarty. Samantha struck her as the kind of woman who would have raucous girls' nights out, and find stripograms hilarious, and flirt drunkenly with everyone else's partner at parties.

"Hi there," said Samantha. She kissed Gavin and smiled at Kay. "Great, you've got drinks. I'll have the same as Kay, Miles."

She turned away to sit down, having already taken stock of the other woman's appearance: Kay was small-breasted and heavy-hipped, and had certainly chosen her black trousers to minimize the size of her bottom. She would have done better, in Samantha's opinion, to wear heels, given the shortness of her legs. Her face was attractive enough, with even-toned olive skin, large dark eyes and a generous mouth; but the closely cropped boy's hair and the resolutely flat shoes were undoubtedly pointers to certain sacrosanct Beliefs. Gavin had done it again: he had gone and picked another humorless, domineering woman who would make his life a misery.

"So!" said Samantha brightly, raising her glass. "Gavin-and-Kay!"

She saw, with satisfaction, Gavin's hangdog wince of a smile; but before she could make him squirm more or weasel private information out of them both to dangle over Shirley's and Maureen's heads, the doorbell rang again.

Mary appeared fragile and angular, especially beside Miles, who ushered her into the room. Her T-shirt hung from protruding collarbones.

"Oh," she said, coming to a startled halt on the threshold. "I didn't realize you were having—"

"Gavin and Kay just dropped in," said Samantha a little wildly. "Come in, Mary, please...have a drink..."

"Mary, this is Kay," said Miles. "Kay, this is Mary Fairbrother."

"Oh," said Kay, thrown; she had thought that it would only be the four of them. "Yes, hello."

Gavin, who could tell that Mary had not meant to drop in on a dinner party and was on the point of walking straight back out again, patted the sofa beside him; Mary sat down with a weak smile. He was overjoyed to see her. Here was his buffer; even Samantha must realize that her particular brand of prurience would be inappropriate in front of a bereaved woman; plus, the constrictive symmetry of a foursome had been broken up.

"How are you?" he said quietly. "I was going to give you a ring, actually...there've been developments with the insurance..."

"Haven't we got any nibbles, Sam?" asked Miles.

Samantha walked from the room, seething at Miles. The smell of scorched meat met her as she opened the kitchen door.

"Oh shit, shit, shit..."

She had completely forgotten the casserole, which had dried out. Desiccated chunks of meat and vegetables sat, forlorn survivors of the catastrophe, on the singed bottom of the pot. Samantha sloshed in wine and stock, chiseling the adhering bits off the pan with her spoon, stirring vigorously, sweating in the heat. Miles' high-pitched laugh rang out from the sitting room. Samantha put on long-stemmed broccoli to steam, drained her glass of wine, ripped open a bag of tortilla chips and a tub of hummus, and upended them into bowls.

Mary and Gavin were still conversing quietly on the sofa when she returned to the sitting room, while Miles was showing Kay a framed aerial photograph of Pagford, and giving her a lesson in the town's history. Samantha set down the bowls on the coffee table, poured herself another drink and settled into the armchair, making no effort to join either conversation. It was awfully uncomfortable to have Mary there; with her grief hanging so heavily around her she might as well have walked in trailing a shroud. Surely, though, she would leave before dinner.

Gavin was determined that Mary should stay. As they discussed the latest developments in their ongoing battle with the insurance company, he felt much more relaxed and in control than he usually did in Miles and Samantha's presence. Nobody was chipping away at him, or patronizing him, and Miles was absolving him temporarily of all responsibility for Kay.

"...and just here, just out of sight," Miles was saying, pointing to a spot two inches past the frame of the picture, "you've got Sweetlove House, the Fawley place. Big Queen Anne manor house, dormers, stone quoins...stunning, you should visit, it's open to the public on Sundays in the summer. Important family locally, the Fawleys."

"Stone quoins?" "Important family, locally?" God, you are an arse, Miles.

Samantha hoisted herself out of her armchair and returned to the kitchen. Though the casserole was watery, the burned flavor dominated. The broccoli was flaccid and tasteless; the mashed potato cool and dry. Past caring, she decanted it all into dishes and slammed it down on the circular dining-room table.

"Dinner's ready!" she called at the sitting-room door.

"Oh, I must go," said Mary, jumping up. "I didn't mean—"

"No, no, no!" said Gavin, in a tone that Kay had never heard before: kindly and cajoling. "It'll do you good to eat—kids'll be all right for an hour."

Miles added his support and Mary looked uncertainly towards Samantha, who was forced to add her voice to theirs, then dashed back through into the dining room to lay another setting.

She invited Mary to sit between Gavin and Miles, because placing her next to a woman seemed to emphasize her husband's absence. Kay and Miles had moved on to discussing social work.

"I don't envy you," he said, serving Kay a large ladle full of casserole; Samantha could see black, scorched flecks in the sauce spreading across the white plate. "Bloody difficult job."

"Well, we're perennially under-resourced," said Kay, "but it can be satisfying, especially when you can feel you're making a difference."

And she thought of the Weedons. Terri's urine sample had tested negative at the clinic yesterday and Robbie had had a full week in nursery. The recollection cheered her, counterbalancing her slight irritation that Gavin's attention was still focused entirely on Mary; that he was doing nothing to help ease her conversation with his friends.

"You've got a daughter, haven't you, Kay?"

"That's right: Gaia. She's sixteen."

"Same age as Lexie; we should get them together," said Miles.

"Divorced?" asked Samantha delicately.

"No," said Kay. "We weren't married. He was a university boyfriend and we split up not long after she was born."

"Yeah, Miles and I had barely left university ourselves," said Samantha.

Kay did not know whether Samantha meant to draw a distinction between herself, who had married the big smug father of her children, and Kay, who had been left...not that Samantha could know that Brendan had left her...

"Gaia's taken a Saturday job with your father, actually," Kay told Miles. "At the new café."

Miles was delighted. He took enormous pleasure in the idea that he and Howard were so much part of the fabric of the place that everybody in Pagford was connected to them, whether as friend or client, customer or employee. Gavin, who was chewing and chewing on a bit of rubbery meat that was refusing to yield to his teeth, experienced a further lowering in the pit of his stomach. It was news to him that Gaia had taken a job with Miles' father. Somehow he had forgotten that Kay possessed in Gaia another powerful device for anchoring herself to Pagford. When not in the immediate vicinity of her slamming doors, her vicious looks and caustic asides, Gavin tended to forget that Gaia had any independent existence at all; that she was not simply part of the uncomfortable backdrop of stale sheets, bad cooking and festering grudges against which his relationship with Kay staggered on.

"Does Gaia like Pagford?" Samantha asked.

"Well, it's a bit quiet compared to Hackney," said Kay, "but she's settling in well."

She took a large gulp of wine to wash out her mouth after disgorging the enormous lie. There had been yet another row before leaving tonight.

("What's the matter with you?" Kay had asked, while Gaia sat at the kitchen table, hunched over her laptop, wearing a dressing gown over her clothes. Four or five boxes of dialogue were open on the screen. Kay knew that Gaia was communicating online with the friends she had left behind in Hackney, friends she had had, in most cases, since she had been in primary school.

"Gaia?"

Refusal to answer was new and ominous. Kay was used to explosions of bile and rage against herself and, particularly, Gavin.

"Gaia, I'm talking to you."

"I know, I can hear you."

"Then kindly have the courtesy to answer me back."

Black dialogue jerked upwards in the boxes on the screen, funny little icons, blinking and waggling.

"Gaia, please will you answer me?"

"What? What do you want?"

"I'm trying to ask about your day."

"My day was shit. Yesterday was shit. Tomorrow will be shit as well."

"When did you get home?"

"The same time I always get home."

Sometimes, even after all these years, Gaia displayed resentment at having to let herself in, at Kay not being at home to meet her like a storybook mother.

"Do you want to tell me why your day was shit?"

"Because you dragged me to live in a shithole."

Kay willed herself not to shout. Lately there had been screaming matches that she was sure the whole street had heard.

"You know that I'm going out with Gavin tonight?"

Gaia muttered something Kay did not catch.

"What?"

"I said, I didn't think he liked taking you out."

"What's that supposed to mean?"

But Gaia did not answer; she simply typed a response into one of the scrolling conversations on the screen. Kay vacillated, both wanting to press her and afraid of what she might hear.

"We'll be back around midnight, I expect."

Gaia had not responded. Kay had gone to wait for Gavin in the hall.)

"Gaia's made friends," Kay told Miles, "with a girl who lives in this street; what's her name—Narinder?"

"Sukhvinder," said Miles and Samantha together.

"She's a nice girl," said Mary.

"Have you met her father?" Samantha asked Kay.

"No," said Kay.

"He's a heart surgeon," said Samantha, who was on her fourth glass of wine. "Absolutely bloody gorgeous."

"Oh," said Kay.

"Like a Bollywood film star."

None of them, Samantha reflected, had bothered to tell her that dinner was tasty, which would have been simple politeness, even though it was awful. If she wasn't allowed to torment Gavin, she ought at least to be able to needle Miles.

"Vikram's the only good thing about living in this godforsaken town, I can tell you," said Samantha. "Sex on legs."

"And his wife's our local GP," said Miles, "and a parish councillor. You'll be employed by Yarvil District Council, Kay, are you?"

"That's right," said Kay. "But I spend most of my time in the Fields. They're technically in Pagford Parish, aren't they?"

Not the Fields, thought Samantha. *Oh, don't mention the bloody Fields.*

"Ah," said Miles, with a meaningful smile. "Yes, well, the Fields do belong to Pagford, *technically.* Technically, they do. Painful subject, Kay."

"Really? Why?" asked Kay, hoping to make conversation general, because Gavin was still talking in an undertone to the widow.

"Well, you see—this is back in the fifties." Miles seemed to be embarking on a well-rehearsed speech. "Yarvil wanted to expand the Cantermill Estate, and instead of building out to the west, where the bypass is now—"

"Gavin? Mary? More wine?" Samantha called over Miles.

"—they were a little bit duplicitous; land was bought without it being very clear what they wanted it for, and then they went and expanded the estate over the border into Pagford Parish."

"Why aren't you mentioning Old Aubrey Fawley, Miles?" asked

Samantha. She had, at last, reached that delicious point of intoxication where her tongue became wicked and she became disengaged from fear of consequences, eager to provoke and to irritate, seeking nothing but her own amusement. "The truth is that Old Aubrey Fawley, who used to own all those lovely stone quoits, or whatever Miles was telling you about, did a deal behind everyone's backs—"

"That's not fair, Sam," said Miles, but she talked over him again.

"—he flogged off the land where the Fields are built, pocketed, I don't know, must have been a quarter of a mil or so—"

"Don't talk rubbish, Sam, back in the fifties?"

"—but then, once he realized everyone was pissed off with him, he pretended he hadn't known it would cause trouble. Upper-class twit. And a drunk," added Samantha.

"*Simply* not true, I'm afraid," Miles said firmly. "To fully understand the problem, Kay, you need to appreciate a bit of local history."

Samantha, holding her chin in her hand, pretended to slide her elbow off the table in boredom. Though she could not like Samantha, Kay laughed, and Gavin and Mary broke off their quiet conversation.

"We're talking about the Fields," said Kay, in a tone intended to remind Gavin that she was there; that he ought to be giving her moral support.

Miles, Samantha and Gavin realized simultaneously that the Fields was a most tactless subject to raise in front of Mary, when they had been such a bone of contention between Barry and Howard.

"Apparently they're a bit of a sore subject locally," said Kay, wanting to force Gavin to express a view, to rope him in.

"Mmm," he replied, and turning back to Mary, he said, "So how's Declan's football coming on?"

Kay experienced a powerful stab of fury: Mary might be recently bereaved, but Gavin's solicitousness seemed unnecessarily pointed. She had imagined this evening quite differently: a foursome in which Gavin would have to acknowledge that they really were a couple; yet nobody looking on would imagine that they enjoyed a closer relationship than acquaintanceship. Also, the food was horrible. Kay put her knife and fork together with three-quarters of her helping untouched—an act that was not lost on Samantha—and addressed Miles again.

"Did you grow up in Pagford?"

"Afraid so," said Miles, smiling complacently. "Born in the old Kelland Hospital along the road. They closed it in the eighties."

"And you?" Kay asked Samantha, who cut across her.

"God, no. I'm here by accident."

"Sorry, I don't know what you do, Samantha?" asked Kay.

"I've got my own busi—"

"She sells outsize bras," said Miles.

Samantha got up abruptly and went to fetch another bottle of wine. When she returned to the table, Miles was telling Kay the humorous anecdote, doubtless intended to illustrate how everyone knew everyone in Pagford, of how he had been pulled over in the car one night by a policeman who turned out to be a friend he had known since primary school. The blow-by-blow reenactment of the banter between himself and Steve Edwards was tediously familiar to Samantha. As she moved around the table replenishing all the glasses, she watched Kay's austere expression; evidently, Kay did not find drink-driving a laughing matter.

"...so Steve's holding out the Breathalyzer, and I'm about to blow in it, and out of nowhere we both start cracking up. His partner's got no idea what the hell's going on; he's like this"—Miles mimed a man turning his head from side to side in astonishment—"and Steve's bent double, pissing himself, because all we can think of is the last time he was holding something steady for me to blow into, which was nigh on twenty years ago, and—"

"It was a blow-up doll," said Samantha, unsmiling, dropping back into her seat beside Miles. "Miles and Steve put it in their friend Ian's parents' beds, during Ian's eighteenth-birthday party. Anyway, in the end Miles was fined a grand and got three points on his license, because it was the second time he'd been caught over the limit. So that was hysterically funny."

Miles' grin remained foolishly in place, like a limp balloon forgotten after a party. A stiff little chill seemed to blow through the temporarily silent room. Though Miles struck her as an almighty bore, Kay was on his side: he was the only one at the table who seemed remotely inclined to ease her passage into Pagford social life.

"I must say, the Fields are pretty rough," she said, reverting to the subject with which Miles seemed most comfortable, and still ignorant that it was in any way inauspicious within Mary's vicinity. "I've worked in the inner cities; I didn't expect to see that kind of deprivation in a rural area, but it's not all that different from London. Less of an ethnic mix, of course."

"Oh, yes, we've got our share of addicts and wasters," said Miles. "I think that's about all I can manage, Sam," he added, pushing his plate away from him with a sizeable amount of food still on it.

Samantha started to clear the table; Mary got up to help.

"No, no, it's fine, Mary, you relax," Samantha said. To Kay's annoyance, Gavin jumped up too, chivalrously insisting on Mary's sitting back down, but Mary insisted too.

"That was lovely, Sam," said Mary, in the kitchen, as they scraped most of the food into the bin.

"No, it wasn't, it was horrible," said Samantha, who was only appreciating how drunk she was now that she was on her feet. "What do you think of Kay?"

"I don't know. She's not what I expected," said Mary.

"She's exactly what I expected," said Samantha, taking out plates for pudding. "She's another Lisa, if you ask me."

"Oh, no, don't say that," said Mary. "He deserves someone nice this time."

This was a most novel point of view to Samantha, who was of the opinion that Gavin's wetness merited constant punishment.

They returned to the dining room to find an animated conversation in progress between Kay and Miles, while Gavin sat in silence.

"...offload responsibility for them, which seems to me to be a pretty self-centered and self-satisfied—"

"Well, I think it's interesting that you use the word 'responsibility,'" said Miles, "because I think that goes to the very heart of the problem, doesn't it? The question is, where exactly do we draw the line?"

"Beyond the Fields, apparently." Kay laughed, with condescension. "You want to draw a line neatly between the home-owning middle classes and the lower—"

"Pagford's full of working-class people, Kay; the difference is, most of them *work*. D'you know what proportion of the Fields lives off benefits? Responsibility, you say: what happened to personal responsibility? We've had them through the local school for years: kids who haven't got a single worker in the family; the concept of earning a living is completely foreign to them; generations of non-workers, and we're expected to subsidize them—"

"So your solution is to shunt off the problem onto Yarvil," said Kay, "not to engage with any of the underlying—"

"Mississippi mud pie?" called Samantha.

Gavin and Mary took slices with thanks; Kay, to Samantha's fury, simply held out her plate as though Samantha were a waitress, her attention all on Miles.

"...the addiction clinic, which is absolutely crucial, and which certain people are apparently lobbying to close—"

"Oh, well, if you're talking about Bellchapel," said Miles, shaking his head and smirking, "I hope you've mugged up on what the success rates are, Kay. Pathetic, frankly, absolutely pathetic. I've seen the figures, I was going through them this morning, and I won't lie to you, the sooner they close—"

"And the figures you're talking about are...?"

"Success rates, Kay, exactly what I said: the number of people who have actually stopped using drugs, gone clean—"

"I'm sorry, but that's a very naive point of view; if you're going to judge success purely—"

"But how on earth else are we supposed to judge an addiction clinic's success?" demanded Miles, incredulous. "As far as I can tell, all they do at Bellchapel is dole out methadone, which half of their clients use alongside heroin anyway."

"The whole problem of addiction is immensely complicated," said Kay, "and it's naive and simplistic to put the problem purely in terms of users and non..."

But Miles was shaking his head, smiling; Kay, who had been

enjoying her verbal duel with this self-satisfied lawyer, was suddenly angry.

"Well, I can give you a very concrete example of what Bellchapel's doing: one family I'm working with—mother, teenage daughter and small son—if the mother wasn't on methadone, she'd be on the streets trying to pay for her habit; the kids are immeasurably better off—"

"They'd be better off away from their mother, by the sound of it," said Miles.

"And where exactly would you propose they go?"

"A decent foster home would be a good start," said Miles.

"Do you know how many foster homes there are, against how many kids needing them?" asked Kay.

"The best solution would have been to have them adopted at birth—"

"Fabulous. I'll hop in my time machine," retorted Kay.

"Well, we know a couple who were desperate to adopt," said Samantha, unexpectedly throwing her weight behind Miles. She would not forgive Kay for the rude outstretched plate; the woman was bolshy and patronizing, exactly like Lisa, who had monopolized every get-together with her political views and her job in family law, despising Samantha for owning a bra shop. "Adam and Janice," she reminded Miles in parenthesis, who nodded; "and they couldn't get a baby for love nor money, could they?"

"Yes, *a baby,*" said Kay, rolling her eyes, "everybody wants a *baby.* Robbie's nearly four. He's not potty-trained, he's developmentally behind for his age and he's almost certainly had inappropriate exposure to sexual behavior. Would your friends like to adopt *him?*"

"But the point is, if he'd been taken from his mother at birth—"

"She was off the drugs when he was born, and making good progress," said Kay. "She loved him and wanted to keep him, and she was meeting his needs at the time. She'd already raised Krystal, with some family support—"

"Krystal!" shrieked Samantha. "Oh my God, are we talking about the *Weedons?*"

Kay was horrified that she had used names; it had never mattered in London, but everyone truly did know everyone in Pagford, it seemed.

"I shouldn't have—"

But Miles and Samantha were laughing, and Mary looked tense. Kay, who had not touched her pie, and had managed very little of the first course, realized that she had drunk too much; she had been sipping wine steadily out of nerves, and now she had committed a prime indiscretion. Still, it was too late to undo that; anger over-rode every other consideration.

"Krystal Weedon is no advert for that woman's mothering skills," said Miles.

"Krystal's trying her damnedest to hold her family together," said Kay. "She loves her little brother very much; she's terrified he'll be taken away—"

"I wouldn't trust Krystal Weedon to look after a boiling egg," said Miles, and Samantha laughed again. "Oh, look, it's to her credit she loves her brother, but he isn't a cuddly toy—"

"Yes, I know that," snapped Kay, remembering Robbie's shitty, crusted bottom, "but he's still loved."

"Krystal bullied our daughter Lexie," said Samantha, "so we've seen a different side of her to the one I'm sure she shows you."

"Look, we all know Krystal's had a rough deal," said Miles, "nobody's denying that. It's the drug-addled mother I've got an issue with."

"As a matter of fact, she's doing very well on the Bellchapel program at the moment."

"But with her *history*," said Miles, "it isn't *rocket science,* is it, to guess that she'll relapse?"

"If you apply that rule across the board, you ought not to have a driving license, because with your *history* you're bound to drink and drive again."

Miles was temporarily baffled, but Samantha said coldly, "I think that's a rather different thing."

"Do you?" said Kay. "It's the same principle."

"Yes, well, principles are sometimes the problem, if you ask me," said Miles. "Often what's needed is a bit of common sense."

"Which is the name people usually give to their prejudices," rejoined Kay.

"According to Nietzsche," said a sharp new voice, making them all jump, "philosophy is the biography of the philosopher."

A miniature Samantha stood at the door into the hall, a busty girl of around sixteen in tight jeans and a T-shirt; she was eating a handful of grapes and looking rather pleased with herself.

"Everyone meet Lexie," said Miles proudly. "Thank you for that, genius."

"You're welcome," said Lexie pertly, and she swept off upstairs.

A heavy silence sank over the table. Without really knowing why, Samantha, Miles and Kay all glanced towards Mary, who looked as though she might be on the verge of tears.

"Coffee," said Samantha, lurching to her feet. Mary disappeared into the bathroom.

"Let's go and sit through," said Miles, conscious that the atmosphere was somewhat charged, but confident that he could, with a few jokes and his habitual bonhomie, steer everyone back into charity with each other. "Bring your glasses."

His inner certainties had been no more rearranged by Kay's arguments than a breeze can move a boulder; yet his feeling towards her was not unkind, but rather pitying. He was the least intoxicated by the constant refilling of glasses, but on reaching the sitting room he realized how very full his bladder was.

"Whack on some music, Gav, and I'll go and get those choccies."

But Gavin made no move towards the vertical stacks of CDs in their sleek Perspex stands. He seemed to be waiting for Kay to start on him. Sure enough, as soon as Miles had vanished from sight, Kay said, "Well, thank you very much, Gav. Thanks for all the support."

Gavin had drunk even more greedily than Kay throughout dinner, enjoying his own private celebration that he had not, after all, been offered up as a sacrifice to Samantha's gladiatorial bullying. He faced Kay squarely, full of a courage born not only of wine but because he had been treated for an hour as somebody important, knowledgeable and supportive, by Mary.

"You seemed to be doing OK on your own," he said.

Indeed, the little he had permitted himself to hear of Kay and Miles' argument had given him a pronounced sense of déjà vu; if he had not had Mary to distract him, he might have fancied himself back on that famous evening, in the identical dining room, when Lisa had told Miles that he epitomized all that was wrong with society, and Miles had laughed in her face, and Lisa had lost her temper and refused to stay for coffee. It was not very long after, that Lisa had admitted that she was sleeping with an associate partner at her firm and advised Gavin to get tested for chlamydia.

"I don't know any of these people," said Kay, "and you haven't done one damn thing to make it any easier for me, have you?"

"What did you want me to do?" asked Gavin. He was wonderfully calm, insulated by the imminent returns of the Mollisons and Mary, and by the copious amounts of Chianti he had consumed. "I didn't want an argument about the Fields. I don't give a monkey's about the Fields. Plus," he added, "it's a touchy subject around Mary; Barry was fighting on the council to keep the Fields part of Pagford."

"Well, then, why couldn't you have told me—given me a hint?"

He laughed, exactly as Miles had laughed at her. Before she could retort, the others returned like the Magi bearing gifts: Samantha carrying a tray of cups, followed by Mary holding the cafetière, and Miles, with Kay's chocolates. Kay saw the flamboyant gold ribbon on the box and remembered how optimistic she had been about tonight when she had bought them. She turned her face away, trying to hide her anger, frantic with the desire to shout at Gavin, and also with a sudden, shocking urge to cry.

"It's been so nice," she heard Mary say, in a thick voice that suggested she, too, might have been crying, "but I won't stay for coffee, I don't want to be late back; Declan's a bit...a bit unsettled at the moment. Thanks so much, Sam, Miles, it's been good to, you know...well, get out for a bit."

"I'll walk you up the—" Miles began, but Gavin was talking firmly over him.

"You stay here, Miles; I'll see Mary back. I'll walk you up the road, Mary. It'll only take five minutes. It's dark up the top there."

Kay was barely breathing; all her being was concentrated in

loathing of complacent Miles, tarty Samantha and fragile, drooping Mary, but most of all of Gavin himself.

"Oh, yes," she heard herself saying, as everybody seemed to look towards her for permission, "yep, you see Mary home, Gav."

She heard the front door close and Gavin had gone. Miles was pouring Kay's coffee. She watched the stream of hot black liquid fall, and felt suddenly, painfully alive to what she had risked in overthrowing her life for the man walking away into the night with another woman.

VIII

Colin Wall saw Gavin and Mary pass under his study window. He recognized Mary's silhouette at once, but had to squint to identify the stringy man at her side, before they moved out of the aureole cast by the streetlight. Crouching, half-raised out of his computer chair, Colin gaped after the figures as they disappeared into the darkness.

He was shocked to his core, having taken it for granted that Mary was in a kind of purdah; that she was receiving only women in the sanctuary of her own home, among them Tessa, who was still visiting every other day. Never had it occurred to him that Mary might be socializing after dark, least of all with a single man. He felt personally betrayed; as though Mary, on some spiritual level, was cuckolding him.

Had Mary permitted Gavin to see Barry's body? Was Gavin spending evenings sitting in Barry's favorite seat by the fire? Were Gavin and Mary…could they possibly be…? Such things happened, after all, every day. Perhaps…perhaps even before Barry's death…?

Colin was perennially appalled by the threadbare state of other people's morals. He tried to insulate himself against shocks by pushing himself to imagine the worst: by conjuring awful visions of depravity and betrayal, rather than waiting for the truth to rip like a shell through his innocent delusions. Life, for Colin, was one long brace against pain and disappointment, and everybody apart from his wife was an enemy until they had proven otherwise.

He was half inclined to rush downstairs to tell Tessa what he had just seen, because she might be able to give him an innocuous explanation of Mary's nighttime stroll, and to reassure him that his best friend's widow had been, and was still, faithful to her husband. Nonetheless, he resisted the urge, because he was angry with Tessa.

Why was she showing such a determined lack of interest in his forthcoming candidacy for the council? Did she not realize how tight a stranglehold his anxiety had gained over him ever since he had sent in his application form? Even though he had expected to feel this way, the pain was not diminished by anticipation, any more than being hit by a train would be less devastating for seeing it approaching down the track; Colin merely suffered twice: in the expectation and in its realization.

His nightmarish new fantasies swirled around the Mollisons and the ways in which they were likely to attack him. Counter-arguments, explanations and extenuations ran constantly through his mind. He saw himself already besieged, fighting for his reputation. The edge of paranoia always apparent in Colin's dealings with the world was becoming more pronounced; and meanwhile, Tessa was pretending to be oblivious, doing absolutely nothing to help alleviate the dreadful, crushing strain.

He knew that she did not think he ought to be standing. Perhaps she too was terrified that Howard Mollison would slit open the bulging gut of their past, and spill its ghastly secrets for all the Pagford vultures to pick over.

Colin had already made a few telephone calls to those whom Barry had counted on for support. He had been surprised and heartened that not one of them had challenged his credentials or interrogated him on the issues. Without exception, they had expressed their profound sorrow at the loss of Barry and their intense dislike of Howard Mollison, or "tha' great smug basturd," as one of the blunter voters had called him. "Tryin' ter crowbar in 'is son. 'E could 'ardly stop hisself grinnin' when 'e 'eard Barry was dead." Colin, who had compiled a list of pro-Fields talking points, had not needed to refer to the paper once. So far, his main appeal as a candidate seemed to be that he was Barry's friend, and that he was not called Mollison.

His miniature black and white face was smiling at him out of the computer monitor. He had been sitting here all evening, trying to compose his election pamphlet, for which he had decided to use the same photograph as was featured on the Winterdown website: full face, with a slightly anodyne grin, his forehead steep and shiny. The image had in its favor the fact that it had already been submitted to the public gaze, and had not brought down ridicule or ruin upon him: a powerful recommendation. But beneath the photograph, where the personal information ought to have been, were only one or two tentative sentences. Colin had spent most of the last two hours composing and then deleting words; at one point he had managed to complete an entire paragraph, only to destroy it, backspace by backspace, with a nervous, jabbing forefinger.

Unable to bear the indecision and solitude, he jumped up and went downstairs. Tessa was lying on the sofa in the sitting room, apparently dozing, with the television on in the background.

"How's it going?" she asked sleepily, opening her eyes.

"Mary's just gone by. Walking up the street with Gavin Hughes."

"Oh," said Tessa. "She said something about going over to Miles and Samantha's, earlier. Gavin must have been there. He's probably walking her home."

Colin was appalled. Mary visiting Miles, the man who sought to fill her husband's shoes, who stood in opposition to all that Barry had fought for?

"What on earth was she doing at the Mollisons'?"

"They went with her to the hospital, you know that," said Tessa, sitting up with a small groan and stretching her short legs. "She hasn't spoken to them properly since. She wanted to thank them. Have you finished your pamphlet?"

"I'm nearly there. Listen, with the information—I mean, as far as the personal information goes—past posts, do you think? Or limit it to Winterdown?"

"I don't think you need say more than where you work now. But why don't you ask Minda? She..." Tessa yawned "...she's done it herself."

"Yes," said Colin. He waited, standing over her, but she did not offer to help, or even to read what he had written so far. "Yes, that's a good idea," he said, more loudly. "I'll get Minda to look over it."

She grunted, massaging her ankles, and he left the room, full of wounded pride. His wife could not possibly realize what a state he was in, how little sleep he was getting, or how his stomach was gnawing itself from within.

Tessa had only pretended to be asleep. Mary and Gavin's footsteps had woken her ten minutes previously.

Tessa barely knew Gavin; he was fifteen years younger than her and Colin, but the main barrier toward intimacy had always been Colin's tendency to be jealous of Barry's other friendships.

"He's been amazing about the insurance," Mary had told Tessa on the telephone earlier. "He's on the phone to them every day, from what I can gather, and he keeps telling me not to worry about fees. Oh God, Tessa, if they don't pay out..."

"Gavin will sort it out for you," said Tessa. "I'm sure he will."

It would have been nice, thought Tessa, stiff and thirsty on the sofa, if she and Colin could have had Mary round to the house, to give her a change of scene and make sure she was eating, but there was one insuperable barrier: Mary found Colin difficult, a strain. This uncomfortable and hitherto concealed fact had emerged slowly in the wake of Barry's death, like flotsam revealed by the ebbing tide. It could not have been plainer that Mary wanted only Tessa; she shied away from suggestions that Colin might help with anything, and avoided talking to him too long on the telephone. They had met so often as a foursome for years, and Mary's antipathy had never surfaced: Barry's good humor must have cloaked it.

Tessa had to manage the new state of affairs with great delicacy. She had successfully persuaded Colin that Mary was happiest in the company of other women. The funeral had been her one failure, because Colin had ambushed Mary as they all left St. Michael's and tried to explain, through racking sobs, that he was going to stand for Barry's seat on the council, to carry on Barry's work, to make sure Barry prevailed posthumously. Tessa had seen Mary's shocked and offended expression, and pulled him away.

Once or twice since, Colin had stated his intention of going over to show Mary all his election materials, to ask whether Barry would have approved of them; even voiced an intention of seeking guidance from Mary as to how Barry would have handled the process of canvassing for votes. In the end Tessa had told him firmly that he must not badger Mary about the Parish Council. He became huffy at this, but it was better, Tessa thought, that he should be angry with her, rather than adding to Mary's distress, or provoking her into a rebuff, as had happened over the viewing of Barry's body.

"The Mollisons, though!" said Colin, reentering the room with a cup of tea. He had not offered Tessa one; he was often selfish in these little ways, too busy with his own worries to notice. "Of all the people for her to have dinner with! They were against everything Barry stood for!"

"That's a bit melodramatic, Col," said Tessa. "Anyway, Mary was never as interested in the Fields as Barry."

But Colin's only understanding of love was of limitless loyalty, boundless tolerance: Mary had fallen, irreparably, in his estimation.

IX

"And where are you going?" asked Simon, planting himself squarely in the middle of the tiny hall.

The front door was open, and the glass porch behind him, full of shoes and coats, was blinding in the bright Saturday morning sun, turning Simon into a silhouette. His shadow rippled up the stairs, just touching the one on which Andrew stood.

"Into town with Fats."

"Homework all finished, is it?"

"Yeah."

It was a lie; but Simon would not bother to check.

"Ruth? *Ruth!*"

She appeared at the kitchen door, wearing an apron, flushed, with her hands covered in flour.

"What?"

"Do we need anything from town?"

"What? No, I don't think so."

"Taking my bike, are you?" demanded Simon of Andrew.

"Yeah, I was going to —"

"Leaving it at Fats' house?"

"Yeah."

"What time do we want him back?" Simon asked, turning to Ruth again.

"Oh, I don't know, Si," said Ruth impatiently. The furthest she ever went in irritation with her husband was on occasions when Simon, though basically in a good mood, started laying down the law for the fun of it. Andrew and Fats often went into town together, on the vague understanding that Andrew would return before it became dark.

"Five o'clock, then," said Simon arbitrarily. "Any later and you're grounded."

"Fine," Andrew replied.

He kept his right hand in his jacket pocket, clenched over a tightly folded wad of paper, intensely aware of it, like a ticking grenade. The fear of losing this piece of paper, on which was inscribed a line of meticulously written code, and a number of crossed-out, reworked and heavily edited sentences, had been plaguing him for a week. He had been keeping it on him at all times, and sleeping with it inside his pillowcase.

Simon barely moved aside, so that Andrew had to edge past him into the porch, his fingers clamped over the paper. He was terrified that Simon would demand that he turn out his pockets, ostensibly looking for cigarettes.

"Bye, then."

Simon did not answer. Andrew proceeded into the garage, where he took out the note, unfolded it and read it. He knew that he was being irrational, that mere proximity to Simon could not have magically switched the papers, but still he made sure. Satisfied that all was safe, he refolded it, tucked it deeper into his pocket, which fastened with a stud, then wheeled the racing bike out of the garage and down through the gate into the lane. He could tell that his father was watching him through the glass door of the porch, hoping, Andrew was sure, to see him fall off or mistreat the bicycle in some way.

Pagford lay below Andrew, slightly hazy in the cool spring sun, the air fresh and tangy. Andrew sensed the point at which Simon's eyes could no longer follow him; it felt as though pressure had been removed from his back.

Down the hill into Pagford he streaked, not touching the brakes; then he turned into Church Row. Approximately halfway along the street he slowed down and cycled decorously into the drive of the Walls' house, taking care to avoid Cubby's car.

"Hello, Andy," said Tessa, opening the front door to him.

"Hi, Mrs. Wall."

Andrew accepted the convention that Fats' parents were laughable. Tessa was plump and plain, her hairstyle was odd and her dress sense embarrassing, while Cubby was comically uptight; yet Andrew could not help but suspect that if the Walls had been his parents, he might have been tempted to like them. They were so civilized, so courteous. You never had the feeling, in their house, that the floor might suddenly give way and plunge you into chaos.

Fats was sitting on the bottom stair, putting on his trainers. A packet of loose tobacco was clearly visible, peeking out of the breast pocket of his jacket.

"Arf."

"Fats."

"D'you want to leave your father's bicycle in the garage, Andy?"

"Yeah, thanks, Mrs. Wall."

(She always, he reflected, said "your father," never "your dad." Andrew knew that Tessa detested Simon; it was one of the things that made him pleased to overlook the horrible shapeless clothes she wore, and the unflattering blunt-cut fringe.

Her antipathy dated from that horrific epoch-making occasion, years and years before, when a six-year-old Fats had come to spend Saturday afternoon at Hilltop House for the first time. Balancing precariously on top of a box in the garage, trying to retrieve a couple of old badminton racquets, the two boys had accidentally knocked down the contents of a rickety shelf.

Andrew remembered the tin of creosote falling, smashing onto the roof of the car and bursting open, and the terror that had engulfed him, and his inability to communicate to his giggling friend what they had brought upon themselves.

Simon had heard the crash. He ran out to the garage and advanced on them with his jaw jutting, making his low, moaning animal noise, before starting to roar threats of dire physical punishment, his fists clenched inches from their small, upturned faces.

Fats had wet himself. A stream of urine had spattered down the inside of his shorts onto the garage floor. Ruth, who had heard the yelling from the kitchen, had run from the house to intervene: "No, Si—Si, no—it was an accident." Fats was white and shaking; he wanted to go home straightaway; he wanted his mum.

Tessa had arrived, and Fats had run to her in his soaking shorts, sobbing. It was the only time in his life that Andrew had seen his father at a loss, backing down. Somehow Tessa had conveyed white-hot fury without raising her voice, without threatening, without hitting. She had written out a check and forced it into Simon's hand, while Ruth said, *"No, no, there's no need, there's no need."* Simon had followed her to her car, trying to laugh it all off; but Tessa had given him a look of contempt while loading the still-sobbing Fats into the passenger seat, and slammed the driver's door in Simon's smiling face. Andrew had seen his parents' expressions: Tessa was taking away with her, down the hill into the town, something that usually remained hidden in the house on top of the hill.)

Fats courted Simon these days. Whenever he came up to Hilltop

House, he went out of his way to make Simon laugh; and in return, Simon welcomed Fats' visits, enjoyed his crudest jokes, liked hearing about his antics. Still, when alone with Andrew, Fats concurred wholeheartedly that Simon was a Grade A, 24-karat cunt.

"I reckon she's a lezzer," said Fats, as they walked past the Old Vicarage, dark in the shadow of the Scots pine, with ivy covering its front.

"Your mum?" asked Andrew, barely listening, lost in his own thoughts.

"What?" yelped Fats, and Andrew saw that he was genuinely outraged. "Fuck off! Sukhvinder Jawanda."

"Oh, yeah. Right."

Andrew laughed, and so, a beat later, did Fats.

The bus into Yarvil was crowded; Andrew and Fats had to sit next to each other, rather than in two double seats, as they preferred. As they passed the end of Hope Street, Andrew glanced along it, but it was deserted. He had not run into Gaia outside school since the afternoon when they had both secured Saturday jobs at the Copper Kettle. The café would open the following weekend; he experienced waves of euphoria every time he thought of it.

"Si-Pie's election campaign on track, is it?" asked Fats, busy making roll-ups. One long leg was stuck out at an angle into the aisle of the bus; people were stepping over it rather than asking him to move. "Cubby's cacking it already, and he's only making his pamphlet."

"Yeah, he's busy," said Andrew, and he bore without flinching a silent eruption of panic in the pit of his stomach.

He thought of his parents at the kitchen table, as they had been, nightly, for the past week; of a box of stupid pamphlets Simon had had printed at work; of the list of talking points Ruth had helped Simon compile, which he used as he made telephone calls, every evening, to every person he knew within the electoral boundary. Simon did all of it with an air of immense effort. He was tightly wound at home, displaying heightened aggression towards his sons; he might have been shouldering a burden that they had shirked. The only topic of conversation at meals was the election, with Simon and Ruth speculating

237

about the forces ranged against Simon. They took it very personally that other candidates were standing for Barry Fairbrother's old seat, and seemed to assume that Colin Wall and Miles Mollison spent most of their time plotting together, staring up at Hilltop House, focused entirely on defeating the man who lived there.

Andrew checked his pocket again for the folded paper. He had not told Fats what he intended to do. He was afraid that Fats might broadcast it; Andrew was not sure how to impress upon his friend the necessity for absolute secrecy, how to remind Fats that the maniac who had made little boys piss themselves was still alive and well, and living in Andrew's house.

"Cubby's not too worried about Si-Pie," said Fats. "He thinks the big competition is Miles Mollison."

"Yeah," said Andrew. He had heard his parents discussing it. Both of them seemed to think that Shirley had betrayed them; that she ought to have forbidden her son from challenging Simon.

"This is a holy fucking crusade for Cubby, y'know," said Fats, rolling a cigarette between forefinger and thumb. "He's picking up the regimental flag for his fallen comrade. Ole Barry Fairbrother."

He poked strands of tobacco into the end of the roll-up with a match.

"Miles Mollison's wife's got gigantic tits," said Fats.

An elderly woman sitting in front of them turned her head to glare at Fats. Andrew began to laugh again.

"Humongous bouncing jubblies," Fats said loudly, into the scowling, crumpled face. "Great big juicy double-F mams."

She turned her red face slowly to face the front of the bus again. Andrew could barely breathe.

They got off the bus in the middle of Yarvil, near the precinct and main pedestrian-only shopping street, and wove their way through the shoppers, smoking Fats' roll-ups. Andrew had virtually no money left: Howard Mollison's wages would be very welcome.

The bright-orange sign of the Internet café seemed to blaze at Andrew from a distance, beckoning him on. He could not concentrate on what Fats was saying. *Are you going to?* he kept asking himself. *Are you going to?*

He did not know. His feet kept moving, and the sign was growing larger and larger, luring him, leering at him.

If I find out you've breathed a word about what's said in this house, I'll skin you alive.

But the alternative...the humiliation of having Simon show what he was to the world; the toll it would take on the family when, after weeks of anticipation and idiocy, he was defeated, as he must be. Then would come rage and spite, and a determination to make everybody else pay for his own lunatic decisions. Only the previous evening Ruth had said brightly, "The boys will go through Pagford and post your pamphlets for you." Andrew had seen, in his peripheral vision, Paul's look of horror and his attempt to make eye contact with his brother.

"I wanna go in here," mumbled Andrew, turning right.

They bought tickets with codes on them, and sat down at different computers, two occupied seats apart. The middle-aged man on Andrew's right stank of body odor and old fags, and kept sniffing.

Andrew logged onto the Internet, and typed in the name of the website: Pagford...Parish...Council...dot...co...dot...uk...

The home page bore the council arms in blue and white, and a picture of Pagford that had been taken from a point close to Hilltop House, with Pargetter Abbey silhouetted against the sky. The site, as Andrew already knew, from looking at it on a school computer, looked dated and amateurish. He had not dared go near it on his own laptop; his father might be immensely ignorant about the Internet, but Andrew did not rule out the possibility that Simon might find somebody at work who could help him investigate, once the thing was done...

Even in this bustling anonymous place, there was no avoiding the fact that today's date would be on the posting, or of pretending that he had not been in Yarvil when it happened; but Simon had never visited an Internet café in his life, and might not be aware that they existed.

The rapid contraction of Andrew's heart was painful. Swiftly, he scrolled down the message board, which did not seem to enjoy a lot of traffic. There were threads entitled: refuse collection — a Query and school catchment areas in Crampton and Little manning? Every tenth entry or so was a posting from the Administrator, attaching Minutes of the Last Council Meeting. Right at the bottom of the page was a thread entitled: Death of Cllr Barry Fairbrother. This had received 152 views and forty-three responses. Then, on the second page of the message board, he found what he hoped to find: a post from the dead man.

A couple of months previously, Andrew's computing set had been supervised by a young supply teacher. He had been trying to look cool, trying to get the class onside. He shouldn't have mentioned SQL injections at all, and Andrew was quite sure that he had not been the only one who went straight home and looked them up. He pulled out the piece of paper on which he had written the code he had researched in odd moments at school, and brought up the log-in page on the council website. Everything hinged on the premise that the site had been set up by an amateur a long time ago; that it had never been protected from the simplest of classical hacks.

Carefully, using only his index finger, he input the magic line of characters.

He read them through twice, making sure that every apostrophe was where it should be, hesitated for a second on the brink, his breathing shallow, then pressed return.

He gasped, as gleeful as a small child, and had to fight the urge to shout out or punch the air. He had penetrated the tin-pot site at his first attempt. There, on the screen in front of him, were Barry Fairbrother's user details: his name, his password, his entire profile.

Andrew smoothed out the magic paper he had kept under his pillow all week, and set to work. Typing up his next paragraph, with its many crossings out and reworkings, was a much more laborious process.

He had been trying for a style that was as impersonal and impenetrable as possible; for the dispassionate tone of a broadsheet journalist.

Aspiring Parish Councillor Simon Price hopes to stand on a platform of cutting wasteful council spending. Mr. Price

is certainly no stranger to keeping down costs, and should
be able to give the council the benefit of his many useful
contacts. He saves money at home by furnishing it with stolen
goods — most recently a PC — and he is the go-to man for
any cut-price printing jobs that may need doing for cash, once
senior management has gone home, at the Harcourt-Walsh
Printworks.

Andrew read the message through twice. He had been over it time
and again in his mind. There were many accusations he could have
leveled at Simon, but the court did not exist in which Andrew
could have laid the real charges against his father, in which he
would have presented as evidence memories of physical terror and
ritual humiliation. All he had were the many petty infractions of
the law of which he had heard Simon boast, and he had selected
these two specific examples—the stolen computer and the out-
of-hours printing jobs done on the sly—because both were firmly
connected to Simon's workplace. People at the printer's knew that
Simon did these things, and they could have talked to anybody:
their friends, their families.

His guts were juddering, the way they did when Simon truly lost
control and laid about anyone within reach. Seeing his betrayal in
black and white on the screen was terrifying.

"What the fuck are you doing?" asked Fats' quiet voice in
his ear.

The stinking, middle-aged man had gone; Fats had moved up;
he was reading what Andrew had written.

"Fucking hell," said Fats.

Andrew's mouth was dry. His hand lay quiescent on the mouse.

"How'd you get in?" Fats whispered.

"SQL injection," said Andrew. "It's all on the Net. Their security's shit."

Fats looked exhilarated; wildly impressed. Andrew was half
pleased, half scared, by the reaction.

"You've gotta keep this to—"

"Lemme do one about Cubby!"

"No!"

Andrew's hand on the mouse skidded away from Fats' reaching fingers. This ugly act of filial disloyalty had sprung from the primordial soup of anger, frustration and fear that had slopped inside him all his rational life, but he knew no better way to convey this to Fats than by saying, "I'm not just having a laugh."

He read the message through a third time, then added a title to the message. He could feel Fats' excitement beside him, as if they were having another porn session. Andrew was seized by a desire to impress further.

"Look," he said, and he changed Barry's username to The_ Ghost_of_Barry_Fairbrother.

Fats laughed loudly. Andrew's fingers twitched on the mouse. He rolled it sideways. Whether he would have gone through with it if Fats had not been watching, he would never know. With a single click, a new thread appeared at the top of the Pagford Parish Council message board: Simon Price Unfit to Stand for Council.

Outside on the pavement, they faced each other, breathless with laughter, slightly overawed by what had happened. Then Andrew borrowed Fats' matches, set fire to the piece of paper on which he had drafted the message, and watched it disintegrate into fragile black flakes, which drifted onto the dirty pavement and vanished under passing feet.

X

Andrew left Yarvil at half past three, to be sure of getting back to Hilltop House before five. Fats accompanied him to the bus stop and then, apparently on a whim, told Andrew that he thought he would stay in town for a bit, after all.

Fats had made a loose arrangement to meet Krystal in the shopping center. He strolled back towards the shops, thinking about what Andrew had done in the Internet café, and trying to disentangle his own reactions.

He had to admit that he was impressed; in fact, he felt somewhat upstaged. Andrew had thought the business through, and kept it to himself, and executed it efficiently: all of this was admirable. Fats experienced a twinge of pique that Andrew had formulated the plan without saying a word to him, and this led Fats to wonder whether, perhaps, he ought not to deplore the undercover nature of Andrew's attack on his father. Was there not something slippery and over-sophisticated about it; would it not have been more authentic to threaten Simon to his face or to take a swing at him?

Yes, Simon was a shit, but he was undoubtedly an authentic shit; he did what he wanted, when he wanted, without submitting to societal constraints or conventional morality. Fats asked himself whether his sympathies ought not to lie with Simon, whom he liked entertaining with crude, crass humor focused mainly on people making tits of themselves or suffering slapstick injuries. Fats often told himself that he would rather have Simon, with his volatility, his unpredictable picking of fights—a worthy opponent, an engaged adversary—than Cubby.

On the other hand, Fats had not forgotten the falling tin of creosote, Simon's brutish face and fists, the terrifying noise he had made, the sensation of hot wet piss running down his own legs, and (perhaps most shameful of all) his wholehearted, desperate yearning for Tessa to come and take him away to safety. Fats was not yet so invulnerable that he was unsympathetic to Andrew's desire for retribution.

So Fats came full circle: Andrew had done something daring, ingenious and potentially explosive in its consequences. Again Fats experienced a small pang of chagrin that it had not been he who had thought of it. He was trying to rid himself of his own acquired middle-class reliance on words, but it was difficult to forgo a sport at which he excelled, and as he trod the polished tiles of the shopping center forecourt, he found himself turning phrases that would blow Cubby's self-important pretensions apart and strip him naked before a jeering public...

He spotted Krystal among a small crowd of Fields kids, grouped around the benches in the middle of the thoroughfare between shops. Nikki, Leanne and Dane Tully were among them. Fats did not hesitate, nor appear to gather himself in the slightest, but continued to walk at the same speed, his hands in his pockets, into the battery of curious critical eyes, raking him from the top of his head to his trainers.

"All righ', Fatboy?" called Leanne.

"All right?" responded Fats. Leanne muttered something to Nikki, who cackled. Krystal was chewing gum energetically, color high in her cheeks, throwing back her hair so that her earrings danced, tugging up her tracksuit bottoms.

"All right?" Fats said to her, individually.

"Yeah," she said.

"Duz yer mum know yer out, Fats?" asked Nikki.

"Yeah, she brought me," said Fats calmly, into the greedy silence. "She's waiting outside in the car; she says I can have a quick shag before we go home for tea."

They all burst out laughing except Krystal, who squealed, "Fuck off, you cheeky bastard!" but looked gratified.

"You smokin' rollies?" grunted Dane Tully, his eyes on Fats' breast pocket. He had a large black scab on his lip.

"Yeah," said Fats.

"Me uncle smokes them," said Dane. "Knackered his fuckin' lungs."

He picked idly at the scab.

"Where're you two goin'?" asked Leanne, squinting from Fats to Krystal.

"Dunno," said Krystal, chewing her gum, glancing sideways at Fats.

He did not enlighten either of them, but indicated the exit of the shopping center with a jerk of his thumb.

"Laters," Krystal said loudly to the rest.

Fats gave them a careless half-raised hand in farewell and walked away, Krystal striding along beside him. He heard more laughter in their wake, but did not care. He knew that he had acquitted himself well.

"Where're we goin'?" asked Krystal.

"Dunno," said Fats. "Where d'you usually go?"

She shrugged, walking and chewing. They left the shopping center and walked on down the high street. They were some distance from the recreation ground, where they had previously gone to find privacy.

"Didjer mum really drop yeh?" Krystal asked.

"Course she bloody didn't. I got the bus in, didn't I?"

Krystal accepted the rebuke without rancor, glancing sideways into the shop windows at their paired reflections. Stringy and strange, Fats was a school celebrity. Even Dane thought he was funny.

"He's on'y usin' yeh, yeh stupid bitch," Ashlee Mellor had spat at her, three days ago, on the corner of Foley Road, "because yer a fuckin' whore, like yer mum."

Ashlee had been a member of Krystal's gang until the two of them had clashed over another boy. Ashlee was notoriously not quite right in the head; she was prone to outbursts of rage and tears, and divided most of her time between learning support and guidance when at Winterdown. If further proof were needed of her inability to think through consequences, she had challenged Krystal on her home turf, where Krystal had backup and she had none. Nikki, Jemma and Leanne had helped corner and hold Ashlee, and Krystal had pummeled and slapped her everywhere she could reach, until her knuckles came away bloody from the other girl's mouth.

Krystal was not worried about repercussions.

"Soft as shite an' twice as runny," she said of Ashlee and her family.

But Ashlee's words had stung a tender, infected place in Krystal's psyche, so it had been balm to her when Fats had sought her out at school the next day and asked her, for the first time, to meet him over the weekend. She had told Nikki and Leanne immediately that she was going out with Fats Wall on Saturday, and had been gratified by their looks of surprise. And to cap it all, he had turned up when he had said he would (or within half an hour of it) right in front of all her mates, and walked away with her. It was like they were properly going out.

"So what've you been up to?" Fats asked, after they had walked fifty yards in silence, back past the Internet café. He knew a conventional need to keep some form of communication going, even while he wondered whether they would find a private place before the rec, a half-hour's walk away. He wanted to screw her while they were both stoned; he was curious to know what that was like.

"I bin ter see my Nana in hospital this mornin', she's 'ad a stroke," said Krystal.

Nana Cath had not tried to speak this time, but Krystal thought she had known that she was there. As Krystal had expected, Terri was refusing to visit, so Krystal had sat beside the bed on her own for an hour until it was time to leave for the precinct.

Fats was curious about the minutiae of Krystal's life; but only insofar as she was an entry point to the real life of the Fields. Particulars such as hospital visits were of no interest to him.

"An'," Krystal added, with an irrepressible spurt of pride, "I've gave an interview to the paper."

"What?" said Fats, startled. "Why?"

"Jus' about the Fields," said Krystal. "What it's like growin' up there."

(The journalist had found her at home at last, and when Terri had given her grudging permission, taken her to a café to talk. She had kept asking her whether being at St. Thomas's had helped Krystal, whether it had changed her life in any way. She had seemed a little impatient and frustrated by Krystal's answers.

"How are your marks at school?" she had said, and Krystal had been evasive and defensive.

"Mr. Fairbrother said that he thought it broadened your horizons."

Krystal did not know what to say about horizons. When she thought of St. Thomas's, it was of her delight in the playing field with the big chestnut tree, which rained enormous glossy conkers on them every year; she had never seen conkers before she went to St. Thomas's. She had liked the uniform at first, liked looking the same as everybody else. She had been excited to see her great-grandfather's name on the war memorial in the middle of the Square: *Pte. Samuel Weedon.* Only one other boy had his surname on the war memorial, and that was a farmer's son, who had been able to drive a tractor at nine, and who had once brought a lamb into class for show and tell. Krystal had never forgotten the sensation of the lamb's fleece under her hand. When she told Nana Cath about it, Nana Cath had said that their family had been farm laborers once.

Krystal had loved the river, green and lush, where they had gone for nature walks. Best of all had been rounders and athletics. She was always first to be picked for any kind of sporting team, and she had delighted in the groan that went up from the other team whenever she was chosen. And she thought sometimes of the special teachers she had been given, especially Miss Jameson, who had been young and trendy, with long blond hair. Krystal had always imagined Anne-Marie to be a little bit like Miss Jameson.

Then there were snippets of information that Krystal had retained in vivid, accurate detail. Volcanoes: they were made by plates shifting in the ground; they had made model ones and filled them with bicarbonate of soda and washing-up liquid, and they had erupted onto plastic trays. Krystal had loved that. She knew about Vikings too: they had longships and horned helmets, though she had forgotten when they arrived in Britain, or why.

But other memories of St. Thomas's included the muttered comments made about her by little girls in her class, one or two of whom she had slapped. When Social Services had allowed her to go back to her mother, her uniform became so tight, short and grubby that letters were sent from school, and Nana Cath and Terri had a big row. The other girls at school had not wanted her in their groups, except for their rounders teams. She could still remember Lexie Mollison handing everyone in the class a little pink envelope containing a party invitation, and walking past Krystal with—as Krystal remembered it—her nose in the air.

Only a couple of people had asked her to parties. She wondered whether Fats or his mother remembered that she had once attended a birthday party at their house. The whole class had been invited, and Nana Cath had bought Krystal a party dress. So she knew that Fats' huge back garden had a pond and a swing and an apple tree. They had eaten jelly and had sack races. Tessa had told Krystal off because, trying desperately hard to win a plastic medal, she had pushed other children out of the way. One of them had had a nosebleed.

"You enjoyed St. Thomas's, though, did you?" the journalist had asked.

"Yeah," said Krystal, but she knew that she had not conveyed what Mr. Fairbrother had wanted her to convey, and wished he could have been there with her to help. "Yeah, I enjoyed it.")

"How come they wanted to talk to you about the Fields?" asked Fats.

"It were Mr. Fairbrother's idea," said Krystal.

After another few minutes, Fats asked, "D'you smoke?"

"Wha', like spliffs? Yeah, I dunnit with Dane."

"I've got some on me," said Fats.

"Get it off Skye Kirby, didja?" asked Krystal. He wondered whether he imagined a trace of amusement in her voice; because Skye was the soft, safe option, the place the middle-class kids went. If so, Fats liked her authentic derision.

"Where d'you get yours, then?" he asked, interested now.

"I dunno, it were Dane's," she said.

"From Obbo?" suggested Fats.

"Tha' fuckin' tosser."

"What's wrong with him?"

But Krystal had no words for what was wrong with Obbo; and even if she had, she would not have wanted to talk about him. Obbo made her flesh crawl; sometimes he came round and shot up with Terri; at other times he fucked her, and Krystal would meet him on the stairs, tugging up his filthy fly, smiling at her through his bottle-bottom glasses. Often Obbo had little jobs to offer Terri, like hiding the computers, or giving strangers a place to stay for a night, or agreeing to perform services of which Krystal did not know the nature, but which took her mother out of the house for hours.

Krystal had had a nightmare, not long ago, in which her mother had become stretched, spread and tied on a kind of frame; she was mostly a vast, gaping hole, like a giant, raw, plucked chicken; and in the dream, Obbo was walking in and out of this cavernous interior, and fiddling with things in there, while Terri's tiny head was frightened and grim. Krystal had woken up feeling sick and angry and disgusted.

"'E's a fucker," said Krystal.

"Is he a tall bloke with a shaved head and tattoos all up the back of his neck?" asked Fats, who had truanted for a second time that week, and sat on a wall for an hour in the Fields, watching. The bald man had interested him, fiddling around in the back of an old white van.

"Nah, tha's Pikey Pritchard," said Krystal, "if yeh saw him down Tarpen Road."

"What does he do?"

"I dunno," said Krystal. "Ask Dane, 'e's mates with Pikey's brother."

But she liked his genuine interest; he had never shown this much inclination to talk to her before.

"Pikey's on probation."

"What for?"

"He glassed a bloke down the Cross Keys."

"Why?"

"'Ow the fuck do I know? I weren't there," said Krystal.

She was happy, which always made her cocky. Setting aside her worry about Nana Cath (who was, after all, still alive, so might yet recover), it had been a good couple of weeks. Terri was adhering to the Bellchapel regime again, and Krystal was making sure that Robbie went to nursery. His bottom had mostly healed over. The social worker seemed as pleased as her sort ever did. Krystal had been to school every day too, though she had not attended either her Monday or her Wednesday morning guidance sessions with Tessa. She did not know why. Sometimes you got out of the habit.

She glanced sideways at Fats again. She had never once thought of fancying him; not until he had targeted her at the disco in the drama hall. Everyone knew Fats; some of his jokes were passed around like funny stuff that happened on the telly. (Krystal pretended to everyone that they had a television at home. She watched enough at friends' houses, and at Nana Cath's, to be able to bluff her way through. "Yeah, it were shit, weren't it?" "I know, I nearly pissed meself," she would say, when the others talked about programs they had seen.)

Fats was imagining how it would feel to be glassed, how the jagged shard would slice through the tender flesh on his face; he could feel the searing nerves and the sting of the air against his ripped skin; the warm wetness as blood gushed. He felt a tickly oversensitivity in the skin around his mouth, as if it was already scarred.

"Is he still carrying a blade, Dane?" he asked.

"'Ow d'you know 'e's gotta blade?" demanded Krystal.

"He threatened Kevin Cooper with it."

"Oh, yeah," Krystal conceded. "Cooper's a twat, innee?"

"Yeah, he is," said Fats.

"Dane's on'y carryin' 'cos o' the Riordon brothers," said Krystal.

Fats liked the matter-of-factness of Krystal's tone; her acceptance of the need for a knife, because there was a grudge and a likelihood of violence. This was the raw reality of life; these were things that actually mattered…before Arf had arrived at the house that day, Cubby had been importuning Tessa to give him an opinion on whether his campaign leaflet should be printed on yellow or white paper…

"What about in there?" suggested Fats, after a while.

To their right was a long stone wall, its gates open to reveal a glimpse of green and stone.

"Yeah, all righ'," said Krystal. She had been in the cemetery once before, with Nikki and Leanne; they had sat on a grave and split a couple of cans, a little self-conscious about what they were doing, until a woman had shouted at them and called them names. Leanne had lobbed an empty can back at the woman as they left.

But it was too exposed, Fats thought, as he and Krystal walked up the broad concreted walkway between the graves: green and flat, the headstones offering virtually no cover. Then he saw barberry hedges along the wall on the far side. He cut a path right across the cemetery, and Krystal followed, hands in her pockets, as they picked their way between rectangular gravel beds, headstones cracked and illegible. It was a large cemetery, wide and well tended. Gradually they reached the newer graves of highly polished black marble with gold lettering, places where fresh flowers had been laid for the recently dead.

To Lyndsey Kyle, September 15 1960–March 26 2008,
Sleep Tight Mum.

"Yeah, we'll be all right in there," said Fats, eyeing the dark gap between the prickly, yellow-flowered bushes and the cemetery wall.

They crawled into the damp shadows, onto the earth, their backs against the cold wall. The headstones marched away from them between the bushes' trunks, but there were no human forms among them. Fats skinned up expertly, hoping that Krystal was watching, and was impressed.

But she was gazing out under the canopy of glossy dark leaves, thinking about Anne-Marie, who (Aunt Cheryl had told her) had come to visit Nana Cath on Thursday. If only she had skipped school and gone at the same time, they could have met at last. She had fantasized, many times, about how she would meet Anne-Marie, and say to her, "I'm yer sister." Anne-Marie, in these fantasies, was always delighted, and they saw each other all the time after that, and eventually Anne-Marie suggested that Krystal move in. The imaginary Anne-Marie had a house like Nana Cath's, neat and clean, except that it was much more modern. Lately, in her fantasies, Krystal had added a sweet little pink baby in a frilly crib.

"There you go," said Fats, handing Krystal the joint. She inhaled, held the smoke in her lungs for a few seconds, and her expression softened into dreaminess as the cannabis worked its magic.

"You ain' got brothers an' sisters," she asked, "'ave yeh?"

"No," said Fats, checking his pocket for the condoms he had brought.

Krystal handed back the joint, her head swimming pleasantly. Fats took an enormous drag and blew smoke rings.

"I'm adopted," he said, after a while.

Krystal goggled at Fats.

"Are yeh adopted, are yeh?"

With the senses a little muffled and cushioned, confidences peeled easily away, everything became easy.

"My sister wuz adopted," said Krystal, marveling at the coincidence, delighted to talk about Anne-Marie.

"Yeah, I probably come from a family like yours," said Fats.

But Krystal was not listening; she wanted to talk.

"I gottan older sister an' an older brother, Liam, but they wuz taken away before I wuz born."

"Why?" asked Fats.

He was suddenly paying close attention.

"Me mum was with Ritchie Adams then," said Krystal. She took a deep drag on the joint and blew out the smoke in a long thin jet. "He's a proper psycho. He's doin' life. He killed a bloke. Proper violent to Mum an' the kids, an' then John an' Sue came an' took 'em, and the social got involved an' it ended up John an' Sue kept 'em."

She drew on the joint again, considering this period of her prelife, which was doused in blood, fury and darkness. She had heard things about Ritchie Adams, mainly from her aunt Cheryl. He had stubbed out cigarettes on one-year-old Anne-Marie's arms, and kicked her until her ribs cracked. He had broken Terri's face; her left cheekbone was still receded, compared to the right. Terri's addiction had spiraled catastrophically. Aunt Cheryl was matter-of-fact about the decision to remove the two brutalized, neglected children from their parents.

"It 'ad to 'appen," said Cheryl.

John and Sue were distant, childless relatives. Krystal had never known where or how they fitted in her complex family tree, or how they had effected what, to hear Terri tell it, sounded like kidnap. After much wrangling with the authorities, they had been allowed to adopt the children. Terri, who had remained with Ritchie until his arrest, never saw Anne-Marie or Liam, for reasons Krystal did not entirely understand; the whole story was clotted and festering with hatred and unforgivable things said and threatened, restraining orders, lots more social workers.

"Who's your dad, then?" asked Fats.

"Banger," said Krystal. She struggled to recall his real name. "Barry," she muttered, though she had a suspicion that was not right. "Barry Coates. O'ny I uses me mum's name, Weedon."

The memory of the dead young man who had overdosed in Terri's bathroom floated back to her through the sweet, heavy smoke. She passed the joint back to Fats and leaned her head against the stone wall, looking up at the sliver of sky, mottled with dark leaves.

Fats was thinking about Ritchie Adams, who had killed a man, and considering the possibility that his own biological father was in prison somewhere too; tattooed, like Pikey, spare and muscled. He mentally compared Cubby with this strong, hard authentic man. Fats knew that he had been parted from his biological mother as a very small baby, because there were pictures of Tessa holding him, frail and birdlike, with a woolly white cap on his head. He had been premature. Tessa had told him a few things, though he had never asked. His real mother had been very young when she had him, he knew that. Perhaps she had been like Krystal; the school bike...

He was properly stoned now. He put his hand behind Krystal's neck and pulled her towards him, kissing her, sticking his tongue into her mouth. With his other hand, he groped for her breast. His brain was fuzzy and his limbs were heavy; even his sense of touch seemed affected. He fumbled a little to get his hand inside her T-shirt, to force it under her bra. Her mouth was hot and tasted of tobacco and dope; her lips were dry and chapped. His excitement was slightly blunted; he seemed to be receiving all sensory information through an invisible blanket. It took longer than the last time to pry her clothes loose from her body, and the condom was difficult, because his fingers had become stiff and slow; then he accidentally placed his elbow, with all his weight behind it, on her soft fleshy underarm and she shrieked in pain.

She was drier than before; he forced his way inside her, determined to accomplish what he had come for. Time was gluelike and slow, but he could hear his own rapid breathing, and it made him edgy, because he imagined someone else, crouching in the dark space with them, watching, panting in his ear. Krystal moaned a little. With her head thrown back, her nose became broad and snoutlike. He pushed up her T-shirt to look at the smooth white breasts, jiggling a little, beneath the loose constraint of the undone bra. He came without expecting it, and his own grunt of satisfaction seemed to belong to the crouching eavesdropper.

He rolled off her, peeled off the condom and threw it aside, then zipped himself up, feeling jittery, looking around to check that they were definitely alone. Krystal was dragging her pants up with one hand, pulling down her T-shirt with the other, reaching behind herself to do up her bra.

It had become cloudy and darker while they had sat behind the bushes. There was a distant buzzing in Fats' ears; he was very hungry; his brain was working slowly, while his ears were hypersensitive. The fear that they had been watched, perhaps over the top of the wall behind them, would not leave him. He wanted to go.

"Let's…" he muttered, and without waiting for her, he crawled out between the bushes and got to his feet, brushing himself down. There was an elderly couple a hundred yards away, crouching at a graveside. He wanted to get right away from phantom eyes that might, or might not, have watched him screw Krystal Weedon; but at the same time, the process of finding the right bus stop and getting on the bus to Pagford seemed almost unbearably onerous. He wished he could simply be transported, this instant, to his attic bedroom.

Krystal had staggered out behind him. She was pulling down the bottom of her T-shirt and staring down at the grassy ground at her feet.

"Fuck," she mumbled.

"What?" said Fats. "C'mon, let's go."

"'S Mr. Fairbrother," she said, without moving.

"What?"

She pointed at the mound in front of them. There was no head-stone yet; but fresh flowers lay all along it.

"See?" she said, crouching over and indicating cards stapled to the cellophane. "Tha' sez Fairbrother." She recognized the name easily from all those letters that had gone home from school, asking her mother to give permission for her to go away on the minibus. "'Ter Barry,'" she read carefully, "an' this sez, 'Ter Dad,'" she sounded out the words slowly, "'from…'"

But Niamh and Siobhan's names defeated her.

"So?" demanded Fats; but in truth, the news gave him the creeps. That wickerwork coffin lay feet below them, and inside it the short body and cheery face of Cubby's dearest friend, so often seen in their house, rotting away in the earth. *The Ghost of Barry Fairbrother*...he was unnerved. It seemed like some kind of retribution.

"C'mon," he said, but Krystal did not move. "What's the matter?"

"I rowed for 'im, di'n I?" snapped Krystal.

"Oh, yeah."

Fats was fidgeting like a restive horse, edging backwards.

Krystal stared down at the mound, hugging herself. She felt empty, sad and dirty. She wished they had not done it there, so close to Mr. Fairbrother. She was cold. Unlike Fats, she had no jacket.

"C'mon," said Fats again.

She followed him out of the cemetery, and they did not speak to each other once. Krystal was thinking about Mr. Fairbrother. He had always called her "Krys," which nobody else had ever done. She had liked being Krys. He had been a good laugh. She wanted to cry.

Fats was thinking about how he would be able to work this into a funny story for Andrew, about being stoned and fucking Krystal and getting paranoid and thinking they were being watched and crawling out almost onto old Barry Fairbrother's grave. But it did not feel funny yet; not yet.

Part Three

Duplicity

7.25 A resolution should not deal with more than
one subject…Disregard of this rule usually
leads to confused discussion and may lead to
confused action…

Charles Arnold-Baker
Local Council Administration,
Seventh Edition

I

"...ran out of here, screaming blue murder, calling her a Paki bitch—and now the paper's called for a comment, because she's..."

Parminder heard the receptionist's voice, barely louder than a whisper, as she passed the door of the staff meeting room, which was ajar. One swift light step, and Parminder had pulled it open to reveal one of the receptionists and the practice nurse in close proximity. Both jumped and spun round.

"Doct' Jawan—"

"You understand the confidentiality agreement you signed when you took this job, don't you, Karen?"

The receptionist looked aghast.

"Yeah, I—I wasn't—Laura already—I was coming to give you this note. The *Yarvil and District Gazette*'s rung. Mrs. Weedon's died and one of her granddaughters is saying—"

"And are those for me?" asked Parminder coldly, pointing at the patient records in Karen's hand.

"Oh—yeah," said Karen, flustered. "He wanted to see Dr. Crawford, but—"

"You'd better get back to the front desk."

Parminder took the patient records and strode back out to reception, fuming. Once there, and facing the patients, she realized that she did not know whom to call, and glanced down at the folder in her hand.

"Mr.—Mr. Mollison."

Howard heaved himself up, smiling, and walked toward her with

259

his familiar rocking gait. Dislike rose like bile in Parminder's throat. She turned and walked back to her surgery, Howard following her.

"All well with Parminder?" he asked, as he closed her door and settled himself, without invitation, on the patient's chair.

It was his habitual greeting, but today it felt like a taunt.

"What's the problem?" she asked brusquely.

"Bit of an irritation," he said. "Just here. Need a cream, or something."

He tugged his shirt out of his trousers and lifted it a few inches. Parminder saw an angry red patch of skin at the edge of the fold where his stomach spilled out over his upper legs.

"You'll need to take your shirt off," she said.

"It's only here that's itching."

"I need to see the whole area."

He sighed and got to his feet. As he unbuttoned his shirt he said, "Did you get the agenda I sent through this morning?"

"No, I haven't checked emails today."

This was a lie. Parminder had read his agenda and was furious about it, but this was not the moment to tell him so. She resented his trying to bring council business into her surgery, his way of reminding her that there was a place where she was his subordinate, even if here, in this room, she could order him to strip.

"Could you, please — I need to look under..."

He hoisted the great apron of flesh upwards; the upper legs of his trousers were revealed, and finally the waistband. With his arms full of his own fat he smiled down at her. She drew her chair nearer, her head level with his belt.

An ugly scaly rash had spread in the hidden crease of Howard's belly: a bright scalded red, it stretched from one side to the other of his torso like a huge, smeared smile. A whiff of rotting meat reached her nostrils.

"Intertrigo," she said, "and lichen simplex there, where you've scratched. All right, you can put your shirt back on."

He dropped his belly and reached for his shirt, unfazed.

"You'll see I've put the Bellchapel building on the agenda. It's generating a bit of press interest at the moment."

She was tapping something into the computer, and did not reply.

"*Yarvil and District Gazette*," Howard said. "I'm doing them an article. Both sides," he said, buttoning up his shirt, "of the question."

She was trying not to listen to him, but the sound of the newspaper's name caused the knot in her stomach to tighten.

"When did you last have your blood pressure done, Howard? I'm not seeing a test in the last six months."

"It'll be fine. I'm on medication for it."

"We should check, though. As you're here."

He sighed again, and laboriously rolled up his sleeve.

"They'll be printing Barry's article before mine," he said. "You know he sent them an article? About the Fields?"

"Yes," she said, against her own better judgment.

"Haven't got a copy, have you? So I don't duplicate anything he's said?"

Her fingers trembled a little on the cuff. It would not meet around Howard's arm. She unfastened it and got up to fetch a bigger one.

"No," she said, her back to him. "I never saw it."

He watched her work the pump, and observed the pressure dial with the indulgent smile of a man observing some pagan ritual.

"Too high," she told him, as the needle registered one hundred and seventy over a hundred.

"I'm on pills for it," he said, scratching where the cuff had been, and letting down his sleeve. "Dr. Crawford seems happy."

She scanned the list of his medications onscreen.

"You're on amlodipine and bendroflumethiazide for your blood pressure, yes? And simvastatin for your heart...no beta-blocker..."

"Because of my asthma," said Howard, tweaking his sleeve straight.

"...right...and aspirin." She turned to face him. "Howard, your weight is the single biggest factor in all of your health problems. Have you ever been referred to the nutritionist?"

"I've run a deli for thirty-five years," he said, still smiling. "I don't need teaching about food."

"A few lifestyle changes could make a big difference. If you were able to lose..."

With the ghost of a wink, he said comfortably, "Keep it simple. All I need is cream for the itch."

Venting her temper on the keyboard, Parminder banged out prescriptions for antifungal and steroid creams, and when they were printed, handed them to Howard without another word.

"Thank you kindly," he said, as he heaved himself out of the chair, "and a very good day to you."

II

"Wha' *d'you* wan'?"

Terri Weedon's shrunken body was dwarfed by her own doorway. She put clawlike hands on either jamb, trying to make herself more imposing, barring the entrance. It was eight in the morning; Krystal had just left with Robbie.

"Wanna talk ter yeh," said her sister. Broad and mannish in her white vest and tracksuit bottoms, Cheryl sucked on a cigarette and squinted at Terri through the smoke. "Nana Cath's died," she said.

"Wha'?"

"Nana Cath's died," repeated Cheryl loudly. "Like you fuckin' care."

But Terri had heard the first time. The news had hit her so hard in the guts that she had asked to hear it again out of confusion.

"Are you blasted?" demanded Cheryl, glaring into the taut and empty face.

"Fuck off. No, I ain't."

It was the truth. Terri had not used that morning; she had not used for three weeks. She took no pride in it; there was no star chart pinned up in the kitchen; she had managed longer than this before, months, even. Obbo had been away for the past fortnight, so it had been easier. But her works were still in the old biscuit tin, and the craving burned like an eternal flame inside her frail body.

"She died yesterday. Danielle on'y fuckin' bothered to lemme know this mornin'," said Cheryl. "An' I were gonna go up the 'ospital an' see 'er again today. Danielle's after the 'ouse. Nana Cath's 'ouse. Greedy bitch."

Terri had not been inside the little terraced house on Hope Street for a long time, but when Cheryl spoke she saw, very vividly, the knickknacks on the sideboard and the net curtains. She imagined Danielle there, pocketing things, ferreting in cupboards.

"Funeral's Tuesday at nine, up the crematorium."

"Right," said Terri.

"It's our 'ouse as much as Danielle's," said Cheryl. "I'll tell 'er we wan' our share. Shall I?"

"Yeah," said Terri.

She watched until Cheryl's canary hair and tattoos had vanished around the corner, then retreated inside.

Nana Cath dead. They had not spoken for a long time. *I'm washin' my 'ands of yeh. I've 'ad enough, Terri, I've 'ad it.* She had never stopped seeing Krystal, though. Krystal had become her blue-eyed girl. She had been to watch Krystal row in her stupid boat races. She had said Krystal's name on her deathbed, not Terri's.

Fine, then, you old bitch. Like I care. Too late now.

Tight-chested and trembling, Terri moved through her stinking kitchen in search of cigarettes, but really craving the spoon, the flame and the needle.

Too late, now, to say to the old lady what she ought to have said. Too late, now, to become again her Terri-Baby. *Big girls don't cry... big girls don't cry...*It had been years before she had realized that the song Nana Cath had sung her, in her rasping smoker's voice, was really "Sherry Baby."

Terri's hands scuttled like vermin through the debris on the work tops, searching for fag packets, ripping them apart, finding them all empty. Krystal had probably had the last of them; she was a greedy little cow, just like Danielle, riffling through Nana Cath's possessions, trying to keep her death quiet from the rest of them.

There was a long stub lying on a greasy plate; Terri wiped it off on her T-shirt and lit it on the gas cooker. Inside her head, she heard her own eleven-year-old voice.

I wish you was my mummy.

She did not want to remember. She leaned up against the sink, smoking, trying to look forward, to imagine the clash that was coming between her two older sisters. Nobody messed with Cheryl and Shane: they were both handy with their fists, and Shane had put burning rags through some poor bastard's letter box not so long ago; it was why he'd done his last stretch, and he would still be inside if the house had not been empty at the time. But Danielle had weapons Cheryl did not: money and her own home, and a landline. She knew official people and how to talk to them. She was the kind that had spare keys, and mysterious bits of paperwork.

Yet Terri doubted that Danielle would get the house, even with her secret weapons. There were more than just the three of them; Nana Cath had had loads of grandchildren and great-grandchildren. After Terri had been taken into care, her father had had more kids. Nine in total, Cheryl reckoned, to five different mothers. Terri had never met her half-siblings, but Krystal had told her that Nana Cath saw them.

"Yeah?" she had retorted. "I hope they rob her blind, the stupid old bitch."

So she saw the rest of the family, but they weren't exactly angels, from all that Terri had heard. It was only she, who had once been Terri-Baby, whom Nana Cath had cut adrift forever.

When you were straight, evil thoughts and memories came pouring up out of the darkness inside you; buzzing black flies clinging to the insides of your skull.

I wish you was my mummy.

In the vest top that Terri was wearing today, her scarred arm, neck and upper back were fully exposed, swirled into unnatural folds and creases like melted ice cream. She had spent six weeks in the burns unit of South West General when she was eleven.

("How did it happen, love?" asked the mother of the child in the next bed.

Her father had thrown a pan of burning chip fat at her. Her Human League T-shirt had caught fire.

"'Naccident," Terri muttered. It was what she had told everyone, including the social worker and the nurses. She would no sooner have shopped her father than chosen to burn alive.

Her mother had walked out shortly after Terri's eleventh birthday, leaving all three daughters behind. Danielle and Cheryl had moved in with their boyfriends' families within days. Terri had been the only one left, trying to make chips for her father, clinging to the hope that her mother would come back. Even through the agony and the terror of those first days and nights in the hospital, she had been glad it had happened, because she was sure that her mum would hear about it and come and get her. Every time there was movement at the end of the ward, Terri's heart would leap.

But in six long weeks of pain and loneliness, the only visitor had been Nana Cath. Through quiet afternoons and evenings, Nana Cath had come to sit beside her granddaughter, reminding her to say thank you to the nurses, grim-faced and strict, yet leaking unexpected tenderness.

She brought Terri a cheap plastic doll in a shiny black mac, but when Terri undressed her, she had nothing on underneath.

"She's got no knickers, Nana."

And Nana Cath had giggled. Nana Cath never giggled.

I wish you was my mummy.

She had wanted Nana Cath to take her home. She had asked her to, and Nana Cath had agreed. Sometimes Terri thought that those weeks in hospital had been the happiest of her life, even with the pain. It had been so safe, and people had been kind to her and looked after her. She had thought that she was going home with Nana Cath, to the house with the pretty net curtains, and not back to her father; not back to the bedroom door flying open in the night, banging off the David Essex poster Cheryl had left behind, and her father with his hand on his fly, approaching the bed where she begged him not to…)

The adult Terri threw the smoking filter of the cigarette stub down onto the kitchen floor and strode to her front door. She needed more than nicotine. Down the path and along the street she marched, walking in the same direction as Cheryl. Out of the corner of her eye she saw them, two of her neighbors chatting on the pavement, watching her go by. *Like a fucking picture? It'll last longer.* Terri knew that she was a perennial subject of gossip; she knew what they said about her; they shouted it after her sometimes. The stuck-up bitch next door was forever whining to the council about the state of Terri's garden. *Fuck them, fuck them, fuck them…*

She was jogging along, trying to outrun the memories.

You don't even know who the father is, do yeh, yer whore? I'm washin' my 'ands of yeh, Terri, I've 'ad enough.

That had been the last time they had ever spoken, and Nana Cath had called her what everyone else called her, and Terri had responded in kind.

Fuck you, then, you miserable old cow, fuck you.

She had never said, "You let me down, Nana Cath." She had never said, "Why didn't you keep me?" She had never said, "I loved you more than anyone, Nana Cath."

She hoped to God Obbo was back. He was supposed to be back today; today or tomorrow. She had to have some. She had to.

"All righ', Terri?"

"Seen Obbo?" she asked the boy who was smoking and drinking on the wall outside the off license. The scars on her back felt as though they were burning again.

He shook his head, chewing, leering at her. She hurried on. Nagging thoughts of the social worker, of Krystal, of Robbie: more buzzing flies, but they were like the staring neighbors, judges all; they did not understand the terrible urgency of her need.

(Nana Cath had collected her from the hospital and taken her home to the spare room. It had been the cleanest, prettiest room Terri had ever slept in. On each of the three evenings she had spent there, she had sat up in bed after Nana Cath had kissed her good night, and rearranged the ornaments beside her on the windowsill. There had been a tinkling bunch of glass flowers in a glass vase, a plastic pink paperweight with a shell in it and Terri's favorite, a rearing pottery horse with a silly smile on its face.

"I like horses," she had told Nana Cath.

There had been a school trip to the agricultural show, in the days before Terri's mother had left. The class had met a gigantic black Shire covered in horse brasses. She was the only one brave enough to stroke it. The smell had intoxicated her. She had hugged its column of a leg, ending in the massive feathered white hoof, and felt the living flesh beneath the hair, while her teacher said, "Careful, Terri, careful!" and the old man with the horse had smiled at her and told her it was quite safe, Samson wouldn't hurt a nice little girl like her.

The pottery horse was a different color: yellow with a black mane and tail.

"You can 'ave it," Nana Cath told her, and Terri had known true ecstasy.

But on the fourth morning her father had arrived.

"You're comin' home," he had said, and the look on his face had terrified her. "You're not stayin' with that fuckin' grassin' old cow. No, you ain't. No, you ain't, you little bitch."

Nana Cath was as frightened as Terri.

"Mikey, no," she kept bleating. Some of the neighbors were peering through the windows. Nana Cath had Terri by one arm, and her father had the other.

"You're coming home with me!"

He blacked Nana Cath's eye. He dragged Terri into his car. When he got her back to the house, he beat and kicked every bit of her he could reach.)

"Seen Obbo?" Terri shouted at Obbo's neighbor, from fifty yards away. "Is 'e back?"

"I dunno," said the woman, turning away.

(When Michael was not beating Terri, he was doing the other things to her, the things she could not talk about. Nana Cath did not come anymore. Terri ran away at thirteen, but not to Nana Cath's; she did not want her father to find her. They caught her anyway, and put her into care.)

Terri thumped on Obbo's door and waited. She tried again, but nobody came. She sank onto the doorstep, shaking, and began to cry.

Two truanting Winterdown girls glanced at her as they passed.

"Tha's Krystal Weedon's mum," one of them said loudly.

"The prozzie?" the other replied at the top of her voice.

Terri could not muster the strength to swear at them, because she was crying so hard. Snorting and giggling, the girls strode out of sight.

"Whore!" one of them called back from the end of the street.

III

Gavin could have invited Mary into his office to discuss the most recent exchange of letters with the insurance company, but decided to visit her at home instead. He had kept the late afternoon free of appointments, on the off-chance that she might ask him to stay for something to eat; she was a fantastic cook.

His instinctive shying away from her naked grief had been dissipated by regular contact. He had always liked Mary, but Barry had eclipsed her in company. Not that she ever appeared to dislike her supporting role; on the contrary, she had seemed delighted to beautify the background, happy laughing at Barry's jokes, happy simply to be with him.

Gavin doubted that Kay had ever been happy to play second fiddle in her life. Crashing the gears as he drove up Church Row, he thought that Kay would have been outraged by any suggestion that she modify her behavior or suppress her opinions for the sake of her partner's enjoyment, his happiness or his self-esteem.

He did not think that he had ever been unhappier in a relationship than he was now. Even in the death throes of the affair with Lisa, there had been temporary truces, laughs, sudden poignant reminders of better times. The situation with Kay was like war. Sometimes he forgot that there was supposed to be any affection between them; did she even like him?

They had had their worst-ever argument by telephone on the

morning after Miles and Samantha's dinner party. Eventually, Kay had slammed down the receiver, cutting Gavin off. For a full twenty-four hours he had believed that their relationship was at an end, and although this was what he wanted he had experienced more fear than relief. In his fantasies, Kay simply disappeared back to London, but the reality was that she had tethered herself to Pagford with a job and a daughter at Winterdown. He faced the prospect of bumping into her wherever he went in the tiny town. Perhaps she was already poisoning the well of gossip against him; he imagined her repeating some of the things she had said to him on the telephone to Samantha, or to that nosy old woman in the delicatessen who gave him gooseflesh.

I uprooted my daughter and left my job and moved house for you, and you treat me like a hooker you don't have to pay.

People would say that he had behaved badly. Perhaps he *had* behaved badly. There must have been a crucial point when he ought to have pulled back, but he had not seen it.

Gavin spent the whole weekend brooding on how it would feel to be seen as the bad guy. He had never been in that position before. After Lisa had left him, everybody had been kind and sympathetic, especially the Fairbrothers. Guilt and dread dogged him until, on Sunday evening, he cracked and called Kay to apologize. Now he was back where he did not want to be, and he hated Kay for it.

Parking his car in the Fairbrothers' drive, as he had done so often when Barry was alive, he headed for the front door, noticing that somebody had mowed the lawn since he had last called. Mary answered his ring on the doorbell almost instantaneously.

"Hi, how—Mary, what's wrong?"

Her whole face was wet, her eyes brimming with diamond-bright tears. She gulped once or twice, shook her head, and then, without quite knowing how it had happened, Gavin found himself holding her in his arms on the doorstep.

"Mary? Has something happened?"

He felt her nod. Acutely aware of their exposed position, of the open road behind him, Gavin maneuvered her inside. She was small and fragile in his arms; her fingers clutched at him, her face pressed into his coat. He relinquished his briefcase as gently as he could, but the sound of it hitting the floor made her withdraw from him, her breath short as she covered her mouth with her hands.

"I'm sorry...I'm sorry...oh *God*, Gav..."

"What's happened?"

His voice sounded different from usual: forceful, take command, more like the way Miles sometimes talked in a crisis at work.

"Someone's put...I don't...someone's put Barry's..."

She beckoned him into the home office, cluttered, shabby and cozy, with Barry's old rowing trophies on the shelves, and a big framed photograph on the wall of eight teenage girls punching the air, with medals around their necks. Mary pointed a trembling finger at the computer screen. Still in his coat, Gavin dropped into the chair and stared at the message board of Pagford Parish Council's website.

"I w-was in the delicatessen this morning, and Maureen Lowe told me that lots of people had put messages of condolence on the site...so I was going to p-post a message to s-say thank you. And—look..."

He spotted it as she spoke. Simon Price Unfit to Stand for Council, posted by The Ghost of Barry Fairbrother.

"Jesus Christ," said Gavin in disgust.

Mary dissolved into tears again. Gavin wanted to put his arms back around her, but was afraid to, especially here, in this snug little room so full of Barry. He compromised by taking hold of her thin wrist and leading her through the hall into the kitchen.

"You need a drink," he told her, in that unfamiliarly strong and commanding voice. "Sod coffee. Where's the proper stuff?"

But he remembered before she answered; he had seen Barry take the bottles out of the cupboard often enough, so he mixed her a small gin and tonic, which was the only thing he had ever known her to drink before dinner.

"Gav, it's four in the afternoon."

"Who gives a damn?" said Gavin, in his new voice. "Get that down you."

An unbalanced laugh broke her sobs; she accepted the glass and sipped. He fetched her kitchen roll to mop her face and eyes.

"You're so kind, Gav. Don't you want anything? Coffee or…or beer?" she asked, on another weak laugh.

He fetched himself a bottle from the fridge, took off his coat and sat down opposite her at the island in the middle of the room. After a while, when she had drunk most of her gin, she became calm and quiet again, the way he always thought of her.

"Who d'you think did it?" she asked him.

"Some total bastard," said Gavin.

"They're all fighting over his council seat, now. Squabbling away over the Fields as usual. And he's still in there, putting his two cents in. The Ghost of Barry Fairbrother. Maybe it really is him, posting on the message board?"

Gavin did not know whether this was meant as a joke, and settled for a slight smile that might be quickly removed.

"You know, I'd love to think that he's worrying about us, wherever he is; about me and the kids. But I doubt it. I'll bet he's still most worried about Krystal Weedon. Do you know what he'd probably say to me if he was here?"

She drained her glass. Gavin had not thought that he had mixed the gin very strong, but there were patches of high color on her cheeks.

"No," he said cautiously.

"He'd tell me that I've got support," said Mary, and to Gavin's astonishment, he heard anger in the voice he always thought of as gentle. "Yeah, he'd probably say, 'You've got all the family and our friends and the kids to comfort you, but Krystal,'" Mary's voice was becoming louder, "'Krystal's got nobody to look out for her.' D'you know what he spent our wedding anniversary doing?"

"No," said Gavin again.

"Writing an article for the local paper about Krystal. Krystal and the Fields. The bloody Fields. If I never hear them mentioned again, it'll be too soon. I want another gin. I don't drink enough."

Gavin picked up her glass automatically and returned to the drinks cupboard, stunned. He had always regarded her and Barry's marriage as literally perfect. Never had it occurred to him that Mary might be other than one hundred percent approving of every venture and crusade with which the ever-busy Barry concerned himself.

"Rowing practice in the evenings, driving them to races at the weekends," she said, over the tinkling of ice he was adding to her glass, "and most nights he was on the computer, trying to get people to support him about the Fields, and getting stuff on the agenda for council meetings. And everyone always said, 'Isn't Barry *marvelous*, the way he does it all, the way he volunteers, he's so involved with the community.'" She took a big gulp of her fresh gin and tonic. "Yes, marvelous. Absolutely marvelous. Until it killed him. All day long, on our wedding anniversary, struggling to meet that stupid deadline. They haven't even printed it yet."

Gavin could not take his eyes off her. Anger and alcohol had restored color to her face. She was sitting upright, instead of cowed and hunched over, as she had been recently.

"That's what killed him," she said clearly, and her voice echoed a little in the kitchen. "He gave everything to everybody. Except to me."

Ever since Barry's funeral, Gavin had dwelled, with a sense of deep inadequacy, on the comparatively small gap that he was sure he would leave behind in his community, should he die. Looking at Mary, he wondered whether it would not be better to leave a huge hole in one person's heart. Had Barry not realized how Mary felt? Had he not realized how lucky he was?

The front door opened with a loud clatter, and he heard the sound of the four children coming in; voices and footsteps and the thumping of shoes and bags.

"Hi, Gav," said eighteen-year-old Fergus, kissing his mother on top of her head. "Are you *drinking*, Mum?"

"It's my fault," said Gavin. "Blame me."

They were such nice kids, the Fairbrother kids. Gavin liked the way they talked to their mother, hugged her, chatted to each other and to him. They were open, polite and funny. He thought of Gaia, her vicious asides, silences like jagged glass, the snarling way she addressed him.

"Gav, we haven't even talked about the insurance," said Mary, as the children surged around the kitchen, finding themselves drinks and snacks.

"It doesn't matter," said Gavin, without thinking, before correcting himself hastily, "Shall we go through to the sitting room or...?"

"Yes, let's."

She wobbled a little getting down from the high kitchen stool, and he caught her arm again.

"Are you staying for dinner, Gav?" called Fergus.

"Do, if you want to," said Mary.

A surge of warmth flooded him.

"I'd love to," he said. "Thanks."

IV

"Very sad," said Howard Mollison, rocking a little on his toes in front of his mantelpiece. "Very sad indeed."

Maureen had just finished telling them all about Catherine Weedon's death; she had heard everything from her friend Karen the receptionist that evening, including the complaint from Cath Weedon's granddaughter. A look of delighted disapproval was crumpling her face; Samantha, who was in a very bad mood, thought she resembled a monkey nut. Miles was making conventional sounds of surprise and pity, but Shirley was staring up at the ceiling with a bland expression on her face; she hated it when Maureen held center stage with news that she ought to have heard first.

"My mother knew the family of old," Howard told Samantha, who already knew it. "Neighbors in Hope Street. Cath was decent enough in her way, you know. The house was always spotless, and she worked until she was into her sixties. Oh, yes, she was one of the world's grafters, Cath Weedon, whatever the rest of the family became."

Howard was enjoying giving credit where credit was due.

"The husband lost his job when they closed the steelworks. Hard drinker. No, she didn't always have it easy, Cath."

Samantha was barely managing to look interested, but fortunately Maureen interrupted.

"And the *Gazette*'s on to Dr. Jawanda!" she croaked. "Imagine how she must be feeling, now the paper's got it! Family's kicking up a stink—well, you can't blame them, alone in that house for three days. D'you know her, Howard? Which one is Danielle Fowler?"

Shirley got up and stalked out of the room in her apron. Samantha slugged a little more wine, smiling.

"Let's think, let's think," said Howard. He prided himself on knowing almost everyone in Pagford, but the later generations of Weedons belonged more to Yarvil. "Can't be a daughter, she had four boys, Cath. Granddaughter, I expect."

"And she wants an inquiry," said Maureen. "Well, it was always going to come to this. It's been on the cards. If anything, I'm surprised it's taken this long. Dr. Jawanda wouldn't give the Hubbards' son antibiotics and he ended up hospitalized for his asthma. Do you know, did she train in India, or—?"

Shirley, who was listening from the kitchen while she stirred the gravy, felt irritated, as she always did, by Maureen's monopolization of the conversation; that, at least, was how Shirley put it to herself. Determined not to return to the room until Maureen had finished, Shirley turned into the study and checked to see whether anyone had sent in apologies for the next Parish Council meeting; as secretary, she was already putting together the agenda.

"Howard—Miles—come and look at this!"

Shirley's voice had lost its usual soft, flutey quality; it rang out shrilly.

Howard waddled out of the sitting room followed by Miles, who was still in the suit he had worn all day at work. Maureen's droopy, bloodshot, heavily mascaraed eyes were fixed on the empty doorway like a bloodhound's; her hunger to know what Shirley had found or seen was almost palpable. Maureen's fingers, a clutch of bulging knuckles covered in translucent leopard-spotted skin, slid the crucifix and wedding ring up and down the chain around her neck. The deep creases running from the corners of Maureen's mouth to her chin always reminded Samantha of a ventriloquist's dummy.

Why are you always here? Samantha asked the older woman loudly, inside her own head. *You couldn't make me lonely enough to live in Howard and Shirley's pocket.*

Disgust rose in Samantha like vomit. She wanted to seize the overwarm cluttered room and mash it between her hands, until the royal china, and the gas fire, and the gilt-framed pictures of Miles broke into jagged pieces; then, with wizened and painted Maureen trapped and squalling inside the wreckage, she wanted to heave it, like a celestial shot-putter, away into the sunset. The crushed lounge and the doomed crone inside it soared in her imagination through the heavens, plunging into the limitless ocean, leaving Samantha alone in the endless stillness of the universe.

She had had a terrible afternoon. There had been another frightening conversation with her accountant; she could not remember much of her drive home from Yarvil. She would have liked to offload on Miles, but after dumping his briefcase and pulling off his tie in the hall he had said, "You haven't started dinner yet, have you?"

He sniffed the air ostentatiously, then answered himself.

"No, you haven't. Well, good, because Mum and Dad have invited us over." And before she could protest, he had added sharply, "It's nothing to do with the council. It's to discuss arrangements for Dad's sixty-fifth."

Anger was almost a relief; it eclipsed her anxiety, her fear. She had followed Miles out to the car, cradling her sense of ill-usage. When he asked, at last, on the corner of Evertree Crescent, "How was your day?" she answered, "Absolutely bloody fantastic."

"Wonder what's up?" said Maureen, breaking the silence in the sitting room.

Samantha shrugged. It was typical of Shirley to have summoned her menfolk and left the women in limbo; Samantha was not going to give her mother-in-law the satisfaction of showing interest.

Howard's elephantine footsteps made the floorboards under the hall carpet creak. Maureen's mouth was slack with anticipation.

"Well, well, well," boomed Howard, lumbering back into the room.

"I was checking the council website for apologies," said Shirley, a little breathless in his wake. "For the next meeting—"

"Someone's posted accusations about Simon Price," Miles told Samantha, pressing past his parents, seizing the role of announcer.

"What kind of accusations?" asked Samantha.

"Receiving stolen goods," said Howard, firmly reclaiming the spotlight, "and diddling his bosses at the printworks."

Samantha was pleased to find herself unmoved. She had only the haziest idea who Simon Price was.

"They've posted under a pseudonym," Howard continued, "and it's not a particularly tasteful pseudonym, either."

"Rude, you mean?" Samantha asked. "Big-Fat-Cock or something?"

Howard's laughter boomed through the room, Maureen gave an affected shriek of horror, but Miles scowled and Shirley looked furious.

"Not *quite* that, Sammy, no," said Howard. "No, they've called themselves 'The Ghost of Barry Fairbrother.'"

"Oh," said Samantha, her grin evaporating. She did not like that. After all, she had been in the ambulance while they had forced needles and tubes into Barry's collapsed body; she had watched him dying beneath the plastic mask; seen Mary clinging to his hand, heard her groans and sobs.

"Oh, no, that's not nice," said Maureen, relish in her bullfrog's voice. "No, that's nasty. Putting words into the mouths of the dead. Taking names in vain. That's not right."

"No," agreed Howard. Almost absentmindedly, he strolled across the room, picked up the wine bottle and returned to Samantha, topping up her empty glass. "But someone out there doesn't care about good taste, it seems, if they can put Simon Price out of the running."

"If you're thinking what I think you're thinking, Dad," said Miles, "wouldn't they have gone for me rather than Price?"

"How do you know they haven't, Miles?"

"Meaning?" asked Miles swiftly.

"Meaning," said Howard, the happy cynosure of all eyes, "that I got sent an anonymous letter about you a couple of weeks ago. Nothing specific. Just said you were unfit to fill Fairbrother's shoes. I'd be very surprised if the letter didn't come from the same source as the online post. The Fairbrother theme in both, you see?"

Samantha tilted her glass a little too enthusiastically, so that wine trickled down the sides of her chin, exactly where her own ventriloquist's doll grooves would no doubt appear in time. She mopped her face with her sleeve.

"Where is this letter?" asked Miles, striving not to look rattled.

"I shredded it. It was anonymous; it didn't count."

"We didn't want to upset you, dear," said Shirley, and she patted Miles' arm.

"Anyway, they can't have anything on you," Howard reassured his son, "or they'd have dished the dirt, the same as they have on Price."

"Simon Price's wife is a lovely girl," said Shirley with gentle regret. "I can't believe Ruth knows anything about it, if her husband's been on the fiddle. She's a friend from the hospital," Shirley elaborated to Maureen. "An agency nurse."

"She wouldn't be the first wife who hasn't spotted what's going on under her nose," retorted Maureen, trumping insider knowledge with worldly wisdom.

"Absolutely brazen, using Barry Fairbrother's name," said Shirley, pretending not to have heard Maureen. "Not a thought for his widow, his family. All that matters is their agenda; they'll sacrifice anything to it."

"Shows you what we're up against," said Howard. He scratched the overfold of his belly, thinking. "Strategically, it's smart. I saw from the get-go that Price was going to split the pro-Fields vote. No flies on Bends-Your-Ear; she's realized it too and she wants him out."

"But," said Samantha, "it mightn't have anything to do with Parminder and that lot at all. It could be from someone we don't know, someone who's got a grudge against Simon Price."

"Oh, Sam," said Shirley, with a tinkling laugh, shaking her head. "It's easy to see you're new to politics."

Oh, fuck off, Shirley.

"So why have they used Barry Fairbrother's name, then?" asked Miles, rounding on his wife.

"Well, it's on the website, isn't it? It's his vacant seat."

"And who's going to trawl through the council website for that kind of information? No," he said gravely, "This is an insider."

An insider...Libby had once told Samantha that there could be thousands of microscopic species inside one drop of pond water. They were all perfectly ridiculous, Samantha thought, sitting here in front of Shirley's commemorative plates as if they were in the Cabinet Room in Downing Street, as though one bit of tittle-tattle on a Parish Council website constituted an organized campaign, as though any of it mattered.

Consciously and defiantly, Samantha withdrew her attention from the lot of them. She fixed her eyes on the window and the clear evening sky beyond, and she thought about Jake, the muscular boy in Libby's favorite band. At lunchtime today, Samantha had gone out for sandwiches, and brought back a music magazine in which Jake and his bandmates were interviewed. There were lots of pictures.

"It's for Libby," Samantha had told the girl who helped her in the shop.

"Wow, look at that. I wouldn't kick him out of bed for eating toast," replied Carly, pointing at Jake, naked from the waist up, his head thrown back to reveal that thick strong neck. "Oh, but he's only twenty-one, look. I'm not a cradle snatcher."

Carly was twenty-six. Samantha did not care to subtract Jake's age from her own. She had eaten her sandwich and read the interview, and studied all the pictures. Jake with his hands on a bar above his head, biceps swelling under a black T-shirt; Jake with his white shirt open, abdominal muscles chiseled above the loose waistband of his jeans.

Samantha drank Howard's wine and stared out at the sky above the black privet hedge, which was a delicate shade of rose pink; the precise shade her nipples had been before they had been darkened and distended by pregnancy and breast-feeding. She imagined herself nineteen to Jake's twenty-one, slender-waisted again, taut curves in the right places, and a strong flat stomach of her own, fitting comfortably into her white, size ten shorts. She vividly recalled how it felt to sit on a young man's lap in those shorts, with the heat and roughness of sun-warmed denim under her bare thighs, and big hands around her lithe waist. She imagined Jake's breath on her neck; she imagined turning to look into the blue eyes, close to the high cheekbones and that firm, carved mouth…

"…at the church hall, and we're getting it catered by Bucknoles," said Howard. "We've invited everyone: Aubrey and Julia—everyone. With luck it will be a double celebration, you on the council, me, another year young…"

Samantha felt tipsy and randy. When were they going to eat? She realized that Shirley had left the room, hopefully to put food on the table.

The telephone rang at Samantha's elbow, and she jumped. Before any of them could move, Shirley had bustled back in. She had one hand in a flowery oven glove, and picked up the receiver with the other.

"Double-two-five-nine?" sang Shirley on a rising inflection. "Oh…hello, Ruth, dear!"

Howard, Miles and Maureen became rigidly attentive. Shirley turned to look at her husband with intensity, as if she were transmitting Ruth's voice through her eyes into her husband's mind.

"Yes," fluted Shirley. "Yes…"

Samantha, sitting closest to the receiver, could hear the other woman's voice but not make out the words.

"Oh, really…?"

Maureen's mouth was hanging open again; she was like an ancient baby bird, or perhaps a pterodactyl, hungering for regurgitated news.

"Yes, dear, I see…oh, that shouldn't be a problem…no, no, I'll explain to Howard. No, no trouble at all."

Shirley's small hazel eyes had not wavered from Howard's big, popping blue ones.

"Ruth, dear," said Shirley, "Ruth, I don't want to worry you, but have you been on the council website today?…Well…it's not very nice, but I think you ought to know…somebody's posted something nasty about Simon…well, I think you'd better read it for yourself, I wouldn't want to…all right, dear. All right. See you Wednesday, I hope. Yes. Bye-bye."

Shirley replaced the receiver.

"She didn't know," Miles stated.

Shirley shook her head.

"Why was she calling?"

"Her son," Shirley told Howard. "Your new potboy. He's got a peanut allergy."

"Very handy, in a delicatessen," said Howard.

"She wanted to ask whether you could store a needleful of Adrenalin in the fridge for him, just in case," said Shirley.

Maureen sniffed.

"They've all got allergies these days, children."

Shirley's ungloved hand was still clutching the receiver. She was subconsciously hoping to feel tremors down the line from Hilltop House.

V

Ruth stood alone in her lamplit sitting room, continuing to grip the telephone she had just replaced in its cradle.

Hilltop House was small and compact. It was always easy to tell the location of each of the four Prices, because voices, footfalls and the sounds of doors opening and shutting carried so effectively in the old house. Ruth knew that her husband was still in the shower, because she could hear the hot water boiler under the stairs hissing and clanking. She had waited for Simon to turn on the water before telephoning Shirley, worried that he might think that even her request about the EpiPen was fraternizing with the enemy.

The family PC was set up in a corner of the sitting room, where Simon could keep an eye on it, and make sure nobody was running up large bills behind his back. Ruth relinquished her grip on the phone and hurried to the keyboard.

It seemed to take a very long time to bring up the Pagford Council website. Ruth pushed her reading glasses up her nose with a trembling hand as she scanned the various pages. At last she found the message board. Her husband's name blazed out at her, in ghastly black and white: Simon Price Unfit to Stand for Council.

She double-clicked the title, brought up the full paragraph and read it. Everything around her seemed to reel and spin.

"Oh God," she whispered.

The boiler had stopped clanking. Simon would be putting on the pajamas he had warmed on the radiator. He had already drawn the sitting-room curtains, turned on the side lamps and lit the wood-burner, so that he could come down and stretch out on the sofa to watch the news.

Ruth knew that she would have to tell him. Not doing so, letting him find out for himself, was simply not an option; she would have been incapable of keeping it to herself. She felt terrified and guilty, though she did not know why.

She heard him jogging down the stairs and then he appeared at the door in his blue brushed-cotton pajamas.

"Si," she whispered.

"What's the matter?" he said, immediately irritated. He knew that something had happened; that his luxurious program of sofa, fire and news was about to be disarranged.

She pointed at the computer monitor, one hand pressed foolishly over her mouth, like a little girl. Her terror infected him. He strode to the PC and scowled down at the screen. He was not a quick reader. He read every word, every line, painstakingly, carefully.

When he had finished, he remained quite still, passing for review, in his mind, all the likely grasses. He thought of the gum-chewing forklift driver, whom he had left stranded in the Fields when they had picked up the new computer. He thought of Jim and Tommy, who did the cash-in-hand jobs on the sly with him. Someone from work must have talked. Rage and fear collided inside him and set off a combustive reaction.

He strode to the foot of the stairs and shouted, "You two! Get down here NOW!"

Ruth still had her hand over her mouth. He had a sadistic urge to slap her hand away, to tell her to fucking pull herself together, it was he who was in the shit.

Andrew entered the room first with Paul behind him. Andrew saw the arms of Pagford Parish Council onscreen, and his mother with her hand over her mouth. Walking barefoot across the old carpet, he had the sensation that he was plummeting through the air in a broken lift.

"Someone," said Simon, glaring at his sons, "has talked about things I've mentioned inside this house."

Paul had brought his chemistry exercise book downstairs with him; he was holding it like a hymnal. Andrew kept his gaze fixed on his father, trying to project an expression of mingled confusion and curiosity.

"Who's told other people we've got a stolen computer?" asked Simon.

"I haven't," said Andrew.

Paul stared at his father blankly, trying to process the question. Andrew willed his brother to speak. Why did he have to be so slow?

"Well?" Simon snarled at Paul.

"I don't think I—"

"You don't *think*? You don't *think* you told anyone?"

"No, I don't think I told any—"

"Oh, this is interesting," said Simon, pacing up and down in front of Paul. "This is interesting."

With a slap he sent Paul's exercise book flying out of his hands.

"Try and think, dipshit," he growled. "Try and fucking think. Did you tell anyone we've got a stolen computer?"

"Not stolen," said Paul. "I never told anyone—I don't think I told anyone we had a new one, even."

"I see," said Simon. "So the news got out by magic then, did it?"

He was pointing at the computer monitor.

"*Someone's* fucking talked!" he yelled, "because it's on the fucking *Internet!* And I'll be fucking lucky not—to—lose—my—job!"

On each of the five last words he thumped Paul on the head with his fist. Paul cowered and ducked; black liquid trickled from his left nostril; he suffered nosebleeds several times a week.

"And what about *you?*" Simon roared at his wife, who was still frozen beside the computer, her eyes wide behind her glasses, her hand clamped like a yashmak over her mouth. "Have *you* been fucking gossiping?"

Ruth ungagged herself.

"No, Si," she whispered, "I mean, the only person I told we had a new computer was Shirley—and she'd never—"

You stupid woman, you stupid fucking woman, what did you have to tell him that for?

"You did what?" asked Simon quietly.

"I told Shirley," whimpered Ruth. "I didn't say it was stolen, though, Si. I only said you were bringing it home—"

"Well, that's fucking it then, isn't it?" roared Simon; his voice became a scream. "Her fucking son's standing for election, of course she wants to get the fucking goods on me!"

"But she's the one who told me, Si, just now, she wouldn't have—"

He ran at her and hit her in the face, exactly as he had wanted to when he had first seen her silly frightened expression; her glasses spun into the air and smashed against the bookcase; he hit her again and she crashed down onto the computer table she had bought so proudly with her first month's wages from South West General.

Andrew had made himself a promise: he seemed to move in slow motion, and everything was cold and clammy and slightly unreal.

"Don't hit her," he said, forcing himself between his parents. "Don't—"

His lip split against his front tooth, Simon's knuckle behind it, and he fell backwards on top of his mother, who was draped over the keyboard; Simon threw another punch, which hit Andew's arms as he protected his face; Andrew was trying to get off his slumped, struggling mother, and Simon was in a frenzy, pummeling both of them wherever he could reach—

"Don't you fucking dare tell me what to do—don't you dare, you cowardly little shit, you spotty streak of piss—"

Andrew dropped to his knees to get out of the way, and Simon kicked him in the ribs. Andrew heard Paul say pathetically, "Stop it!" Simon's foot swung for Andrew's rib cage again, but Andrew dodged it; Simon's toes collided with the brick fireplace and he was suddenly, absurdly, howling in pain.

Andrew scrambled out of the way; Simon was gripping the end of his foot, hopping on the spot and swearing in a high-pitched voice; Ruth had collapsed into the swivel chair, sobbing into her hands. Andrew got to his feet; he could taste his own blood.

"Anyone could have talked about that computer," he panted, braced for further violence; he felt braver now that it had begun, now that the fight was really on; it was waiting that told on your nerves, watching Simon's jaw begin to jut, and hearing the urge for violence building in his voice. "You told us a security guard got beaten up. Anyone could have talked. It's not us—"

"Don't you—fucking little shit—I've broken my fucking toe!" Simon gasped, falling backwards into an armchair, still nursing his foot. He seemed to expect sympathy.

Andrew imagined picking up a gun and shooting Simon in the face, watching his features blast apart, his brains spattering the room.

"And Pauline's got her fucking period again!" Simon yelled at Paul, who was trying to contain the blood dripping through his fingers from his nose. "Get off the carpet! Get off the fucking carpet, you little pansy!"

Paul scuttled out of the room. Andrew pressed the hem of his T-shirt to his stinging mouth.

"What about all the cash-in-hand jobs?" Ruth sobbed, her cheek pink from his punch, tears dripping from her chin. Andrew hated to see her humiliated and pathetic like this; but he half hated her too for landing herself in it, when any idiot could have seen…"It says about the cash-in-hand jobs. Shirley doesn't know about them, how could she? Someone at the printworks has put that on there. I told you, Si, I told you you shouldn't do those jobs, they've always worried the living daylights out of—"

"Fucking shut up, you whining cow, you didn't mind spending the money!" yelled Simon, his jaw jutting again; and Andrew wanted to roar at his mother to stay silent: she blabbed when any idiot could have told her she should keep quiet, and she kept quiet when she might have done good by speaking out; she never learned, she never saw any of it coming.

Nobody spoke for a minute. Ruth dabbed at her eyes with the back of her hand and sniffed intermittently. Simon clutched his toe, his jaw clenched, breathing loudly. Andrew licked the blood from his stinging lip, which he could feel swelling.

"This'll cost me my fucking job," said Simon, staring wild-eyed around the room, as if there might be somebody there he had forgotten to hit. "They're already talking about fucking redundancies. This'll be it. This'll—" He slapped the lamp off the end table, but it didn't break, merely rolled on the floor. He picked it up, tugged the lead out of the wall socket, raised it over his head and threw it at Andrew, who dodged.

"Who's fucking talked?" Simon yelled, as the lamp base broke apart on the wall. "Someone's fucking talked!"

"It's some bastard at the printworks, isn't it?" Andrew shouted back; his lip was thick and throbbing; it felt like a tangerine segment. "D'you think we'd have—d'you think we don't know how to keep our mouths shut by now?"

It was like trying to read a wild animal. He could see the muscles working in his father's jaw, but he could tell that Simon was considering Andrew's words.

"When was that put on there?" he roared at Ruth. "Look at it! What's the date on it?"

Still sobbing, she peered at the screen, needing to approach the tip of her nose within two inches of it, now that her glasses were broken.

"The fifteenth," she whispered.

"Fifteenth...Sunday," said Simon. "Sunday, wasn't it?"

Neither Andrew nor Ruth put him right. Andrew could not believe his luck; nor did he believe it would hold.

"Sunday," said Simon, "So anyone could've—my fucking *toe*," he yelled, as he pulled himself up and limped exaggeratedly toward Ruth. "Get out of my way!"

She hastened out of the chair and watched him read the paragraph through again. He kept snorting like an animal to clear his airways. Andrew thought that he might be able to garrote his father as he sat there, if only there was a wire to hand.

"Someone's got all this from work," said Simon, as if he had just reached this conclusion, and had not heard his wife or son urging the hypothesis on him. He placed his hands on the keyboard and turned to Andrew. "How do I get rid of it?"

"What?"

"You do fucking computing! How do I get this off here?"

"You can't get—you can't," said Andrew. "You'd need to be the administrator."

"Make yourself the administrator, then," said Simon, jumping up and pointing Andrew into the swivel chair.

"I can't make myself the administrator," said Andrew. He was afraid that Simon was working himself up into a second bout of violence. "You need to input the right user name and passwords."

"You're a real fucking waste of space, aren't you?"

Simon shoved Andrew in the middle of his sternum as he limped past, knocking him back into the mantelpiece.

"Pass me the phone!" Simon shouted at his wife, as he sat back down in the armchair.

Ruth took the telephone and carried it the few feet to Simon. He ripped it out of her hands and punched in a number.

Andrew and Ruth waited in silence as Simon called, first Jim, and then Tommy, the men with whom he had completed the after-hours jobs at the printworks. Simon's fury, his suspicion of his own accomplices, was funneled down the telephone in curt short sentences full of swearwords.

Paul had not returned. Perhaps he was still trying to stanch his bleeding nose, but more likely he was too scared. Andrew thought his brother unwise. It was safest to leave only after Simon had given you permission.

His calls completed, Simon held out the telephone to Ruth without speaking; she took it and hurried it back into its stand.

Simon sat thinking while his fractured toe pulsated, sweating in the heat of the wood-burner, awash with impotent fury. The beating to which he had subjected his wife and son was nothing, he did not give them a thought; a terrible thing had just happened to him, and naturally his rage had exploded on those nearest him; that was how life worked. In any case, Ruth, the silly bitch, had admitted to telling Shirley...

Simon was building his own chain of evidence, as he thought things must have happened. Some fucker (and he suspected that gum-chewing forklift driver, whose expression, as Simon had sped away from him in the Fields, had been outraged) talking about him to the Mollisons (somehow, illogically, Ruth's admission that she had mentioned the computer to Shirley made this seem more likely), and they (the Mollisons, the establishment, the smooth and the snide, guarding their access to power) had put up this message on their website (Shirley, the old cow, managed the site, which set the seal on the theory).

"It's your fucking friend," Simon told his wet-faced, trembling-lipped wife. "It's your fucking Shirley. She's done this. She's got some dirt on me to get me off her son's case. That's who it is."

"But Si—"

Shut up, shut up, you silly cow, thought Andrew.

"Still on her side, are you?" roared Simon, making to stand again.

"No!" squealed Ruth, and he sank back into the chair, glad to keep the weight off his pounding foot.

The Harcourt-Walsh management would not be happy about those after-hours jobs, Simon thought. He wouldn't put it past the bloody police to come nosing around the computer. A desire for urgent action filled him.

"You," he said, pointing at Andrew. "Unplug that computer. All of it, the leads and everything. You're coming with me."

VI

Things denied, things untold, things hidden and disguised.

The muddy River Orr gushed over the wreckage of the stolen computer, thrown from the old stone bridge at midnight. Simon limped to work on his fractured toe and told everyone that he had slipped on the garden path. Ruth pressed ice to her bruises and concealed them inexpertly with an old tube of foundation; Andrew's lip scabbed over, like Dane Tully's, and Paul had another nosebleed on the bus and had to go straight to the nurse on arrival at school.

Shirley Mollison, who had been shopping in Yarvil, did not answer Ruth's repeated telephone calls until late afternoon, by which time Ruth's sons had arrived home from school. Andrew listened to the one-sided conversation from the stairs outside the sitting room. He knew that Ruth was trying to take care of the problem before Simon came home, because Simon was more than capable of seizing the receiver from her and shouting and swearing at her friend.

"…just silly lies," she was saying brightly, "but we'd be very grateful if you could remove it, Shirley."

He scowled and the cut on his fat lip threatened to burst open again. He hated hearing his mother asking the woman for a favor. In that moment he was irrationally annoyed that the post had not been taken down already; then he remembered that he had written it, that he had caused everything: his mother's battered face, his own cut lip and the atmosphere of dread that pervaded the house at the prospect of Simon's return.

"I do understand you've got a lot of things on…" Ruth was saying cravenly, "but you can see how this might do Simon damage, if people believe…"

This, Andrew thought, was how Ruth spoke to Simon on the rare occasions when she felt obliged to challenge him: subservient, apologetic, tentative. Why did his mother not demand that the woman take down the post at once? Why was she always so craven, so apologetic? *Why did she not leave his father?*

He had always seen Ruth as separate, good and untainted. As a child, his parents had appeared to him as starkly black and white, the one bad and frightening, the other good and kind. Yet as he had grown older, he kept coming up hard in his mind against Ruth's willing blindness, to her constant apologia for his father, to the unshakable allegiance to her false idol.

Andrew heard her put down the receiver, and he continued noisily down the stairs, meeting Ruth as she left the sitting room.

"Calling the website woman?"

"Yes." Ruth sounded tired. "She's going to take those things about Dad off the site so, hopefully, that'll be the end of it."

Andrew knew his mother to be intelligent, and much handier around the house than his ham-fisted father. She was capable of earning her own living.

"Why didn't she take the post down straightaway, if you're friends?" he asked, following her into the kitchen. For the first time in his life, his pity for Ruth was mingled with a feeling of frustration that amounted to anger.

"She's been busy," snapped Ruth.

One of her eyes was bloodshot from Simon's punch.

"Did you tell her she could be in trouble for leaving defamatory stuff on there, if she moderates the boards? We did that stuff in comput—"

"I've told you, she's taking it down, Andrew," said Ruth angrily.

She was not frightened of showing temper to her sons. Was it because they did not hit her, or for some other reason? Andrew knew that her face must ache as badly as his own.

"So who d'you reckon wrote that stuff about Dad?" he asked her recklessly.

She turned a face of fury upon him.

"*I* don't know," she said, "but whoever they are, it was a despicable, cowardly thing to do. *Everyone's* got something they'd like to hide. How would it be if Dad put some of the things *he* knows about other people on the Internet? But he wouldn't do it."

"That'd be against his moral code, would it?" said Andrew.

"You don't know your father as well as you think you do!"

shouted Ruth with tears in her eyes. "Get out—go and do your homework—I don't care—just get out!"

Andrew returned to his bedroom hungry, because he had been heading for the kitchen to take some food, and lay for a long while on his bed, wondering whether the post had been a terrible mistake, and also wondering how badly Simon would have to injure anyone in the family before his mother realized that he recognized no moral code whatsoever.

Meanwhile, in the study of her bungalow, a mile away from Hilltop House, Shirley Mollison was trying to remember how to delete a post from the message board. Posts were so infrequent that she usually left them there for up to three years. At last she dug out of a filing cabinet in the corner the simple guide to administering the site that she had made for herself when she started, and managed, after several fumbled attempts, to remove the accusations against Simon. She did it only because Ruth, whom she liked, had asked her to; she felt no personal responsibility in the matter.

Yet the deletion of the post could not remove it from the consciousness of those who were passionately interested in the forthcoming contest for Barry's seat. Parminder Jawanda had copied the message about Simon Price onto her computer, and kept opening it, subjecting each sentence to the scrutiny of a forensic scientist examining fibers on a corpse, searching for traces of Howard Mollison's literary DNA. He would have done all he could to disguise his distinctive phraseology, but she was sure that she recognized his pomposity in "Mr. Price is certainly no stranger to keeping down costs," and in "The benefit of his many useful contacts."

"Minda, you don't know Simon Price," said Tessa Wall. She and Colin were having supper with the Jawandas in the Old Vicarage kitchen, and Parminder had started on the subject of the post almost the moment they had crossed the threshold. "He's a very unpleasant man and he could have upset any number of people. I honestly don't think it's Howard Mollison. I can't see him doing anything so obvious."

"Don't kid yourself, Tessa," said Parminder. "Howard will do anything to make sure Miles is elected. You watch. He'll go for Colin next."

Tessa saw Colin's knuckles whiten on his fork handle, and wished that Parminder would think before she spoke. She, of anyone, knew what Colin was like; she prescribed his Prozac.

Vikram was sitting at the end of the table in silence. His beautiful face fell naturally into a slightly sardonic smile. Tessa had always been intimidated by the surgeon, as she was by all very good-looking men. Although Parminder was one of Tessa's best friends, she barely knew Vikram, who worked long hours and involved himself much less in Pagford matters than his wife.

"I told you about the agenda, didn't I?" Parminder rattled on. "For the next meeting? He's proposing a motion on the Fields, for us to pass to the Yarvil committee doing the boundary review, *and* a resolution on forcing the drug clinic out of their building. He's trying to rush it all through, while Barry's seat's empty."

She kept leaving the table to fetch things, opening more cupboard doors than was necessary, distracted and unfocused. Twice she forgot why she had got up, and sat down again, empty-handed. Vikram watched her, everywhere she moved, from beneath his thick eyelashes.

"I rang Howard last night," Parminder said, "and I told him we ought to wait until we're back up to the full complement of councillors before we vote on such big issues. He laughed; he says we can't wait. Yarvil wants to hear our views, he said, with the boundary review coming up. What he's really scared of is that Colin's going to win Barry's seat, because it won't be so easy to foist it all on us then. I've emailed everyone I think will vote with us, to see if they can't put pressure on him to delay the votes, for one meeting…

"'The Ghost of Barry Fairbrother,'" Parminder added breathlessly. "The *bastard*. He's not using Barry's death to beat him. Not if I can help it."

Tessa thought she saw Vikram's lips twitch. Old Pagford, led by Howard Mollison, generally forgave Vikram the crimes that it could not forget in his wife: brownness, cleverness and affluence (all of which, to Shirley Mollison's nostrils, had the whiff of a gloat). It was, Tessa thought, grossly unfair: Parminder worked hard at every aspect of her Pagford life: school fetes and sponsored bakes, the local surgery and the Parish Council, and her reward was implacable dislike from the Pagford old guard; Vikram, who rarely joined or participated in anything, was fawned upon, flattered and spoken of with proprietary approval.

"Mollison's a megalomaniac," Parminder said, pushing food nervously around her plate. "A bully and a megalomaniac."

Vikram laid down his knife and fork and sat back in his chair.

"So why," he asked, "is he happy being chair of the Parish Council? Why hasn't he tried to get on the District Council?"

"Because he thinks that Pagford is the epicenter of the universe," snapped Parminder. "You don't understand: he wouldn't swap being chair of Pagford Parish Council for being Prime Minister. Anyway, he doesn't *need* to be on the council in Yarvil; he's already got Aubrey Fawley there, pushing through the big agenda. All revved up for the boundary review. They're working together."

Parminder felt Barry's absence like a ghost at the table. He would have explained it all to Vikram and made him laugh in the process; Barry had been a superb mimic of Howard's speech patterns, of his rolling, waddling walk, of his sudden gastrointestinal interruptions.

"I keep telling her, she's letting herself get too stressed," Vikram told Tessa, who was appalled to find herself blushing slightly, with his dark eyes upon her. "You know about this stupid complaint—the old woman with emphysema?"

"Yes, Tessa knows. Everyone knows. Do we have to discuss it at the dinner table?" snapped Parminder, and she jumped to her feet and began clearing the plates.

Tessa tried to help, but Parminder told her crossly to stay where she was. Vikram gave Tessa a small smile of solidarity that made her stomach flutter. She could not help remembering, as Parminder clattered around the table, that Vikram and Parminder had had an arranged marriage.

("It's only an introduction through the family," Parminder had told her, in the early days of their friendship, defensive and annoyed at something she had seen in Tessa's face. "Nobody *makes* you marry, you know."

But she had spoken, at other times, of the immense pressure from her mother to take a husband.

"All Sikh parents want their kids married. It's an obsession," Parminder said bitterly.)

Colin saw his plate snatched away without regret. The nausea churning in his stomach was even worse than when he and Tessa had arrived. He might have been encased in a thick glass bubble, so separate did he feel from his three dining companions. It was a sensation with which he was only too familiar, that of walking in a giant sphere of worry, enclosed by it, watching his own terrors roll by, obscuring the outside world.

Tessa was no help: she was being deliberately cool and unsympathetic about his campaign for Barry's seat. The whole point of this supper was so that Colin could consult Parminder on the little leaflets he had produced, advertising his candidacy. Tessa was refusing to get involved, blocking discussion of the fear that was slowly engulfing him. She was refusing him an outlet.

Trying to emulate her coolness, pretending that he was not, after all, caving under self-imposed pressure, he had not told her about the telephone call from the *Yarvil and District Gazette* that he had received at school that day. The journalist on the end of the line had wanted to talk about Krystal Weedon.

Had he touched her?

Colin had told the woman that the school could not possibly discuss a pupil and that Krystal must be approached through her parents.

"I've already talked to Krystal," said the voice on the end of the line. "I only wanted to get your—"

But he had put the receiver down, and terror had blotted out everything.

Why did they want to talk about Krystal? Why had they called him? Had he done something? Had he touched her? Had she complained?

The psychologist had taught him not to try and confirm or disprove the content of such thoughts. He was supposed to acknowledge their existence, then carry on as normal, but it was like trying not to scratch the worst itch you had ever known. The public unveiling of Simon Price's dirty secrets on the council web-site had stunned him: the terror of exposure, which had dominated so much of Colin's life, now wore a face, its features those of an aging cherub, with a demonic brain seething beneath a deerstalker on tight gray curls, behind bulging inquisitive eyes. He kept remembering Barry's tales of the delicatessen owner's formidable strategic brain, and of the intricate web of alliances that bound the sixteen members of Pagford Parish Council.

Colin had often imagined how he would find out that the game was up: a guarded article in the paper; faces turned away from him when he entered Mollison and Lowe's; the headmistress calling him into her office for a quiet word. He had visualized his downfall a thousand times: his shame exposed and hung around his neck like a leper's bell, so that no concealment would be possible, ever again. He would be sacked. He might end up in prison.

"Colin," Tessa prompted quietly; Vikram was offering him wine.

She knew what was going on inside that big domed forehead; not the specifics, but the theme of his anxiety had been constant for years. She knew that Colin could not help it; it was the way he was made. Many years before, she had read, and recognized as true, the words of W. B. Yeats: "A pity beyond all telling is hid at the heart of love." She had smiled over the poem, and stroked the page, because she had known both that she loved Colin, and that compassion formed a huge part of her love.

Sometimes, though, her patience wore thin. Sometimes *she* wanted a little concern and reassurance too. Colin had erupted into a predictable panic when she had told him that she had received a firm diagnosis of Type 2 diabetes, but once she had convinced him that she was not in imminent danger of dying, she had been taken aback by how quickly he dropped the subject, how completely he reimmersed himself in his election plans.

(That morning, at breakfast, she had tested her blood sugar with the glucometer for the first time, then taken out the prefilled needle and inserted it into her own belly. It had hurt much more than when deft Parminder did it.

Fats had seized his cereal bowl and swung round in his chair away from her, sloshing milk over the table, the sleeve of his school shirt and onto the kitchen floor. Colin had let out an inchoate shout of annoyance as Fats spat his mouthful of cornflakes back into his bowl, and demanded of his mother, "Have you got to do that at the bloody table?"

"Don't be so damn rude and disgusting!" shouted Colin. "Sit up properly! Wipe up that mess! How dare you speak to your mother like that? Apologize!"

Tessa withdrew the needle too fast; she had made herself bleed.

"I'm sorry that you shooting up at breakfast makes me want to puke, Tess," said Fats from under the table, where he was wiping the floor with a bit of kitchen roll.

"Your mother isn't 'Shooting up,' she's got a medical condition!" shouted Colin. "And don't call her 'Tess'!"

"I know you don't like needles, Stu," said Tessa, but her eyes were stinging; she had hurt herself, and felt shaken and angry with both of them, feelings that were still with her this evening.)

Tessa wondered why Parminder did not appreciate Vikram's concern. Colin never noticed when *she* was stressed. *Perhaps,* Tessa thought angrily, *there's something in this arranged marriage business... my mother certainly wouldn't have chosen Colin for me...*

Parminder was shoving bowls of cut fruit across the table for pudding. Tessa wondered a little resentfully what she would have offered a guest who was not diabetic, and comforted herself with the thought of a bar of chocolate lying at home in the fridge.

Parminder, who had talked five times as much as anybody else all through supper, had started ranting about her daughter, Sukhvinder. She had already told Tessa on the telephone about the girl's betrayal; she went through it all again at the table.

"Waitressing with Howard Mollison. I don't, I really *don't* know what she's thinking. But Vikram——"

"They don't think, Minda," Colin proclaimed, breaking his long silence. "That's teenagers. They don't care. They're all the same."

"Colin, what rubbish," snapped Tessa. "They aren't all the same at all. We'd be delighted if Stu went and got himself a Saturday job—not that there's the remotest chance of that."

"—but Vikram doesn't mind," Parminder pressed on, ignoring the interruption. "He can't see anything wrong with it, can you?"

Vikram answered easily: "It's work experience. She probably won't make university; there's no shame in it. It's not for everyone. I can see Jolly married early, quite happy."

"*Waitressing...*"

"Well, they can't all be academic, can they?"

"No, she certainly isn't academic," said Parminder, who was almost quivering with anger and tension. "Her marks are absolutely atrocious—no aspiration, no ambition—*waitressing*—'let's face it, I'm not going to get into uni'—no, you certainly *won't*, with that attitude—with *Howard Mollison*...oh, he must have absolutely loved it—my daughter going cap in hand for a job. What was she thinking—*what* was she thinking?"

"You wouldn't like it if Stu took a job with someone like Mollison," Colin told Tessa.

"I wouldn't care," said Tessa. "I'd be thrilled he was showing any kind of work ethic. As far as I can tell, all he seems to care about is computer games and—"

But Colin did not know that Stuart smoked; she broke off, and Colin said, "Actually, this would be exactly the kind of thing Stuart would do. Insinuate himself with somebody he knew we didn't like, to get at us. He'd love that."

"For goodness sake, Colin, Sukhvinder isn't trying to *get at* Minda," said Tessa.

"So you think I'm being unreasonable?" Parminder shot at Tessa.

"No, no," said Tessa, appalled at how quickly they had been sucked into the family row. "I'm just saying, there aren't many places for kids to work in Pagford, are there?"

"And why does she need to work at all?" said Parminder, raising her hands in a gesture of furious exasperation. "Don't we give her enough money?"

"Money you earn yourself is always different, you know that," said Tessa.

Tessa's chair faced a wall that was covered in photographs of the Jawanda children. She had sat here often, and had counted how many appearances each child made: Jaswant, eighteen; Rajpal, nineteen; and Sukhvinder, nine. There was only one photograph on the wall celebrating Sukhvinder's individual achievements: the picture of the Winterdown rowing team on the day that they had beaten St. Anne's. Barry had given all the parents an enlarged copy of this picture, in which Sukhvinder and Krystal Weedon were in the middle of the line of eight, with their arms around each other's shoulders, beaming and jumping up and down so that they were both slightly blurred.

Barry, she thought, *would have helped Parminder see things the right way.* He had been a bridge between mother and daughter, both of whom had adored him.

Not for the first time, Tessa wondered how much difference it made that she had not given birth to her son. Did she find it easier to accept him as a separate individual than if he had been made from her flesh and blood? Her glucose-heavy, tainted blood…

Fats had recently stopped calling her "Mum." She had to pretend not to care, because it made Colin so angry; but every time Fats said "Tessa" it was like a needle jab to her heart.

The four of them finished their cold fruit in silence.

VII

Up in the little white house that sat high above the town, Simon Price fretted and brooded. Days passed. The accusatory post had vanished from the message boards, but Simon remained paralyzed. To withdraw his candidacy might seem like an admission of guilt. The police had not come knocking about the computer; Simon half regretted throwing it off the old bridge now. On the other hand, he could not decide whether he had imagined a knowing grin from the man behind the till when he handed over his credit card in the garage at the foot of the hill. There was a lot of talk about redundancies at work, and Simon was still afraid of the contents of that post coming to the bosses' ears, that they might save themselves redundancy pay by sacking himself, Jim and Tommy.

Andrew watched and waited, losing hope every day. He had tried to show the world what his father was, and the world, it seemed, had merely shrugged. Andrew had imagined that someone from the printworks or the council would rise up and tell Simon firmly, "no"; that he was not fit to set himself up in competition with other people, that he was unsuitable and substandard, and must not disgrace himself or his family. Yet nothing had happened, except that Simon stopped talking about the council or making telephone calls in the hope of garnering votes, and the leaflets that he had had printed out of hours at work sat untouched in a box in the porch.

Then, without warning or fanfare, came victory. Heading down the dark stairs in search of food on Friday evening, Andrew heard Simon talking stiffly on the telephone in the sitting room, and paused to listen.

"...withdraw my candidacy," he was saying. "Yes. Well, my personal circumstances have changed. Yes. Yes. Yeah, that's right. OK. Thank you."

Andrew heard Simon replace the receiver.

"Well, that's that," his father said to his mother. "I'm well out of it, if that's the kind of shit they're throwing around."

He heard his mother return some muffled, approving rejoinder, and before Andrew had time to move, Simon had emerged into the hall below, drawn breath into his lungs and yelled the first syllable of Andrew's name, before realizing that his son was right in front of him.

"What are you doing?"

Simon's face was half in shadow, lit only by the light escaping the sitting room.

"I wanted a drink," Andrew lied; his father did not like the boys helping themselves to food.

"You start work with Mollison this weekend, don't you?"

"Yeah."

"Right, well, you listen to me. I want anything you can get on that bastard, d'you hear me? All the dirt you can get. And on his son, if you hear anything."

"All right," said Andrew.

"And I'll put it up on the fucking website for them," said Simon, and he walked back into the sitting room. "*Barry Fairbrother's fucking ghost.*"

As he scavenged an assortment of food that might not be missed, skimming off slices here, handfuls there, a jubilant jingle ran through Andrew's mind: *I stopped you, you bastard. I stopped you.*

He had done exactly what he had set out to do: Simon had no idea who had brought his ambitions to dust. The silly sod was even demanding Andrew's help in getting his revenge; a complete about-turn, because when Andrew had first told his parents that he had a job at the delicatessen, Simon had been furious.

"You stupid little tit. What about your fucking allergy?"

"I thought I'd try not eating any of the nuts," said Andrew.

"Don't get smart with me, Pizza Face. What if you eat one accidentally, like at St. Thomas's? D'you think we want to go through that crap again?"

But Ruth had supported Andrew, telling Simon that Andrew was old enough to take care, to know better. When Simon had left the room, she had tried to tell Andrew that Simon was only worried about him.

"The only thing he's worried about is that he'd have to miss bloody *Match of the Day* to take me to hospital."

Andrew returned to his bedroom, where he sat shoveling food into his mouth with one hand and texting Fats with the other.

He thought that it was all over, finished, done with. Andrew had never yet had reason to observe the first tiny bubble of fermenting yeast, in which was contained an inevitable, alchemical transformation.

VIII

The move to Pagford had been the worst thing that had ever happened to Gaia Bawden. Excepting occasional visits to her father in Reading, London was all that she had ever known. So incredulous had Gaia been, when Kay had first said that she wanted to move to a tiny West Country town, that it had been weeks before she took the threat seriously. She had thought it one of Kay's mad ideas, like the two chickens she had bought for their tiny back garden in Hackney (killed by a fox a week after purchase), or deciding to ruin half their saucepans and permanently scar her own hand by making marmalade, when she hardly ever cooked.

Wrenched from friends she had had since primary school, from the house she had known since she was eight, from weekends that were, increasingly, about every kind of urban fun, Gaia had been plunged, over her pleas, threats and protests, into a life she had never dreamed existed. Cobbled streets and no shops open past six o'clock, a communal life that seemed to revolve around the church, and where you could often hear birdsong and nothing else: Gaia felt as though she had fallen through a portal into a land lost in time.

She and Kay had clung tightly to each other all Gaia's life (for her father had never lived with them, and Kay's two successive relationships had never been formalized), bickering, condoling and growing steadily more like flatmates with the passing years. Now, though, Gaia saw nothing but an enemy when she looked across the kitchen table. Her only ambition was to return to London, by any means possible, and to make Kay as unhappy as she could, in revenge. She could not decide whether it would punish Kay more to fail all her GCSEs, or to pass them, and try and get her father to agree to house her, while she attended a sixth-form college in London. In the meantime, she had to exist in alien territory, where her looks and her accent, once instant passports to the most select social circles, had become foreign currency.

Gaia had no desire to become one of the popular students at Winterdown: she thought they were embarrassing, with their West

Country accents and their pathetic ideas of what constituted entertainment. Her determined pursuit of Sukhvinder Jawanda was, in part, a way of showing the in-crowd that she found them laughable, and partly because she was in a mood to feel kinship with anybody who seemed to have outsider status.

The fact that Sukhvinder had agreed to join Gaia as a waitress had moved their friendship to a different level. In their next period of double biology, Gaia unbent as she had never done before, and Sukhvinder glimpsed, at last, part of the mysterious reason why this beautiful, cool newcomer had selected her as a friend. Adjusting the focus on their shared microscope, Gaia muttered, "It's so frigging *white* here, isn't it?"

Sukhvinder heard herself saying "yeah" before she had fully considered the question. Gaia was still talking, but Sukhvinder was only half listening. "So frigging white." She supposed that it was.

At St. Thomas's, she had been made to get up, the only brown person in the class, and talk about the Sikh religion. She had stood obediently at the front of the class and told the story of the Sikh religion's founder Guru Nanak, who disappeared into a river, and was believed drowned, but reemerged after three days underwater to announce: "There is no Hindu, there is no Moslem."

The other children had sniggered at the idea of anyone surviving underwater for three days. Sukhvinder had not had the courage to point out that Jesus had died and then come back to life. She had cut the story of Guru Nanak short, desperate to get back to her seat. She had only ever visited a gurdwara a handful of times in her life; there was none in Pagford, and the one in Yarvil was tiny and dominated, according to her parents, by Chamars, a different caste from their own. Sukhvinder did not even know why that mattered, because she knew that Guru Nanak explicitly forbade caste distinctions. It was all very confusing, and she continued to enjoy Easter eggs and decorating the Christmas tree, and found the books that Parminder pressed upon her children, explaining the lives of the gurus and the tenets of Khalsa, extremely difficult to read.

Visits to her mother's family in Birmingham, to the streets where nearly everyone was brown, and the shops full of saris and Indian spices, made Sukhvinder feel dislocated and inadequate. Her cousins spoke Punjabi as well as English; they lived a cool city life; her female cousins were good-looking and trendy. They laughed at her West Country burr and her lack of fashion sense, and Sukhvinder hated being laughed at. Before Fats Wall had begun his regime of daily torture, before their year had been streamed into sets and she had found herself in daily contact with Dane Tully, she had always liked returning to Pagford. It had felt, then, like a haven.

While they were fiddling with slides, keeping their heads low to escape Mrs. Knight's attention, Gaia told Sukhvinder more than ever before about her life at Gravener Secondary in Hackney; the words had poured out of her in a slightly nervy stream. She described the friends she had left behind; one of them, Harpreet, had the same name as Sukhvinder's oldest cousin. She talked about Sherelle, who was black, and the cleverest girl in their gang; and about Jen, whose brother had been Gaia's first boyfriend.

Though passionately interested in all that Gaia was telling her, Sukhvinder's thoughts strayed, imagining a school assembly where your eye struggled to pick out individual components of a kaleidoscope composed of every shade of skin from porridge right through to mahogany. Here at Winterdown, the blue-black hair of the Asian kids stood out clearly in the sea of mouse and dun. At a place like Gravener, the likes of Fats Wall and Dane Tully might be in a minority themselves.

Sukhvinder asked a timid question.

"Why did you move?"

"Because my mother wanted to be near her twat of a boyfriend," muttered Gaia. "Gavin Hughes, d'you know him?"

Sukhvinder shook her head.

"You've probably heard them shagging," said Gaia. "The whole street hears when they're at it. Just keep your windows open some night."

Sukhvinder tried not to look shocked, but the idea of overhearing her parents, her married parents, having sex was quite bad enough. Gaia herself was flushed; not, Sukhvinder thought, with embarrassment but with anger. "He's going to ditch her. She's so deluded. He can't wait to leave after they've done it."

Sukhvinder would never have talked about her mother like this, and nor would the Fairbrother twins (still, in theory, her best friends). Niamh and Siobhan were working together at a microscope not far away. Since their father had died, they seemed to have closed in on themselves, choosing each other's company, drifting away from Sukhvinder.

Andrew Price was staring almost constantly at Gaia through a gap in the white faces all around them. Sukhvinder, who had noticed this, thought that Gaia had not, but she was wrong. Gaia was simply not bothering to stare back or preen herself, because she was used to boys staring at her; it had been happening since she was twelve. Two boys in the lower sixth kept turning up in the corridors as she moved between classes, far more often than the law of averages would seem to dictate, and both were better-looking than Andrew. However, none of them could compare to the boy to whom Gaia had lost her virginity shortly before moving to Pagford.

Gaia could hardly bear that Marco de Luca was still physically alive in the universe, and separated from her by a hundred and thirty-two miles of aching, useless space.

"He's eighteen," she told Sukhvinder. "He's half Italian. He plays football really well. He's supposed to be getting a tryout for Arsenal's youth squad."

Gaia had had sex with Marco four times before leaving Hackney, each time stealing condoms out of Kay's bedside table. She had half wanted Kay to know to what lengths she was driven, to brand herself on Marco's memory because she was being forced to leave him.

Sukhvinder listened, fascinated, but not admitting to Gaia that she had already seen Marco on her new friend's Facebook page. There was nobody like that in the whole of Winterdown: he looked like Johnny Depp.

Gaia slumped against the desk, playing absentmindedly with the focus on the microscope, and across the room Andrew Price continued to stare at Gaia whenever he thought Fats would not notice.

"Maybe he'll be faithful. Sherelle's having a party on Saturday night. She's invited him. She's sworn she won't let him get up to anything. But shit, I wish…"

She stared at the desk with her flecked eyes out of focus and Sukhvinder watched her humbly, marveling at her good looks, lost in admiration for her life. The idea of having another world where you belonged completely, where you had a footballer boyfriend and a gang of cool, devoted friends, seemed to her, even if you had been forcibly removed from it all, an awe-inspiring and enviable state of affairs.

They walked together to the shops at lunchtime, something Sukhvinder almost never did; she and the Fairbrother twins usually ate in the canteen.

As they hung about on the pavement outside the newsagent's where they had bought sandwiches, they heard words uttered in a piercing scream.

"Your fucking mum killed my Nan!"

All the Winterdown students clustered by the newsagent's looked around for the source of the shouting, puzzled, and Sukhvinder imitated them, as confused as everyone else. Then she spotted Krystal Weedon, who was standing on the other side of the road, pointing a stubby finger like a gun. She had four other girls with her, all of them strung along the pavement in a line, held back by the traffic.

"Your fucking mum killed my Nan! She's gonna get fucking done and so are you!"

Sukhvinder's stomach seemed to melt clean away. People were staring at her. A couple of third-year girls scuttled out of sight. Sukhvinder sensed the bystanders nearby transforming into a watchful, eager pack. Krystal and her gang were dancing on tiptoes, waiting for a break in the cars.

"What's she talking about?" Gaia asked Sukhvinder, whose mouth was so dry that she could not reply. There was no point in running. She would never make it. Leanne Carter was the fastest girl in their year. All that seemed to move in the world were the passing cars, giving her a few final seconds of safety.

And then Jaswant appeared, accompanied by several sixth-year boys.

"All right, Jolly?" she said. "What's up?"

Jaswant had not heard Krystal; it was mere luck that she had drifted this way with her entourage. Over the road, Krystal and her friends had gone into a huddle.

"Nothing much," said Sukhvinder, dizzy with relief at her temporary reprieve. She could not tell Jaz what was happening in front of the boys. Two of them were nearly six feet tall. All were staring at Gaia.

Jaz and her friends moved toward the newsagent's door, and Sukhvinder, with an urgent look at Gaia, followed them. She and Gaia watched through the window as Krystal and her gang moved on, glancing back every few steps.

"What was that about?" Gaia asked.

"Her great-gran was my mum's patient, and she died," said Sukhvinder. She wanted to cry so much that the muscles in her throat were painful.

"Silly bitch," said Gaia.

But Sukhvinder's suppressed sobs were born not only from the shaky aftermath of fear. She had liked Krystal very much, and she knew that Krystal had liked her too. All those afternoons on the canal, all those journeys in the minibus; she knew the anatomy of Krystal's back and shoulders better than she knew her own.

They returned to school with Jaswant and her friends. The best-looking of the boys struck up a conversation with Gaia. By the time they had turned in at the gates, he was teasing her about her London accent. Sukhvinder could not see Krystal anywhere, but she spotted Fats Wall at a distance, loping along with Andrew Price. She would have known his shape and his walk anywhere, the way something primal inside you helped you recognize a spider moving across a shadowy floor.

Wave upon wave of nausea rippled through her as she approached the school building. There would be two of them from now on: Fats and Krystal together. Everyone knew that they were seeing each other. And into Sukhvinder's mind dropped a vividly colored picture of herself bleeding on the floor, and Krystal and her gang kicking her, and Fats Wall watching, laughing.

"Need the loo," she told Gaia. "Meet you up there."

She dived into the first girls' bathroom they passed, locked herself in a cubicle and sat down on the closed seat. If she could have died...if she could have disappeared forever...but the solid surface of things refused to dissolve around her, and her body, her hateful hermaphrodite's body, continued, in its stubborn, lumpen way, to live...

She heard the bell for the start of afternoon lessons, jumped up and hurried out of the bathroom. Queues were forming along the corridor. She turned her back on all of them and marched out of the building.

Other people truanted. Krystal did it and so did Fats Wall. If she could only get away and stay away this afternoon, she might be able to think of something to protect her before she had to go back in. Or she could walk in front of a car. She imagined it slamming into her body and her bones shattering. How quickly would she die, broken in the road? She still preferred the thought of drowning, of cool clean water putting her to sleep forever: a sleep without dreams...

"Sukhvinder? *Sukhvinder!*"

Her stomach turned over. Tessa Wall was hurrying toward her across the car park. For one mad moment Sukhvinder considered running, but then the futility of it overwhelmed her, and she stood waiting for Tessa to reach her, hating her, with her stupid plain face and her evil son.

"Sukhvinder, what are you doing? Where are you going?"

She could not even think of a lie. With a hopeless gesture of her shoulders, she surrendered.

Tessa had no appointments until three. She ought to have taken Sukhvinder to the office and reported her attempted flight; instead, she took Sukhvinder upstairs to the guidance room, with its Nepalese wall-hanging and the posters for ChildLine. Sukhvinder had never been there before.

Tessa spoke, and left inviting little pauses, then spoke again, and Sukhvinder sat with sweaty palms, her gaze fixed on her shoes. Tessa knew her mother—Tessa would tell Parminder that she had tried to truant—but if she explained why? Would Tessa, could Tessa, intercede? Not with her son; she could not control Fats, that was common knowledge. But with Krystal? Krystal came to guidance...

How bad would the beating be, if she told? But there would be a beating even if she did not tell. Krystal had been ready to set her whole gang on her...

"...anything happened, Sukhvinder?"

She nodded. Tessa said encouragingly, "Can you tell me what it was?"

So Sukhvinder told.

She was sure she could read, in the minute contraction of Tessa's brow as she listened, something other than sympathy for herself. Perhaps Tessa was thinking about how Parminder might react to the news that her treatment of Mrs. Catherine Weedon was being screamed about in the street. Sukhvinder had not forgotten to worry about that as she had sat in the bathroom cubicle, wishing for death. Or perhaps Tessa's look of unease was reluctance to tackle Krystal Weedon; doubtless Krystal was her favorite too, as she had been Mr. Fairbrother's.

A fierce, stinging sense of injustice burst through Sukhvinder's misery, her fear and her self-loathing; it swept aside that tangle of worries and terrors that encased her daily; she thought of Krystal and her mates, waiting to charge; she thought of Fats, whispering poisonous words from behind her in every maths lesson, and of the message that she had wiped off her Facebook page the previous evening:

Les-bian-ism n. Sexual orientation of women to women. Also called Sapphism. A native or inhabitant of Lesbos.

"I don't know how she knows," said Sukhvinder, with the blood thrumming in her ears.

"Knows...?" asked Tessa, her expression still troubled.

"That there's been a complaint about Mum and her great-gran. Krystal and her mum don't talk to the rest of the family. Maybe," said Sukhvinder, "Fats told her?"

"Fats?" Tessa repeated uncomprehendingly.

"You know, because they're seeing each other," said Sukhvinder. "Him and Krystal? Going out together? So maybe he told her."

It gave her some bitter satisfaction to see every vestige of professional calm drain from Tessa's face.

IX

Kay Bawden never wanted to set foot in Miles and Samantha's house again. She could not forgive them for witnessing Gavin's parade of indifference, nor could she forget Miles' patronizing laughter, his attitude to Bellchapel, or the sneery way that he and Samantha had spoken about Krystal Weedon.

In spite of Gavin's apology and his tepid assurances of affection, Kay could not stop picturing him nose to nose with Mary on the sofa; jumping up to help her with the plates; walking her home in the dark. When Gavin told her, a few days later, that he had had dinner at Mary's house, she had to fight down an angry response, because he had never eaten more than toast at her house in Hope Street.

She might not be allowed to say anything bad about The Widow, about whom Gavin spoke as though she were the Holy Mother, but the Mollisons were different.

"I can't say I like Miles very much."

"He's not exactly my best mate."

"If you ask me, it'll be a catastrophe for the addiction clinic if he gets elected."

"I doubt it'll make any difference."

Gavin's apathy, his indifference to other people's pain, always infuriated Kay.

"Isn't there anyone who'll stick up for Bellchapel?"

"Colin Wall, I suppose," said Gavin.

So, at eight o'clock on Monday evening, Kay walked up the Walls' drive and rang their doorbell. From the front step, she could make out Samantha Mollison's red Ford Fiesta, parked in the drive three houses along. The sight added a little extra zest to her desire for a fight.

The Walls' door was opened by a short plain dumpy woman in a tie-dyed skirt.

"Hello," said Kay. "My name's Kay Bawden, and I was wondering whether I could speak to Colin Wall?"

For a split second, Tessa simply stared at the attractive young woman on the doorstep whom she had never seen before. The strangest idea flashed across her mind: that Colin was having an affair and that his lover had come to tell her so.

"Oh—yes—come in. I'm Tessa."

Kay wiped her feet conscientiously on the doormat and followed Tessa into a sitting room that was smaller, shabbier but cosier than the Mollisons'. A tall, balding man with a high forehead was sitting in an armchair with a notebook in his lap and a pen in his hand.

"Colin, this is Kay Bawden," said Tessa. "She'd like to speak to you."

Tessa saw Colin's startled and wary expression, and knew at once that the woman was a stranger to him. *Really*, she thought, a little ashamed, *what were you thinking?*

"I'm sorry to barge in on you like this, unannounced," said Kay, as Colin stood up to shake her hand. "I would have telephoned, but you're—"

"We're ex-directory, yes," said Colin. He towered over Kay, his eyes tiny behind the lenses of his glasses. "Please, sit down."

"Thank you. It's about the election," said Kay. "This Parish Council election. You're standing, aren't you, against Miles Mollison?"

"That's right," said Colin nervously. He knew who she must be: the reporter who had wanted to talk to Krystal. They had tracked him down—Tessa ought not to have let her in.

"I was wondering whether I could help in any way," said Kay. "I'm a social worker, mostly working in the Fields. There are some facts and figures I could give you about the Bellchapel Addiction Clinic, which Mollison seems quite keen on closing. I've been told that you're for the clinic? That you'd like to keep it open?"

The onrush of relief and pleasure made him almost giddy.

"Oh, yes," said Colin, "yes, I would. Yes, that was my pre-decessor's—that's to say, the previous holder of the seat—Barry Fairbrother—was certainly opposed to closing the clinic. And I am, too."

"Well, I've had a conversation with Miles Mollison, and he made it quite clear that he doesn't think the clinic's worth keeping open. Frankly, I think he's rather ignorant and naive about the causes and treatment of addiction, and about the very real difference

Bellchapel is making. If the Parish refuses to renew the lease on the building, and the District cuts funding, then there's a danger that some very vulnerable people will be left without support."

"Yes, yes, I see," said Colin. "Oh, yes, I agree."

He was astonished and flattered that this attractive young woman would have walked through the evening to find him and offer herself as an ally.

"Would you like a cup of tea or coffee, Kay?" asked Tessa.

"Oh, thanks very much," said Kay. "Tea, please, Tessa. No sugar."

Fats was in the kitchen, helping himself from the fridge. He ate copiously and continually, but remained scrawny, never putting on an ounce of weight. In spite of his openly declared disgust for them, he seemed unaffected by Tessa's pack of ready-filled syringes, which sat in a clinical white box next to the cheese.

Tessa moved to the kettle, and her thoughts returned to the subject that had consumed her ever since Sukhvinder had suggested it earlier: that Fats and Krystal were "seeing each other." She had not questioned Fats, and she had not told Colin.

The more that Tessa thought about it, the more certain she was that it could not be true. She was sure that Fats held himself in such high regard that no girl would be good enough, especially a girl like Krystal. Surely he would not...

Demean himself? Is that it? Is that what you think?

"Who's here?" Fats asked Tessa, through a mouthful of cold chicken, as she put on the kettle.

"A woman who wants to help Dad get elected to the council," replied Tessa, foraging in the cupboard for biscuits.

"Why? Does she fancy him?"

"Grow up, Stu," said Tessa crossly.

He plucked several slices of thin ham out of an open pack and poked them, bit by bit, into his crammed mouth, like a magician inserting silk handkerchiefs into his fist. Fats sometimes stood for ten minutes at a time at the open fridge, ripping open clingfilm and packets and putting chunks of food directly into his mouth. It was a habit Colin deprecated, along with almost every other aspect of Fats' behavior.

"Why's she want to help him, seriously?" he asked, having swallowed his mouthful of meat.

"She wants the Bellchapel Addiction Clinic to stay open."

"What, a junkie, is she?"

"No, she isn't a junkie," said Tessa, noting with annoyance that Fats had finished the last three chocolate biscuits and left the empty wrappings on the shelf. "She's a social worker, and she thinks the clinic is doing a good job. Dad wants to keep it open, but Miles Mollison doesn't think it's very effective."

"It can't be doing that well. The Fields are full of glue-sniffers and smackheads."

Tessa knew that if she had said that Colin wanted to close the clinic, Fats would have instantly produced an argument for its continuation.

"You ought to be a barrister, Stu," she said as the kettle lid started to rattle.

When Tessa returned to the sitting room with her tray, she found Kay talking Colin through a sheaf of printed material she had brought out of her big tote bag.

"...two drugs workers part funded by the council, and partly by Action on Addiction, which is a really good charity. Then there's a social worker attached to the clinic, Nina, she's the one who gave me all this—oh, thanks very much," said Kay, beaming up at Tessa, who had set down a mug of tea on the table beside her.

Kay had taken to the Walls, in just a few minutes, as she had not taken to anybody else in Pagford. There had been no sweeping up-and-down glance from Tessa as she walked in, no gimlet-eyed assessment of her physical imperfections and dress sense. Her husband, though nervous, seemed decent and earnest in his determination to obstruct the abandonment of the Fields.

"Is that a London accent, Kay?" asked Tessa, dunking a plain biscuit in her tea. Kay nodded.

"What brings you to Pagford?"

"A relationship," said Kay. She took no pleasure saying it, even though she and Gavin were officially reconciled. She turned back to Colin.

"I don't quite understand the situation with regards to the Parish Council and the clinic."

"Oh, it owns the building," said Colin. "It's an old church. The lease is coming up for renewal."

"So that would be an easy way to force them out."

"Exactly. When did you say you'd spoken to Miles Mollison?" asked Colin, both hoping and dreading to hear that Miles had mentioned him.

"We had dinner, Friday before last," Kay explained, "Gavin and I—"

"Oh, you're *Gavin's* girlfriend!" interjected Tessa.

"Yes; and, anyway, the subject of the Fields came up—"

"It would," said Tessa.

"—and Miles mentioned Bellchapel, and I was quite—quite *dismayed* by the way he talked about the issues involved. I told him I'm dealing with a family at the moment," Kay remembered her indiscreet mention of the Weedons' names and proceeded carefully, "and if the mother is deprived of methadone, she'll almost certainly end up back on the game."

"That sounds like the Weedons," said Tessa, with a lowering sensation.

"I—yes, I am talking about the Weedons, actually," said Kay.

Tessa reached for another biscuit.

"I'm Krystal's guidance teacher. This must be the second time her mother's been through Bellchapel, is it?"

"Third," said Kay.

"We've known Krystal since she was five: she was in our son's class at primary school," Tessa said. "She's had an awful life, really."

"Absolutely," said Kay. "It's astounding she's as sweet as she is, actually."

"Oh, I agree," said Colin heartily.

Remembering Colin's absolute refusal to rescind Krystal's detention after the squawking incident in assembly, Tessa raised her eyebrows. Then she wondered, with a sick lurch in her stomach, what Colin would say if Sukhvinder was not lying or mistaken. But surely Sukhvinder was wrong. She was a shy, naive girl. Probably she had got the wrong end of the stick…misheard something…

"The point is, about the only thing that motivates Terri is the fear of losing her kids," said Kay. "She's back on track at the moment; her key worker at the clinic told me she senses a bit of a breakthrough in Terri's attitude. If Bellchapel closes, it all goes belly-up again, and God knows what'll happen to the family."

"This is all very useful," said Colin, nodding importantly, and starting to make notes on a clean page in his notebook. "Very useful indeed. Did you say you've got statistics on people going clean?"

Kay shuffled the printed pages, looking for the information. Tessa had the impression that Colin wanted to reclaim Kay's attention for himself. He had always been susceptible to good looks and a sympathetic manner.

Tessa munched another biscuit, still thinking about Krystal. Their recent guidance sessions had not been very satisfactory. Krystal had been standoffish. Today's had been no different. She had extracted a promise from Krystal that she would not pursue or harass Sukhvinder Jawanda again, but Krystal's demeanor suggested that Tessa had let her down, that trust was broken. Possibly Colin's detention was to blame. Tessa had thought that she and Krystal had forged a bond strong enough to withstand that, although it had never been quite like the one Krystal had with Barry.

(Tessa had been there, on the spot, the day that Barry had come into school with a rowing machine, looking for recruits to the crew he was trying to start. She had been summoned from the staff room to the gym, because the PE teacher was off sick, and the only supply teacher they could find at such short notice was male.

The fourth-year girls, in their shorts and Aertex tops, had been giggly when they had arrived in the gym to find Miss Jarvis absent, replaced by two strange men. Tessa had had to reprimand Krystal, Nikki and Leanne, who had pushed to the front of the class and were making lewd suggestive remarks about the supply teacher; he was a handsome young man with an unfortunate tendency to blush.

Barry, short, ginger-haired and bearded, was wearing a tracksuit. He had taken a morning off work to do this. Everybody thought his idea was strange and unrealistic: schools like Winterdown did not have rowing eights. Niamh and Siobhan had seemed half amused, half mortified by their dad's presence.

Barry explained what he was trying to do: put together crews. He had secured the use of the old boathouse down on the canal at Yarvil; it was a fabulous sport, and an opportunity to shine, for themselves, for their school. Tessa had positioned herself right next to Krystal and her friends to keep them in check; the worst of their giggling had subsided, but was not entirely quelled.

Barry demonstrated the rowing machine and asked for volunteers. Nobody stepped forward.

"Krystal Weedon," said Barry, pointing at her. "I've seen you dangling off the monkey bars down the park; that's proper upper body strength you've got there. Come here and give it a go."

Krystal was only too happy to step into the spotlight; she swaggered up to the machine and sat down on it. Even with Tessa glowering beside them, Nikki and Leanne had howled with laughter and the rest of the class joined in.

Barry showed Krystal what to do. The silent supply teacher had watched in professional alarm as Barry positioned her hands on the wooden handle.

She heaved on the handle, making a stupid face at Nikki and Leanne, and everyone laughed again.

"Look at that," Barry had said, beaming. "She's a natural."

Had Krystal really been a natural? Tessa did not know anything about rowing; she could not tell.

"Straighten your back," Barry told Krystal, "or you'll injure it. That's it. Pull...pull...look at that technique...have you done this before?"

Then Krystal really had straightened her back, and she really had done it properly. She stopped looking at Nikki and Leanne. She hit a rhythm.

"Excellent," said Barry. "Look at that...*excellent*. That's how you do it! Atta girl. And again. And again. And—"

"It 'urts!" shouted Krystal.

"I know it does. That's how you end up with arms like Jennifer Aniston, doing that," said Barry.

There had been a little ripple of laughter, but this time they laughed with him. What was it that Barry had had? He was always so present, so natural, so entirely without self-consciousness. Teenagers, Tessa knew, were riven with the fear of ridicule. Those who were without it, and God knew there were few enough of them in the adult world, had natural authority among the young; they ought to be forced to teach.

"And rest!" Barry said, and Krystal slumped, red in the face and rubbing her arms.

"You'll have to give up the fags, Krystal," said Barry, and he got a big laugh this time. "OK, who else wants a try?"

When Krystal rejoined her watching classmates, she was no longer laughing. She watched each new rower jealously, her eyes darting constantly to Barry's bearded face to see what he thought of them. When Carmen Lewis messed it up completely, Barry said, "Show 'em, Krystal," and her face lit up as she returned to the machine.

But at the end of the exhibition, when Barry asked those who were interested in trying out for the team to raise their hands, Krystal kept her arms folded. Tessa watched her shake her head, sneering, as Nikki muttered to her. Barry carefully noted down the names of the interested girls, then looked up.

"And *you*, Krystal Weedon," he said, pointing at her. "You're coming too. Don't you shake your head at me. I'll be very annoyed if I don't see *you*. That's natural talent you've got there. I don't like seeing natural talent wasted. Krys-tal," he said loudly, inscribing her name, "Wee-*don*."

Had Krystal thought about her natural talent as she showered at the end of the lesson? Had she carried the thought of her new aptitude around with her that day, like an unexpected Valentine? Tessa did not know; but to the amazement of all, except perhaps Barry, Krystal had turned up at tryouts.)

Colin was nodding vigorously as Kay took him through relapse rates at Bellchapel.

"Parminder should see this," he said. "I'll make sure she gets a copy. Yes, yes, very useful indeed."

Feeling slightly sick, Tessa took a fourth biscuit.

X

Parminder worked late on Monday evenings, and as Vikram was usually at the hospital, the three Jawanda children laid the table and cooked for themselves. Sometimes they squabbled; occasionally they had a laugh; but today, each was absorbed in their own particular thoughts, and the job was completed with unusual efficiency in near silence.

Sukhvinder had not told her brother or her sister that she had tried to truant, or about Krystal Weedon's threat to beat her up. The habit of secrecy was very strong in her these days. She was actively frightened of imparting confidences, because she feared that they might betray the world of oddness that lived inside her, the world that Fats Wall seemed able to penetrate with such terrifying ease. All the same, she knew that the events of the day could not be kept quiet indefinitely. Tessa had told her that she intended to telephone Parminder.

"I'm going to have to call your mum, Sukhvinder, it's what we always do, but I'm going to explain to her why you did it."

Sukhvinder had felt almost warm toward Tessa, even though she was Fats Wall's mother. Frightened though she was of her mother's reaction, a tiny little glow of hope had kindled inside her at the thought of Tessa interceding for her. Would the realization of Sukhvinder's desperation lead, at last, to some crack in her mother's implacable disapproval, her disappointment, her endless stone-faced criticism?

When the front door opened at last, she heard her mother speaking Punjabi.

"Oh, not the bloody farm again," groaned Jaswant, who had cocked an ear to the door.

The Jawandas owned a patch of ancestral land in the Punjab, which Parminder, the oldest, had inherited from their father in the absence of sons. The farm occupied a place in the family consciousness that Jaswant and Sukhvinder had sometimes discussed. To their slightly amused astonishment, a few of their older relatives seemed to live in the expectation that the whole family would move back there one day. Parminder's father had sent money back to the farm all his life. It was tenanted and worked by second cousins, who seemed surly and embittered. The farm caused regular arguments among her mother's family.

"Nani's gone off on one again," interpreted Jaswant, as Parminder's muffled voice penetrated the door.

Parminder had taught her first-born some Punjabi, and Jaz had picked up a lot more from their cousins. Sukhvinder's dyslexia had been too severe to enable her to learn two languages and the attempt had been abandoned.

"...Harpreet still wants to sell off that bit for the road..."

Sukhvinder heard Parminder kicking off her shoes. She wished that her mother had not been bothered about the farm tonight of all nights; it never put her into a good mood; and when Parminder pushed open the kitchen door and she saw her mother's tight mask-like face, her courage failed her completely.

Parminder acknowledged Jaswant and Rajpal with a slight wave of her hand, but she pointed at Sukhvinder and then toward a kitchen chair, indicating that she was to sit down and wait for the call to end.

Jaswant and Rajpal drifted back upstairs. Sukhvinder waited beneath the wall of photographs, in which her relative inadequacy was displayed for the world to see, pinned to her chair by her mother's silent command. On and on went the call, until at long last Parminder said good-bye and cut the connection.

When she turned to look at her daughter Sukhvinder knew, instantly, before a word was spoken, that she had been wrong to hope.

"So," said Parminder. "I had a call from Tessa while I was at work. I expect you know what it was about."

Sukhvinder nodded. Her mouth seemed to be full of cotton wool.

Parminder's rage crashed over her like a tidal wave, dragging Sukhvinder with it, so that she was unable to find her feet or right herself.

"Why? *Why?* Is this copying the London girl, again—are

you trying to impress her? Jaz and Raj never behave like this, never—why do you? What's wrong with you? Are you proud of being lazy and sloppy? Do you think it's cool to act like a delinquent? How do you think I felt when Tessa told me? Called at work—I've never been so ashamed—I'm disgusted by you, do you hear me? Do we not give you enough? Do we not help you enough? *What is wrong with you, Sukhvinder?*"

In desperation, Sukhvinder tried to break through her mother's tirade, and mentioned the name Krystal Weedon—

"Krystal Weedon!" shouted Parminder. "That stupid girl! Why are you paying attention to anything she says? Did you tell her I tried to keep her damn great-grandmother alive? Did you tell her that?"

"I—no—"

"If you're going to care about what the likes of Krystal Weedon says, there's no hope for you! Perhaps that's your natural level, is it, Sukhvinder? You want to play truant and work in a café and waste all your opportunities for education, because that's easier? Is that what being in a team with Krystal Weedon taught you—to sink to her level?"

Sukhvinder thought of Krystal and her gang, raring to go on the opposite curb, waiting for a break in the cars. What would it take to make her mother understand? An hour ago she had had the tiniest fantasy that she might confide in her mother, at last, about Fats Wall...

"Get out of my sight! Go! I'll speak to your father when he comes in—go!"

Sukhvinder walked upstairs. Jaswant called from her bedroom: "What was all that shouting about?"

Sukhvinder did not answer. She proceeded to her own room, where she closed the door and sat down on the edge of her bed.

What's wrong with you, Sukhvinder?

You disgust me.

Are you proud of being lazy and sloppy?

What had she expected? Warm encircling arms and comfort? When had she ever been hugged and held by Parminder? There was more comfort to be had from the razor blade hidden in her stuffed rabbit; but the desire, mounting to a need, to cut and bleed, could not be satisfied by daylight, with the family awake and her father on his way.

The dark lake of desperation and pain that lived in Sukhvinder and yearned for release was in flames, as if it had been fuel all along.

Let her see how it feels.

She got up, crossed her bedroom in a few strides, and dropping into the chair by her desk, pounded at the keyboard of her computer.

Sukhvinder had been just as interested as Andrew Price when that stupid supply teacher had tried to impress them with his cool in computing. Unlike Andrew and a couple of the other boys, Sukhvinder had not plied the teacher with questions about the hacking; she had merely gone home quietly and looked it all up online. Nearly every modern website was proof against a classic SQL injection, but when Sukhvinder had heard her mother discussing the anonymous attack on the Pagford Parish Council website, it had occurred to Sukhvinder that the security on that feeble old site was probably minimal.

Sukhvinder always found it much easier to type than to write, and computer code easier to read than long strings of words. It did not take very long for her to retrieve a site that gave explicit instructions for the simplest form of SQL injection. Then she brought up the Parish Council website.

It took her five minutes to hack the site, and then only because she had transcribed the code wrong the first time. To her astonishment, she discovered that whoever was administering the site had not removed the user details of The_Ghost_of_Barry_Fairbrother from the database, but merely deleted the post. It would be child's play, therefore, to post in the same name.

It took Sukhvinder much longer to compose the message than it had to hack into the site. She had carried the secret accusation with her for months, ever since New Year's Eve, when she had noticed with wonder her mother's face, at ten to midnight, from the corner of the party where she was hiding. She typed slowly. Autocorrect helped with her spelling.

She was not afraid that Parminder would check her computer history; her mother knew so little about her, and about what went on in this bedroom, that she would never suspect her lazy, stupid, sloppy daughter.

Sukhvinder pressed the mouse like a trigger.

XI

Krystal did not take Robbie to nursery on Tuesday morning, but dressed him for Nana Cath's funeral instead. As she pulled up his least ripped trousers, which were a good two inches too short in the leg, she tried to explain to him who Nana Cath had been, but she might as well have saved her breath. Robbie had no memory of Nana Cath; he had no idea what Nana meant; no concept of any relative other than mother and sister. In spite of her shifting hints and stories, Krystal knew that Terri had no idea who his father was.

Krystal heard her mother's footsteps on the stairs.

"Leave it," she snapped at Robbie, who had reached for an empty beer can lying beneath Terri's usual armchair. "C'm'ere."

She pulled Robbie by the hand into the hall. Terri was still wearing the pajama bottoms and dirty T-shirt in which she had spent the night, and her feet were bare.

"Why intcha changed?" demanded Krystal.

"I ain't goin'," said Terri, pushing past her son and daughter into the kitchen. "Changed me mind."

"Why?"

"I don' wanna," said Terri. She was lighting a cigarette off the ring of the cooker. "Don' fuckin' 'ave to."

Krystal was still holding Robbie's hand, as he tugged and swung.

"They're all goin'," said Krystal. "Cheryl an' Shane an' all."

"So?" said Terri aggressively.

Krystal had been afraid that her mother would pull out at the last minute. The funeral would bring her face-to-face with Danielle, the sister who pretended that Terri did not exist, not to mention all the other relatives who had disowned them. Anne-Marie might be there. Krystal had been holding on to that hope, like a torch in the darkness, through the nights she had sobbed for Nana Cath and Mr. Fairbrother.

"You gotta go," said Krystal.

"No, I ain'."

"It's Nana Cath, innit," said Krystal.

"So?" said Terri, again.

"She done loads fer us," said Krystal.

"No, she ain'," snapped Terri.

"She did," said Krystal, her face hot and her hand clutching Robbie's.

"Fer you, maybe," said Terri. "She done fuck-all for me. Go an' fuckin' bawl all over 'er fuckin' grave if yeh want. I'm waitin' in."

"Wha' for?" said Krystal.

"My bus'ness, innit."

The old familiar shadow fell.

"Obbo's comin' round, is 'e?"

"My bus'ness," repeated Terri, with pathetic dignity.

"Come to the funeral," said Krystal loudly.

"You go."

"Don' go fuckin' usin'," said Krystal, her voice an octave higher.

"I ain'," said Terri, but she turned away, looking out of the dirty back window over the patch of overgrown litter-strewn grass they called the back garden.

Robbie tugged his hand out of Krystal's and disappeared into the sitting room. With her fists deep in her trackie pockets, shoulders squared, Krystal tried to decide what to do. She wanted to cry at the thought of not going to the funeral, but her distress was edged with relief that she would not have to face the battery of hostile eyes she had sometimes met at Nana Cath's. She was angry with Terri, and yet felt strangely on her side. *You don't even know who the father is, do yeh, yer whore?* She wanted to meet Anne-Marie, but was scared.

"All righ', then, I'll stay an' all."

"You don' 'ave ter. Go, if yeh wan'. I don' fuckin' care."

But Krystal, certain that Obbo would appear, stayed. Obbo had been away for more than a week, for some nefarious purpose of his own. Krystal wished that he had died, that he would never come back.

For something to do, she began to tidy the house, while smoking one of the roll-ups Fats Wall had given her. She didn't like them, but she liked that he had given them to her. She had been keeping them in Nikki's plastic jewelry box, along with Tessa's watch.

She had thought that she might not see Fats anymore, after their shag in the cemetery, because he had been almost silent afterwards and left her with barely a good-bye, but they had since met up on the rec. She could tell that he had enjoyed this time more than the last; they had not been stoned, and he had lasted longer. He lay beside her in the grass beneath the bushes, smoking, and when she had told him about Nana Cath dying, he had told her that Sukhvinder Jawanda's mother had given Nana Cath the wrong drugs or something; he was not clear exactly what had happened.

Krystal had been horrified. So Nana Cath need not have died; she might still have been in the neat little house on Hope Street, there in case Krystal needed her, offering a refuge with a comfortable clean-sheeted bed, the tiny kitchen full of food and mismatched china, and the little TV in the corner of the sitting room: *I don' wanna watch no filth, Krystal, turn that off.*

Krystal had liked Sukhvinder, but Sukhvinder's mother had killed Nana Cath. You did not differentiate between members of an enemy tribe. It had been Krystal's avowed intention to pulverize Sukhvinder; but then Tessa Wall had intervened. Krystal could not remember the details of what Tessa had told her; but it seemed that Fats had got the story wrong or, at least, not exactly right. She had given Tessa a grudging promise not to go after Sukhvinder, but such promises could only ever be stopgaps in Krystal's frantic ever-changing world.

"Put it down!" Krystal shouted at Robbie, because he was trying to prise the lid off the biscuit tin where Terri kept her works.

Krystal snatched the tin from him and held it in her hands like a living creature, something that would fight to stay alive, whose destruction would have tremendous consequences. There was a scratched picture on the lid: a carriage with luggage piled high on the roof, drawn through the snow by four chestnut horses, a coachman in a top hat carrying a bugle. She carried the tin upstairs with her, while Terri sat in the kitchen smoking, and hid it in her bedroom. Robbie trailed after her.

"Wanna go play park."

She sometimes took him and pushed him on the swings and the roundabout.

"Not today, Robbie."

He whined until she shouted at him to shut up.

Later, when it was dark—after Krystal had made Robbie his tea of spaghetti hoops and given him a bath; when the funeral was long since over—Obbo rapped on the front door. Krystal saw him from Robbie's bedroom window and tried to get there first, but Terri beat her to it.

"All righ', Ter?" he said, over the threshold before anyone had invited him in. "'Eard you was lookin' fer me las' week."

Although she had told him to stay put, Robbie had followed Krystal downstairs. She could smell his shampooed hair over the smell of fags and stale sweat that clung to Obbo in his ancient leather jacket. Obbo had had a few; when he leered at her, she smelled the beer fumes.

"All righ', Obbo?" said Terri, with the note in her voice Krystal never heard otherwise. It was conciliating, accommodating; it conceded that he had rights in their house. "Where you bin, then?"

"Bristol," he said. "How's you, Ter?"

"She don' wan' nuthin'," said Krystal.

He blinked at her through his thick glasses. Robbie was clutching Krystal's leg so tightly that she could feel his nails in her skin.

"'Oo's this, Ter?" asked Obbo. "Yer mum?"

Terri laughed. Krystal glared at him, Robbie's grip tight on her thigh. Obbo's bleary gaze dropped to him.

"An' 'ow's me boy?"

"He ain' your fuckin' boy," said Krystal.

"'Ow d'you know?" Obbo asked her quietly, grinning.

"Fuck off. She don' wan' nuthin'. Tell 'im," Krystal virtually shouted at Terri. "Tell 'im you don' wan' nuthin'."

Daunted, caught between two wills much stronger than her own, Terri said, "'E on'y come rounda see—"

"No, 'e ain't," said Krystal. "No, 'e fuckin' ain't. Tell 'im. She don' wan' nuthin'," she said fiercely into Obbo's grinning face. "She's bin off it fer weeks."

"Is tha' right, Terri?" said Obbo, still smiling.

"Yeah, it is," said Krystal, when Terri did not answer. "She's still at Bellchapel."

"Noffur much longer," said Obbo.

"Fuck off," said Krystal, outraged.

"Closin' it," said Obbo.

"Are they?" said Terri in sudden panic. "They ain't, are they?"

"Course they are," said Obbo. "Cuts, innit?"

"You don't know nuthin'," Krystal told Obbo. "It's bollocks," she told her mother. "They 'aven' said nuthin', 'ave they?"

"Cuts," repeated Obbo, patting his bulging pockets for cigarettes.

"We got the case review," Krystal reminded Terri. "Yeh can't use. Yeh can't."

"Wha's that?" asked Obbo, fiddling with his lighter, but neither woman enlightened him. Terri met her daughter's gaze for a bare two seconds; her eyes fell, reluctantly, to Robbie in his pajamas, still clinging tightly to Krystal's leg.

"Yeah, I wuz gonna go ter bed, Obbo," she mumbled, without looking at him. "I'll mebbe see yer another time."

"I 'eard your Nan died," he said. "Cheryl wuz tellin' me."

Pain contorted Terri's face; she looked as old as Nana Cath herself.

"Yeah, I'm goin' ter bed. C'mon, Robbie. Come wi' me, Robbie."

Robbie did not want to let go of Krystal while Obbo was still there. Terri held out her claw-like hand.

"Yeah, go on, Robbie," Krystal urged him. In certain moods, Terri clutched her son like a teddy bear; better Robbie than smack. "Go on. Go wi' Mum."

He was reassured by something in Krystal's voice, and allowed Terri to take him upstairs.

"See yeh," said Krystal, without looking at Obbo, but stalking away from him into the kitchen, pulling the last of Fats Wall's roll-ups out of her pocket and bending to light it off the gas ring. She heard the front door close and felt triumphant. *Fuck him.*

"You got a lovely arse, Krystal."

She jumped so violently that a plate slipped off the heaped side and smashed on the filthy floor. He had not gone, but had followed her. He was staring at her chest in its tight T-shirt.

"Fuck off," she said.

"Big girl, intcha?"

"Fuck off."

"I 'eard you give it away free," said Obbo, closing in. "You could make better money'n yer mum."

"Fuck—"

His hand was on her left breast. She tried to knock it away; he seized her wrist in his other hand. Her lit cigarette grazed his face and he punched her, twice, to the side of the head; more plates shattered on the filthy floor and then, as they wrestled, she slipped and fell; the back of her head smacked on the floor, and he was on top of her: she could feel his hand at the waistband of her tracksuit bottoms, pulling.

"No—fuck—no!"

His knuckles in her belly as he undid his own fly—she tried to scream and he smacked her across the face—the smell of him was thick in her nostrils as he growled in her ear, "Fuckin' shout and I'll cut yer."

He was inside her and it hurt; she could hear him grunting and her own tiny whimper; she was ashamed of the noise she made, so frightened and so small.

He came and clambered off her. At once she pulled up her track-suit bottoms and jumped up to face him, tears pouring down her face as he leered at her.

"I'll tell Mist' Fairbrother," she heard herself sob. She did not know where it came from. It was a stupid thing to say.

"The fuck's he?" Obbo tugged up his fly, lit a cigarette, taking his time, blocking her exit. "You fuckin' 'im too, are yeh? Little slapper."

He sauntered up the hall and was gone.

She was shaking as she had never done in her life. She thought she might be sick; she could smell him all over her. The back of her head throbbed; there was a pain inside her, and wetness seeping into her pants. She ran out of the room into the living room and stood, shivering, with her arms wrapped around herself; then she knew a moment of terror, that he would come back, and hurried to the front door to lock it.

Back in the sitting room she found a long stub in the ashtray and lit it. Smoking, shaking and sobbing, she sank into Terri's usual chair, then jumped up because she heard footsteps on the stairs: Terri had reappeared, looking confused and wary.

"Wha'ssa matter with you?"

Krystal gagged on the words.

"He jus'—he jus' fucked me."

"Wha'?" said Terri.

"Obbo—'e jus'—"

"'E wouldn'."

It was the instinctive denial with which Terri met all of life: *he wouldn't, no, I never, no, I didn't.*

Krystal flew at her and pushed her; emaciated as she was, Terri crumpled backwards into the hall, shrieking and swearing; Krystal ran to the door she had just locked, fumbled to unfasten it and wrenched it open.

Still sobbing, she was twenty yards along the dark street before she realized that Obbo might be waiting out here, watching. She cut across a neighbor's garden at a run and took a zigzag route through back ways in the direction of Nikki's house, and all the time the wetness spread in her pants and she thought she might throw up.

Krystal knew that it was rape, what he had done. It had happened to Leanne's older sister in the car park of a nightclub in Bristol. Some people would have gone to the police, she knew that; but you did not invite the police into your life when your mother was Terri Weedon.

I'll tell Mist' Fairbrother.

Her sobs came faster and faster. She could have told Mr. Fairbrother. He had known what real life was like. One of his brothers had done time. He had told Krystal stories of his youth. It had not been like her youth—nobody was as low as her, she knew that—but like Nikki's, like Leanne's. Money had run out; his mother had bought her council house and then been unable to keep up the payments; they had lived for a while in a caravan lent by an uncle.

Mr. Fairbrother took care of things; he sorted things out. He had come to their house and talked to Terri about Krystal and rowing, because there had been an argument and Terri was refusing to sign forms for Krystal to go away with the team. He had not been disgusted, or he had not shown it, which came to the same thing. Terri, who liked and trusted nobody, had said, "'E seems all righ'," and she had signed.

Mr. Fairbrother had once said to her, "It'll be tougher for you than these others, Krys; it was tougher for me. But you can do better. You don't have to go the same way."

He had meant working hard at school and stuff, but it was too late for that and, anyway, it was all bollocks. How would reading help her now?

'Ow's me boy?

He ain' your fuckin' boy.

'Ow d'you know?

Leanne's sister had had to get the morning-after pill. Krystal would ask Leanne about the pill and go and get it. She could not have Obbo's baby. The thought of it made her retch.

I gotta get out of here.

She thought fleetingly of Kay, and then discarded her: as bad as the police, to tell a social worker that Obbo walked in and out of their house, raping people. She would take Robbie for sure, if she knew that.

A clear lucid voice in Krystal's head was speaking to Mr. Fairbrother, who was the only adult who had ever talked to her the way she needed, unlike Mrs. Wall, so well-intentioned and so blinkered, and Nana Cath, refusing to hear the whole truth.

I gotta get Robbie out of here. How can I get away? I gotta get away.

Her one sure refuge, the little house in Hope Street, was already being gobbled up by squabbling relatives...

She scurried around a corner underneath a streetlamp, looking over her shoulder in case he was watching her, following.

And then the answer came to her, as though Mr. Fairbrother had shown her the way.

If she got knocked up by Fats Wall, she would be able to get her own place from the council. She would be able to take Robbie to live with her and the baby if Terri used again. And Obbo would never enter her house, not ever. There would be bolts and chains and locks on the door, and her house would be clean, always clean, like Nana Cath's house.

Half running along the dark street, Krystal's sobs slowed and subsided.

The Walls would probably give her money. They were like that. She could imagine Tessa's plain, concerned face, bending over a cot. Krystal would have their grandchild.

She would lose Fats in getting pregnant; they always went, once you were expecting; she had watched it happen nearly every time in the Fields. But perhaps he would be interested; he was so strange. It did not much matter to her either way. Her interest in him, except as the essential component in her plan, had dwindled to almost nothing. What she wanted was the baby: the baby was more than a means to an end. She liked babies; she had always loved Robbie. She would keep the two of them safe, together; she would be like a better, kinder, younger Nana Cath to her family.

Anne-Marie might come and visit, once she was away from Terri. Their children would be cousins. A very vivid image of herself and Anne-Marie came to Krystal; they were standing at the school gates of St. Thomas's in Pagford, waving off two little girls in pale blue dresses and ankle socks.

The lights were on in Nikki's house, as they always were. Krystal broke into a run.

Part Four

Lunacy

5.11 At common law, idiots are subject to a permanent legal incapacity to vote, but persons of unsound mind may vote during lucid intervals.

Charles Arnold-Baker
Local Council Administration,
Seventh Edition

I

Samantha Mollison had now bought herself all three of the DVDs released by Libby's favorite boy band. She kept them hidden in her socks and tights drawer, beside her diaphragm. She had her story ready, if Miles spotted them: they were a gift for Libby. Sometimes at work, where business was slower than ever, she searched the Internet for pictures of Jake. It was during one of these trawling sessions—Jake in a suit but with no shirt, Jake in jeans and a white vest—that she discovered that the band was playing at Wembley in a fortnight's time.

She had a friend from university who lived in West Ealing. She could stay over, sell it to Libby as a treat, a chance to spend time together. With more genuine excitement than she had felt in a long time, Samantha managed to buy two very expensive tickets for the concert. When she let herself into the house that evening, she glowed with a delicious secret, almost as though she were coming home from a date.

Miles was already in the kitchen, still in his work suit, with the phone in his hand. He stared at her as she entered, and his expression was strange, difficult to read.

"What?" said Samantha, a little defensively.

"I can't get hold of Dad," said Miles. "His bloody phone's engaged. There's been another post."

And when Samantha looked nonplussed, he said with a trace of impatience, "Barry Fairbrother's Ghost! Another message! On the council website!"

"Oh," said Samantha, unwinding her scarf. "Right."

"Yeah, I met Betty Rossiter just now, coming up the street; she was full of it. I've checked the message board, but I can't see it. Mum must've taken it down already—well, I bloody hope she has, she'll be in the firing line if Bends-Your-Ear goes to a lawyer."

"About Parminder Jawanda, was it?" asked Samantha, her tone deliberately casual. She did not ask what the accusation had been, first, because she was determined not to be a nosy, gossiping old bag like Shirley and Maureen, and secondly, because she thought she already knew: that Parminder had caused the death of old Cath Weedon. After a moment or two, she asked, sounding vaguely amused, "Did you say your mother might be in the firing line?"

"Well, she's the site administrator, so she's liable if she doesn't get rid of defamatory or potentially defamatory statements. I'm not sure she and Dad understand how serious this could be."

"You could defend your mother, she'd like that."

But Miles had not heard; he was pressing redial and scowling, because his father's mobile was still engaged.

"This is getting serious," he said.

"You were all quite happy when it was Simon Price who was getting attacked. Why's this any different?"

"If it's a campaign against anyone on the council, or standing for council…"

Samantha turned away to hide her grin. His concern was not about Shirley after all.

"But why would anyone write stuff about you?" she asked innocently. "You haven't got any guilty secrets."

You might be more bloody interesting if you had.

"What about that letter?"

"What letter?"

"For God's—Mum and Dad said there was a letter, an anonymous letter about me! Saying I wasn't fit to fill Barry Fairbrother's shoes!"

Samantha opened the freezer and stared at the unappetizing contents, aware that Miles could no longer see her expression with the door open.

"You don't think anyone's got anything on you, do you?" she asked.

"No—but I'm a lawyer, aren't I? There might be people with a grudge. I don't think this kind of anonymous stuff...I mean, so far it's all about the other side, but there could be reprisals...I don't like the way this thing's going."

"Well, that's politics, Miles," said Samantha, openly amused. "Dirty business."

Miles stalked out of the room, but she did not care; her thoughts had already returned to chiseled cheekbones, winged eyebrows and taut, tight abdominal muscles. She could sing along with most of the songs now. She would buy a band T-shirt to wear—and one for Libby too. Jake would be undulating mere yards away from her. It would be more fun than she had had in years.

Howard, meanwhile, was pacing up and down the closed delicatessen with his mobile phone clamped to his ear. The blinds were down, the lights were on, and through the archway in the wall Shirley and Maureen were busy in the soon-to-be-opened café, unpacking china and glasses, talking in excited undertones and half listening to Howard's almost monosyllabic contributions to his conversation.

"Yes...mm, hmm...yes..."

"Screaming at me," said Shirley. "Screaming *and* swearing. 'Take it *bloody* down,' she said. I said, 'I'm taking it down, Dr. Jawanda, and I'll thank you not to swear at me.'"

"I'd've left it up there for another couple of hours if she'd sworn at me," said Maureen.

Shirley smiled. As it happened, she had chosen to go and make herself a cup of tea, leaving the anonymous post about Parminder up on the site for an extra forty-five minutes before removing it. She and Maureen had already picked over the topic of the post until it was ragged and bare; there was plenty of scope for further dissection, but the immediate urge was sated. Instead, Shirley looked ahead, greedily, to Parminder's reaction to having her secret spilled in public.

"It can't have been her who did that post about Simon Price, after all," said Maureen.

"No, obviously not," said Shirley, as she wiped over the pretty blue and white china that she had chosen, overruling Maureen's preference for pink. Sometimes, though not directly involved in the business, Shirley liked to remind Maureen that she still had huge influence, as Howard's wife.

"Yes," said Howard, on the telephone. "But wouldn't it be better to…? Mm, hmm…"

"So who do you think it is?" asked Maureen.

"I really don't know," said Shirley, in a genteel voice, as though such knowledge or suspicions were beneath her.

"Someone who knows the Prices and the Jawandas," said Maureen.

"Obviously," said Shirley again.

Howard hung up at last.

"Aubrey agrees," he told the two women, waddling through into the café. He was clutching today's edition of the *Yarvil and District Gazette.* "Very weak piece. Very weak indeed."

It took the two women several seconds to recollect that they were supposed to be interested in the posthumous article by Barry Fairbrother in the local newspaper. His ghost was so much more interesting.

"Oh, yes; well, I thought it was very poor when I read it," said Shirley, hurriedly catching up.

"The interview with Krystal Weedon was funny," guffawed Maureen. "Making out she enjoyed art. I suppose that's what she calls graffitiing the desks."

Howard laughed. As an excuse to turn her back, Shirley picked up Andrew Price's spare EpiPen from the counter, which Ruth had dropped into the delicatessen that morning. Shirley had looked up EpiPens on her favorite medical website, and felt fully competent to explain how Adrenalin worked. Nobody asked, though, so she put the small white tube away in the cupboard and closed the door as noisily as she could to try and disrupt Maureen's further witticisms.

The phone in Howard's huge hand rang.

"Yes, hello? Oh, Miles, yes…yes, we know all about it…Mum saw it this morning…" He laughed. "Yes, she's taken it down…I don't know...I think it was posted yesterday...Oh, I wouldn't say that...we've all known about Bends-Your-Ear for years..."

But Howard's jocularity faded as Miles talked. After a while he said, "Ah...yes, I see. Yes. No, I hadn't considered it from... perhaps we should get someone to have a look at security..."

The sound of a car in the darkening square outside went virtually unremarked by the three in the delicatessen, but its driver noticed the enormous shadow of Howard Mollison moving behind the cream blinds. Gavin put his foot down, eager to get to Mary. She had sounded desperate on the telephone.

"Who's doing this? Who's doing it? Who hates me this much?"

"Nobody hates you," he had said. "Who could hate you? Stay there...I'm coming over."

He parked outside the house, slammed the door and hurried up the footpath. She opened the front door before he had even knocked. Her eyes were puffy with tears again, and she was wearing a floor-length woolen dressing gown that dwarfed her. It was not at all seductive; the very antithesis of Kay's scarlet kimono, but its homeliness, its very shabbiness, represented a new level of intimacy.

Mary's four children were all in the sitting room. Mary gestured him through into the kitchen.

"Do they know?" he asked her.

"Fergus does. Somebody at school told him. I've asked him not to tell the others. Honestly, Gavin...I'm about at the end of my tether. The spite—"

"It isn't true," he said, and then, his curiosity getting the better of him, "is it?"

"No!" she said, outraged. "I mean...I don't know...I don't really know her. But to make him *talk* like that...Putting the words in his mouth...Don't they *care* what it's like for me?"

She dissolved into tears again. He felt that he shouldn't hug her while she was wearing her dressing gown, and was glad that he had not, when eighteen-year-old Fergus entered the kitchen a moment later.

"Hey, Gav."

The boy looked tired, older than his years. Gavin watched him put an arm around Mary and saw her lean her head against his shoulder, mopping her eyes on her baggy sleeve like a child.

"I don't think it was the same person," Fergus told them, without preamble. "I've been looking at it again. The style of the message is different."

He had it on his mobile phone, and began to read aloud:

"*'Parish Councillor Dr. Parminder Jawanda, who pretends to be so keen on looking after the poor and needy of the area, has always had a secret motive. Until I died—'*"

"Fergus, don't," said Mary, slumping down at the kitchen table. "I can't take it. I honestly can't. And his article in the paper today too."

As she covered her face with her hands and sobbed silently, Gavin noticed the *Yarvil and District Gazette* lying there. He never read it. Without asking or offering, he moved across to the cupboard to make her a drink.

"Thanks, Gav," she said thickly, when he pushed the glass into her hand.

"It might be Howard Mollison," suggested Gavin, sitting down beside her. "From what Barry said about him."

"I don't think so," said Mary, dabbing at her eyes. "It's so crude. He never did anything like that when Barry was—" she hiccuped "—alive." And then she snapped at her son, "Throw that paper away, Fergus."

The boy looked confused and hurt.

"It's got Dad's"—

"Throw it away!" said Mary, with an edge of hysteria in her voice. "I can read it off the computer if I want to, the last thing he ever did—on our anniversary!"

Fergus took the newspaper off the table and stood for a moment watching his mother, who had buried her face in her hands again. Then, with a glance at Gavin, he walked out of the room still holding the *Gazette*.

After a while, when Gavin judged that Fergus was not coming back, he put out a consoling hand and rubbed Mary's arm. They sat in silence for some time, and Gavin felt much happier with the newspaper gone from the table.

II

Parminder was not supposed to be working the next morning, but she had a meeting in Yarvil. Once the children had left for school she moved methodically around the house, making sure that she had everything she needed, but when the telephone rang, she jumped so much that she dropped her bag.

"Yes?" she yelped, sounding almost frightened. Tessa, on the other end of the line, was taken aback.

"Minda, it's me—are you all right?"

"Yes—yes—the phone made me jump," said Parminder, looking at the kitchen floor now littered with keys, papers, loose change and tampons. "What is it?"

"Nothing really," said Tessa. "Just calling for a chat. See how you are."

The subject of the anonymous post hung between them like some jeering monster, dangling from the line. Parminder had barely allowed Tessa to talk about it during yesterday's call. She had shouted, *"It's a lie, a filthy lie, and don't tell me Howard Mollison didn't do it!"*

Tessa had not dared pursue the subject.

"I can't talk," said Parminder. "I've got a meeting in Yarvil. A case review for a little boy on the at-risk register."

"Oh, right. Sorry. Maybe later?"

"Yes," said Parminder. "Great. Good-bye."

She scooped up the contents of her bag and hurried from the house, running back from the garden gate to check that she had closed the front door properly.

Every so often, as she drove, she realized that she had no recollection of traveling the last mile, and told herself fiercely to concentrate. But the malicious words of the anonymous post kept coming back to her. She already knew them by heart.

Parish Councillor Dr. Parminder Jawanda, who pretends to be so keen on looking after the poor and needy of the area, has always had a secret motive. Until I died, she was in love with me, which she could barely hide whenever she laid eyes on me, and she would vote however I told her to, whenever there was a council meeting. Now that I am gone, she will be useless as a councillor, because she has lost her brain.

She had first seen it the previous morning, when she opened up the council website to check the minutes of the last meeting. The shock had been almost physical; her breathing had become very fast and shallow, as it had been during the most excruciating parts of childbirth, when she had tried to lift herself over the pain, to disengage from the agonizing present.

Everyone would know by now. There was nowhere to hide.

The oddest thoughts kept coming to her. For instance, what her grandmother would have said if she had known that Parminder had been accused of loving another woman's husband, and a *gora* to boot, in a public forum. She could almost see *bebe* covering her face with a fold of her sari, shaking her head, rocking backwards and forwards as she had always done when a harsh blow had hit the family.

"Some husbands," Vikram had said to her late last night, with a strange new twist to his sardonic smile, "might want to know whether it was true."

"Of course it isn't true!" Parminder had said, with her own shaking hand over her mouth. "How can you ask me that? Of course it isn't! You knew him! He was my friend—just a friend!"

She was already passing the Bellchapel Addiction Clinic. How had she traveled so far, without realizing it? She was becoming a dangerous driver. She was not paying attention.

She remembered the evening that she and Vikram had gone to the restaurant, nearly twenty years ago, the night they had agreed to marry. She had told him about all the fuss the family had made when she had walked home with Stephen Hoyle, and he had agreed how silly it was. He had understood then. But he did not understand when it was Howard Mollison who accused her instead of her own hidebound relatives. Apparently he did not realize that *goras* could be narrow, and untruthful, and full of malice…

She had missed the turning. She must concentrate. She must pay attention.

"Am I late?" she called, as she hurried at last across the car park towards Kay Bawden. She had met the social worker once before, when she had come in for a renewal of her prescription for the pill.

"Not at all," said Kay. "I thought I'd show you up to the office, because it's a rabbit warren in here…"

The building that housed Yarvil Social Services was an ugly 1970s office block. As the two women traveled up in the lift, Parminder wondered whether Kay knew about the anonymous post on the council website, or about the accusations made against her by Catherine Weedon's family. She imagined the lift doors sliding open to reveal a line of people in suits, waiting to accuse and condemn her. Imagine if this review about Robbie Weedon's welfare were a ruse, and it was to her own tribunal she was traveling…

Kay led her down a shabby, deserted institutional corridor into a meeting room. Three more women were already sitting there; they greeted Parminder with smiles.

"This is Nina, who works with Robbie's mother at Bellchapel," said Kay, sitting down with her back to the venetian-blinded windows. "And this is my supervisor Gillian, and this is Louise Harper, who oversees the Anchor Road Nursery. Dr. Parminder Jawanda, Robbie's GP," Kay added.

Parminder accepted coffee. The other four women began talking, without involving her.

(*Parish Councillor Dr. Parminder Jawanda, who pretends to be so keen on looking after the poor and needy of the area…*

Who *pretends* to be so keen. You bastard, Howard Mollison. But he had always seen her as a hypocrite; Barry had said so.

"He thinks that because I came from the Fields, I want Pagford overrun by Yarvillians. But you're proper professional class, so he doesn't think you've got any right to be on the side of the Fields. He thinks you're a hypocrite or making trouble for fun.")

"…understand why the family's registered with a GP in Pagford?" said one of the three unfamiliar social workers, whose names Parminder had already forgotten.

"Several families in the Fields are registered with us," said Parminder at once. "But wasn't there some trouble with the Weedons and their previous—?"

"Yeah, the Cantermill practice threw them out," said Kay, in front of whom sat a pile of notes thicker than either of her colleagues'. "Terri assaulted a nurse there. So they've been registered with you, how long?"

"Nearly five years," said Parminder, who had looked up all the details at the surgery.

(She had seen Howard in church, at Barry's funeral, pretending to pray, with his big fat hands clasped in front of him, and the Fawleys kneeling beside him. Parminder knew what Christians were supposed to believe in. *Love thy neighbor as thyself*...if Howard had been more honest, he would have turned sideways and prayed to Aubrey...

Until I died, she was in love with me, which she could barely hide whenever she laid eyes on me...

Had she really not been able to hide it?)

"...last seen him, Parminder?" asked Kay.

"When his sister brought him in for antibiotics for an ear infection," said Parminder. "About eight weeks ago."

"And how was his physical condition then?" asked one of the other women.

"Well, he's not failing to thrive," said Parminder, withdrawing a slim sheaf of photocopied notes from her handbag. "I checked him quite thoroughly, because—well, I know the family history. He's a good weight, although I doubt his diet's anything to write home about. No lice or nits or anything of that description. His bottom was a bit sore, and I remember his sister said that he still wets himself sometimes."

"They keep putting him back in nappies," said Kay.

"But you wouldn't," asked the woman who had first questioned Parminder, "have any major concerns health-wise?"

"There was no sign of abuse," said Parminder. "I remember, I took off his vest to check, and there were no bruises or other injuries."

"There's no man in the house," interjected Kay.

"And this ear infection?" her supervisor prompted Parminder.

"It was a fairly run-of-the-mill bacterial infection following a virus. Nothing odd about it. Typical of kids his age."

"So, all in all—"

"I've seen much worse," said Parminder.

"You said it was the sister who brought him in, not the mother? Are you Terri's doctor, too?"

"I don't think we've seen Terri for five years," said Parminder, and the supervisor turned to Nina instead.

"How's she doing on methadone?"

(*Until I died, she was in love with me...*

Parminder thought, *Perhaps it's Shirley, or Maureen, who's the ghost, not Howard—they would be much more likely to watch her when she was with Barry, hoping to see something with their dirty old-womanish minds...*)

"...longest she's lasted on the program so far," said Nina. "She's mentioned the case review quite a lot. I get the feeling she knows that this is it, that she's running out of chances. She doesn't want to lose Robbie. She's said that a few times. I'd have to say you've got through to her, Kay. I really do see her taking some responsibility for the situation, for the first time since I've known her."

"Thank you, but I'm not going to get overexcited. The situation's still pretty precarious." Kay's dampening words were at odds with her tiny irrepressible smile of satisfaction. "How are things going at nursery, Louise?"

"Well, he's back again," said the fourth social worker. "He's been in full attendance for the past three weeks, which is a dramatic change. The teenage sister brings him. His clothes are too small and usually dirty, but he talks about bath and meal times at home."

"And behaviorally?"

"He's developmentally delayed. His language skills are very poor. He doesn't like men coming into the nursery. When fathers turn up, he won't go near them; he hangs around the nursery workers and becomes very anxious. And once or twice," she said, turning a page in her notes, "he's mimicked what are clearly sexual acts on or near little girls."

"I don't think, whatever we decide, there can be any question of taking him off the at-risk register," said Kay, to a murmur of agreement.

"It sounds like everything hinges on Terri staying on your program," said the supervisor to Nina, "and staying off the game."

"That's key, certainly," Kay agreed, "but I'm concerned that even when she's heroin-free, she doesn't provide much mothering to Robbie. Krystal seems to be raising him, and she's sixteen and got plenty of her own issues…"

(Parminder remembered what she had said to Sukhvinder a couple of nights previously.

Krystal Weedon! That stupid girl! Is that what being in a team with Krystal Weedon taught you—to sink to her level?

Barry had liked Krystal. He had seen things in her that were invisible to other people's eyes.

Once, long ago, Parminder had told Barry the story of Bhai Kanhaiya, the Sikh hero who had administered to the needs of those wounded in combat, whether friend or foe. When asked why he gave aid indiscriminately, Bhai Kanhaiya had replied that the light of God shone from every soul, and that he had been unable to distinguish between them.

The light of God shone from every soul.

She had called Krystal Weedon stupid and implied that she was low.

Barry would never have said it.

She was ashamed.)

"…when there was a great-grandmother who seemed to provide some backup in care, but—"

"She died," said Parminder, rushing to say it before anyone else could. "Emphysema and stroke."

"Yeah," said Kay, still looking at her notes. "So we go back to Terri. She came out of care herself. Has she ever attended parenting classes?"

"We offer them, but she's never been in a fit state to attend," said the woman from the nursery.

"If she agreed to take them and actually turned up, it would be a massive step forward," said Kay.

"If they close us down," sighed Nina from Bellchapel, addressing Parminder, "I suppose she'll have to come to you for her methadone."

"I'm concerned that she wouldn't," said Kay, before Parminder could answer.

"What do you mean?" asked Parminder angrily.

The other women stared at her.

"Just that catching buses and remembering appointments isn't Terri's forte," said Kay. "She only has to walk up the road to Bellchapel."

"Oh," said Parminder, mortified. "Yes. Sorry. Yes, you're probably right."

(She had thought that Kay was making a reference to the complaint about Catherine Weedon's death; that she did not think Terri Weedon would trust her.

Concentrate on what they're saying. What's wrong with you?)

"So, big picture," said the supervisor, looking down at her notes. "We've got neglectful parenting interspersed with some adequate care." She sighed, but there was more exasperation than sadness in the sound. "The immediate crisis is over—she's stopped using—Robbie's back in nursery, where we can keep a proper eye on him—and there's no immediate concern for his safety. As Kay says, he stays on the at-risk register...I certainly think we'll need another meeting in four weeks..."

It was another forty minutes before the meeting broke up. Kay walked Parminder back down to the car park.

"It was very good of you to come in person; most GPs send through a report."

"It was my morning off," said Parminder. She meant it as an explanation for her attendance, because she hated sitting at home alone with nothing to do, but Kay seemed to think that she was asking for more praise and gave it.

At Parminder's car, Kay said, "You're the parish councillor, aren't you? Did Colin pass you the figures on Bellchapel I gave him?"

"Yes, he did," said Parminder. "It would be good to have a talk about that sometime. It's on the agenda for the next meeting."

But when Kay had given her her number, and left, with renewed thanks, Parminder's thoughts reverted to Barry, the Ghost and the

Mollisons. She was driving through the Fields when the simple thought that she had tried to bury, to drown out, slipped past her lowered defenses at last.

Perhaps I did love him.

III

Andrew had spent hours deciding which clothes he ought to wear for his first day's work at the Copper Kettle. His final choice was draped over the back of the chair in his bedroom. A particularly angry acne pustule had chosen to bring itself to a shiny tight peak on his left cheek, and Andrew had gone so far as to experiment with Ruth's foundation, which he had sneaked out of her dressing-table drawer.

He was laying the kitchen table on Friday evening, his mind full of Gaia and the seven solid hours of close proximity to her that were within touching distance, when his father returned from work in a state that Andrew had never seen before. Simon seemed subdued, almost disoriented.

"Where's your mother?"

Ruth came bustling out of the walk-in pantry.

"Hello Si-Pie! How — what's wrong?"

"They've made me redundant."

Ruth clapped her hands to her face in horror, then dashed to her husband, threw her arms around his neck and drew him close.

"Why?" she whispered.

"That message," said Simon. "On that fucking website. They pulled in Jim and Tommy too. It was take redundancy or we'll sack you. And it's a shitty deal. It's not even what they gave Brian Grant."

Andrew stood perfectly still, calcifying slowly into a monument of guilt.

"Fuck," said Simon, into Ruth's shoulder.

"You'll get something else," she whispered.

"Not round here," said Simon.

He sat down at a kitchen chair, still in his coat, and stared across the room, apparently too stunned to speak. Ruth hovered around him, dismayed, affectionate and tearful. Andrew was glad to detect in Simon's catatonic gaze a whiff of his usual ham theatrics. It made him feel slightly less guilty. He continued to lay the table without saying a word.

Dinner was a subdued affair. Paul, apprised of the family news, looked terrified, as though his father might accuse him of causing it all. Simon acted like a Christian martyr through the first course, wounded but dignified in the face of unwarranted persecution, but then—"I'll pay someone to punch the fucker's fat face through the back of his neck," he burst out as he spooned apple crumble into himself; and the family knew that he meant Howard Mollison.

"You know, there's been another message on that council website," said Ruth breathlessly. "It's not only you who's had it, Si. Shir—somebody told me at work. The same person—The Ghost of Barry Fairbrother—has put up something horrible about Dr. Jawanda. So Howard and Shirley got someone in to look at the site, and he realized that whoever's doing these messages has been using Barry Fairbrother's log-in details, so to be safe, they've taken them off the—the database or something—"

"And will any of this get me my fucking job back?"

Ruth did not speak again for several minutes.

Andrew was unnerved by what his mother had said. It was worrying that The_Ghost_of_Barry_Fairbrother was being investigated, and unnerving that somebody else had followed his lead.

Who else would have thought of using Barry Fairbrother's log-in details but Fats? Yet why would Fats go for Dr. Jawanda? Or was it just another way of getting at Sukhvinder? Andrew did not like it at all...

"What's the matter with you?" Simon barked across the table.

"Nothing," Andrew muttered, and then, backtracking, "it's a shock, isn't it...your job..."

"Oh, you're *shocked,* are you?" shouted Simon, and Paul dropped his spoon and dribbled ice cream down himself. "(Clean it up, Pauline, you little pansy!) Well, this is the real world, Pizza Face!" he shouted at Andrew. "Fuckers everywhere trying to do you down! So *you*," he pointed across the table at his eldest son, "you get some dirt on Mollison, or don't bother coming home tomorrow!"

"Si—"

Simon pushed his chair away from the table, threw down his own spoon, which bounced onto the floor with a clatter, and stalked from the room, slamming the door behind him. Andrew waited for the inevitable, and was not disappointed.

"It's a terrible shock for him," a shaken Ruth whispered at her sons. "After all the years he's given that company...he's worried how he's going to look after us all..."

When the alarm rang at six thirty the next morning, Andrew slammed it off within seconds and virtually leaped out of bed. Feeling as though it was Christmas Day, he washed and dressed at speed, then spent forty minutes on his hair and face, dabbing minuscule amounts of foundation onto the most obvious of his spots.

He half expected Simon to waylay him as he crept past his parents' room, but he met nobody, and after a hasty breakfast he wheeled Simon's racing bicycle out of the garage and sped off down the hill toward Pagford.

It was a misty morning that promised sunshine later. The blinds were still down in the delicatessen, but the door tinkled and gave when he pushed it.

"Not this way!" shouted Howard, waddling toward him. "You come in round the back! You can leave the bike by the bins, get it away from the front!"

The rear of the delicatessen, reached by a narrow passageway, comprised a tiny dank patch of stone-paved yard, bordered by high walls, sheds with industrial-sized metal bins and a trapdoor that led down vertiginous steps to a cellar.

"You can chain it up somewhere there, out of the way," said Howard, who had appeared at the back door, wheezing and sweaty-faced. While Andrew fumbled with the padlock on the chain, Howard dabbed at his forehead with his apron.

"Right, we'll start with the cellar," he said, when Andrew had secured the bicycle. He pointed at the trapdoor. "Get down there and see the layout."

He bent over the hatch as Andrew climbed down the steps. Howard had not been able to climb down into his own cellar for years. Maureen usually tottered up and down the steps a couple of times a week; but now that it was fully stocked with goods for the café, younger legs were indispensible.

"Have a good look around," he shouted at the out-of-sight Andrew. "See where we've got the gateaux and all the baked goods? See the big bags of coffee beans and the boxes of tea bags? And in the corner—the toilet rolls and the bin bags?"

"Yeah," Andrew's voice echoed up from the depths.

"You can call me Mr. Mollison," said Howard, with a slightly tart edge to his wheezy voice.

Down in the cellar, Andrew wondered whether he ought to start straight away.

"OK...Mr. Mollison."

It sounded sarcastic. He hastened to make amends with a polite question.

"What's in these big cupboards?"

"Have a look," said Howard impatiently. "That's what you're down there for. To know where you put everything and where you get it from."

Howard listened to the muffled sounds of Andrew opening the heavy doors, and hoped that the boy would not prove gormless or need a lot of direction. Howard's asthma was particularly bad today; the pollen count was unseasonably high, on top of all the extra work, and the excitement and petty frustrations of the opening. The way he was sweating, he might need to ring Shirley to bring him a new shirt before they unlocked the doors.

"Here's the van!" Howard shouted, hearing a rumble at the other end of the passageway. "Get up here! You're to carry the stuff down to the cellar and put it away, all right? And bring a couple of gallons of milk through to me in the café. You got that?"

"Yeah...Mr. Mollison," said Andrew's voice from below.

Howard walked slowly back inside to fetch the inhaler that he kept in his jacket, which was hanging up in the staff room behind the delicatessen counter. Several deep breaths later, he felt much better. Wiping his face on his apron again, he sat down on one of the creaking chairs to rest.

Several times since he had been to see her about his skin rash, Howard had thought about what Dr. Jawanda had said about his weight: that it was the source of all his health problems.

Nonsense, obviously. Look at the Hubbards' boy: built like a beanpole, and shocking asthma. Howard had always been big, as far back as he could remember. In the very few photographs taken of him with his father, who had left the family when Howard was four or five, he was merely chubby. After his father had left, his mother had sat him at the head of the table, between herself and his grandmother, and been hurt if he did not take seconds. Steadily he had grown to fill the space between the two women, as heavy at twelve as the father who had left them. Howard had come to associate a hearty appetite with manliness. His bulk was one of his defining characteristics. It had been built with pleasure, by the women who loved him, and he thought it was absolutely characteristic of Bends-Your-Ear, that emasculating killjoy, that she wanted to strip him of it.

But sometimes, in moments of weakness, when it became difficult to breathe or to move, Howard knew fear. It was all very well for Shirley to act as though he had never been in danger, but he remembered long nights in the hospital after his bypass, when he had not been able to sleep for worry that his heart might falter and stop. Whenever he caught sight of Vikram Jawanda, he remembered that those long dark fingers had actually touched his naked, beating heart; the bonhomie with which he brimmed at each encounter was a way of driving out that primitive, instinctive terror. They had told him at the hospital afterwards that he needed to lose some weight, but he had dropped two stone naturally while he was forced to live off their dreadful food, and Shirley had been intent on fattening him up again once he was out...

Howard sat for a moment more, enjoying the ease with which

he breathed after using his inhaler. Today meant a great deal to him. Thirty-five years previously, he had introduced fine dining to Pagford with the élan of a sixteenth-century adventurer returning with delicacies from the other side of the world, and Pagford, after initial wariness, had soon begun to nose curiously and timidly into his polystyrene pots. He thought wistfully of his late mother, who had been so proud of him and his thriving business. He wished that she could have seen the café. Howard heaved himself back to his feet, took his deerstalker from its hook and placed it carefully on his head in an act of self-coronation.

His new waitresses arrived together at half-past eight. He had a surprise for them.

"Here you are," he said, holding out the uniforms: black dresses with frilly white aprons, exactly as he had imagined. "Ought to fit. Maureen reckoned she knew your sizes. She's wearing one herself."

Gaia forced back a laugh as Maureen stalked into the delicatessen from the café, smiling at them. She was wearing Dr. Scholl's sandals over her black stockings. Her dress finished two inches above her wrinkled knees.

"You can change in the staff room, girls," she said, indicating the place from which Howard had just emerged.

Gaia was already pulling off her jeans beside the staff toilet when she saw Sukhvinder's expression.

"Whassamatter, Sooks?" she asked.

The new nickname gave Sukhvinder the courage to say what she might otherwise have been unable to voice.

"I can't wear this," she whispered.

"Why?" asked Gaia. "You'll look OK."

But the black dress had short sleeves.

"I can't."

"But wh—Jesus," said Gaia.

Sukhvinder had pulled back the sleeves of her sweatshirt. Her inner arms were covered in ugly crisscross scars, and angry fresh-clotted cuts traveled up from her wrist to her inner arm.

"Sooks," said Gaia quietly. "What are you playing at, mate?"

Sukhvinder shook her head, with her eyes full of tears.

Gaia thought for a moment, then said, "I know—come here."
She was stripping off her long-sleeved T-shirt.

The door suffered a big blow and the imperfectly closed bolt shot open: a sweating Andrew was halfway inside, carrying two weighty packs of toilet rolls, when Gaia's angry shout stopped him in his tracks. He tripped out backwards, into Maureen.

"They're changing in there," she said, in sour disapproval.

"Mr. Mollison told me to put these in the staff bathroom."

Holy shit, holy shit. She had been stripped to her bra and pants. He had seen nearly everything.

"Sorry," Andrew yelled at the closed door. His whole face was throbbing with the force of his blush.

"Wanker," muttered Gaia, on the other side. She was holding out her T-shirt to Sukhvinder. "Put it on underneath the dress."

"That'll look weird."

"Never mind. You can get a black one for next week, it'll look like you're wearing long sleeves. We'll tell him some story…"

"She's got eczema," Gaia announced, when she and Sukhvinder emerged from the staff room, fully dressed and aproned. "All up her arms. It's a bit scabby."

"Ah," said Howard, glancing at Sukhvinder's white T-shirted arms and then back at Gaia, who looked every bit as gorgeous as he had hoped.

"I'll get a black one for next week," said Sukhvinder, unable to look Howard in the eye.

"Fine," he said, patting Gaia in the small of her back as he sent the pair of them through to the café. "Brace yourselves," he called to his staff at large. "We're nearly there…Doors open, please, Maureen!"

There was already a little knot of customers waiting on the pavement. A sign outside read: *The Copper Kettle, Opening Today—First Coffee Free!*

Andrew did not see Gaia again for hours. Howard kept him busy heaving milk and fruit juices up and down the steep cellar steps, and swabbing the floor of the small kitchen area at the back. He was given a lunch break earlier than either of the waitresses. The next glimpse he got of her was when Howard summoned him to the counter of the café, and they passed within inches of each other as she walked in the other direction, toward the backroom.

"We're swamped, Mr. Price!" said Howard, in high good humor. "Get yourself a clean apron and mop down some of these tables for me while Gaia has her lunch!"

Miles and Samantha Mollison had sat down with their two daughters and Shirley at a table in the window.

"It seems to be going awfully well, doesn't it?" Shirley said, looking around. "But what on earth is that Jawanda girl wearing under her dress?"

"Bandages?" suggested Miles, squinting across the room.

"Hi, Sukhvinder!" called Lexie, who knew her from primary school.

"Don't shout, darling," Shirley reproved her granddaughter, and Samantha bristled.

Maureen emerged from behind the counter in her short black dress and frilly apron, and Shirley corpsed into her coffee.

"Oh dear," she said quietly, as Maureen walked towards them, beaming.

It was true, Samantha thought, Maureen looked ridiculous, especially next to a pair of sixteen-year-olds in identical dresses, but she was not going to give Shirley the satisfaction of agreeing with her. She turned ostentatiously away, watching the boy mopping tables nearby. He was spare but reasonably broad-shouldered. She could see his muscles working under the loose T-shirt. Incredible to think that Miles' big fat backside could ever have been that small and tight—then the boy turned into the light and she saw his acne.

"Not half bad, is it?" Maureen was croaking to Miles. "We've been full all day."

"All right, girls," Miles addressed his family, "what'll we have to keep up Grandpa's profits?"

Samantha listlessly ordered a bowl of soup, as Howard waddled through from the delicatessen; he had been striding in and out of the café every ten minutes all day, greeting customers and checking the flow of cash into the till.

"Roaring success," he told Miles, squeezing in at their table. "What d'you think of the place, Sammy? You haven't seen it before, have you? Like the mural? Like the china?"

"Mm," said Samantha. "Lovely."

"I was thinking about having my sixty-fifth here," said Howard, absentmindedly scratching at the itch Parminder's creams had not yet cured, "but it's not big enough. I think we'll stick with the church hall."

"When's that, Grandpa?" piped up Lexie. "Am I coming?"

"Twenty-ninth, and what are you now—sixteen? Course you can come," said Howard happily.

"The twenty-ninth?" said Samantha. "Oh, but…"

Shirley looked at her sharply.

"Howard's been planning this for months. We've all been talking about it for ages."

"…that's the night of Libby's concert," said Samantha.

"A school thing, is it?" asked Howard.

"No," said Libby, "Mum's got me tickets for my favorite group. It's in London."

"And I'm going with her," said Samantha. "She can't go alone."

"Harriet's mum says she could—"

"*I'm* taking you, Libby, if you're going to London."

"The twenty-ninth?" said Miles, looking hard at Samantha. "The day after the election?"

Samantha let loose the derisive laugh that she had spared Maureen.

"It's the Parish Council, Miles. It's not as though you'll be giving press conferences."

"Well, we'll miss you, Sammy," said Howard, as he hauled himself up with the aid of the back of her chair. "Best get on…All right, Andrew, you're done here…go and see if we need anything up from the cellar."

Andrew was forced to wait beside the counter while people passed to and from the bathroom. Maureen was loading up Sukhvinder with plates of sandwiches.

"How's your mother?" she asked the girl abruptly, as though the thought had just occurred to her.

"Fine," said Sukhvinder, her color rising.

"Not too upset by that nasty business on the council website?"

"No," said Sukhvinder, her eyes watering.

Andrew proceeded out into the dank yard, which, in the early afternoon, had become warm and sunny. He had hoped that Gaia might be there, taking a breath of fresh air, but she must have gone into the staff room in the deli. Disappointed, he lit up a cigarette. He had barely inhaled when Gaia emerged from the café, finishing her lunch with a can of fizzy drink.

"Hi," said Andrew, his mouth dry.

"Hi," she said. Then, after a moment or two: "Hey, why's that friend of yours such a shit to Sukhvinder? Is it personal or is he racist?"

"He isn't racist," said Andrew. He removed the cigarette from his mouth, trying to keep his hands from trembling, but could not think of anything else to say. The sunshine reflected off the bins warmed his sweaty back; close proximity to her in the tight black dress was almost overwhelming, especially now that he had glimpsed what lay beneath. He took another drag of the cigarette, not knowing when he had felt so bedazzled or so alive.

"What's she ever done to him, though?"

The curve of her hips to her tiny waist; the perfection of her wide, flecked eyes over the can of Sprite. Andrew felt like saying, *Nothing, he's a bastard, I'll hit him if you let me touch you...*

Sukhvinder emerged into the yard, blinking in the sunlight; she looked uncomfortable and hot in Gaia's top.

"He wants you back in," she said to Gaia.

"He can wait," said Gaia coolly. "I'm finishing this. I've only had forty minutes."

Andrew and Sukhvinder contemplated her as she sipped her drink, awed by her arrogance and her beauty.

"Was that old bitch saying something to you just then, about your mum?" Gaia asked Sukhvinder.

Sukhvinder nodded.

"I think it might've been *his* mate," she said, staring at Andrew again, and he found her emphasis on *his* positively erotic, even if she meant it to be derogatory, "who put that message about your mum on that website."

"Can't've been," said Andrew, and his voice wobbled slightly. "Whoever did it went after my old man, too. Couple of weeks ago."

"What?" asked Gaia. "The same person posted something about your dad?"

He nodded, relishing her interest.

"Something about stealing, wasn't it?" asked Sukhvinder, with considerable daring.

"Yeah," said Andrew. "And he got the sack for it yesterday. So her mum," he met Gaia's blinding gaze almost steadily, "isn't the only one who's suffered."

"Bloody hell," said Gaia, upending the can and throwing it into a bin. "People round here are effing mental."

IV

The post about Parminder on the council website had driven Colin Wall's fears to a nightmarish new level. He could only guess how the Mollisons were getting their information, but if they knew that about Parminder…

"For God's sake, Colin!" Tessa had said. "It's just malicious gossip! There's nothing in it!"

But Colin did not dare believe her. He was constitutionally prone to believing that others too lived with secrets that drove them half-demented. He could not even take comfort in knowing that he had spent most of his adult life in dread of calamities that had not materialized, because, by the law of averages, one of them was bound to come true one day.

He was thinking about his imminent exposure, as he thought about it constantly, while walking back from the butcher's at half past two, and it was not until the hubbub from the new café caught his startled attention that he realized where he was. He would have crossed to the other side of the Square if he had not been already level with the Copper Kettle's windows; mere proximity to any Mollison frightened him now. Then he saw something through the glass that made him do a double take.

When he entered their kitchen ten minutes later, Tessa was on the telephone to her sister. Colin deposited the leg of lamb in the fridge and marched upstairs, all the way to Fats' loft conversion. Flinging open the door, he saw, as he had expected, a deserted room.

He could not remember the last time he had been in here. The floor was covered in dirty clothes. There was an odd smell, even though Fats had left the skylight propped open. Colin noticed a large matchbox on Fats' desk. He slid it open, and saw a mass of twisted cardboard stubs. A packet of Rizlas lay brazenly on the desk beside the computer.

Colin's heart seemed to have toppled down out of his chest to thump against his guts.

"Colin?" came Tessa's voice, from the landing below. "Where are you?"

"Up here!" he roared.

She appeared at Fats' door looking frightened and anxious. Wordlessly, he picked up the matchbox and showed her the contents.

"Oh," said Tessa weakly.

"He said he was going out with Andrew Price today," said Colin. Tessa was frightened by the muscle working in Colin's jaw, an angry little bump moving from side to side. "I've just been past that new café in the Square, and Andrew Price is working in there, mopping tables. So where's Stuart?"

For weeks, Tessa had been pretending to believe Fats when-ever he said that he was going out with Andrew. For days she had been telling herself that Sukhvinder must be mistaken in thinking that Fats was going out (would condescend, ever, to go out) with Krystal Weedon.

"I don't know," she said. "Come down and have a cup of tea. I'll ring him."

"I think I'll wait here," said Colin, and he sat down on Fats' unmade bed.

"Come on, Colin—come downstairs," said Tessa.

She was scared of leaving him here. She did not know what he might find in the drawers or in Fats' schoolbag. She did not want him to look on the computer or under the bed. Refusing to probe dark corners had become her sole modus operandi.

"Come downstairs, Col," she urged him.

"No," said Colin, and he crossed his arms like a mutinous child, but with that muscle working in his jaw. "Drugs in his bin. The son of the deputy headmaster."

Tessa, who had sat down on Fats' computer chair, felt a familiar thrill of anger. She knew that self-preoccupation was an inevitable consequence of his illness, but sometimes…

"Plenty of teenagers experiment," she said.

"Still defending him, are you? Doesn't it ever occur to you that it's your constant excuses for him that make him think he can get away with blue murder?"

She was trying to keep a curb on her temper, because she must be a buffer between them.

"I'm sorry, Colin, but you and your job aren't the be-all and end—"

"I see—so if I get the sack—"

"Why on earth would you get the sack?"

"For God's sake!" shouted Colin, outraged. "It all reflects on me—it's already bad enough—he's already one of the biggest problem students in the—"

"That's not true!" shouted Tessa. "Nobody but you thinks Stuart's anything other than a normal teenager. He's not Dane Tully!"

"He's going the same way as Tully—drugs in his bin—"

"I told you we should have sent him to Paxton High! I *knew* you'd make everything he did all about you, if he went to Winterdown! Is it any wonder he rebels, when his every movement is supposed to be a credit to you? I never wanted him to go to your school!"

"And I," bellowed Colin, jumping to his feet, "never bloody wanted him at all!"

"Don't say that!" gasped Tessa. "I know you're angry—but don't say that!"

The front door slammed two floors below them. Tessa looked around, frightened, as though Fats might materialize instantly beside them. It wasn't merely the noise that had made her start. Stuart never slammed the front door; he usually slipped in and out like a shape-shifter.

His familiar tread on the stairs; did he know, or suspect they were in his room? Colin was waiting, with his fists clenched by his sides. Tessa heard the creak of the halfway step, and then Fats stood before them. She was sure he had arranged his expression in advance: a mixture of boredom and disdain.

"Afternoon," he said, looking from his mother to his rigid, tense father. He had all the self-possession that Colin had never had. "This is a surprise."

Desperate, Tessa tried to show him the way.

"Dad was worried about where you are," she said, with a plea in her voice. "You said you were going to be with Arf today, but Dad saw—"

"Yeah, change of plan," said Fats.

He glanced towards the place where the matchbox had been.

"So, do you want to tell us where you've been?" asked Colin. There were white patches around his mouth.

"Yeah, if you like," said Fats, and he waited.

"Stu," said Tessa, half whisper, half groan.

"I've been out with Krystal Weedon," said Fats.

Oh God, no, thought Tessa. *No, no, no...*

"You've what?" said Colin, so taken aback that he forgot to sound aggressive.

"I've been out with Krystal Weedon," Fats repeated, a little more loudly.

"And since when," said Colin, after an infinitesimal pause, "has she been a friend of yours?"

"A while," said Fats.

Tessa could see Colin struggling to formulate a question too grotesque to utter.

"You should have told us, Stu," she said.

"Told you what?" he said.

She was frightened that he was going to push the argument to a dangerous place.

"Where you were going," she said, standing up and trying to look matter-of-fact. "Next time, call us."

She looked toward Colin in the hope that he might follow her lead and move towards the door. He remained fixed in the middle of the room, staring at Fats in horror.

"Are you...involved with Krystal Weedon?" Colin asked.

They faced each other, Colin taller by a few inches, but Fats holding all the power.

"'Involved'?" Fats repeated. "What d'you mean, 'involved'?"

"You know what I mean!" said Colin, his face growing red.

"D'you mean, am I shagging her?" asked Fats.

Tessa's little cry of "Stu!" was drowned by Colin shouting, "How bloody dare you!"

Fats merely looked at Colin, smirking. Everything about him was a taunt and a challenge.

"What?" said Fats.

"Are you—" Colin was struggling to find the words, growing redder all the time, "—are you sleeping with Krystal Weedon?"

"It wouldn't be a problem if I was, would it?" Fats asked, and he glanced at his mother as he said it. "You're all for helping Krystal, aren't you?"

"Helping—"

"Aren't you trying to keep that addiction clinic open so you can help Krystal's family?"

"What's that got to do—?"

"I can't see what the problem is with me going out with her."

"And *are* you going out with her?" asked Tessa sharply. If Fats wanted to take the row into this territory, she would meet him there. "Do you actually *go* anywhere with her, Stuart?"

His smirk sickened her. He was not prepared even to pretend to some decency.

"Well, we don't do it in either of our houses, do—"

Colin had raised one of his stiff, clench-fisted arms and swung it. He connected with Fats' cheek, and Fats, whose attention had been on his mother, was caught off guard; he staggered sideways, hit the desk and slid, momentarily, to the floor. A moment later he had jumped to his feet again, but Tessa had already placed herself between the pair of them, facing her son.

Behind her, Colin was repeating, "You little bastard. You little bastard."

"Yeah?" said Fats, and he was no longer smirking. "I'd rather be a little bastard than be you, you arsehole!"

"No!" shouted Tessa. "Colin, get out. *Get out!*"

Horrified, furious and shaken, Colin lingered for a moment, then marched from the room; they heard him stumble a little on the stairs.

"How could you?" Tessa whispered to her son.

"How could I fucking what?" said Stuart, and the look on his face alarmed her so much that she hurried to close and bar the bedroom door.

"You're taking advantage of that girl, Stuart, and you know it, and the way you just spoke to your—"

"The fuck I am," said Fats, pacing up and down, every semblance of cool gone. "The fuck I'm taking advantage of her. She knows exactly what she wants—just because she lives in the fucking Fields, it doesn't—the truth is, you and Cubby don't want me to shag her because you think she's beneath—"

"That's not true!" said Tessa, even though it was, and for all her concern about Krystal, she would still have been glad to know that Fats had sense enough to wear a condom.

"You're fucking hypocrites, you and Cubby," he said, still pacing the length of the bedroom. "All the bollocks the pair of you spout about wanting to help the Weedons, but you don't want—"

"That's enough!" shouted Tessa. "Don't you dare speak to me like that! Don't you realize—don't you understand—are you so damn selfish...?"

Words failed her. She turned, tugged open his door and was gone, slamming it behind her.

Her exit had an odd effect on Fats, who stopped pacing and stared at the closed door for several seconds. Then he searched his pockets, drew out a cigarette and lit it, not bothering to blow the smoke out of the skylight. Round and round his room he walked, and he had no control of his own thoughts: jerky, unedited images filled his brain, sweeping past on a tide of fury.

He remembered the Friday evening, nearly a year previously, when Tessa had come up here to his bedroom to tell him that his father wanted to take him out to play football with Barry and his sons next day.

("What?" Fats had been staggered. The suggestion was unprecedented.

"For fun. A kick-around," Tessa had said, avoiding Fats' glare by scowling down at the clothes littering the floor.

"Why?"

"Because Dad thought it might be nice," said Tessa, bending to pick up a school shirt. "Declan wants a practice, or something. He's got a match."

Fats was quite good at football. People found it surprising; they expected him to dislike sport, to disdain teams. He played as he talked, skillfully, with many a feint, fooling the clumsy, daring to take chances, unconcerned if they did not come off.

"I didn't even know he could play."

"Dad can play very well, he was playing twice a week when we met," said Tessa, riled. "Ten o'clock tomorrow morning, all right? I'll wash your tracksuit bottoms.")

Fats sucked on his cigarette, remembering against his will. Why had he gone along with it? Today, he would have simply refused to participate in Cubby's little charade, but remained in bed until the shouting died away. A year ago he had not yet understood about authenticity.

(Instead he had left the house with Cubby and endured a silent five-minute walk, each equally aware of the enormous shortfall that filled all the space between them.

The playing field belonged to St. Thomas's. It had been sunny and deserted. They had divided into two teams of three, because

Declan had a friend staying for the weekend. The friend, who clearly hero-worshipped Fats, had joined Fats and Cubby's team.

Fats and Cubby passed to each other in silence, while Barry, easily the worst player, had yelled, cajoled and cheered in his Yarvil accent as he tore up and down the pitch they had marked out with sweatshirts. When Fergus scored, Barry had run at him for a flying chest bump, mistimed it and smashed Fergus on the jaw with the top of his head. The two of them had fallen to the ground, Fergus groaning in pain and laughing, while Barry sat apologizing through his roars of mirth. Fats had found himself grinning, then heard Cubby's awkward, booming laugh and turned away, scowling.

And then had come that moment, that cringeworthy, pitiful moment, with the scores equal and nearly time to go, when Fats had successfully wrested the ball from Fergus, and Cubby had shouted, "Come on, Stu, lad!"

"Lad." Cubby had never said "lad" in his life. It sounded pitiful, hollow and unnatural. He was trying to be like Barry; imitating Barry's easy, unself-conscious encouragement of his sons; trying to impress Barry.

The ball had flown like a cannonball from Fats' foot and there was time, before it hit Cubby full in his unsuspecting, foolish face, before his glasses cracked, and a single drop of blood bloomed beneath his eye, to realize his own intent; to know that he had hoped to hit Cubby, and that the ball had been dispatched for retribution.)

They had never played football again. The doomed little experiment in father-son togetherness had been shelved, like a dozen before it.

And I never wanted him at all!

He was sure he had heard it. Cubby must have been talking about him. They had been in his room. Who else could Cubby have been talking about?

Like I give a shit, thought Fats. It was what he'd always suspected. He did not know why this sensation of spreading cold had filled his chest.

Fats pulled the computer chair back into position, from the place where it had been knocked when Cubby had hit him. The authentic reaction would have been to shove his mother out of the way and punch Cubby in the face. Crack his glasses again. Make him bleed. Fats was disgusted with himself that he had not done it.

But there were other ways. He had overheard things for years. He knew much more about his father's ludicrous fears than they thought.

Fats' fingers were clumsier than usual. Ash spilled onto the keyboard from the cigarette in his mouth as he brought up the Parish Council website. Weeks previously, he had looked up SQL injections and found the line of code that Andrew had refused to share. After studying the council message board for a few minutes, he logged himself in, without difficulty, as Betty Rossiter, changed her username to The_Ghost_of_Barry_Fairbrother, and began to type.

V

Shirley Mollison was convinced that her husband and son were overstating the danger to the council of leaving the Ghost's posts online. She could not see how the messages were worse than gossip, and that, she knew, was not yet punishable by law; nor did she believe that the law would be foolish and unreasonable enough to punish her for what somebody else had written: that would be monstrously unfair. Proud as she was of Miles' law degree, she was sure that he must have this bit wrong.

She was checking the message boards even more frequently than Miles and Howard had advised, but not because she was afraid of legal consequences. Certain as she was that Barry Fairbrother's Ghost had not yet finished his self-appointed task of crushing the pro-Fielders, she was eager to be the first to set eyes on his next post. Several times a day she scurried into Patricia's old room, and clicked on the web page. Sometimes a little frisson would run through her while she was hoovering or peeling potatoes and she would race to the study, only to be disappointed again.

Shirley felt a special, secret kinship with the Ghost. He had chosen her website as the forum where he would expose the hypocrisy of Howard's opponents, and this, she felt, entitled her to the pride of the naturalist who has constructed a habitat in which a rare species deigns to nest. But there was more to it than that. Shirley relished the Ghost's anger, his savagery and his audacity. She wondered who he might be, visualizing a strong, shadowy man standing behind herself and Howard, on their side, cutting a path for them through the opponents who crumpled as he slayed them with their own ugly truths.

Somehow, none of the men in Pagford seemed worthy to be the Ghost; she would have felt disappointed to learn that it was any of the anti-Fielders she knew.

"That's *if* it's a man," said Maureen.

"Good point," said Howard.

"I think it's a man," said Shirley coolly.

When Howard left for the café on Sunday morning, Shirley, still in her dressing gown, and holding her cup of tea, padded automatically to the study and brought up the website.

Fantasies of a Deputy Headmaster posted by The_Ghost_of_ Barry_ Fairbrother.

She set down her tea with trembling hands, clicked on the post and read it, openmouthed. Then she ran to the lounge, seized the telephone and called the café, but the number was engaged.

A mere five minutes later, Parminder Jawanda, who had also developed a habit of looking at the council message boards much more frequently than usual, opened up the site and saw the post. Like Shirley, her immediate reaction was to seize a telephone.

The Walls were breakfasting without their son, who was still asleep upstairs. When Tessa picked up, Parminder cut across her friend's greeting.

"There's a post about Colin on the council website. Don't let him see it, whatever you do."

Tessa's frightened eyes swiveled to her husband, but he was a mere three feet from the receiver and had already heard every word that Parminder had spoken so loudly and clearly.

"I'll call you back," said Tessa urgently. "Colin," she said, fumbling to replace the receiver, "Colin, wait—"

But he had already stalked out of the room, bobbing up and down, his arms stiff by his side, and Tessa had to jog to catch him up.

"Perhaps it's better not to look," she urged him, as his big, knobble-knuckled hand moved the mouse across the desk, "or I can read it and—"

Fantasies of a Deputy Headmaster
One of the men hoping to represent the community at
Parish Council level is Colin Wall, Deputy Headmaster
at Winterdown Comprehensive School. Voters might be
interested to know that Wall, a strict disciplinarian, has a very
unusual fantasy life. Mr. Wall is so frightened that a pupil
might accuse him of inappropriate sexual behavior that he
has often needed time off work to calm himself down again.
Whether Mr. Wall has actually fondled a first year, the Ghost
can only guess. The fervor of his feverish fantasies suggests
that, even if he hasn't, he would like to.

Stuart wrote that, thought Tessa, at once.

Colin's face was ghastly in the light pouring out of the monitor. It was how she imagined he would look if he had had a stroke.

"Colin—"

"I suppose Fiona Shawcross has told people," he whispered.

The catastrophe he had always feared was upon him. It was the end of everything. He had always imagined taking sleeping tablets. He wondered whether they had enough in the house.

Tessa, who had been momentarily thrown by the mention of the headmistress, said, "Fiona wouldn't—anyway, she doesn't know—"

"She knows I've got OCD."

"Yes, but she doesn't know what you—what you're afraid of—"

"She does," said Colin. "I told her, before the last time I needed sick leave."

"Why?" Tessa burst out. "What on earth did you tell her for?"

"I wanted to explain why it was so important I had time off," said Colin, almost humbly. "I thought she needed to know how serious it was."

Tessa fought down a powerful desire to shout at him. The tinge of distaste with which Fiona treated him and talked about him was explained; Tessa had never liked her, always thought her hard and unsympathetic.

"Be that as it may," she said, "I don't think Fiona's got anything to do—"

"Not directly," said Colin, pressing a trembling hand to his sweating upper lip. "But Mollison's heard gossip from somewhere."

It wasn't Mollison. Stuart wrote that, I know he did. Tessa recognized her son in every line. She was even astonished that Colin could not see it, that he had not connected the message with yesterday's row, with hitting his son. *He couldn't even resist a bit of alliteration. He must have done all of them—Simon Price. Parminder.* Tessa was horror-struck.

But Colin was not thinking about Stuart. He was recalling thoughts that were as vivid as memories, as sensory impressions, violent, vile ideas: a hand seizing and squeezing as he passed through densely packed young bodies; a cry of pain, a child's face contorted. And then asking himself, again and again: had he done it? Had he enjoyed it? He could not remember. He only knew that he kept thinking about it, seeing it happen, feeling it happen. Soft flesh through a thin cotton blouse; seize, squeeze, pain and shock; a violation. How many times? He did not know. He had spent hours wondering how many of the children knew he did it, whether they had spoken to each other, how long it would be until he was exposed.

Not knowing how many times he had offended, and unable to trust himself, he burdened himself with so many papers and files that he had no hands free to attack as he moved through the corridors. He shouted at the swarming children to get out of the way, to stand clear, as he passed. None of it helped. There were always stragglers, running past him, up against him, and with his hands burdened he imagined other ways to have improper contact with them: a swiftly repositioned elbow brushing against a breast; a side-step to ensure bodily contact; a leg accidentally entangled, so that the child's groin made contact with his flesh.

"Colin," said Tessa.

But he had started to cry again, great sobs shaking his big, ungainly body, and when she put her arms around him and pressed her face to his her own tears wet his skin.

A few miles away, in Hilltop House, Simon Price was sitting at a brand-new family computer in the sitting room. Watching Andrew cycle away to his weekend job with Howard Mollison, and the reflection that he had been forced to pay full market price for this computer, made him feel irritable and additionally hard done by. Simon had not looked at the Parish Council website once since the night that he had thrown out the stolen PC, but it occurred to him, by an association of ideas, to check whether the message that had cost him his job was still on the site and thus viewable by potential employers.

It was not. Simon did not know that he owed this to his wife, because Ruth was scared of admitting that she had telephoned Shirley, even to request the removal of the post. Slightly cheered by its absence, Simon looked for the post about Parminder, but that was gone too.

He was about to close the site, when he saw the newest post, which was entitled Fantasies of a Deputy Headmaster.

He read it through twice and then, alone in the sitting room, he began to laugh. It was a savage triumphant laugh. He had never taken to that big, bobbing man with his massive forehead. It was good to know that he, Simon, had got off very lightly indeed by comparison.

Ruth came into the room, smiling timidly; she was glad to hear Simon laughing, because he had been in a dreadful mood since losing his job.

"What's funny?"

"You know Fats' old man? Wall, the deputy headmaster? He's only a bloody pedo."

Ruth's smile slipped. She hurried forward to read the post.

366

"I'm going to shower," said Simon, in high good humor.

Ruth waited until he had left the room before trying to call her friend Shirley, and alert her to this new scandal, but the Mollisons' telephone was engaged.

Shirley had, at last, reached Howard at the delicatessen. She was still in her dressing gown; he was pacing up and down the little backroom, behind the counter.

"...been trying to get you for ages—"

"Mo was using the phone. What did it say? Slowly."

Shirley read the message about Colin, enunciating like a newsreader. She had not reached the end, when he cut across her.

"Did you copy this down or something?"

"Sorry?" she said.

"Are you reading it off the screen? Is it still on there? Have you taken it off?"

"I'm dealing with it now," lied Shirley, unnerved. "I thought you'd like to—"

"Get it off there now! God above, Shirley, this is getting out of hand—we can't have stuff like that on there!"

"I just thought you ought to—"

"Make sure you've got rid of it, and we'll talk about it when I get home!" Howard shouted.

Shirley was furious: they never raised their voices to each other.

VI

The next Parish Council meeting, the first since Barry had died, would be crucial in the ongoing battle over the Fields. Howard had refused to postpone the votes on the future of Bellchapel Addiction Clinic, or the town's wish to transfer jurisdiction of the estate to Yarvil.

Parminder therefore suggested that she, Colin and Kay ought to meet up the evening before the meeting to discuss strategy.

"Pagford can't unilaterally decide to alter the parish boundary, can it?" asked Kay.

"No," said Parminder patiently (Kay could not help being a newcomer), "but the District Council has asked for Pagford's opinion, and Howard's determined to make sure it's *his* opinion that gets passed on."

They were holding their meeting in the Walls' sitting room, because Tessa had put subtle pressure on Colin to invite the other two where she could listen in. Tessa handed around glasses of wine, put a large bowl of crisps on the coffee table, then sat back in silence, while the other three talked.

She was exhausted and angry. The anonymous post about Colin had brought on one of his most debilitating attacks of acute anxiety, so severe that he had been unable to go to school. Parminder knew how ill he was—she had signed him off work—yet she invited him to participate in this pre-meeting, not caring, it seemed, what fresh effusions of paranoia and distress Tessa would have to deal with tonight.

"There's definitely resentment out there about the way the Mollisons are handling things," Colin was saying, in the lofty, knowledgeable tone he sometimes adopted when pretending to be a stranger to fear and paranoia. "I think it's starting to get up people's noses, the way they think that they can speak for the town. I've got that impression, you know, while I've been canvassing."

It would have been nice, thought Tessa bitterly, if Colin could have summoned these powers of dissimulation for *her* benefit occasionally. Once, long ago, she had liked being Colin's sole confidante, the only repository of his terrors and the font of all reassurance, but she no longer found it flattering. He had kept her awake from two o'clock until half past three that morning, rocking backwards and forwards on the edge of the bed, moaning and crying, saying that he wished he were dead, that he could not take it, that he wished he had never stood for the seat, that he was ruined...

Tessa heard Fats on the stairs, and tensed, but her son passed the open door on his way to the kitchen with nothing worse than a scathing glance at Colin, who was perched in front of the fire on a leather pouf, his knees level with his chest.

"Maybe Miles' standing for the empty seat will really antagonize people — even the Mollisons' natural supporters?" said Kay hopefully.

"I think it might," said Colin, nodding.

Kay turned to Parminder.

"D'you think the council will really vote to force Bellchapel out of their building? I know people get uptight about discarded needles, and addicts hanging around the neighborhood, but the clinic's miles away...why does Pagford care?"

"Howard and Aubrey are scratching each other's backs," explained Parminder, whose face was taut, with dark brown patches under her eyes. (It was she who would have to attend the council meeting the next day, and fight Howard Mollison and his cronies without Barry by her side.) "They need to make cuts in spending at District level. If Howard turfs the clinic out of its cheap building, it'll be much more expensive to run and Fawley can say the costs have increased, and justify cutting council funding. Then Fawley will do his best to make sure that the Fields get reassigned to Yarvil."

Tired of explaining, Parminder pretended to examine the new stack of papers about Bellchapel that Kay had brought with her, easing herself out of the conversation.

Why am I doing this? she asked herself.

She could have been sitting at home with Vikram, who had been watching comedy on television with Jaswant and Rajpal as she left. The sound of their laughter had jarred on her; when had she last laughed? Why was she here, drinking nasty warm wine, fighting for a clinic that she would never need and a housing development inhabited by people she would probably dislike if she met them? She was not Bhai Kanhaiya, who could not see a difference between the souls of allies and enemies; she saw no light of God shining from Howard Mollison. She derived more pleasure from the thought of Howard losing, than from the thought of Fields children continuing to attend St. Thomas's, or from Fields people being able to break their addictions at Bellchapel, although, in a distant and dispassionate way, she thought that these were good things...

(But she knew why she was doing it, really. She wanted to win for Barry. He had told her all about coming to St. Thomas's. His classmates had invited him home to play; he, who had been living in a caravan with his mother and two brothers, had relished the neat and comfortable houses of Hope Street, and been awed by the big Victorian houses on Church Row. He had even attended a birthday party in that very cow-faced house that he had subsequently bought, and where he had raised his four children.

He had fallen in love with Pagford, with the river and the fields and the solid-walled houses. He had fantasized about having a garden to play in, a tree from which to hang a swing, space and greenness everywhere. He had collected conkers and taken them back to the Fields. After shining at St. Thomas's, top of his class, Barry had gone on to be the first in his family to go to university.

Love and hate, Parminder thought, a little frightened by her own honesty. *Love and hate, that's why I'm here…*)

She turned over a page of Kay's documents, feigning concentration.

Kay was pleased that the doctor was scrutinizing her papers so carefully, because she had put a lot of time and thought into them. She could not believe that anybody reading her material would not be convinced that the Bellchapel clinic ought to remain in situ.

But through all the statistics, the anonymous case studies and first-person testimonies, Kay really thought of the clinic in terms of only one patient: Terri Weedon. There had been a change in Terri, Kay could feel it, and it made her both proud and frightened. Terri was showing faint glimmerings of an awakened sense of control over her life. Twice lately, Terri had said to Kay, "They ain' takin' Robbie, I won' lerrem," and these had not been impotent railings against fate, but statements of intent.

"I took 'im ter nursery yest'day," she told Kay, who had made the mistake of looking astonished. "Why's tha' so fuckin' shockin'? Aren' I good enough ter go ter the fuckin' nurs'ry?"

If Bellchapel's door was slammed shut against Terri, Kay was sure it would blow to pieces that delicate structure they were trying to build out of the wreckage of a life. Terri seemed to have a visceral fear of Pagford that Kay did not understand.

"I 'ate that fuckin' place," she had said, when Kay had mentioned it in passing.

Beyond the fact that her dead grandmother had lived there, Kay knew nothing of Terri's history with the town, but she was afraid that if Terri was asked to travel there weekly for her methadone her self-control would crumble, and with it the family's fragile new safety.

Colin had taken over from Parminder, explaining the history of the Fields; Kay nodded, bored, and said "mm," but her thoughts were a long way away.

Colin was deeply flattered by the way this attractive young woman was hanging on his every word. He felt calmer tonight than at any point since he had read that awful post, which was gone from the website. None of the cataclysms that Colin had imagined in the small hours had come to pass. He was not sacked. There was no angry mob outside his front door. Nobody on the Pagford Council website, or indeed anywhere else on the Internet (he had performed several Google searches), was demanding his arrest or incarceration.

Fats walked back past the open door, spooning yogurt into his mouth as he went. He glanced into the room, and for a fleeting moment met Colin's gaze. Colin immediately lost the thread of what he had been saying.

"…and…yes, well, that's it in a nutshell," he finished lamely. He glanced toward Tessa for reassurance, but his wife was staring stonily into space. Colin was a little hurt; he would have thought that Tessa would be glad to see him feeling so much better, so much more in control, after their wretched, sleepless night. Dreadful swooping sensations of dread were agitating his stomach, but he drew much comfort from the proximity of his fellow underdog and scapegoat Parminder, and from the sympathetic attention of the attractive social worker.

Unlike Kay, Tessa had listened to every word that Colin had just said about the Fields' right to remain joined to Pagford. There was, in her opinion, no conviction behind his words. He wanted to believe what Barry had believed, and he wanted to defeat the Mollisons, because that was what Barry had wanted. Colin did not like Krystal Weedon, but Barry had liked her, so he assumed that there was more worth in her than he could see. Tessa knew her husband to be a strange mixture of arrogance and humility, of unshakable conviction and insecurity.

They're completely deluded, Tessa thought, looking at the other three, who were poring over some graph that Parminder had extracted from Kay's notes. *They think they'll reverse sixty years of anger and resentment with a few sheets of statistics.* None of them was Barry. He had been a living example of what they proposed in theory: the advancement, through education, from poverty to affluence, from powerlessness and dependency to valuable contributor to society. Did they not see what hopeless advocates they were, compared to the man who had died?

"People are definitely getting irritable with the Mollisons trying to run everything," Colin was saying.

"I do think," said Kay, "that they'll be hard-pushed, if they read this stuff, to pretend that the clinic isn't doing crucial work."

"Not everybody's forgotten Barry, on the council," said Parminder, in a slightly shaky voice.

Tessa realized that her greasy fingers were groping vainly in space. While the others had talked, she had singlehandedly finished the entire bowl of crisps.

VII

It was a bright, balmy morning, and the computing lab at Winterdown Comprehensive became stuffy as lunchtime approached, the dirty windows speckling the dusty monitors with distracting spots of light. Even though there was no Fats or Gaia here to distract him, Andrew Price could not concentrate. He could think of nothing but what he had overheard his parents discussing the previous evening.

They had been talking, quite seriously, about moving to Reading, where Ruth's sister and brother-in-law lived. With his ear turned towards the open kitchen door, Andrew had hovered in the tiny dark hall and listened: Simon, it appeared, had been offered a job, or the possibility of a job, by the uncle whom Andrew and Paul barely knew, because Simon disliked him so much.

"It's less money," Simon had said.

"You don't know that. He hasn't said—"

"Bound to be. And it'll be more expensive all round, living there."

Ruth made a noncommital noise. Scarcely daring to breathe in the hall, Andrew could tell, by the mere fact that his mother was not rushing to agree with Simon, that she wanted to go.

Andrew found it impossible to imagine his parents in any house but Hilltop House, or against any backdrop but Pagford. He had taken it for granted that they would remain there forever. He, Andrew, would leave one day for London, but Simon and Ruth would remain rooted to the hillside like trees, until they died.

He had crept back upstairs to his bedroom and stared out of the window at the twinkling lights of Pagford, cupped in the deep black hollow between the hills. He felt as though he had never seen the view before. Somewhere down there, Fats was smoking in his attic room, probably looking at porn on his computer. Gaia was there too, absorbed in the mysterious rites of her gender. It occurred to Andrew that she had been through this; she had been torn away from the place she knew and transplanted. They had something profoundly in common at last; there was almost melancholy pleasure in the idea that, in leaving, he would share something with her.

But she had not caused her own displacement. With a squirming unease in his guts, he had picked up his mobile and texted Fats: Si-Pie offered job in Reading. Might take it.

Fats had still not responded, and Andrew had not seen him all morning, because they shared none of their classes. He had not seen Fats for the previous two weekends either, because he had been working at the Copper Kettle. Their longest conversation, recently, had concerned Fats' posting about Cubby on the council website.

"I think Tessa suspects," Fats had told Andrew casually. "She keeps looking at me like she knows."

"What're you gonna say?" Andrew had muttered, scared.

He knew Fats' desire for glory and credit, and he knew Fats' passion for wielding the truth as a weapon, but he was not sure that his friend understood that his own pivotal role in the activities of the Ghost of Barry Fairbrother must never be revealed. It had never been easy to explain to Fats the reality of having Simon as a father, and, somehow, Fats was becoming more difficult to explain things to.

When his IT teacher had passed by out of sight, Andrew looked up Reading on the Internet. It was huge compared with Pagford. It had an annual music festival. It was only forty miles from London. He contemplated the train service. Perhaps he would go up to the capital at weekends, the way he currently took the bus to Yarvil. But the whole thing seemed unreal: Pagford was all he had ever known; he still could not imagine his family existing anywhere else.

At lunchtime Andrew headed straight out of school, looking for Fats. He lit up a cigarette just out of sight of the grounds, and was delighted to hear, as he was slipping his lighter casually back into his pocket, a female voice that said, "Hey." Gaia and Sukhvinder caught up with him.

"All right," he said, blowing smoke away from Gaia's beautiful face.

The three of them had something these days that nobody else had. Two weekends' work at the café had created a fragile bond between them. They knew Howard's stock phrases, and had endured Maureen's prurient interest in all of their home lives; they had smirked together at her wrinkled knees in the too-short waitress's dress and had exchanged, like traders in a foreign land, small nuggets of personal information. Thus the girls knew that Andrew's father had been sacked; Andrew and Sukhvinder knew that Gaia was working to save for a train ticket back to Hackney; and he and Gaia knew that Sukhvinder's mother hated her working for Howard Mollison.

"Where's your Fat friend?" she asked, as the three of them fell into step together.

"Dunno," said Andrew. "Haven't seen him."

"No loss," said Gaia. "How many of those do you smoke a day?"

"Don't count," said Andrew, elated by her interest. "D'you want one?"

"No," said Gaia. "I don't like smoking."

He wondered instantly whether the dislike extended to kissing people who smoked. Niamh Fairbrother had not complained when he had stuck his tongue into her mouth at the school disco.

"Doesn't Marco smoke?" asked Sukhvinder.

"No, he's always in training," said Gaia.

Andrew had become almost inured to the thought of Marco de Luca by now. There were advantages to Gaia being safeguarded, as it were, by an allegiance beyond Pagford. The power of the photographs of them together on her Facebook page had been blunted by his familiarity with them. He did not think it was his own wishful thinking that the messages she and Marco left for each other were becoming less frequent and less friendly. He could not know what was happening by telephone or email, but he was sure that Gaia's air, when he was mentioned, was dispirited.

"Oh, there he is," said Gaia.

It was not the handsome Marco who had come into view, but Fats Wall, who was talking to Dane Tully outside the newsagent's.

Sukhvinder braked, but Gaia grabbed her upper arm.

"You can walk where you like," she said, tugging her gently onwards, her flecked green eyes narrowing as they approached the place where Fats and Dane were smoking.

"All right, Arf," called Fats, as the three of them came close.

"Fats," said Andrew.

Trying to head off trouble, especially Fats bullying Sukhvinder in front of Gaia, he asked, "Did you get my text?"

"What text?" said Fats. "Oh yeah—that thing about Si? You leaving, then, are you?"

It was said with a cavalier indifference that Andrew could only attribute to the presence of Dane Tully.

"Yeah, maybe," said Andrew.

"Where are you going?" asked Gaia.

"My old man's been offered a job in Reading," said Andrew.

"Oh, that's where my dad lives!" said Gaia in surprise. "We could hang out when I go and stay. The festival's awesome. D'you wanna get a sandwich, then, Sooks?"

Andrew was so stupefied by her voluntary offer to spend time with him, that she had disappeared into the newsagent's before he could gather his wits and agree. For a moment, the dirty bus stop, the newsagent's, even Dane Tully, tattooed and shabby in a T-shirt and tracksuit bottoms, seemed to glow with an almost celestial light.

"Well, I got things to do," said Fats.

Dane sniggered. Before Andrew could say anything or offer to accompany him, he had loped away.

Fats was sure that Andrew would be nonplussed and hurt by his cool attitude, and he was glad of it. Fats did not ask himself why he was glad, or why a general desire to cause pain had become his overriding emotion in the last few days. He had lately decided that questioning your own motives was inauthentic; a refinement of his personal philosophy that had made it altogether easier to follow.

As he headed into the Fields, Fats thought about what had happened at home the previous evening, when his mother had entered his bedroom for the first time since Cubby had punched him.

("That message about your father on the Parish Council website," she had said. "I've got to ask you this, Stuart, and I wish—Stuart, did you write it?"

It had taken her a few days to summon the courage to accuse him, and he was prepared.

"No," he said.

Perhaps it would have been more authentic to say yes, but he had preferred not to, and he did not see why he should have to justify himself.

"You didn't?" she repeated, with no change of tone or expression.

"No," he repeated.

"Because very, very few people know what Dad…what he worries about."

"Well, it wasn't me."

"The post went up the same evening that Dad and you had the row, and Dad hit—"

"I've told you, I didn't do it."

"You know he's ill, Stuart."

"Yeah, so you keep telling me."

"I keep telling you because it's true! He can't help it—he's got a serious mental illness that causes him untold distress and misery."

Fats' mobile had beeped, and he had glanced down at a text from Andrew. He read it and experienced an air punch to the midriff: Arf leaving for good.

"I'm talking to you, Stuart—"

"I know—what?"

"All these posts—Simon Price, Parminder, Dad—these are all people you know. If you're behind all this—"

"I've told you, I'm not."

"—you're causing untold damage. Serious, awful damage, Stuart, to people's lives."

Fats was trying to imagine life without Andrew. They had known each other since they were four.

"It's not me," he had said.)

Serious, awful damage to people's lives.

They had made their lives, Fats thought scornfully as he turned into Foley Road. The victims of the Ghost of Barry Fairbrother were mired in hypocrisy and lies, and they didn't like the exposure. They were stupid bugs running from bright light. They knew nothing about real life.

He could see a house ahead that had a bald tire lying on the grass in front of it. He had a strong suspicion that that was Krystal's, and when he saw the number, he knew he was right. He had never been here before. He would never have agreed to meet her at her home during the lunch hour a couple of weeks ago, but things changed. He had changed.

They said that her mother was a prostitute. She was certainly a junkie. Krystal had told him that the house would be empty because her mother would be at Bellchapel Addiction Clinic, receiving her allotted amount of methadone. Fats walked up the garden path without slowing, but with unexpected trepidation.

Krystal had been on the watch for him, from her bedroom

window. She had closed the doors of every room downstairs, so that all he would see was the hall; she had thrown everything that had spilled into it back into the sitting room and kitchen. The carpet was gritty and burned in places, and the wallpaper stained, but she could do nothing about that. There had been none of the pine-scented disinfectant left, but she had found some bleach and sloshed that around the kitchen and bathroom, both of them sources of the worst smells in the house.

When he knocked, she ran downstairs. They did not have long; Terri would probably be back with Robbie at one. Not long to make a baby.

"Hiya," she said, when she opened the door.

"All right?" said Fats, blowing out smoke through his nostrils.

He did not know what he had expected. His first glimpse of the interior of the house was of a grimy bare box. There was no furniture. The closed doors to his left and ahead were strangely ominous.

"Are we the only ones here?" he asked as he crossed the threshold.

"Yeah," said Krystal. "We c'n go upstairs. My room."

She led the way. The deeper inside they went, the worse the smell became: mingled bleach and filth. Fats tried not to care. All doors were closed on the landing, except one. Krystal went inside.

Fats did not want to be shocked, but there was nothing in the room except a mattress, which was covered with a sheet and a bare duvet, and a small pile of clothes heaped up in a corner. A few pictures ripped from tabloid newspapers were sellotaped to the wall; a mixture of pop stars and celebrities.

Krystal had made her collage the previous day, in imitation of the one on Nikki's bedroom wall. Knowing that Fats was coming over, she had wanted to make the room more hospitable. She had drawn the thin curtains. They gave a bluish tinge to daylight.

"Gimme a fag," she said. "I'm gasping."

He lit it for her. She was more nervous than he had ever seen her; he preferred her cocky and worldly.

"We ain' got long," she told him, and with the cigarette in her mouth, she began to strip. "Me mum'll be back."

"Yeah, at Bellchapel, isn't she?" said Fats, somehow trying to harden Krystal up again in his mind.

"Yeah," said Krystal, sitting on the mattress and pulling off her tracksuit bottoms.

"What if they close it?" asked Fats, taking off his blazer. "I heard they're thinking about it."

"I dunno," said Krystal, but she was frightened. Her mother's willpower, fragile and vulnerable as a fledgling chick, could fail at the slightest provocation.

She had already stripped to her underwear. Fats was taking off his shoes when he noticed something nestled beside her heaped clothes: a small plastic jewelry box lying open, and curled inside, a familiar watch.

"Is that my mum's?" he said, in surprise.

"What?" Krystal panicked. "No," she lied. "It was my Nana Cath's. Don't—!"

But he had already pulled it out of the box.

"It is hers," he said. He recognized the strap.

"It fuckin' ain't!"

She was terrified. She had almost forgotten that she had stolen it, where it had come from. Fats was silent, and she did not like it.

The watch in Fats' hand seemed to be both challenging and reproaching him. In quick succession he imagined walking out, slipping it casually into his pocket, or handing it back to Krystal with a shrug.

"It's mine," she said.

He did not want to be a policeman. He wanted to be lawless. But it took the recollection that the watch had been Cubby's gift to make him hand it back to her and carry on taking off his clothes. Scarlet in the face, Krystal tugged off bra and pants and slipped, naked, beneath the duvet.

Fats approached her in his boxer shorts, a wrapped condom in his hand.

"We don' need that," said Krystal thickly. "I'm takin' the pill now."

"Are you?"

She moved over on the mattress for him. Fats slid under the

duvet. As he pulled off his boxers, he wondered whether she was lying about the pill, like the watch. But he had wanted to try without a condom for a while.

"Go on," she whispered, and she tugged the little foil square out of his hand and threw it on top of his blazer, crumpled on the floor.

He imagined Krystal pregnant with his child; the faces of Tessa and Cubby when they heard. His kid in the Fields, his flesh and blood. It would be more than Cubby had ever managed.

He climbed on top of her; this, he knew, was real life.

VIII

At half past six that evening, Howard and Shirley Mollison entered Pagford Church Hall. Shirley was carrying an armful of papers and Howard was wearing the chain of office decorated with the blue and white Pagford crest.

The floorboards creaked beneath Howard's massive weight as he moved to the head of the scratched tables that had already been set end to end. Howard was almost as fond of this hall as he was of his own shop. The Brownies used it on Tuesdays, and the Women's Institute on Wednesdays. It had hosted jumble sales and Jubilee celebrations, wedding receptions and wakes, and it smelled of all of these things: of stale clothes and coffee urns, and the ghosts of home-baked cakes and meat salads; of dust and human bodies; but primarily of aged wood and stone. Beaten-brass lights hung from the rafters on thick black flexes, and the kitchen was reached through ornate mahogany doors.

Shirley bustled from place to place, setting out papers. She adored council meetings. Quite apart from the pride and enjoyment she derived from listening to Howard chair them, Maureen was necessarily absent; with no official role, she had to be content with the pickings Shirley deigned to share.

Howard's fellow councillors arrived singly and in pairs. He boomed out greetings, his voice echoing from the rafters. The full complement of sixteen councillors rarely attended; he was expecting twelve of them today.

The table was half full when Aubrey Fawley arrived, walking, as he always did, as if into a high wind, with an air of reluctant forcefulness, slightly stooped, his head bowed.

"Aubrey!" called Howard joyfully, and for the first time he moved forward to greet the newcomer. "How are you? How's Julia? Did you get my invitation?"

"Sorry, I don't—"

"To my sixty-fifth? Here—Saturday—day after the election."

"Oh, yes, yes. Howard, there's a young woman outside—she says she's from the *Yarvil and District Gazette*. Alison something?"

"Oh," said Howard. "Strange. I've just sent her my article, you know, the one answering Fairbrother's...Maybe it's something to do...I'll go and see."

He waddled away, full of vague misgivings. Parminder Jawanda entered as he approached the door; scowling as usual, she walked straight past without greeting him, and for once Howard did not ask "How's Parminder?"

Out on the pavement he found a young blonde woman, stocky and square, with an aura of impermeable cheerfulness that Howard recognized immediately as determination of his own brand. She was holding a notebook and looking up at the Sweetlove initials carved over the double doors.

"Hello, hello," said Howard, his breathing a little labored. "Alison, is it? Howard Mollison. Have you come all this way to tell me I can't write for toffee?"

She beamed, and shook the hand he proffered.

"Oh, no, we like the article," she assured him. "I thought, as things are getting so interesting, I'd come and sit in on the meeting. You don't mind? Press are allowed, I think. I've looked up all the regulations."

She was moving toward the door as she spoke.

"Yes, yes, press are allowed," said Howard, following her and pausing courteously at the entrance to let her through first. "Unless we have to deal with anything in camera, that is."

She glanced back at him, and he could make out her teeth, even in the fading light.

"Like all those anonymous accusations on your message board? From the Ghost of Barry Fairbrother?"

"Oh dear," wheezed Howard, smiling back at her. "*They're* not news, surely? A couple of silly comments on the Internet?"

"Has it only been a couple? Somebody told me the bulk of them had been taken off the site."

"No, no, somebody's got that wrong," said Howard. "There have only been two or three, to my knowledge. Nasty nonsense. Personally," he said, improvising on the spot, "I think it's some kid."

"A kid?"

"You know. Teenager having fun."

"Would teenagers target Parish councillors?" she asked, still smiling. "I heard, actually, that one of the victims has lost his job. Possibly as a result of the allegations made against him on your site."

"News to me," said Howard untruthfully. Shirley had seen Ruth at the hospital the previous day and reported back to him.

"I see on the agenda," said Alison, as the pair of them entered the brightly lit hall, "That you'll be discussing Bellchapel. You and Mr. Fairbrother made good points on both sides of the argument in your articles…we had quite a few letters to the paper after we printed Mr. Fairbrother's piece. My editor liked that. Anything that makes people write letters…"

"Yes, I saw those," said Howard. "Nobody seemed to have much good to say about the clinic, did they?"

The councillors at the table were watching the pair of them. Alison Jenkins returned their gaze, still smiling imperturbably.

"Let me get you a chair," said Howard, puffing slightly as he lifted one down from a nearby stack and settling Alison some twelve feet from the table.

"Thank you." She pulled it six feet forward.

"Ladies and gentlemen," called Howard, "we've got a press gallery here tonight. Miss Alison Jenkins of the *Yarvil and District Gazette*."

A few of them seemed interested and gratified by Alison's appearance, but most looked suspicious. Howard stumped back to the head of the table, where Aubrey and Shirley were questioning him with their eyes.

"Barry Fairbrother's Ghost," he told them in an undertone, as he lowered himself gingerly into the plastic chair (one of them had collapsed under him two meetings ago). "And Bellchapel. And there's Tony!" he shouted, making Aubrey jump. "Come on in, Tony... we'll give Henry and Sheila another couple of minutes, shall we?"

The murmur of talk around the table was slightly more subdued than usual. Alison Jenkins was already writing in her notebook. Howard thought angrily, *This is all bloody Fairbrother's fault*. He was the one who had invited the press in. For a split second, Howard thought of Barry and the Ghost as one and the same, a troublemaker alive and dead.

Like Shirley, Parminder had brought a stack of papers with her to the meeting, and these were piled up underneath the agenda she was pretending to read so that she did not have to speak to anybody. In reality, she was thinking about the woman sitting almost directly behind her. The *Yarvil and District Gazette* had written about Catherine Weedon's collapse, and the family's complaints against their GP. Parminder had not been named, but doubtless the journalist knew who she was. Perhaps Alison had got wind of the anonymous post about Parminder on the Parish Council website too.

Calm down. You're getting like Colin.

Howard was already taking apologies and asking for revisions to the last set of minutes, but Parminder could barely hear over the sound of her own blood thudding in her ears.

"Now, unless anybody's got any objections," said Howard, "we're going to deal with items eight and nine first, because District Councillor Fawley's got news on both, and he can't stay long—"

"Got until eight thirty," said Aubrey, checking his watch.

"—yes, so unless there are objections—no?—floor's yours, Aubrey."

Aubrey stated the position simply and without emotion. There was a new boundary review coming and, for the first time, there was an appetite beyond Pagford to reassign the Fields to Yarvil. Absorbing Pagford's relatively small costs seemed worthwhile to those who hoped to add antigovernment votes to Yarvil's tally, where they might make a difference, as opposed to being wasted in Pagford, which had been a safe Conservative seat since the 1950s. The whole thing could be done under the guise of simplifying and streamlining: Yarvil provided almost all services for the place as it was.

Aubrey concluded by saying that it would be helpful, should Pagford wish to cut the estate away, for the town to express its wishes for the benefit of the District Council.

"...a good, clear message from you," he said, "and I really think that this time—"

"It's never worked before," said a farmer, to muttered agreement.

"Well, now, John, we've never been invited to state our position before," said Howard.

"Shouldn't we decide what our position is, before we declare it publicly?" asked Parminder, in an icy voice.

"All right," said Howard blandly. "Would you like to kick off, Dr. Jawanda?"

"I don't know how many people saw Barry's article in the *Gazette,*" said Parminder. Every face was turned towards her, and she tried not to think about the anonymous post or the journalist sitting behind her. "I thought it made the arguments for keeping the Fields part of Pagford very well."

Parminder saw Shirley, who was writing busily, give her pen a tiny smile.

"By telling us the likes of Krystal Weedon benefit?" said an elderly woman called Betty, from the end of the table. Parminder had always detested her.

"By reminding us that people living in the Fields are part of our community too," she answered.

"They think of themselves as from Yarvil," said the farmer. "Always have."

"I remember," said Betty, "when Krystal Weedon pushed another child into the river on a nature walk."

384

"No, she didn't," said Parminder angrily, "my daughter was there—that was two boys who were fighting—anyway—"

"I heard it was Krystal Weedon," said Betty.

"You heard wrong," said Parminder, except that she did not say it, she shouted it.

They were shocked. She had shocked herself. The echo hummed off the old walls. Parminder could barely swallow; she kept her head down, staring at the agenda, and heard John's voice from a long way off.

"Barry would've done better to talk about himself, not that girl. He got a lot out of St. Thomas's."

"Trouble is, for every Barry," said another woman, "you get a load of yobs."

"They're Yarvil people, bottom line," said a man, "They belong to Yarvil."

"That's not true," said Parminder, keeping her voice deliberately low, but they all fell silent to listen to her, waiting for her to shout again. "It's simply not true. Look at the Weedons. That was the whole point of Barry's article. They were a Pagford family going back years, but—"

"They moved to Yarvil!" said Betty.

"There was no housing here," said Parminder, fighting her own temper, "none of you wanted a new development on the outskirts of town."

"You weren't here, I'm sorry," said Betty, pink in the face, looking ostentatiously away from Parminder. "You don't know the history."

Talk had become general: the meeting had broken into several little knots of conversation, and Parminder could not make out any of it. Her throat was tight and she did not dare meet anyone's eyes.

"Shall we have a show of hands?" Howard shouted down the table, and silence fell again. "Those in favor of telling the District Council that Pagford will be happy for the parish boundary to be redrawn, to take the Fields out of our jurisdiction?"

Parminder's fists were clenched in her lap and the nails of both her hands were embedded in their palms. There was a rustle of sleeves all around her.

"Excellent!" said Howard, and the jubilation in his voice rang triumphantly from the rafters. "Well, I'll draft something with Tony and Helen and we'll send it round for everyone to see, and we'll get it off. Excellent!"

A couple of councillors clapped. Parminder's vision blurred and she blinked hard. The agenda swam in and out of focus. The silence went on so long that finally she looked up: Howard, in his excitement, had had recourse to his inhaler, and most of the councillors were watching solicitously.

"All right, then," wheezed Howard, putting the inhaler away again, red in the face and beaming, "unless anyone's got anything else to add—"an infinitesimal pause "—item nine. Bellchapel. And Aubrey's got something to tell us here too."

Barry wouldn't have let it happen. He'd have argued. He'd have made John laugh and vote with us. He ought to have written about himself, not Krystal...I've let him down.

"Thank you, Howard," said Aubrey, as the blood pounded in Parminder's ears, and she dug her nails still more deeply into her palms. "As you know, we're having to make some pretty drastic cuts at District level..."

She was in love with me, which she could barely hide whenever she laid eyes on me...

"...and one of the projects we've got to look at is Bellchapel," said Aubrey. "I thought I'd have a word, because, as you all know, it's the Parish that owns the building —"

"—and the lease is almost up," said Howard. "That's right."

"But nobody else is interested in that old place, are they?" asked a retired accountant from the end of the table. "It's in a bad state, from what I've heard."

"Oh, I'm sure we could find a new tenant," said Howard comfortably, "but that's not really the issue. The point is whether we think the clinic is doing a good —"

"That's not the point at all," said Parminder, cutting across him. "It isn't the Parish Council's job to decide whether or not the clinic's doing a good job. We don't fund their work. They're not our responsibility."

"But we own the building," said Howard, still smiling, still polite, "So I think it's natural for us to want to consider—"

"If we're going to look at information on the clinic's work, I think it's very important that we get a balanced picture," said Parminder.

"I'm terribly sorry," said Shirley, blinking down the table at Parminder, "but could you try not to interrupt the Chair, Dr. Jawanda? It's awfully difficult to take notes if people talk over other people. And now I've interrupted," she added with a smile. "Sorry!"

"I presume the Parish wants to keep getting revenue from the building," said Parminder, ignoring Shirley. "And we have no other potential tenant lined up, as far as I know. So I'm wondering why we are even considering terminating the clinic's lease."

"They don't cure them," said Betty. "They just give them more drugs. I'd be very happy to see them out."

"We're having to make some very difficult decisions at District Council level," said Aubrey Fawley. "The government's looking for more than a billion in savings from local government. We cannot continue to provide services the way we have done. That's the reality."

Parminder hated the way that her fellow councillors acted around Aubrey, drinking in his deep modulated voice, nodding gently as he talked. She was well aware that some of them called her "Bends-Your-Ear."

"Research indicates that illegal drug use increases during recessions," said Parminder.

"It's their choice," said Betty. "Nobody makes them take drugs." She looked around the table for support. Shirley smiled at her.

"We're having to make some tough choices," said Aubrey.

"So you've got together with Howard," Parminder talked over him, "and decided that you can give the clinic a little push by forcing them out of the building."

"I can think of better ways to spend money than on a bunch of criminals," said the accountant.

"I'd cut off all their benefits, personally," said Betty.

"I was invited to this meeting to put you all in the picture about what's happening at District level," said Aubrey calmly. "Nothing more than that, Dr. Jawanda."

"Helen," said Howard loudly, pointing to another councillor, whose hand was raised, and who had been trying to make her views heard for a minute.

Parminder heard nothing of what the woman said. She had quite forgotten about the stack of papers lying underneath her agenda, on which Kay Bawden had spent so much time: the statistics, the profiles of successful cases, the explanation of the benefits of methadone as against heroin; studies showing the cost, financial and social, of heroin addiction. Everything around her had become slightly liquid, unreal; she knew that she was going to erupt as she had never erupted in her life, and there was no room to regret it, or to prevent it, or do anything except watch it happen; it was too late, far too late…

"…culture of entitlement," said Aubrey Fawley. "People who have literally not worked a day in their lives."

"And, let's face it," said Howard, "this is a problem with a simple solution. *Stop taking the drugs.*"

He turned, smiling and conciliating, to Parminder. "They call it 'cold turkey,' isn't that right, Dr. Jawanda?"

"Oh, you think that they should take responsibility for their addiction and change their behavior?" said Parminder.

"In a nutshell, yes."

"Before they cost the state any more money."

"Exact—"

"And you," said Parminder loudly, as the silent eruption engulfed her, "do you know how many tens of thousands of pounds *you,* Howard Mollison, have cost the health service, because of your total inability to stop gorging yourself?"

A rich, red claret stain was spreading up Howard's neck into his cheeks.

"Do you know how much your bypass cost, and your drugs, and your long stay in hospital? And the doctor's appointments you take up with your asthma and your blood pressure and the nasty skin rash, which are all caused by your refusal to lose weight?"

As Parminder's voice became a scream, other councillors began to protest on Howard's behalf; Shirley was on her feet; Parminder was still shouting, clawing together the papers that had somehow been scattered as she gesticulated.

"What about patient confidentiality?" shouted Shirley. "Outrageous! Absolutely outrageous!"

Parminder was at the door of the hall and striding through it, and she heard, over her own furious sobs, Betty calling for her immediate expulsion from the council; she was half running away from the hall, and she knew that she had done something cataclysmic, and she wanted nothing more than to be swallowed up by the darkness and to disappear forever.

IX

The *Yarvil and District Gazette* erred on the side of caution in reporting what had been said during the most acrimonious Pagford Parish Council meeting in living memory. It made little difference; the bowdlerized report, augmented by the vivid eyewitness descriptions offered by all who had attended, still created widespread gossip. To make matters worse, a front-page story detailed the anonymous Internet attacks in the dead man's name that had, to quote Alison Jenkins, *"caused considerable speculation and anger. See page four for full report."* While the names of the accused and the details of their supposed misdemeanors were not given, the sight of "serious allegations" and "criminal activity" in newsprint disturbed Howard even more than the original posts.

"We should have beefed up security on the site as soon as that first post appeared," he said, addressing his wife and business partner from in front of his gas fire.

Silent spring rain sprinkled the window, and the back lawn glistened with tiny red pinpricks of light. Howard was feeling shivery, and was hogging all the heat emanating from the fake coal. For several days, nearly every visitor to the delicatessen and the café had been gossiping about the anonymous posts, about the Ghost of Barry Fairbrother and about Parminder Jawanda's outburst at the council meeting. Howard hated the things that she had shouted being bandied about in public. For the first time in his life, he felt uncomfortable in his own shop, and concerned about his previously unassailable position in Pagford. The election for the replacement of Barry Fairbrother would take place the following day, and where Howard had felt sanguine and excited, he was worried and twitchy.

"This has done a lot of damage. A *lot* of damage," he repeated.

His hand strayed to his belly to scratch, but he pulled it away, enduring the itch with a martyr's expression. He would not soon forget what Dr. Jawanda had screamed to the council and the press. He and Shirley had already checked the details of the General Medical Council, gone to see Dr. Crawford, and made a formal complaint. Parminder had not been seen at work since, so no doubt she was already regretting her outburst. Nevertheless, Howard could not rid himself of the sight of her expression as she screamed at him. It had shaken him to see such hatred on another human's face.

"It'll all blow over," said Shirley reassuringly.

"I'm not so sure," said Howard. "I'm not so sure. It doesn't make us look good. The council. Rows in front of the press. We look divided. Aubrey says they're not happy, at District level. This whole thing's undermined our statement about the Fields. Squabbling in public, everything getting dirty…it doesn't look like the council's speaking for the town."

"But we are," said Shirley, with a little laugh. "Nobody in Pagford wants the Fields—hardly anyone."

"The article makes it look like our side went after pro-Fielders. Tried to intimidate them," said Howard, succumbing to the temptation to scratch, and doing it fiercely. "All right, Aubrey knows it wasn't any of our side, but that's not how that journalist made it look. And I'll tell you this: if Yarvil makes us look inept or dirty…they've been looking for a chance to take us over for years."

"That won't happen," said Shirley at once. "That couldn't happen."

"I thought it was over," said Howard, ignoring his wife, and thinking of the Fields. "I thought we'd done it. I thought we'd got rid of them."

The article over which he had spent so much time, explaining why the estate and the Bellchapel Addiction Clinic were drains and blots on Pagford, had been completely overshadowed by the scandals of Parminder's outburst, and the Ghost of Barry Fairbrother. Howard had completely forgotten now how much pleasure the accusations against Simon Price had given him, and that it had not occurred to him to remove them until Price's wife had asked.

"District Council's emailed me," he told Maureen, "with a bunch of questions about the website. They want to hear what steps we've taken against defamation. They think the security's lax."

Shirley, who detected a personal reproof in all of this, said coldly, "I've told you, I've taken care of it, Howard."

The nephew of friends of Howard and Shirley's had come round the previous day, while Howard was at work. The boy was halfway through a degree in computing. His recommendation to Shirley had been that they take down the immensely hackable website, bring in "Someone who knows what they're doing" and set up a new one.

Shirley had understood barely one word in ten of the technical jargon that the young man had spewed at her. She knew that "hack" meant to breach illegally, and when the student stopped talking his gibberish, she was left with the confused impression that the Ghost had somehow managed to find out people's passwords, maybe by questioning them cunningly in casual conversation.

She had therefore emailed everybody to request that they change their password and make sure not to share the new one with anybody. This was what she meant by "I've taken care of it."

As to the suggestion of closing down the site, of which she was guardian and curator, she had taken no steps, nor had she mentioned the idea to Howard. Shirley was afraid that a site containing all the security measures that the superior young man had suggested would be way beyond the scope of her managerial and technical skills. She was already stretched to the limits of her abilities, and she was determined to cling to the post of administrator.

"If Miles is elected—" Shirley began, but Maureen interrupted, in her deep voice. "Let's hope it hasn't hurt him, this nasty stuff. Let's hope there isn't a backlash against him."

"People will know Miles had nothing to do with it," said Shirley coolly.

"Will they, though?" said Maureen, and Shirley simply hated her. How dare she sit in Shirley's lounge and contradict her? And what was worse, Howard was nodding his agreement with Maureen.

"That's my worry," he said, "and we need Miles more than ever now. Get some cohesion back on the council. After Bends-Your-Ear said what she said—after all the uproar—we didn't even take the vote on Bellchapel. We need Miles."

Shirley had already walked out of the room in silent protest at Howard's siding with Maureen. She busied herself with the teacups in the kitchen, silently fuming, wondering why she did not set out only two cups to give Maureen the hint that she so richly deserved.

Shirley continued to feel nothing but defiant admiration for the Ghost. His accusations had exposed the truth about people whom she disliked and despised, people who were destructive and wrongheaded. She was sure that the electorate of Pagford would see things her way and vote for Miles, rather than that disgusting man, Colin Wall.

"When shall we go and vote?" Shirley asked Howard, reentering the room with the tinkling tea tray, and pointedly ignoring Maureen (for it was their son whose name they would tick on the ballot).

But to her intense irritation, Howard suggested that all three of them go after closing time.

Miles Mollison was quite as concerned as his father that the unprecedented ill humor surrounding next day's vote would affect his electoral chances. That very morning he had entered the newsagent's behind the Square and caught a snatch of conversation between the woman behind the till and her elderly customer.

"...Mollison's always thought he was king of Pagford," the old man was saying, oblivious to the wooden expression on the shopkeeper's face. "I liked Barry Fairbrother. Tragedy, that was.

Tragedy. The Mollison boy did our wills and I thought he was very pleased with himself."

Miles had lost his nerve at that and slipped back out of the shop, his face glowing like a schoolboy's. He wondered whether the well-spoken old man was the originator of that anonymous letter. Miles' comfortable belief in his own likability was shaken, and he kept trying to imagine how it would feel if nobody voted for him the following day.

As he undressed for bed that night, he watched his silent wife's reflection in the dressing-table mirror. For days, Samantha had been nothing but sarcastic if he mentioned the election. He could have done with some support, some comfort, this evening. He also felt randy. It had been a long time. Thinking back, he supposed that it had been the night before Barry Fairbrother dropped dead. She had been a little bit drunk. It often took a little bit of drink, these days.

"How was work?" he asked, watching her undo her bra in the mirror.

Samantha did not answer immediately. She rubbed the deep red grooves in the flesh beneath her arms left by the tight bra, then said, without looking at Miles, "I've been meaning to talk to you about that, actually."

She hated having to say it. She had been trying to avoid doing so for several weeks.

"Roy thinks I ought to close the shop. It's not doing well."

Exactly how badly the shop was doing would be a shock to Miles. It had been a shock to her, when her accountant had laid out the position in the baldest terms. She had both known and not known. It was strange how your brain could know what your heart refused to accept.

"Oh," said Miles. "But you'd keep the website?"

"Yeah," she said. "We'd keep the website."

"Well, that's good," said Miles encouragingly. He waited for almost a minute, out of respect for the death of her shop. Then he said, "I don't suppose you saw the *Gazette* today?"

She reached over for the nightdress on her pillow and he had a satisfying glimpse of her breasts. Sex would definitely help relax him.

"It's a real shame, Sam," he said, crawling across the bed behind her, and waiting to put his arms around her as she wriggled into the nightdress. "About the shop. It was a great little place. And you've had it, what—ten years?"

"Fourteen," said Samantha.

She knew what he wanted. She considered telling him to go and screw himself, and decamping to the spare room, but the trouble was that there would then be a row and an atmosphere, and what she wanted more than anything in the world was to be able to head off to London with Libby in two days' time, wearing the T-shirts that she had bought them both, and to be within close proximity of Jake and his bandmates for a whole evening. This excursion constituted the entire sum of Samantha's current happiness. What was more, sex might assuage Miles' continuing annoyance that she was missing Howard's birthday party.

So she let him embrace and then kiss her. She closed her eyes, climbed on top of him, and imagined herself riding Jake on a deserted white beach, nineteen years old to his twenty-one. She came while imagining Miles watching them, furiously, through binoculars, from a distant pedalo.

X

At nine o'clock on the morning of the election for Barry's seat, Parminder left the Old Vicarage and walked up Church Row to the Walls' house. She rapped on the door and waited until, at last, Colin appeared.

There were shadows around his bloodshot eyes and beneath his cheekbones; his skin seemed to have thinned and his clothes grown too big. He had not yet returned to work. The news that Parminder had screamed confidential medical information about Howard in public had set back his tentative recovery; the more robust Colin of a few nights ago, who had sat on the leather pouf and pretended to be confident of victory, might never have been.

"Is everything all right?" he asked, closing the door behind her, looking wary.

"Yes, fine," she said. "I thought you might like to walk down the church hall with me, to vote."

"I—no," he said weakly. "I'm sorry."

"I know how you feel, Colin," said Parminder, in a small tight voice. "But if you don't vote, it means they've won. I'm not going to let them win. I'm going to go down there and vote for you, and I want you to come with me."

Parminder was effectively suspended from work. The Mollisons had complained to every professional body for which they could find an address, and Dr. Crawford had advised Parminder to take time off. To her great surprise, she felt strangely liberated.

But Colin was shaking his head. She thought she saw tears in his eyes.

"I can't, Minda."

"You can!" she said. "You *can*, Colin! You've got to stand up to them! Think of Barry!"

"I can't—I'm sorry—I…"

He made a choking noise and burst into tears. Colin had cried in her surgery before now; sobbed in desperation at the burden of fear he carried with him every day of his life.

"Come on," she said, unembarrassed, and she took his arm and steered him through to the kitchen, where she handed him kitchen roll and let him sob himself into hiccups again. "Where's Tessa?"

"At work," he gasped, mopping his eyes.

There was an invitation to Howard Mollison's sixty-fifth birthday party lying on the kitchen table; somebody had torn it neatly in two.

"I got one of those, as well," said Parminder. "Before I shouted at him. Listen, Colin. Voting—"

"I can't," whispered Colin.

"—shows them they haven't beaten us."

"But they have," said Colin.

Parminder burst out laughing. After contemplating her with his mouth open for a moment, Colin started to laugh too: a big, booming guffaw, like the bark of a mastiff.

"All right, they've run us out of our jobs," said Parminder, "and neither of us wants to leave the house but, other than that, I think we're in very good shape indeed."

Colin took off his glasses and dabbed his wet eyes, grinning.

"Come *on,* Colin. I want to vote for you. It isn't over yet. After I blew my top, and told Howard Mollison he was no better than a junkie in front of the whole council and the local press—"

He burst out laughing again and she was delighted; she had not heard him laugh so much since New Year, and then it had been Barry making him do it.

"—they forgot to vote on forcing the addiction clinic out of Bellchapel. So, please. Get your coat. We'll walk down there together."

Colin's snorts and giggles died away. He stared down at the big hands fumbled over each other, as if he were washing them clean.

"Colin, it's not over. You've made a difference. People don't like the Mollisons. If you get in, we'd be in a much stronger position to fight. Please, Colin."

"All right," he said, after a few moments, awed by his own daring.

It was a short walk, in the fresh clean air, each of them clutching their voter registration cards. The church hall was empty of voters apart from themselves. Each put a thick pencil cross beside Colin's name and left with the sense that they had got away with something.

Miles Mollison did not vote until midday. He paused at his partner's door on the way out.

"I'm off to vote, Gav," he said.

Gavin indicated the telephone pressed against his ear; he was on hold with Mary's insurance company.

"Oh—right—I'm off to vote, Shona," said Miles, turning to their secretary.

There was no harm in reminding them both that he was in need of their support. Miles jogged downstairs and proceeded to the Copper Kettle, where, during a brief postcoital chat, he had arranged to meet his wife so that they could go down to the church hall together.

Samantha had spent the morning at home, leaving her assistant in charge at the shop. She knew that she could no longer put off telling Carly that they were out of business, and that Carly was out of a job, but she could not bring herself to do it before the weekend and the concert in London. When Miles appeared, and she saw his excited little grin, she experienced a rush of fury.

"Dad not coming?" were his first words.

"They're going down after closing time," said Samantha.

There were two old ladies in the voting booths when she and Miles got there. Samantha waited, looking at the backs of their iron-gray perms, their thick coats and their thicker ankles. That was how she would look one day. The more crooked of the two old women noticed Miles as they left, beamed, and said, "I've just voted for you!"

"Well, thank you very much!" said Miles, delighted.

Samantha entered the booth and stared down at the two names: Miles Mollison and Colin Wall, the pencil, tied to the end of a piece of string, in her hand. Then she scribbled "I hate bloody Pagford" across the paper, folded it over, crossed to the ballot box and dropped it, unsmiling, through the slot.

"Thanks, love," said Miles quietly, with a pat on her back.

Tessa Wall, who had never failed to vote in an election before, drove past the church hall on her way back home from school and did not stop. Ruth and Simon Price spent the day talking more seriously than ever about the possibility of moving to Reading. Ruth threw out their voter registration cards while clearing the kitchen table for supper.

Gavin had never intended to vote; if Barry had been alive to stand, he might have done so, but he had no desire to help Miles achieve another of his life's goals. At half past five he packed up his briefcase, irritable and depressed, because he had finally run out of excuses not to have dinner at Kay's. It was particularly irksome, because there were hopeful signs that the insurance company was shifting in Mary's favor, and he had very much wanted to go over and tell her so. This meant that he would have to store up the news until tomorrow; he did not want to waste it on the telephone.

When Kay opened the door to him, she launched at once into the rapid, quick-fire talk that usually meant she was in a bad mood.

"Sorry, it's been a dreadful day," she said, although he had not complained, and they had barely exchanged greetings. "I was late back, I meant to be further on with dinner, come through."

From upstairs came the insistent crash of drums and a loud bass line. Gavin was surprised that the neighbors were not complaining. Kay saw him glance up at the ceiling and said, "Oh, Gaia's furious because some boy she liked back in Hackney has started going out with another girl."

She seized the glass of wine she was already drinking and took a big gulp. Her conscience had hurt her when she called Marco de Luca "Some boy." He had virtually moved into their house in the weeks before they had left London. Kay had found him charming, considerate and helpful. She would have liked a son like Marco.

"She'll live," said Kay, pushing the memories away, and she returned to the potatoes she was boiling. "She's sixteen. You bounce at that age. Help yourself to wine."

Gavin sat down at the table, wishing that Kay would make Gaia turn the music down. She had virtually to shout at him over the vibration of the bass, the rattling saucepan lids and the noisy extractor fan. He yearned again for the melancholy calm of Mary's big kitchen, for Mary's gratitude, her need for him.

"What?" he said loudly, because he could tell that Kay had just asked him something.

"I said, did you vote?"

"Vote?"

"In the council election!" she said.

"No," he replied. "Couldn't care less."

He was not sure whether she had heard. She was talking again, and only when she turned to the table with knives and forks could he hear her clearly.

"...absolutely disgusting, actually, that the parish is colluding with Aubrey Fawley. I expect Bellchapel will be finished if Miles gets in..."

She drained the potatoes and the splatter and crash drowned her temporarily again.

" …if that silly woman hadn't lost her temper, we might be in with a better shot. I gave her masses of stuff on the clinic and I don't think she used any of it. She just screamed at Howard Mollison that he was too fat. Talk about unprofessional…"

Gavin had heard rumors about Dr. Jawanda's public outburst. He had found it mildly amusing.

"…all this uncertainty's very damaging to the people who work at that clinic, not to mention the clients."

But Gavin could muster neither pity nor indignation; all he felt was dismay at the firm grip Kay seemed to have on the intricacies and personalities involved in this esoteric local issue. It was yet another indication of how she was driving roots deeper and deeper into Pagford. It would take a lot to dislodge her now.

He turned his head and gazed out of the window onto the overgrown garden beyond. He had offered to help Fergus with Mary's garden this weekend. With luck, he thought, Mary would invite him to stay for dinner again, and if she did, he would skip Howard Mollison's sixty-fifth birthday party, to which Miles seemed to think he was looking forward with excitement.

"…wanted to keep the Weedons, but no, Gillian says we can't cherry-pick. Would *you* call that cherry-picking?"

"Sorry, what?" asked Gavin.

"Mattie's back," she said, and he had to struggle to recollect that this was a colleague of hers, whose cases she had been covering. "I wanted to keep working with the Weedons, because sometimes you do get a particular feeling for a family, but Gillian won't let me. It's crazy."

"You must be the only person in the world who ever wanted to keep the Weedons," said Gavin. "From what I've heard, anyway."

It took nearly all Kay's willpower not to snap at him. She pulled the salmon fillets she had been baking out of the oven. Gaia's music was so loud that she could feel it vibrating through the tray, which she slammed down on the hob.

"Gaia!" she screamed, making Gavin jump as she strode past him to the foot of the stairs. "GAIA! Turn it down! I mean it! TURN IT DOWN!"

The volume diminished by perhaps a decibel. Kay marched back into the kitchen, fuming. The row with Gaia, before Gavin arrived, had been one of their worst ever. Gaia had stated her intention of telephoning her father and asking to move in with him.

"Well, good luck with that!" Kay had shouted.

But perhaps Brendan would say yes. He had left her when Gaia was only a month old. Brendan was married now, with three other children. He had a huge house and a good job. What if he said yes?

Gavin was glad that he did not have to talk as they ate; the thumping music filled the silence, and he could think about Mary in peace. He would tell her tomorrow that the insurance company was making conciliatory noises, and receive her gratitude and admiration…

He had almost cleared his plate when he realized that Kay had not eaten a single mouthful. She was staring at him across the table, and her expression alarmed him. Perhaps he had somehow revealed his inner thoughts…

Gaia's music came to an abrupt halt overhead. The throbbing quiet was dreadful to Gavin; he wished that Gaia would put something else on, quickly.

"You don't even try," Kay said miserably. "You don't even pretend to care, Gavin."

He attempted to take the easy way out.

"Kay, I've had a long day," he said. "I'm sorry if I'm not up to the minutiae of local politics the second I walk—"

"I'm not talking about local politics," she said. "You sit there looking as if you'd rather be anywhere else—it's—it's offensive. What do you want, Gavin?"

He saw Mary's kitchen, and her sweet face.

"I have to beg to see you," Kay said, "and when you come round here you couldn't make it clearer that you don't want to come."

She wanted him to say "That's not true." The last point at which a denial might have counted slunk past. They were sliding, at increasing speed, towards that crisis which Gavin both urgently desired and dreaded.

"Tell me what you want," she said wearily. "Just tell me."

Both could feel the relationship crumbling to pieces beneath the weight of everything that Gavin refused to say. It was with a sense of putting them both out of their misery that he reached for words that he had not intended to speak aloud, perhaps ever, but which, in some way, seemed to excuse both of them.

"I didn't want this to happen," Gavin said earnestly. "I didn't mean it to. Kay, I'm really sorry, but I think I'm in love with Mary Fairbrother."

He saw from her expression that she had not been prepared for this.

"Mary Fairbrother?" she repeated.

"I think," he said (and there was a bittersweet pleasure in talking about it, even though he knew he was wounding her; he had not been able to say it to anyone else), "it's been there for a long time. I never acknowledged — I mean, when Barry was alive I'd never have —"

"I thought he was your best friend," whispered Kay.

"He was."

"He's only been dead a few weeks!"

Gavin did not like hearing that.

"Look," he said, "I'm trying to be honest with you. I'm trying to be fair."

"You're trying to be *fair?*"

He had always imagined it ending in a blaze of fury, but she simply watched him putting on his coat with tears in her eyes.

"I'm sorry," he said, and walked out of her house for the last time.

On the pavement, he experienced a rush of elation, and hurried to his car. He would be able to tell Mary about the insurance company tonight, after all.

Part Five

Privilege

7.32 A person who has made a defamatory statement may claim privilege for it if he can show that he made it without malice and in pursuit of a public duty.

Charles Arnold-Baker
Local Council Administration,
Seventh Edition

I

Terri Weedon was used to people leaving her. The first and greatest
departure had been her mother's, who had never said good-bye,
but had simply walked out one day with a suitcase while Terri was
at school.

There had been lots of social workers and care workers after she
ran away at fourteen, and some of them had been nice enough, but
they all left at the end of the working day. Every fresh departure
added a fine new layer to the crust building over her core.

She had had friends in care, but at sixteen they were all on their
own, and life had scattered them. She met Ritchie Adams, and she
bore him two children. Tiny little pink things, pure and beautiful
like nothing in the whole world: and they had come out of her,
and for shining hours in the hospital, twice, it had been like her
own rebirth.

And then they took the children from her, and she never saw
them again, either.

Banger had left her. Nana Cath had left her. Nearly everybody
went, hardly anyone stayed. She ought to be used to it by now.

When Mattie, her regular social worker, reappeared, Terri
demanded, "Where's the other one?"

"Kay? She was only covering for me while I was ill," said Mattie.
"So, where's Liam? No...I mean Robbie, don't I?"

Terri did not like Mattie. For one thing, she did not have kids,
and how could people who didn't have kids tell you how to raise
them, how could they understand? She had not liked Kay, exactly,

either…except that Kay gave you a funny feeling, the same feeling that Nana Cath had once given Terri, before she had called her a whore and told her she never wanted to see her again…you felt, with Kay—even though she carried folders, like the rest of them, even though she had instituted the case review—you felt that she wanted things to go right for you, and not only for the forms. You really did feel that. But she was gone, *and she probably don't even think about us now,* thought Terri furiously.

On Friday afternoon, Mattie told Terri that Bellchapel would almost certainly close.

"It's political," she said briskly. "They want to save money, but methadone treatment's unpopular with the District Council. Plus, Pagford wants them out of the building. It was all in the local paper, maybe you saw it?"

Sometimes she spoke to Terri like that, veering into a kind of after-all-we're-in-this-together small-talk that jarred, because it sat alongside inquiries as to whether Terri was remembering to feed her son. But this time it was what she said, rather than how she said it, that upset Terri.

"They're closin' it?" she repeated.

"It looks that way," said Mattie breezily, "but it won't make any difference to you. Well, obviously…"

Three times Terri had embarked upon the program at Bellchapel. The dusty interior of the converted church with its partition walls and its flyers, the bathroom with its neon-blue light (so you could not find veins and shoot up in there), had become familiar and almost friendly. Lately, she had begun to sense in the workers there a change in the way they spoke to her. They had all expected her to fail again, in the beginning, but they had started talking to her the way Kay had talked: as if they knew a real person lived inside her pockmarked, burned body.

" …obviously, it *will* be different, but you can get your methadone from your GP instead," said Mattie. She flipped over pages in the distended file that was the state's record of Terri's life. "You're registered with Dr. Jawanda in Pagford, right? Pagford…why are you going all the way out there?"

"I smacked a nurse at Cantermill," said Terri, almost absent-mindedly.

After Mattie had left, Terri sat for a long time in her filthy chair in the sitting room, gnawing at her nails until they bled.

The moment Krystal came home, bringing Robbie back from nursery, she told her that they were closing Bellchapel.

"They ain't decided yet," said Krystal with authority.

"The fuck do you know?" demanded Terri. "They're closin' it, and now they say I've gotta go to fuckin' Pagford to that bitch that killed Nana Cath. Well, I fuckin' ain't."

"You gotta," said Krystal.

Krystal had been like this for days; bossing her mother, acting as though she, Krystal, was the grown-up.

"I ain' gotta do fuckin' anythin'," said Terri furiously. "Cheeky little bitch," she added, for good measure.

"If you start fuckin' usin' again," said Krystal, scarlet in the face, "They'll take Robbie away."

He was still holding Krystal's hand, and burst into tears.

"See?" both women shouted at each other.

"You're fuckin' doin' it to him!" shouted Krystal. "An' anyway, that doctor didn' do nuthin' to Nana Cath, that's all jus' Cheryl an' them talking shit!"

"Fuckin' little know-it-all, ain't yeh?" yelled Terri. "You know fuck-all—"

Krystal spat at her.

"Get the fuck out!" screamed Terri, and because Krystal was bigger and heavier she seized a shoe lying on the floor and brandished it. "Gerrout!"

"I fuckin' will!" yelled Krystal. "An' I'll take Robbie an' all, an' you can stay here an' fuckin' screw Obbo an' make another one!"

She dragged the wailing Robbie out with her before Terri could stop her.

Krystal marched him all the way to her usual refuge, forgetting that at this time in the afternoon, Nikki would still be hanging around outside somewhere, not at home. It was Nikki's mum who opened the door, in her Asda uniform.

"He ain' stayin' 'ere," she told Krystal firmly, while Robbie whined and tried to pull his hand from Krystal's tight grip. "Where's your mum?"

"Home," said Krystal, and everything else she wanted to say evaporated in the older woman's stern gaze.

So she returned to Foley Road with Robbie, where Terri, bitterly triumphant, grabbed her son's arm, pulled him inside and blocked Krystal from entering.

"'Ad enough of him already, 'ave yeh?" Terri jeered, over Robbie's wails. "Fuck off."

And she slammed the door.

Terri had Robbie sleep beside her on her own mattress that night. She lay awake and thought about how little she needed Krystal, and ached for her as badly as she had ever craved smack.

Krystal had been angry for days. The thing that Krystal had said about Obbo…

("She said *what?*" he had laughed, incredulously, when they had met in the street, and Terri had muttered something about Krystal being upset.)

…he wouldn't have done it. He couldn't have.

Obbo was one of the few people who had hung around. Terri had known him since she was fifteen. They had gone to school together, hung out in Yarvil while she was in care, swigged cider together beneath the trees on the footpath that cut its way through the small patch of remaining farmland beside the Fields. They had shared their first joint.

Krystal had never liked him. *Jealous,* thought Terri, watching Robbie sleep in the street light pouring through the thin curtains. *Just jealous. He's done more for me than anyone,* thought Terri defiantly, because when she tallied kindnesses she subtracted abandonment. Thus all of Nana Cath's care had been annihilated by her rejection.

But Obbo had hidden her, once, from Ritchie, the father of her first two children, when she had fled the house barefoot and bleeding. Sometimes he gave her free bags of smack. She saw them as equivalent kindnesses. His refuges were more reliable than the little house in Hope Street that she had once, for three glorious days, thought was home.

Krystal did not return on Saturday morning, but that was nothing new; Terri knew she must be at Nikki's. In a rage, because they were low on food, and she was out of cigarettes, and Robbie was whining for his sister, she stormed into her daughter's room and kicked her clothes around, searching for money or the odd, overlooked fag. Something clattered as she threw aside Krystal's crumpled old rowing kit, and she saw the little plastic jewelry box, upended, with the rowing medal that Krystal had won, and Tessa Wall's watch lying beneath it.

Terri picked up the watch and stared at it. She had never seen it before. She wondered where Krystal had got it. Her first assumption was that Krystal had stolen it, but then she wondered whether she might have been given it by Nana Cath, or even left it in Nana Cath's will. That was a much more troubling thought than the idea of the watch being stolen. The idea of the sneaky little bitch hiding it away, treasuring it, never mentioning it…

Terri put the watch inside the pocket of her tracksuit bottoms and bellowed for Robbie to come with her to the shops. It took ages to get him into his shoes, and Terri lost her temper and slapped him. She wished she could go to the shop alone, but the social workers did not like you leaving kids behind in the house, even though you could get things done much quicker without them.

"Where's Krystal?" wailed Robbie, as she manhandled him out of the door. "I wan' Krystal!"

"I dunno where the little tart is," snapped Terri, dragging him along the road.

Obbo was on the corner beside the supermarket, talking to two men. When he saw her he raised a hand in greeting, and his two companions walked away.

"'Ow's Ter?" he said.

"N'bad," she lied. "Robbie, leggo."

He was digging his fingers so tightly into her thin leg that it hurt.

"Listen," said Obbo, "couldja keep a bit more stuff for me fer a bit?"

"Kinda stuff?" asked Terri, prying Robbie off her leg and holding his hand instead.

"Coupla bags o' stuff," said Obbo. "Really help me out, Ter."

"'Ow long for?"

"Few days. Bring it round this evenin'. Will yeh?"

Terri thought of Krystal, and what she would say if she knew.

"Yeah, go on then," said Terri.

She remembered something else, and pulled Tessa's watch out of her pocket. "Gonna sell this, whaddaya reckon?"

"Not bad," said Obbo, weighing it in his hand. "I'll give yeh twenty for it. Bring it over tonight?"

Terri had thought the watch might be worth more, but she did not like to challenge him.

"Yeah, all righ' then."

She took a few steps toward the supermarket entrance, hand in hand with Robbie, but then turned abruptly.

"I ain' usin' though," she said. "So don' bring…"

"Still on the mixture?" he said, grinning at her through his thick glasses. "Bellchapel's done for, mind. All in the paper."

"Yeah," she said miserably, and she tugged Robbie toward the entrance of the supermarket. "I know."

I ain't going to Pagford, she thought, as she picked biscuits off the shelf. *I ain't going there.*

She was almost inured to constant criticism and assessment, to the sideways glance of passersby, to abuse from the neighbors, but she was not going to go all the way to that smug little town to get double helpings; to travel back in time, once a week, to the place where Nana Cath had said she would keep her, but let her go. She would have to pass that pretty little school that had sent horrible letters home about Krystal, saying that her clothes were too small and too dirty, that her behavior was unacceptable. She was afraid of long-forgotten relatives emerging from Hope Street, as they squabbled over Nana Cath's house, and of what Cheryl would say, if she knew that Terri had entered into voluntary dealings with the Paki bitch who had killed Nana Cath. Another mark against her, in the family that despised her.

"They ain't making me go to fuckin' Pagford," Terri muttered aloud, pulling Robbie toward the checkout.

II

"Brace yourself," teased Howard Mollison at midday on Saturday. "Mum's about to post the results on the website. Want to wait and see it made public or shall I tell you now?"

Miles turned away instinctively from Samantha, who was sitting opposite him at the island in the middle of the kitchen. They were having a last coffee before she and Libby set off for the station and the concert in London. With the handset pressed tightly to his ear, he said, "Go on."

"You won. Comfortably. Pretty much two to one over Wall."

Miles grinned at the kitchen door.

"OK," he said, keeping his voice as steady as he could. "Good to know."

"Hang on," said Howard. "Mum wants a word."

"Well done, darling," said Shirley gleefully. "Absolutely wonderful news. I knew you'd do it."

"Thanks, Mum," said Miles.

Those two words told Samantha everything, but she had resolved not to be scornful or sarcastic. Her band T-shirt was packed; she had had her hair done and she had bought new heels. She could hardly wait to leave.

"Parish Councillor Mollison then, is it?" she said, when he had hung up.

"That's right," he said a little warily.

"Congratulations," she said. "It's going to be a real celebration tonight, then. I'm sorry I'm missing it, actually," she lied, out of excitement at her imminent escape. Touched, Miles leaned forward and squeezed her hand.

Libby appeared in the kitchen in tears. She was clutching her mobile in her hand.

"What?" said Samantha, startled.

"Please will you call Harriet's mum?"

"Why?"

"Please will you?"

"But why, Libby?"

"Because she wants to talk to you, because," Libby wiped her eyes and nose on the back of her hand, "Harriet and I've had a big row. Please will you call her?"

Samantha took the telephone through to the sitting room. She had only the haziest idea who this woman was. Since the girls had started at boarding school she had virtually no contact with their friends' parents.

"I'm so *desperately* sorry to do this," said Harriet's mother. "I told Harriet I'd speak to you, because I've been *telling* her it's not that *Libby* doesn't want her to go...you know how close they are, and I hate seeing them like this..."

Samantha checked her watch. They needed to leave in ten minutes at the latest.

"Harriet's got it into her head that Libby had a spare ticket, but didn't want to take her. I've told her it's not true—you're taking the ticket because you don't want Libby going alone, aren't you?"

"Well, naturally," said Samantha, "She can't go alone."

"I knew it," said the other woman. She sounded strangely triumphant. "And I *absolutely* understand your protectiveness, and I would *never* suggest it if I didn't think it would save you an awful lot of bother. It's just that the girls are so close—and Harriet's absolutely wild about this silly group—and I think, from what Libby's just told Harriet on the phone, that Libby's really *desperate* for her to go too. I *totally* understand why you want to keep an eye on Libby, but the thing is, my sister's taking *her* two girls, so there would be an adult there with them. I could drive Libby and Harriet up together this afternoon, we'd meet up with the others outside the stadium and we could all stay overnight at my sister's place. I absolutely guarantee that my sister or I will be with Libby at all times."

"Oh...that's so kind. But my friend," said Samantha, with a strange ringing in her ears, "is expecting us, you see..."

"But if you still wanted to go and visit your friend...all I'm saying is there's really no need for you to attend, is there, if somebody else is with the girls?...And Harriet's absolutely desperate—really desperate—I wasn't going to get involved, but now it's putting a strain on their friendship..."

Then, on a less gushing note, "We'd buy the ticket from you, of course."

There was nowhere to go, nowhere to hide.

"Oh," said Samantha. "Yes. I just thought it might be nice to go with her—"

"They'd much prefer to be with each other," said Harriet's mother firmly. "And you won't have to crouch down and hide among all the little teenyboppers, ha ha—it's all right for my sister, she's only five foot two."

III

To Gavin's disappointment, it seemed that he would have to attend Howard Mollison's birthday party after all. If Mary, a client of the firm and the widow of his best friend, had asked him to stay for dinner, he would have considered himself more than justified in skipping it...but Mary had not asked him to stay. She had family visiting, and she had been oddly flustered when he had turned up.

She doesn't want them to know, he thought, taking comfort in her self-consciousness as she ushered him toward the door.

He drove back to the Smithy, replaying his conversation with Kay in his mind.

I thought he was your best friend. He's only been dead a few weeks!

Yeah, and I was looking after her for Barry, he retorted in his head, *which is what he'd have wanted. Neither of us expected this to happen. Barry's dead. It can't hurt him now.*

Alone in the Smithy he looked out a clean suit for the party, because the invitation said "formal," and tried to imagine gossipy little Pagford relishing the story of Gavin and Mary.

So what? he thought, staggered by his own bravery. *Is she supposed to be alone forever? It happens. I was looking after her.*

And in spite of his reluctance to attend a party that was sure to be dull and exhausting, he was buoyed inside by a little bubble of excitement and happiness.

Up in Hilltop House, Andrew Price was styling his hair with his mother's blow-dryer. He had never looked forward to a disco or a party as much as he had longed for tonight. He, Gaia and Sukhvinder were being paid by Howard to serve food and drinks at the party. Howard had hired him a uniform for the occasion: a white shirt, black trousers and a bow tie. He would be working alongside Gaia, not as potboy but as a waiter.

But there was more to his anticipation than this. Gaia had split up with the legendary Marco de Luca. He had found her crying about it in the backyard of the Copper Kettle that afternoon, when he had gone outside for a smoke.

"His loss," Andrew had said, trying to keep the delight out of his voice.

And she had sniffed and said, "Cheers, Andy."

"You little poofter," said Simon, when Andrew finally turned off the dryer. He had been waiting to say it for several minutes, standing on the dark landing, staring through the gap in the door, which was ajar, watching Andrew preen himself in the mirror. Andrew jumped, then laughed. His good humor discomposed Simon.

"Look at you," he jeered, as Andrew passed him on the landing in his shirt and bow tie. "With your dicky bow. You look a twat."

And you're unemployed, and I did it to you, dickhead.

Andrew's feelings about what he had done to his father changed almost hourly. Sometimes the guilt would bear down on him, tainting everything, but then it would melt away, leaving him glorying in his secret triumph. Tonight, the thought of it gave extra heat to the excitement burning beneath Andrew's thin white shirt, an additional tingle to the gooseflesh caused by the rush of evening air as he sped, on Simon's racing bike, down the hill into town. He was excited, full of hope. Gaia was available and vulnerable. Her father lived in Reading.

Shirley Mollison was standing in a party dress outside the church hall when he cycled up, tying giant gold helium balloons in the shapes of fives and sixes to the railings.

"Hello, Andrew," she trilled. "Bike away from the entrance, please."

He wheeled it along to the corner, passing a brand-new, racing green BMW convertible parked feet away. He walked around the car on his way inside, taking in the luxurious inner fittings.

"And here's Andy!"

Andrew saw at once that his boss's good humor and excitement were equal to his own. Howard was striding down the hall, wearing an immense velvet dinner jacket; he resembled a conjurer. There were only five or six other people dotted around: the party would not start for twenty minutes. Blue, white and gold balloons had been fastened up everywhere. There was a massive trestle table largely covered in plates draped with tea towels, and at the top of the hall a middle-aged DJ setting up his equipment.

"Go help Maureen, Andy, will you?"

She was laying out glasses at one end of the long table, caught gaudily in a stream of light from an overhead lamp.

"Don't you look handsome!" she croaked as he approached.

She was wearing a scant, stretchy shiny dress that revealed every contour of the bony body to which unexpected little rolls and pads of flesh still clung, exposed by the unforgiving fabric. From somewhere out of sight came a small "hi"; Gaia was crouching over a box of plates on the floor.

"Glasses out of boxes, please, Andy," said Maureen, "and set them up here, where we're having the bar."

He did as he was told. As he unpacked the box, a woman he had never seen before approached, carrying several bottles of champagne.

"These should go in the fridge, if there is one."

She had Howard's straight nose, Howard's big blue eyes and Howard's curly fair hair, but whereas his features were womanish, softened by fat, his daughter—she had to be his daughter—was unpretty yet striking, with low brows, big eyes and a cleft chin. She was wearing trousers and an open-necked silk shirt. After dumping the bottles onto the table she turned away. Her demeanor, and something about the quality of her clothing, made Andrew sure that she was the owner of the BMW outside.

"That's Patricia," whispered Gaia in his ear, and his skin tingled again as though she carried an electric charge. "Howard's daughter."

"Yeah, I thought so," he said, but he was much more interested to see that Gaia was unscrewing the cap of a bottle of vodka and pouring out a measure. As he watched, she drank it straight off with a little shudder. She had barely replaced the top when Maureen reappeared beside them with an ice bucket.

"Bloody old slapper," said Gaia, as Maureen walked away, and Andrew smelled the spirits on her breath. "*Look* at the state of her."

He laughed, turned and stopped abruptly, because Shirley was right beside them, smiling her pussycat smile.

"Has Miss Jawanda not arrived yet?" she asked.

"She's on her way, she just texted me," said Gaia.

But Shirley did not really care where Sukhvinder was. She had overheard Andrew and Gaia's little exchange about Maureen, and it had completely restored the good mood that had been dented by Maureen's evident delight in her own *toilette*. It was difficult to satisfactorily puncture self-esteem so obtuse, so deluded, but as Shirley walked away from the teenagers toward the DJ, she planned what she would say to Howard the next time she saw him alone.

I'm afraid the young ones were, well, laughing at Maureen...it's such a pity she wore that dress...I hate seeing her make a fool of herself.

There was plenty to be pleased about, Shirley reminded herself, for she needed a little bolstering tonight. She and Howard and Miles were all going to be on the council together; it would be marvelous, simply marvelous.

She checked that the DJ knew that Howard's favorite song was "The Green, Green Grass of Home," Tom Jones' version, and looked around for more little jobs to do: but instead her gaze fell upon the reason that her happiness, tonight, had not quite that perfect quality she had anticipated.

Patricia was standing alone, staring up at the Pagford coat of arms on the wall, and making no effort to talk to anybody. Shirley wished that Patricia would wear a skirt sometimes; but at least she had arrived alone. Shirley had been afraid that the BMW might contain another person, and that absence was something gained.

You weren't supposed to dislike your own child; you were supposed to like them no matter what, even if they were not what you wanted, even if they turned out to be the kind of person that you would have crossed the street to avoid had you not been related. Howard took a large view of the whole matter; he even joked about it, in a mild way, beyond Patricia's hearing. Shirley could not rise to those heights of detachment. She felt compelled to join Patricia, in the vague, unconscious hope that she might dilute the strangeness she was afraid everyone else would smell by her own exemplary dress and behavior.

"Do you want a drink, darling?"

"Not yet," said Patricia, still staring up at the Pagford arms. "I had a heavy night last night. Probably still over the limit. We were out drinking with Melly's office pals."

Shirley smiled vaguely up at the crest above them.

"Melly's fine, thanks for asking," said Patricia.

"Oh, good," said Shirley.

"I liked the invitation," said Patricia. "Pat and *guest.*"

"I'm sorry, darling, but that's just what you put, you know, when people aren't married—"

"Ah, that's what it says in *Debrett's,* does it? Well, Melly didn't want to come if she wasn't even named on the invitation, so we had a massive row, and here I am, alone. Result, eh?"

Patricia stalked away toward the drinks, leaving Shirley a little shaken behind her. Patricia's rages had been frightening even as a child.

"You're late, Miss Jawanda," she called, recovering her composure as a flustered Sukhvinder came hurrying toward her. In Shirley's opinion, the girl was demonstrating a kind of insolence turning up at all, after what her mother had said to Howard, here, in this very hall. She watched her hurry to join Andrew and Gaia, and thought that she would tell Howard that they ought to let Sukhvinder go. She was tardy, and there was probably a hygiene issue with the eczema she was hiding under the long-sleeved black

T-shirt; Shirley made a mental note to check whether it was contagious, on her favorite medical website.

Guests began to arrive promptly at eight o'clock. Howard told Gaia to come and stand beside him and collect coats, because he wanted everyone to see him ordering her around by name, in that little black dress and frilly apron. But there were soon too many coats for her to carry alone, so he summoned Andrew to help.

"Nick a bottle," Gaia ordered Andrew, as they hung coats three and four deep in the tiny cloakroom, "and hide it in the kitchen. We can take it in turns to go and have some."

"OK," said Andrew, elated.

"Gavin!" cried Howard, as his son's partner came through the door alone at half past eight.

"Kay not with you, Gavin?" asked Shirley swiftly (Maureen was changing into sparkly stilettos behind the trestle table, so there was very little time to steal a march on her).

"No, she couldn't make it, unfortunately," said Gavin; then, to his horror, he came face-to-face with Gaia, who was waiting to take his coat.

"Mum could have made it," said Gaia, in a clear, carrying voice, as she glared at him. "But Gavin's dumped her, haven't you, Gav?"

Howard clapped Gavin on the shoulder, pretending he had not heard, and boomed, "Great to see you, go get yourself a drink."

Shirley's expression remained impassive, but the thrill of the moment did not subside quickly, and she was a little dazed and dreamy, greeting the next few guests. When Maureen tottered over in her awful dress to join the greeting party, Shirley took immense pleasure in telling her quietly: "We've had a *very* awkward little scene. *Very* awkward. Gavin and Gaia's mother…oh, dear…if we'd known…"

"What? What's happened?"

But Shirley shook her head, savoring the exquisite pleasure of Maureen's frustrated curiosity, and opened her arms wide as Miles, Samantha and Lexie entered the hall.

"Here he is! Parish Councillor Miles Mollison!"

Samantha watched Shirley hugging Miles as though from a great distance. She had moved so abruptly from happiness and anticipation to shock and disappointment that her thoughts had become white noise, against which she had to fight to take in the exterior world.

(Miles had said: "That's great! You can come to Dad's party, you were only just saying—"

"Yes," she had replied, "I know. It is great, isn't it?"

But when he had seen her dressed in the jeans and band T-shirt she had been visualizing herself in for over a week, he had been perplexed.

"It's formal."

"Miles, it's the church hall in Pagford."

"I know, but the invitation—"

"I'm wearing this.")

"Hello, Sammy," said Howard. "Look at you. You needn't have dressed up."

But his embrace was as lascivious as ever, and he patted her tightly jeaned backside.

Samantha gave Shirley a cold tight smile and walked past her towards the drinks. A nasty voice inside her head was asking: *but what did you think was going to happen at the concert, anyway? What was the point? What were you after?*

Nothing. A bit of fun.

The dream of strong young arms and laughter, which was to have had some kind of catharsis tonight; her own thin waist encircled again, and the sharp taste of the new, the unexplored; her fantasy had lost wings, it was plummeting back to earth…

I only wanted to look.

"Looking good, Sammy."

"Cheers, Pat."

She had not met her sister-in-law for over a year.

I like you more than anyone else in this family, Pat.

Miles had caught up with her; he kissed his sister.

"How are you? How's Mel? Isn't she here?"

"No, she didn't want to come," said Patricia. She was drinking champagne, but from her expression, it might have been vinegar. "The invitation said *Pat and guest are invited*…huge bloody row. One up to Mum."

"Oh, Pat, come on," said Miles, smiling.

"Oh, Pat, fucking come on what, Miles?"

A furious delight took hold of Samantha: a pretext to attack.

"That's a bloody rude way to invite your sister's partner and you know it, Miles. Your mother could do with some lessons in manners, if you ask me."

He was fatter, surely, than he had been a year ago. She could see his neck bulging over the collar of his shirt. His breath went sour quickly. He had a little trick of bouncing on his toes that he had caught from his father. She experienced a surge of physical disgust and walked away to the end of the trestle table, where Andrew and Sukhvinder were busy filling and handing out glasses.

"Have you got any gin?" Samantha asked. "Give me a big one."

She barely recognized Andrew. He poured her a measure, trying not to look at her breasts, boundlessly exposed in the T-shirt, but it was like trying not to squint in direct sunlight.

"Do you know them?" Samantha asked, after downing half a glass of gin and tonic.

A blush had risen before Andrew could marshal his thoughts. To his horror, she gave a reckless cackle, and said, "The band. I'm talking about the band."

"Yeah, I—yeah, I've heard of them. I don't...not my kind of thing."

"Is that right?" she said, throwing back the rest of her drink. "I'll have another one of those, please."

She realized who he was: the mousy boy from the delicatessen. His uniform made him look older. Maybe a couple of weeks of lugging pallets up and down the cellar steps had built some muscle.

"Oh, look," said Samantha, spotting a figure heading away from her into the growing crowd, "There's Gavin. The second-most boring man in Pagford. After my husband, obviously."

She strode off, pleased with herself, holding her new drink; the gin had hit her where she most needed it, anesthetizing and stimulating at the same time, and as she walked she thought: *he liked my tits; let's see what he thinks of my arse.*

Gavin saw Samantha coming and tried to deflect her by joining somebody else's conversation, anybody's; the nearest person was Howard and he insinuated himself hastily into the group around his host.

"I took a risk," Howard was saying to three other men; he was waving a cigar, and a little ash had dribbled down the front of his velvet jacket. "I took a risk and I put in the graft. Simple as that. No magic formula. Nobody handed me—oh, here's Sammy. Who are those young men, Samantha?"

While four elderly men stared at the pop group stretched across her breasts, Samantha turned to Gavin.

"Hi," she said, leaning in and forcing him to kiss her. "Kay not here?"

"No," said Gavin shortly.

"Talking about business, Sammy," said Howard happily, and Samantha thought of her shop, failed and finished. "I was a self-starter," he informed the group, reprising what was clearly an established theme. "That's all there is to it. That's all you need. I was a self-starter."

Massive and globular, he was like a miniature velvety sun, radiating satisfaction and contentment. His tones were already rounded and mellowed by the brandy in his hand. "I was ready to take a risk—could've lost everything."

"Well, your mum could have lost everything," Samantha corrected him. "Didn't Hilda mortgage her house to put up half the deposit on the shop?"

She saw the tiny flicker in Howard's eyes, but his smile remained constant.

"All credit to my mother, then," he said, "for working and scrimping and saving, and giving her son a start. I multiply what I was given, and I give back to the family—pay for your girls to go to St. Anne's—what goes round, comes round, eh, Sammy?"

She expected this from Shirley, but not from Howard. Both of them drained their glasses, and Samantha watched Gavin drift away without trying to stop him.

Gavin was wondering whether it would be possible to slip out unnoticed. He was nervous, and the noise was making it worse.

A horrible idea had taken possession of him since meeting Gaia at the door. What if Kay had told her daughter everything? What if the girl knew that he was in love with Mary Fairbrother, and told other people? It was the sort of thing that a vengeful sixteen-year-old might do.

The very last thing he wanted was for Pagford to know that he was in love with Mary before he had a chance to tell her himself. He had imagined doing it months and months hence, perhaps a year down the line...letting the first anniversary of Barry's death slip by...and, in the meantime, nurturing the tiny shoots of trust and reliance that were already there, so that the reality of her feelings stole gradually upon her, as they had upon him...

"You haven't got a drink, Gav!" said Miles. "That situation must be remedied!"

He led his partner firmly to the drinks table and poured him a beer, talking all the while, and, like Howard, giving off an almost visible glow of happiness and pride.

"You heard I won the seat?"

Gavin had not, but he did not feel equal to feigning surprise.

"Yeah. Congratulations."

"How's Mary?" asked Miles expansively; he was a friend to the whole town tonight, because it had elected him. "She doing OK?"

"Yeah, I think—"

"I heard she might be going to Liverpool. Might be for the best."

"What?" said Gavin sharply.

"Maureen was saying this morning; apparently, Mary's sister's trying to persuade Mary to go home with the kids. She's still got a lot of family in Liver—"

"This is her home."

"I think it was Barry who liked Pagford. I'm not sure Mary will want to stay without him."

Gaia was watching Gavin through a chink in the kitchen door. She was clutching a paper cup containing several fingers of the vodka that Andrew had stolen for her.

"He's such a bastard," she said. "We'd still be in Hackney if he hadn't led Mum on. She's so bloody stupid. I could have told her

422

he wasn't that interested. He never took her out. He couldn't wait to leave after they'd shagged."

Andrew, who was piling additional sandwiches on an almost empty platter behind her, could hardly believe that she was using words like shagged. The chimeric Gaia who filled his fantasies was a sexually inventive and adventurous virgin. He did not know what the real Gaia had done, or not done, with Marco de Luca. Her judgment on her mother made it sound as if she knew how men behaved after sex, if they *were* interested...

"Drink something," she told Andrew as he approached the door with the platter, and she held up her own polystyrene cup to his lips, and he drank some of her vodka. Giggling a little, she backed away to let him out and called after him: "Make Sooks come in here and get some!"

The hall was crowded and noisy. Andrew put the pile of fresh sandwiches on the table, but interest in the food seemed to have waned; Sukhvinder was struggling to keep up with demand at the drinks table, and many people had started pouring their own.

"Gaia wants you in the kitchen," Andrew told Sukhvinder, and he took over from her. There was no point acting like a bartender; instead, he filled as many glasses as he could find, and left them on the table for people to help themselves.

"Hi, Peanut!" said Lexie Mollison. "Can I have some champagne?"

They had been at St. Thomas's together, but he had not seen her for a long time. Her accent had changed since she had been at St. Anne's. He hated being called Peanut.

"It's there in front of you," he said, pointing.

"Lexie, you're not drinking," snapped Samantha, appearing out of the crowd. "Absolutely not."

"Grandad said—"

"I don't care."

"Everyone else—"

"I said no!"

Lexie stomped away. Andrew, glad to see her go, smiled at Samantha, and was surprised when she beamed at him.

"Do you talk back to your parents?"

"Yeah," he said, and she laughed. Her breasts really were enormous.

"Ladies and gentlemen!" boomed a voice through the microphone, and everyone stopped talking to listen to Howard. "Wanted to say a few words…most of you probably know by now that my son Miles has just been elected to the Parish Council!"

There was a smattering of applause and Miles raised his drink high above his head to acknowledge it. Andrew was startled to hear Samantha say quite clearly under her breath, "Hoo-fucking-ray."

Nobody was coming for drinks now. Andrew slipped back into the kitchen. Gaia and Sukhvinder were alone in there, drinking and laughing, and when they saw Andrew they both shouted, *"Andy!"*

He laughed too.

"Are you both pissed?"

"Yes," said Gaia, and "No," said Sukhvinder. "*She* is, though."

"I don't care," said Gaia. "Mollison can sack me if he wants. No point saving up for a ticket to Hackney anymore."

"He won't sack you," said Andrew, helping himself to some of the vodka. "You're his favorite."

"Yeah," said Gaia. "Creepy old bastard."

And the three of them laughed again.

Through the glass doors, amplified by the microphone, came Maureen's croaky voice.

"Come on, then, Howard! Come on—a duet for your birthday! Go on—ladies and gentlemen—Howard's favorite song!"

The teenagers gazed at each other in tantalized horror. Gaia tripped forward, giggling, and pushed the door open.

The first few bars of "The Green, Green Grass of Home" blared out, and then, in Howard's bass and Maureen's gravelly alto:

> *The old home town looks the same,*
> *As I step down from the train…*

Gavin was the only one who heard the giggles and snorts, but when he turned around all he saw were the double doors to the kitchen, swinging a little on their hinges.

Miles had left to chat with Aubrey and Julia Fawley, who had arrived late, wreathed in polite smiles. Gavin was in the grip of a familiar mixture of dread and anxiety. His brief sunlit haze of freedom and happiness had been overcast by the twin threats of Gaia blabbing what he had said to her mother, and of Mary leaving Pagford forever. What was he going to do?

Down the lane I walk, with my sweet Mary,
Hair of gold and lips like cherries...

"Kay not here?"

Samantha had arrived, leaning against the table beside him, smirking.

"You already asked me that," said Gavin. "No."

"Everything OK with you two?"

"Is that really any of your business?"

It slipped out of him before he could stop it; he was sick of her constant probing and jeering. For once, it was just the two of them; Miles was still busy with the Fawleys.

She overacted being taken aback. Her eyes were bloodshot and her speech was deliberate; for the first time, Gavin felt more dislike than intimidation.

"I'm sorry. I was only—"

"Asking. Yeah," he said, as Howard and Maureen swayed, arm in arm.

"I'd like to see you settled down. You and Kay seemed good together."

"Yeah, well, I like my freedom," said Gavin. "I don't know many happily married couples."

Samantha had drunk too much to feel the full force of the dig, but she had the impression that one had been made.

"Marriages are always a mystery to outsiders," she said carefully. "Nobody can ever really know except the two people involved. So you shouldn't judge, Gavin."

"Thanks for the insight," he said, and irritated past endurance he set down his empty beer can and headed toward the cloakroom.

Samantha watched him leave, sure that she had had the best of the encounter, and turned her attention to her mother-in-law, whom she could see through a gap in the crowd, watching Howard and Maureen sing. Samantha relished Shirley's anger, which was expressed in the tightest, coldest smile she had worn all evening. Howard and Maureen had performed together many a time over the years; Howard loved to sing, and Maureen had once performed backing vocals for a local skiffle band. When the song finished, Shirley clapped her hands together once; she might have been summoning a flunky, and Samantha laughed out loud and moved along to the bar end of the table, which she was disappointed to find unmanned by the boy in the bow tie.

Andrew, Gaia and Sukhvinder were still convulsed in the kitchen. They laughed because of Howard and Maureen's duet, and because they had finished two-thirds of the vodka, but mostly they laughed because they laughed, feeding off each other until they could barely stand.

The little window over the sink, propped ajar so that the kitchen did not become too steamy, rattled and clattered, and Fats' head appeared through it.

"Evening," he said. Evidently he had climbed onto something outside, because, with a noise of scraping and a heavy object falling over, more and more of him emerged through the window until he landed heavily on the draining board, knocking several glasses to the ground, where they shattered.

Sukhvinder walked straight out of the kitchen. Andrew knew immediately that he did not want Fats there. Only Gaia seemed unperturbed. Still giggling, she said, "There's a door, you know."

"No shit?" said Fats. "Where's the drink?"

"This is ours," said Gaia, cradling the vodka in her arms. "Andy nicked it. You'll have to get your own."

"Not a problem," said Fats coolly, and he walked through the doors into the hall.

"Need the loo…" mumbled Gaia, and she stowed the vodka bottle back under the sink, and left the kitchen too.

Andrew followed. Sukhvinder had returned to the bar area, Gaia was disappearing into the bathroom, and Fats was leaning against the trestle table with a beer in one hand and a sandwich in the other.

"Didn't think you'd want to come to this," said Andrew.

"I was invited, mate," said Fats. "It was on the invitation. Whole Wall family."

"Does Cubby know you're here?"

"Dunno," said Fats. "He's in hiding. Didn't get ol' Barry's seat after all. The whole social fabric'll collapse now Cubby's not holding it together. Fucking hell, that's horrible," he added, spitting out a mouthful of sandwich. "Wanna fag?"

The hall was so noisy, and the guests so raucously drunk, that nobody seemed to care where Andrew went anymore. When they got outside, they found Patricia Mollison, alone beside her sports car, looking up at the clear starry sky, smoking.

"You can have one of these," she said, offering her packet, "if you want."

After she had lit their cigarettes, she stood at her ease with one hand balled deep in her pocket. There was something about her that Andrew found intimidating; he could not even bring himself to glance at Fats, to gauge his reaction.

"I'm Pat," she told them, after a little while. "Howard and Shirley's daughter."

"Hi," said Andrew. "'M Andrew."

"Stuart," said Fats.

She did not seem to need to prolong conversation. Andrew felt it as a kind of compliment and tried to emulate her indifference. The silence was broken by footsteps and the sound of muffled girls' voices.

Gaia was dragging Sukhvinder outside by the hand. She was laughing, and Andrew could tell that the full effect of the vodka was still intensifying inside her.

"You," said Gaia, to Fats, "are really horrible to Sukhvinder."

"Stop it," said Sukhvinder, tugging against Gaia's hand. "I'm serious—let me—"

"He is!" said Gaia breathlessly. "You are! Do you put stuff on her Facebook?"

"Stop it!" shouted Sukhvinder. She wrenched herself free and plunged back inside the party.

"You *are* horrible to her," said Gaia, grabbing on to the railings for support. "Calling her a lesbian and stuff…"

"Nothing wrong with being a lesbian," said Patricia, her eyes narrowed through the smoke she was inhaling. "But then, I would say that."

Andrew saw Fats look at Pat sideways.

"I never said there was anything wrong with it. It's only jokes," he said.

Gaia slid down the rails to sit on the chilly pavement, her head in her arms.

"You all right?" Andrew asked. If Fats had not been there, he would have sat down too.

"Pissed," she muttered.

"Might do better to stick your fingers down your throat," suggested Patricia, looking down at her dispassionately.

"Nice car," Fats said, eyeing the BMW.

"Yeah," said Patricia. "New. I make double what my brother makes," she said, "but Miles is the Christ Child. Miles the Messiah…Parish Councillor Mollison the Second…of Pagford. Do you like Pagford?" she asked Fats, while Andrew watched Gaia breathing deeply, her head between her knees.

"No," said Fats. "It's a shithole."

"Yeah, well…I couldn't wait to leave, personally. Did you know Barry Fairbrother?"

"A bit," said Fats.

Something in his voice made Andrew worried.

"He was my reading mentor at St. Thomas's," said Patricia, with her eyes still on the end of the street. "Lovely bloke. I would have come back for the funeral, but Melly and I were in Zermatt. What's all this stuff my mother's been gloating about…this Barry's Ghost stuff?"

"Someone putting stuff on the Parish Council website," said Andrew hastily, afraid of what Fats might say, if he let him. "Rumors and stuff."

"Yeah, my mother would love that," said Patricia.

"Wonder what the Ghost'll say next?" Fats asked, with a sidelong glance at Andrew.

"Probably stop now the election's over," muttered Andrew.

"Oh, I dunno," said Fats. "If there's stuff old Barry's Ghost is still pissed off about…"

He knew that he was making Andrew anxious and he was glad of it. Andrew was spending all his time at his poxy job these days, and he would soon be moving. Fats did not owe Andrew anything. True authenticity could not exist alongside guilt and obligation.

"You all right down there?" Patricia asked Gaia, who nodded, with her face still hidden. "What was it, the drink or the duet that made you feel sick?"

Andrew laughed a little bit, out of politeness and because he wanted to keep the subject away from the Ghost of Barry Fairbrother.

"Turned my stomach too," said Patricia. "Old Maureen and my father singing along together. Arm in arm." Patricia took a final fierce drag on her cigarette and threw the end down, grinding it beneath her heel. "I walked in on her blowing him when I was twelve," she said. "And he gave me a fiver not to tell my mother."

Andrew and Fats stood transfixed, scared even to look at each other. Patricia wiped her face on the back of her hand: she was crying.

"Shouldn't have bloody come," she said. "Knew I shouldn't."

She got into the BMW, and the two boys watched, stunned, as she turned on the engine, reversed out of her parking space and drove away into the night.

"Fuck me," said Fats.

"I think I might be sick," whispered Gaia.

"Mr. Mollison wants you back inside—for the drinks."

Her message delivered, Sukhvinder darted away again.

"I can't," whispered Gaia.

Andrew left her there. The din in the hall hit him as he opened the inner doors. The disco was in full swing. He had to move aside to allow Aubrey and Julia Fawley room to leave. Both, with their backs to the party, looked grimly pleased to be going.

Samantha Mollison was not dancing, but was leaning up against the trestle table where, so recently, there had been rows and rows of drinks. While Sukhvinder rushed around collecting glasses, Andrew unpacked the last box of clean ones, set them out and filled them.

"Your bow tie's crooked," Samantha told him, and she leaned across the table and straightened it for him. Embarrassed, he ducked into the kitchen as soon as she let go. Between each load of glasses he put in the dishwasher, Andrew took another swig of the vodka he had stolen. He wanted to be drunk like Gaia; he wanted to return to that moment when they had been laughing uncontrollably together, before Fats had appeared.

After ten minutes, he checked the drinks table again; Samantha was still propped up against it, glassy-eyed, and there were plenty of fresh-poured drinks left for her to enjoy. Howard was bobbing in the middle of the dance floor, sweat pouring down his face, roaring with laughter at something Maureen had said to him. Andrew wound his way through the crowd and back outside.

He could not see where she was at first: then he spotted them. Gaia and Fats were locked together ten yards away from the door, leaning up against the railings, bodies pressed tight against each other, tongues working in each other's mouths.

"Look, I'm sorry, but I can't do it all," said Sukhvinder desperately from behind him. Then she spotted Fats and Gaia and let out something between a yelp and a sob. Andrew walked back into the hall with her, completely numb. In the kitchen, he poured the remainder of the vodka into a glass and downed it in one. Mechanically he filled the sink and set to washing out the glasses that could not fit in the dishwasher.

The alcohol was not like dope. It made him feel empty, but also keen to hit someone: Fats, for instance.

After a while, he realized that the plastic clock on the kitchen wall had leaped from midnight to one and that people were leaving.

He was supposed to find coats. He tried for a while, but then lurched off to the kitchen again, leaving Sukhvinder in charge.

Samantha was leaning up against the fridge, on her own, with a glass in her hand. Andrew's vision was strangely jerky, like a series of stills. Gaia had not come back. She was doubtless long gone with Fats. Samantha was talking to him. She was drunk too. He was not embarrassed by her anymore. He suspected that he might be sick quite soon.

"…hate bloody Pagford…" said Samantha, and, "but you're young enough to get out."

"Yeah," he said, unable to feel his lips. "An' I will. 'Nigh will."

She pushed his hair off his forehead and called him sweet. The image of Gaia with her tongue in Fats' mouth threatened to obliterate everything. He could smell Samantha's perfume, coming in waves from her hot skin.

"That band's shit," he said, pointing at her chest, but he did not think she heard him.

Her mouth was chapped and warm, and her breasts were huge, pressed against his chest; her back was as broad as his—

"What the fuck?"

Andrew was slumped against the draining board and Samantha was being dragged out of the kitchen by a big man with short graying hair. Andrew had a dim idea that something bad had happened, but the strange flickering quality of reality was becoming more and more pronounced, until the only thing to do was to stagger across the room to the bin and throw up again and again and again…

"Sorry, you can't come in!" he heard Sukhvinder tell someone. "Stuff piled up against the door!"

He tied the bin bag tightly on his own vomit. Sukhvinder helped him clear the kitchen. He needed to throw up twice more, but both times managed to get to the bathroom.

It was nearly two o'clock by the time Howard, sweaty but smiling, thanked them and said good night.

"Very good work," he said. "See you tomorrow, then. Very good…where's Miss Bawden, by the way?"

Andrew left Sukhvinder to come up with a lie. Out in the street, he unchained Simon's bicycle and wheeled it away into the darkness.

The long cold walk back to Hilltop House cleared his head, but assuaged neither his bitterness nor his misery.

Had he ever told Fats that he fancied Gaia? Maybe not, but Fats knew. He *knew* that Fats knew…were they, perhaps, shagging right now?

I'm moving, anyway, Andrew thought, bent over and shivering as he pushed the bicycle up the hill. *So fuck them…*

Then he thought: *I'd better be moving…*Had he just snogged Lexie Mollison's mother? Had her husband walked in on them? Had that really happened?

He was scared of Miles, but he also wanted to tell Fats about it, to see his face…

When he let himself into the house, exhausted, Simon's voice came out of the darkness from the kitchen.

"Have you put my bike in the garage?"

He was sitting at the kitchen table, eating a bowl of cereal. It was nearly half past two in the morning.

"Couldn't sleep," said Simon.

For once, he was not angry. Ruth was not there, so he did not have to prove himself bigger or smarter than his sons. He seemed weary and small.

"Think we're gonna have to move to Reading, Pizza Face," said Simon. It was almost a term of endearment.

Shivering slightly, feeling old and shell-shocked, and immensely guilty, Andrew wanted to give his father something to make up for what he had done. It was time to redress balances and claim Simon as an ally. They were a family. They had to move together. Perhaps it could be better, somewhere else.

"I've got something for you," he said. "Come through here. Found out how to do it at school…"

And he led the way to the computer.

IV

A misty blue sky stretched like a dome over Pagford and the Fields. Dawn light shone upon the old stone war memorial in the Square, on the cracked concrete facades of Foley Road, and turned the white walls of Hilltop House pale gold. As Ruth Price climbed into her car ready for another long shift at the hospital, she looked down at the River Orr, shining like a silver ribbon in the distance, and felt how completely unjust it was that somebody else would soon have her house and her view.

A mile below, in Church Row, Samantha Mollison was still sound asleep in the spare bedroom. There was no lock on the door, but she had barricaded it with an armchair before collapsing, semidressed, onto the bed. The beginnings of a vicious headache disturbed her slumber, and the sliver of sunshine that had penetrated the gap in the curtains fell like a laser beam across the corner of one eye. She twitched a little, in the depths of her dry-mouthed, anxious half sleep, and her dreams were guilty and strange.

Downstairs, among the clean, bright surfaces of the kitchen, Miles sat bolt upright and alone with an untouched mug of tea in front of him, staring at the fridge, and stumbling again, in his mind's eye, upon his drunken wife locked in the embrace of a sixteen-year-old schoolboy.

Three houses away, Fats Wall lay smoking in his bedroom in the clothes he had worn to Howard Mollison's birthday party. He had wanted to stay awake all night, and he had done it. His mouth was slightly numb and tingly from all the cigarettes he had smoked, but his tiredness had had the reverse effect of the one he had hoped: he was unable to think very clearly, but his unhappiness and unease were as acute as ever.

Colin Wall woke, drenched in sweat, from another of the nightmares that had tormented him for years. He had always done terrible things in the dreams, the kinds of things that he spent his waking life dreading, and this time he had killed Barry Fairbrother, and the authorities had only just found out, and had come to tell him that they knew, that they had dug up Barry and found the poison that Colin had administered.

Staring up at the lampshade's familiar shadow on the ceiling, Colin wondered why he had never considered the possibility that he had killed Barry; and at once, the question presented itself to him: *How do you know you didn't?*

Downstairs, Tessa was injecting insulin into her stomach. She knew that Fats had come home the previous evening, because she could smell the cigarette smoke at the bottom of the stairs to his attic bedroom. Where he had been and what time he had come in, she did not know, and it frightened her. How had things come to this?

Howard Mollison was sleeping soundly and happily in his double bed. The patterned curtains dappled him with pink petals and protected him from a rude awakening, but his rattling wheezing snores had roused his wife. Shirley was eating toast and drinking coffee in the kitchen, wearing her glasses and her candlewick dressing gown. She visualized Maureen swaying arm in arm with her husband in the village hall and experienced a concentrated loathing that took the taste from every mouthful.

In the Smithy, a few miles outside Pagford, Gavin Hughes soaped himself under a hot shower and wondered why he had never had the courage of other men, and how they managed to make the right choices among almost infinite alternatives. There was a yearning inside him for a life he had glimpsed but never tasted, yet he was afraid. Choice was dangerous: you had to forgo all other possibilities when you chose.

Kay Bawden was lying awake and exhausted in bed in Hope Street, listening to the early morning quiet of Pagford and watching Gaia, who was asleep beside her in the double bed, pale and drained in the early daylight. There was a bucket next to Gaia on the floor, placed there by Kay, who had half carried her daughter from bathroom to bedroom in the early hours, after holding her hair out of the toilet for an hour.

"Why did you make us come here?" Gaia had wailed, as she choked and retched over the bowl. "Get off me. Get off. I fuck—*I hate you.*"

Kay watched the sleeping face and recalled the beautiful little baby who had slept beside her, sixteen years ago. She remembered the tears that Gaia had shed when Kay had split up with Steve, her live-in partner of eight years. Steve had attended Gaia's parents' evenings and taught her to ride a bicycle. Kay remembered the fantasy she had nurtured (with hindsight, as silly as four-year-old Gaia's wish for a unicorn) that she would settle down with Gavin and give Gaia, at last, a permanent stepfather, and a beautiful house in the country. How desperate she had been for a storybook ending, and a life to which Gaia would always want to return; because her daughter's departure was hurtling toward Kay like a meteorite, and she foresaw the loss of Gaia as a calamity that would shatter her world.

Kay reached out a hand beneath the duvet and held Gaia's. The feel of the warm flesh that she had accidentally brought into the world made Kay start to weep, quietly, but so violently that the mattress shook.

And at the bottom of Church Row, Parminder Jawanda slipped a coat on over her nightdress and took her coffee into the back garden. Sitting in the chilly sunlight on a wooden bench, she saw that it was promising to be a beautiful day, but there seemed to be a blockage between her eyes and her heart. The heavy weight on her chest deadened everything.

The news that Miles Mollison had won Barry's seat on the Parish Council had not been a surprise, but on seeing Shirley's neat little announcement on the website, she had known another flicker of that madness that had overtaken her at the last meeting: a desire to attack, superseded almost at once by stifling hopelessness.

"I'm going to resign from the council," she told Vikram. "What's the point?"

"But you like it," he had said.

She had liked it when Barry had been there too. It was easy to conjure him up this morning, when everything was quiet and still. A little, ginger-bearded man; she had been taller than him by half a head. She had never felt the slightest physical attraction towards him. *What was love, after all?* thought Parminder, as a gentle breeze ruffled the tall hedge of Leyland cypresses that enclosed the

Jawandas' big back lawn. Was it love when somebody filled a space in your life that yawned inside you, once they had gone?

I did love laughing, thought Parminder. *I really miss laughing.*

And it was the memory of laughter that, at last, made the tears flow from her eyes. They trickled down her nose and into her coffee, where they made little bullet holes, swiftly erased. She was crying because she never seemed to laugh anymore, and also because the previous evening, while they had been listening to the jubilant distant thump of the disco in the church hall, Vikram had said, "Why don't we visit Amritsar this summer?"

The Golden Temple, the holiest shrine of the religion to which he was indifferent. She had known at once what Vikram was doing. Time lay slack and empty on her hands as never before in her life. Neither of them knew what the GMC would decide to do with her, once it had considered her ethical breach toward Howard Mollison.

"Mandeep says it's a big tourist trap," she had replied, dismissing Amritsar at a stroke.

Why did I say that? Parminder wondered, crying harder than ever in the garden, with her coffee cooling in her hand. *It'd be good to show the children Amritsar. He was trying to be kind. Why didn't I say yes?*

She felt dimly that she had betrayed something, in refusing the Golden Temple. A vision of it swam through her tears, its lotus-flower dome reflected in a sheet of water, honey-bright against a backdrop of white marble.

"Mum."

Sukhvinder had crossed the lawn without Parminder noticing. She was dressed in jeans and a baggy sweatshirt. Parminder hastily wiped her face and squinted at Sukhvinder, who had her back to the sun.

"I don't want to go to work today."

Parminder responded at once, in the same spirit of automatic contradiction that had made her turn down Amritsar. "You've made a commitment, Sukhvinder."

"I don't feel well."

"You mean you're tired. You're the one who wanted this job. Now you fulfill your obligations."

"But—"

"You're going to work," snapped Parminder, and she might have been pronouncing sentence. "You're not giving the Mollisons another reason to complain."

After Sukhvinder walked back to the house Parminder felt guilty. She almost called her daughter back, but instead she made a mental note that she must try and find time to sit down with her and talk to her without arguing.

V

Krystal was walking along Foley Road in the early morning sunlight, eating a banana. It was an unfamiliar taste and texture, and she could not make up her mind whether she liked it or not. Terri and Krystal never bought fruit.

Nikki's mother had just turfed her unceremoniously out of the house.

"We got things to do, Krystal," she had said. "We're going to Nikki's gran's for dinner."

As an afterthought, she had handed Krystal the banana to eat for breakfast. Krystal had left without protest. There was barely enough room for Nikki's family around the kitchen table.

The Fields were not improved by sunshine, which merely showed up the dirt and the damage, the cracks in the concrete walls, the boarded windows and the litter.

The Square in Pagford looked freshly painted whenever the sun shone. Twice a year, the primary school children had walked through the middle of town, crocodile fashion, on their way to church for Christmas and Easter services. (Nobody had ever wanted to hold Krystal's hand. Fats had told them all that she had fleas. She wondered whether he remembered.) There had been hanging baskets full of flowers; splashes of purple, pink and green, and every time Krystal had passed one of the planted troughs outside the Black Canon, she had pulled off a petal. Each one had been cool and slippery in her fingers, swiftly becoming slimy and brown as she clutched it, and she usually wiped it off on the underside of a warm wooden pew in St. Michael's.

She let herself into her house and saw at once, through the open door to her left, that Terri had not gone to bed. She was sitting in her armchair with her eyes closed and her mouth open. Krystal closed the door with a snap, but Terri did not stir.

Krystal was at Terri's side in four strides, shaking her thin arm. Terri's head fell forwards onto her shrunken chest. She snored.

Krystal let go of her. The vision of a dead man in the bathroom swam back into her subconscious.

"Silly bitch," she said.

Then it occurred to her that Robbie was not there. She pounded up the stairs, shouting for him.

"'M'ere," she heard him say, from behind her own closed bedroom door.

When she shouldered it open, she saw Robbie standing there, naked. Behind him, scratching his bare chest, lying on her own mattress, was Obbo.

"All righ', Krys?" he said, grinning.

She seized Robbie and pulled him into his own room. Her hands trembled so badly that it took her ages to dress him.

"Did 'e do somethin' to yer?" she whispered to Robbie.

"'M'ungry," said Robbie.

When he was dressed, she picked him up and ran downstairs. She could hear Obbo moving around in her bedroom.

"Why's 'e 'ere?" she shouted at Terri, who was drowsily awake in her chair. "Why's 'e with Robbie?"

Robbie fought to get out of her arms; he hated shouting.

"An' wha' the fuck's that?" screamed Krystal, spotting, for the first time, two black holdalls lying beside Terri's armchair.

"S'nuthin'," said Terri vaguely.

But Krystal had already forced one of the zips open.

"*S'nuthin'!*" shouted Terri.

Big, bricklike blocks of hashish wrapped neatly in sheets of polythene: Krystal, who could barely read, who could not have identified half the vegetables in a supermarket, who could not have named the Prime Minister, knew that the contents of the bag, if discovered on the premises, meant prison for her mother. Then she saw the tin, with the coachman and horses on the lid, half protruding from the chair on which Terri was sitting.

"Yeh've used," said Krystal breathlessly, as disaster rained invisibly around her and everything collapsed. "Yeh've fuckin'—"

She heard Obbo on the stairs and she snatched up Robbie again. He wailed and struggled in her arms, frightened by her anger, but Krystal's grip was unbreakable.

"Fuckin' lerrim go," called Terri fruitlessly. Krystal had opened the front door and was running as fast as she could, encumbered by Robbie who was resisting and moaning, back along the road.

VI

Shirley showered and pulled clothes out of the wardrobe while Howard slept noisily on. The church bell of St. Michael and All Saints, ringing for ten o'clock matins, reached her as she buttoned up her cardigan. She always thought how loud it must be for the Jawandas, living right opposite, and hoped that it struck them as a loud proclamation of Pagford's adherence to the old ways and traditions of which they, so conspicuously, were not a part.

Automatically, because it was what she so often did, Shirley walked along the hall, turned into Patricia's old bedroom and sat down at the computer.

Patricia ought to be here, sleeping on the sofa bed that Shirley had made up for her. It was a relief not to have to deal with her this morning. Howard, who had still been humming "The Green,

Green Grass of Home" when they arrived at Ambleside in the early hours, had not realized that Patricia was absent until Shirley had had the key in the front door.

"Where's Pat?" he had wheezed, leaning against the porch.

"Oh, she was upset that Melly didn't want to come," sighed Shirley. "They had a row or something…I expect she's gone home to try and patch things up."

"Never a dull moment," said Howard, bouncing lightly off alternate walls of the narrow hallway as he navigated his way carefully toward the bedroom.

Shirley brought up her favorite medical website. When she typed in the first letter of the condition she wished to investigate, the site offered its explanation of EpiPens again, so Shirley swiftly revised their use and content, because she might yet have an opportunity to save their potboy's life. Next, she carefully typed in "eczema," and learned, somewhat to her disappointment, that the condition was not infectious, and could not, therefore, be used as an excuse to sack Sukhvinder Jawanda.

From sheer force of habit, she then typed in the address of the Pagford Parish Council website, and clicked onto the message board.

She had grown to recognize at a glance the shape and length of the user name The_Ghost_of_Barry_Fairbrother, just as a besotted lover knows at once the back of their beloved's head, or the set of their shoulders, or the tilt of their walk.

A single glimpse at the topmost message sufficed: excitement exploded; he had not forsaken her. She had known that Dr. Jawanda's outburst could not go unpunished.

Affair of the First Citizen of Pagford

She read it, but did not, at first, understand: she had been expecting to see Parminder's name. She read it again, and gave the suffocated gasp of a woman being hit by icy water.

Howard Mollison, First Citizen of Pagford, and long-standing resident Maureen Lowe have been more than business partners for many years. It is common knowledge that Maureen holds regular tastings of Howard's finest salami. The only person who appears not to be in on the secret is Shirley, Howard's wife.

Completely motionless in her chair, Shirley thought: *it's not true.* It could not be true.

Yes, she had once or twice suspected…had hinted, sometimes, to Howard…

No, she would not believe it. She could not believe it.

But other people would. They would believe the Ghost. Everybody believed him.

Her hands were like empty gloves, fumbling and feeble, as she tried, with many a blunder, to remove the message from the site. Every second that it remained there, somebody else might be reading it, believing it, laughing about it, passing it to the local newspaper…Howard and Maureen, Howard and Maureen…

The message was gone. Shirley sat and stared at the computer monitor, her thoughts scurrying like mice in a glass bowl, trying to escape, but there was no way out, no firm foothold, no way of climbing back to the happy place she had occupied before she saw that dreadful thing, written in public for the world to see…

He had laughed at Maureen.

No, *she* had laughed at Maureen. Howard had laughed at Kenneth.

Always together: holidays and workdays and weekend excursions…

…only person who appears not to be in on the secret…

*…*she and Howard did not need sex: separate beds for years, they had a silent understanding…

…holds regular tastings of Howard's finest salami…

(Shirley's mother was alive in the room with her: cackling and jeering, a glass slopping wine...Shirley could not bear dirty laughter. She had never been able to bear ribaldry or ridicule.)

She jumped up, tripping over the chair legs, and hurried back to the bedroom. Howard was still asleep, lying on his back, making rumbling, porcine noises.

"Howard," she said. *"Howard."*

It took a whole minute to rouse him. He was confused and disoriented, but as she stood over him, she saw him still as a knight protector who could save her.

"Howard, the Ghost of Barry Fairbrother's put up another message."

Disgruntled at his rude awakening, Howard made a growling groaning noise into the pillow.

"About you," said Shirley.

They did very little plain speaking, she and Howard. She had always liked that. But today she was driven to it.

"About you," she repeated, "and Maureen. It says you've been — having an affair."

His big hand slid up over his face and he rubbed his eyes. He rubbed them longer, she was convinced, than he needed.

"What?" he said, his face shielded.

"You and Maureen, having an affair."

"Where's he get that from?"

No denial, no outrage, no scathing laughter. Merely a cautious request for a source.

Ever afterwards, Shirley would remember this moment as a death; a life truly ended.

VII

"Fuckin' shurrup, Robbie! Shurrup!"

Krystal had dragged Robbie to a bus stop several streets away, so that neither Obbo nor Terri could find them. She was not sure she had enough money for the fare, but she was determined to get to Pagford. Nana Cath was gone, Mr. Fairbrother was gone, but Fats Wall was there, and she needed to make a baby.

"Why wuz 'e in the room with yeh?" Krystal shouted at Robbie, who grizzled and did not answer.

There was only a tiny amount of battery power left on Terri's mobile phone. Krystal called Fats' number, but it went to voice mail.

In Church Row, Fats was busy eating toast and listening to his parents having one of their familiar, bizarre conversations in the study across the hall. It was a welcome distraction from his own thoughts. The mobile in his pocket vibrated but he did not answer it. There was nobody he wanted to talk to. It would not be Andrew. Not after last night.

"Colin, you know what you're supposed to do," his mother was saying. She sounded exhausted. "Please, Colin—"

"We had dinner with them on Saturday night. The night before he died. I cooked. What if—"

"Colin, *you didn't put anything in the food*—for God's sake, now I'm doing it—I'm not supposed to do this, Colin, you know I'm not supposed to get into it. This is your OCD talking."

"But I might've, Tess, I suddenly thought, what if I put some-thing—"

"Then why are we alive, you, me and Mary? They did a post-mortem, Colin!"

"Nobody told us the details. Mary never told us. I think that's why she doesn't want to talk to me anymore. She suspects."

"Colin, for Christ's sake—"

Tessa's voice became an urgent whisper, too quiet to hear. Fats' mobile vibrated again. He pulled it out of his pocket. Krystal's number. He answered.

"Hiya," said Krystal, over what sounded like a kid shouting. "D'you wanna meet up?"

"Dunno," yawned Fats. He had been intending to go to bed.

"I'm comin' into Pagford on the bus. We could hook up."

Last night he had pressed Gaia Bawden into the railings outside the town hall, until she had pulled away from him and thrown up. Then she had started to berate him again, so he had left her there and walked home.

"I dunno," he said. He felt so tired, so miserable.

"Go on," she said.

From the study, he heard Colin. "You say that, but would it show up? What if I—"

"Colin, we shouldn't be going into this—you're not supposed to take these ideas seriously."

"How can you say that to me? How can I not take it seriously? If I'm responsible—"

"Yeah, all right," said Fats to Krystal. "I'll meet you in twenty, front of the pub in the Square."

VIII

Samantha was driven from the spare room at last by her urgent need to pee. She drank cold water from the tap in the bathroom until she felt sick, gulped down two paracetamol from the cabinet over the sink, then took a shower.

She dressed without looking at herself in the mirror. Through everything she did, she was alert for some noise that would indicate the whereabouts of Miles, but the house seemed to be silent. Perhaps, she thought, he had taken Lexie out somewhere, away from her drunken, lecherous, cradle-snatching mother…

("He was in Lexie's class at school!" Miles had spat at her, once they

444

were alone in their bedroom. She had waited for him to move away from the door, then wrenched it back open and run to the spare room.)

Nausea and mortification came over her in waves. She wished she could forget, that she had blacked out, but she could still see the boy's face as she launched herself at him…she could remember the feel of his body pressed against her, so skinny, so young…

If it had been Vikram Jawanda, there might have been some dignity in it…She had to get coffee. She could not stay in the bathroom forever. But as she turned to open the door, she saw herself in the mirror, and her courage almost failed. Her face was puffy, her eyes hooded, the lines in her face etched more deeply by pressure and dehydration.

Oh God, what must he have thought of me…

Miles was sitting in the kitchen when she entered. She did not look at him, but crossed straight to the cupboard where the coffee was. Before she had touched the handle, he said, "I've got some here."

"Thanks," she muttered, and poured herself out a mug, avoiding eye contact.

"I've sent Lexie over to Mum and Dad's," said Miles. "We need to talk."

Samantha sat down at the kitchen table.

"Go on, then," she said.

"Go on—is that all you can say?"

"You're the one who wants to talk."

"Last night," said Miles, "at my father's birthday party, I came to look for you, and I found you snogging a sixteen-year—"

"Sixteen-year-old, yes," said Samantha. "Legal. One good thing."

He stared at her, appalled.

"You think this is funny? If you'd found me so drunk that I didn't even realize—"

"I did realize," said Samantha.

She refused to be Shirley, to cover everything up with a frilly little tablecloth of polite fiction. She wanted to be honest, and she wanted to penetrate that thick coating of complacency through which she no longer recognized a young man she had loved.

"You did realize—what?" said Miles.

He had so plainly expected embarrassment and contrition that she almost laughed.

"I did realize that I was kissing him," she said.

He stared at her, and her courage seeped away, because she knew what he was going to say next.

"And if Lexie had walked in?"

Samantha had no answer to that. The thought of Lexie knowing what had happened made her want to run away and not come back—and what if the boy told her? They had been at school together. She had forgotten what Pagford was like...

"What the hell's going on with you?" asked Miles.

"I'm...unhappy," said Samantha.

"Why?" asked Miles, but then he added quickly, "Is it the shop? Is it that?"

"A bit," said Samantha. "But I hate living in Pagford. I hate living on top of your parents. And sometimes," she said slowly, "I hate waking up next to you."

She thought he might get angry, but instead he asked, quite calmly, "Are you saying you don't love me anymore?"

"I don't know," said Samantha.

He seemed thinner in his open-necked shirt. For the first time in a long while, she thought she glimpsed somebody familiar and vulnerable inside the aging body across the table. *And he still wants me,* she thought, with wonder, recalling the crumpled face in the mirror upstairs.

"But I was glad," she added, "the night that Barry Fairbrother died, that you were still alive. I think I dreamed you weren't, and I woke up, and I know I was happy when I heard you breathing."

"And that's—that's all you've got to say to me, is it? You're glad I'm not dead?"

She had been wrong to think that he was not angry. He had simply been in shock.

"*That's all you've got to say to me?* You get absolutely ratted at my father's birthday—"

"Would it have been better if it hadn't been your bloody father's party?" she shouted, his anger igniting hers. "Was that the real problem, that I showed you up in front of Mummy and Daddy?"

"You were kissing a *sixteen-year-old boy*—"

"Maybe he'll be the first of many!" yelled Samantha, getting up from the table and slamming her mug down in the sink; the handle came off in her hand. "Don't you get it, Miles? I've had enough! I hate our fucking life and I hate your fucking parents—"

"—you don't mind them paying for the girls' education—"

"—I hate you turning into your father in front of me—"

"—absolute bollocks, you just don't like me being happy when you're not—"

"—whereas my darling husband doesn't give a shit how I feel—"

"—plenty for you to do round here, but you'd rather sit at home and sulk—"

"—I don't intend to sit at home anymore, Miles—"

"—not going to apologize for getting involved with the community—"

"—well, I meant what I said— *you're not fit to fill his shoes!*"

"What?" he said, and his chair fell over as he jumped to his feet, while Samantha strode to the kitchen door.

"You heard me," she shouted. "Like my letter said, Miles, you're not fit to fill Barry Fairbrother's shoes. He was sincere."

"*Your* letter?" he said.

"Yep," she said breathlessly, with her hand on the doorknob. "*I* sent that letter. Too much to drink one evening, while you were on the phone to your mother. And," she pulled the door open, "I didn't vote for you either."

The look on his face unnerved her. Out in the hall, she slipped on clogs, the first pair of shoes she could find, and was through the front door before he could catch up.

The journey took Krystal back to her childhood. She had made this trip daily to St. Thomas's, all on her own, on the bus. She knew when the abbey would come into sight, and she pointed it out to Robbie.

"See the big ruin' castle?"

Robbie was hungry, but slightly distracted by the excitement of being on a bus. Krystal held his hand tightly. She had promised him food when they got off at the other end, but she did not know where she would get it. Perhaps she could borrow money from Fats for a bag of crisps, not to mention the return bus fare.

"I wen' ter school 'ere," she told Robbie, while he wiped his fingers on the dirty windows, making abstract patterns. "An' you'll go to school 'ere too."

When they rehoused her, because of her pregnancy, they were almost certain to give her another Fields house; nobody wanted to buy them, they were so run down. But Krystal saw this as a good thing, because in spite of their dilapidation it would put Robbie and the baby in the catchment area for St. Thomas's. Anyway, Fats' parents would almost certainly give her enough money for a washing machine once she had their grandchild. They might even get a television.

The bus rolled down a slope toward Pagford, and Krystal caught a glimpse of the glittering river, briefly visible before the road sank too low. She had been disappointed, when she joined the rowing team, that they did not train on the Orr, but on the dirty old canal in Yarvil.

"'Ere we are," Krystal told Robbie, as the bus turned slowly into the flower-decked square.

Fats had forgotten that waiting in front of the Black Canon meant standing opposite Mollison and Lowe's and the Copper Kettle. There was more than an hour to go until midday, when the café opened on Sundays, but Fats did not know how early Andrew had to arrive for work. He had no desire to see his oldest friend this morning, so he skulked down the side of the pub out of sight, and only emerged when the bus arrived.

It pulled away, revealing Krystal and a small dirty-looking boy. Nonplussed, Fats loped towards them.

"'E's my brother," said Krystal aggressively, in response to something she had seen in Fats' face.

Fats made another mental adjustment to what gritty and authentic life meant. He had been fleetingly taken with the idea of knocking Krystal up (and showing Cubby what real men were able to achieve casually, without effort) but this little boy clinging to his sister's hand and leg disconcerted him.

Fats wished that he had not agreed to meet her. She was making him ridiculous. He would rather have gone back to that stinking, squalid house of hers, now that he saw her in the Square.

"'Ave yeh got any money?" Krystal demanded.

"What?" said Fats. His wits were slow with tiredness. He could not remember now why he had wanted to sit up all night; his tongue was throbbing with all the cigarettes he had smoked.

"Money," repeated Krystal. "'E's 'ungry an' I've lost a fiver. Pay yeh back."

Fats stuck a hand in his jeans pocket and touched a crumpled banknote. Somehow he did not want to look too flush in front of Krystal, so he ferreted deeper for change, and finally came up with a small amount of silver and coppers.

They went to the tiny newsagent's two streets from the Square, and Fats hung around outside while Krystal bought Robbie crisps and a packet of Rolos. None of them said a word, not even Robbie, who seemed fearful of Fats. At last, when Krystal had handed her brother the crisps, she said to Fats, "Where'll we go?"

Surely, he thought, she could not mean that they were going to shag. Not with the boy there. He had had some idea of taking her to the Cubby Hole: it was private, and it would be a final desecration of his and Andrew's friendship; he owed nothing to anyone, anymore. But he balked at the idea of fucking in front of a three-year-old.

"'E'll be all right," said Krystal. "'E's got chocolates now. No, later," she said to Robbie, who was whining for the Rolos still in her hand. "When you've 'ad the crisps."

They walked off down the road in the direction of the old stone bridge.

"'E'll be all right," Krystal repeated. "'E does as 'e's told. Dontcha?" she said loudly to Robbie.

"Wan' chocolates," he said.

"Yeah, in a minute."

She could tell that Fats needed cajoling today. She had known, on the bus, that bringing Robbie, however necessary, would be difficult.

"Whatcha bin up ter?" she asked.

"Party last night," said Fats.

"Yeah? Who wuz there?"

He yawned widely, and she had to wait for an answer.

"Arf Price. Sukhvinder Jawanda. Gaia Bawden."

"Does she live in Pagford?" asked Krystal sharply.

"Yeah, in Hope Street," said Fats.

He knew, because Andrew had let it slip, where she lived. Andrew had never said that he liked her, but Fats had watched him watching Gaia almost constantly in the few classes they shared. He had noticed Andrew's extreme self-consciousness around her, and whenever she was mentioned.

Krystal, though, was thinking about Gaia's mother: the only social worker she had ever liked, the only one who had got through to her mother. She lived in Hope Street, the same as Nana Cath. She was probably there right now. What if...

But Kay had left them. Mattie was their social worker again. Anyway, you weren't supposed to bother them at home. Shane Tully had once followed his social worker to her house, and he'd got a restraining order for his pains. But then, Shane had earlier tried to heave a brick through the woman's car window...

And, Krystal reasoned, squinting as the road turned, and the river dazzled her eyes with thousands of blinding white spots of light, Kay was still the keeper of folders, the scorekeeper and the judge. She had seemed all right, but none of her solutions would keep Krystal and Robbie together...

"We could go down there," she suggested to Fats, pointing at the overgrown stretch of bank, a little way along from the bridge. "An' Robbie could wait up there, on the bench."

She would be able to keep an eye on him from there, she thought, and she would make sure he didn't see anything. Not that it was anything he had not seen before, in the days that Terri brought strangers home...

But, exhausted as he was, Fats was revolted. He could not do it in the grass, under the eye of a small boy.

"Nah," he said, trying to sound offhand.

"'E won' bother," said Krystal. "'E's got 'is Rolos. 'E won' even know," she said, although she thought that was a lie. Robbie knew too much. There had been trouble at nursery when he'd mimicked doing it doggy-style on another child.

Krystal's mother, Fats remembered, was a prostitute. He hated the idea of what she was suggesting, but was that not inauthenticity?

"Whassamatter?" Krystal asked him aggressively.

"Nothing," he said.

Dane Tully would do it. Pikey Pritchard would do it. Cubby, not in a million years.

Krystal walked Robbie to the bench. Fats bent to peer over the back of it, down to the overgrown patch of weeds and bushes, and thought that the kid might not see anything, but that he would be as quick as he could, in any case.

"'Ere y'are," Krystal told Robbie, pulling out the long tube of Rolos while he reached for them excitedly. "Yeh can 'ave all of 'em if yeh jus' sit 'ere fer a minute, all righ'? Yeh jus' sit 'ere, Robbie, an' I'll be in them bushes. D'yeh understand, Robbie?"

"Yeah," he said happily, his cheeks already full of chocolate and toffee.

Krystal slipped and slid down the bank toward the patch of undergrowth, hoping that Fats was not going to make any difficulties about doing it without a condom.

X

Gavin was wearing sunglasses against the glare of the morning sun, but that was no disguise: Samantha Mollison was sure to recognize his car. When he caught sight of her, striding along the pavement alone with her hands in her pockets and her head down, Gavin made a sharp left turn, and instead of continuing along the road to Mary's, crossed the old stone bridge, and parked up a side lane on the other side of the river.

He did not want Samantha to see him parking outside Mary's house. It did not matter on workdays, when he wore a suit and carried a briefcase; it had not mattered before he had admitted to himself what he felt about Mary, but it mattered now. In any case, the morning was glorious and a walk bought him time.

Still keeping my options open, he thought, as he crossed the bridge on foot. There was a small boy sitting by himself on a bench, eating sweets, below him. *I don't have to say anything…I'll play it by ear…*

But his palms were wet. The thought of Gaia telling the Fairbrother twins that he was in love with their mother had haunted him all through a restless night.

Mary seemed pleased to see him.

"Where's your car?" she asked, peering over his shoulder.

"Parked it down by the river," he said. "Lovely morning. I fancied a walk, and then it occurred to me that I could mow the lawn if you—"

"Oh, Graham did it for me," she said, "but that's so sweet of you. Come in and have a coffee."

She chatted as she moved around the kitchen. She was wearing old cutoff jeans and a T-shirt; they showed how thin she was, but her hair was shiny again, the way he usually thought of it. He could see the twin girls, lying out on the freshly mown lawn on a blanket, both with headphones in, listening to their iPods.

"How are you?" Mary asked, sitting down beside him.

He could not think why she sounded so concerned; then he

remembered that he had found time to tell her, yesterday, during his brief visit, that he and Kay had split up.

"I'm OK," he said. "Probably for the best."

She smiled and patted his arm.

"I heard last night," he said, his mouth a little dry, "That you might be moving."

"News travels fast in Pagford," she said. "It's just an idea. Theresa wants me to move back to Liverpool."

"And how do the kids feel about that?"

"Well, I'd wait for the girls and Fergus to do their exams in June. Declan's not so much of a problem. I mean, none of us wants to leave…"

She melted into tears in front of him, but he was so happy that he reached out to touch her delicate wrist.

"Of course you don't…"

"…Barry's grave."

"Ah," said Gavin, his happiness snuffed out like a candle.

Mary wiped her streaming eyes on the back of her hand. Gavin found her a little morbid. His family cremated their dead. Barry's burial had only been the second he had ever attended, and he had hated everything about it. Gavin saw a grave purely as a marker for the place where a corpse was decomposing; a nasty thought, yet people took it into their heads to visit and bring flowers, as though it might yet recover.

She had got up to get tissues. Outside on the lawn, the twins had switched to sharing a set of headphones, their heads bobbing up and down in time to the same song.

"So Miles got Barry's seat," she said. "I could hear the celebrations all the way up here last night."

"Well, it was Howard's…yeah, that's right," said Gavin.

"And Pagford's nearly rid of the Fields," she said.

"Yeah, looks like it."

"And now Miles is on the council, it'll be easier to close Bellchapel," she said.

Gavin always had to remind himself what Bellchapel was; he had no interest in these issues at all.

"Yeah, I suppose so."

"So everything Barry wanted is finished," she said.

Her tears had dried up, and the patches of high angry color had returned to her cheeks.

"I know," he said. "It's really sad."

"I don't know," she said, still flushed and angry. "Why should Pagford pick up the bills for the Fields? Barry only ever saw one side of it. He thought everyone in the Fields was like him. He thought Krystal Weedon was like him, but she wasn't. It never occurred to him that people in the Fields might be happy where they are."

"Yeah," said Gavin, overjoyed that she disagreed with Barry, and feeling as if the shadow of his grave had lifted from between them, "I know what you mean. From all I've heard about Krystal Weedon—"

"She got more of his time and his attention than his own daughters," said Mary. "And she never even gave a penny for his wreath. The girls told me. The whole rowing team chipped in, except Krystal. And she didn't come to his funeral, even, after all he'd done for her."

"Yeah, well, that shows—"

"I'm sorry, but I can't stop thinking about it all," she said frenetically. "I can't stop thinking that he'd still want me to worry about bloody Krystal Weedon. I can't get past it. All the last day of his life, and he had a headache and he didn't do anything about it, writing that bloody article!"

"I know," said Gavin. "I know. I think," he said, with a sense of putting his foot tentatively on an old rope bridge, "it's a bloke thing. Miles is the same. Samantha didn't want him to stand for the council, but he went ahead anyway. You know, some men really like a bit of power—"

"Barry wasn't in it for power," said Mary, and Gavin hastily retreated.

"No, no, Barry wasn't. He was in it for—"

"He couldn't help himself," she said. "He thought everyone was like him, that if you gave them a hand they'd start bettering themselves."

"Yeah," said Gavin, "but the point is, there are other people who could use a hand—people at home…"

"Well, exactly!" said Mary, dissolving yet again into tears.

"Mary," said Gavin, leaving his chair, moving to her side (on the rope bridge now, with a sense of mingled panic and anticipation), "look…it's really early…I mean, it's far too soon…but you'll meet someone else."

"At forty," sobbed Mary, "with four children…"

"Plenty of men," he began, but that was no good; he would rather she did not think she had too many options. "The right man," he corrected himself, "won't care that you've got kids. Anyway, they're such nice kids…anyone would be glad to take them on."

"Oh, Gavin, you're so sweet," she said, dabbing her eyes again.

He put his arm around her, and she did not shrug it off. They stood without speaking while she blew her nose, and then he felt her tense to move away, and he said, "Mary…"

"What?"

"I've got to—Mary, I think I'm in love with you."

He knew for a few seconds the glorious pride of the skydiver who pushes off firm floor into limitless space.

Then she pulled away.

"Gavin. I—"

"I'm sorry," he said, observing with alarm her repulsed expression. "I wanted you to hear it from me. I told Kay that's why I wanted to split up, and I was scared you'd hear it from someone else. I wouldn't have said anything for months. Years," he added, trying to bring back her smile and the mood in which she found him sweet.

But Mary was shaking her head, arms folded over her thin chest.

"Gavin, I never, ever—"

"Forget I said anything," he said foolishly. "Let's just forget it."

"I thought you understood," she said.

He gathered that he should have known that she was encased in the invisible armor of grief, and that it ought to have protected her.

"I do understand," he lied. "I wouldn't have told you, only—"

"Barry always said you fancied me," said Mary.

"I didn't," he said frantically.

"Gavin, I think you're such a nice man," she said breathlessly. "But I don't—I mean, even if—"

"No," he said loudly, trying to drown her out. "I understand. Listen, I'm going to go."

"There's no need…"

But he almost hated her now. He had heard what she was trying to say: *even if I weren't grieving for my husband, I wouldn't want you.*

His visit had been so brief that when Mary, slightly shaky, poured away his coffee it was still hot.

XI

Howard had told Shirley that he did not feel well, that he thought he had better stay in bed and rest, and that the Copper Kettle could run without him for an afternoon.

"I'll call Mo," he said.

"No, I'll call her," said Shirley sharply.

As she closed the bedroom door on him, Shirley thought, *He's using his heart.*

He had said, "Don't be silly, Shirl," and then, "It's rubbish, bloody rubbish," and she had not pressed him. Years of genteel avoidance of grisly topics (Shirley had been literally struck dumb when twenty-three-year-old Patricia had said: "I'm gay, Mum.") seemed to have muzzled something inside her.

The doorbell rang. Lexie said, "Dad told me to come round here. He and Mum have got something to do. Where's Grandad?"

"In bed," said Shirley. "He overdid it a bit last night."

"It was a good party, wasn't it?" said Lexie.

"Yes, lovely," said Shirley, with a tempest building inside her.

After a while, her granddaughter's prattling wore Shirley down.

"Let's have lunch at the café," she suggested. "Howard," she called through the closed bedroom door, "I'm taking Lexie for lunch at the Copper Kettle."

He sounded worried, and she was glad. She was not afraid of Maureen. She would look Maureen right in the face…

But it occurred to Shirley, as she walked, that Howard might have telephoned Maureen the moment she had left the bungalow. She was so stupid…somehow, she had thought that, in calling Maureen herself about Howard's illness, she had stopped them communicating…she was forgetting…

The familiar, well-loved streets seemed different, strange. She had taken a regular inventory of the window she presented to this lovely little world: wife and mother, hospital volunteer, secretary to the Parish Council, First Citizeness; and Pagford had been her mirror, reflecting, in its polite respect, her value and her worth. But the Ghost had taken a rubber stamp and smeared across the pristine surface of her life a revelation that would nullify it all: "her husband was sleeping with his business partner, and she never knew…"

It would be all that anyone said, when she was mentioned; all that they ever remembered about her.

She pushed open the door of the café; the bell tinkled, and Lexie said, "There's Peanut Price."

"Howard all right?" croaked Maureen.

"Just tired," said Shirley, moving smoothly to a table and sitting down, her heart beating so fast that she wondered whether she might have a coronary herself.

"Tell him neither of the girls has turned up," said Maureen crossly, lingering by their table, "and neither of them bothered to call in either. It's lucky we're not busy."

Lexie went to the counter to talk to Andrew, who had been put on waiter duty. Conscious of her unusual solitude, as she sat alone at the table, Shirley remembered Mary Fairbrother, erect and gaunt at Barry's funeral, widowhood draped around her like a queen's train; the pity, the admiration. In losing her husband, Mary had become the silent passive recipient of admiration, whereas she, shackled to a man who had betrayed her, was cloaked in grubbiness, a target of derision…

(Long ago, in Yarvil, men had subjected Shirley to smutty jokes because of her mother's reputation, even though she, Shirley, had been as pure as it was possible to be.)

"Grandad's feeling ill," Lexie was telling Andrew. "What's in those cakes?"

He bent down behind the counter, hiding his red face.

I snogged your mum.

Andrew had almost skived off work. He had been afraid that Howard might sack him on the spot for kissing his daughter-in-law, and was downright terrified that Miles Mollison might storm in, looking for him. At the same time, he was not so naive that he did not know that Samantha, who must, he thought ruthlessly, be well over forty, would figure as the villain of the piece. His defense was simple. "She was pissed and she grabbed me."

There was a tiny glimmer of pride in his embarrassment. He had been anxious to see Gaia; he wanted to tell her that a grown woman had pounced on him. He had hoped that they might laugh about it, the way that they laughed about Maureen, but that she might be secretly impressed; and also that in the course of laughing, he might find out exactly what she had done with Fats; how far she had let him go. He was prepared to forgive her. She had been pissed too. But she had not turned up.

He went to fetch a napkin for Lexie and almost collided with his boss's wife, who was standing behind the counter, holding his EpiPen.

"Howard wanted me to check something," Shirley told him. "And this needle shouldn't be kept in here. I'll put it in the back."

XII

Halfway down his packet of Rolos, Robbie became extremely thirsty. Krystal had not bought him a drink. He climbed off the bench and crouched down in the warm grass, where he could still see her outline in the bushes with the stranger. After a while, he scrambled down the bank toward them.

"'M thirsty," he whined.

"Robbie, get out of it!" screamed Krystal. "Go an' sit on the bench!"

"Wanna drink!"

"Fuckin'—go an' wai' by the bench, an' I'll gerra drink in a minute! Go 'way, Robbie!"

Crying, he climbed back up the slippery bank to the bench. He was accustomed to not being given what he wanted, and disobedient by habit, because grown-ups were arbitrary in their wrath and their rules, so he had learned to seize his tiny pleasures wherever and whenever he could.

Angry at Krystal, he wandered a little way from the bench along the road. A man in sunglasses was walking along the pavement toward him.

(Gavin had forgotten where he had parked the car. He had marched out of Mary's and walked straight down Church Row, only realizing that he was heading in the wrong direction when he drew level with Miles and Samantha's house. Not wanting to pass the Fairbrothers' again, he had taken a circuitous route back to the bridge.

He saw the boy, chocolate-stained, ill-kempt and unappealing, and walked past, with his happiness in tatters, half wishing that he could have gone to Kay's house and been silently cradled…she had always been nicest to him when he was miserable, it was what had attracted him to her in the first place.)

The rushing of the river increased Robbie's thirst. He cried a bit more as he changed direction and headed away from the bridge, back past the place where Krystal was hidden. The bushes had started shaking. He walked on, wanting a drink, then noticed a hole in a long hedge on the left of the road. When he drew level, he spotted a playing field beyond.

Robbie wriggled through the hole and contemplated the wide green space with its spreading chestnut tree and goalposts. Robbie knew what they were, because his cousin Dane had showed him how to kick a football at the play park. He had never seen so much greenness.

A woman came striding across the field, with her arms folded and her head bowed.

(Samantha had been walking at random, walking and walking, anywhere as long as it was nowhere near Church Row. She had been asking herself many questions and coming up with few answers; and one of the questions she asked herself was whether she might not have gone too far in telling Miles about that stupid, drunken letter, which she had sent out of spite, and which seemed much less clever now...

She glanced up and her eyes met Robbie's. Children often wriggled through the hole in the hedge to play in the field at weekends. Her own girls had done it when they were younger.

She climbed over the gate and turned away from the river toward the Square. Self-disgust clung to her, no matter how hard she tried to outrun it.)

Robbie went back through the hole in the hedge and walked a little way along the road after the striding lady, but she was soon out of sight. The half packet of remaining Rolos were melting in his hand, and he did not want to put them down, but he was so thirsty. Maybe Krystal had finished. He wandered back in the opposite direction.

When he reached the first patch of bushes on the bank, he saw that they were not moving, so he thought it was all right to approach.

"Krystal," he said.

But the bushes were empty. Krystal was gone.

Robbie started to wail and shout for Krystal. He clambered back up the bank and looked wildly up and down the road, but there was no sign of her.

"Krystal!" he yelled.

A woman with short silver hair glanced at him, frowning, as she trotted briskly along the opposite pavement.

Shirley had left Lexie at the Copper Kettle, where she seemed happy, but a short way across the Square she had caught a glimpse of Samantha, who was the very last person she wanted to meet, so she had taken off in the opposite direction.

The boy's wails and squawks echoed behind her as she hurried along. Shirley's fist was clutched tightly around the EpiPen in her pocket. She would not be a dirty joke. She wanted to be pure and pitied, like Mary Fairbrother. Her rage was so enormous, so dangerous, that she could not think coherently: she wanted to act, to punish, to finish.

Just before the old stone bridge, a patch of bushes shivered to Shirley's left. She glanced down and caught a disgusting glimpse of something sordid and vile, and it drove her on.

XIII

Sukhvinder had been walking around Pagford longer than Samantha. She had left the Old Vicarage shortly after her mother had told her she must go to work, and since then had been wandering the streets, observing invisible exclusion zones around Church Row, Hope Street and the Square.

She had nearly fifty pounds in her pocket, which represented her wages from the café and the party, and the razor blade. She had wanted to take her building society passbook, which resided in a little filing cabinet in her father's study, but Vikram had been at his desk. She had waited for a while at the bus stop where you could catch a bus into Yarvil, but then she had spotted Shirley and Lexie Mollison coming down the road, and dived out of sight.

Gaia's betrayal had been brutal and unexpected. Pulling Fats Wall…he would drop Krystal now that he had Gaia. Any boy would drop any girl for Gaia, she knew that. But she could not bear to go to work and hear her one ally trying to tell her that Fats was all right, really.

Her mobile buzzed. Gaia had already texted her twice.

How pissed was I last nite?
R u going 2 work?

Nothing about Fats Wall. Nothing about snogging Sukhvinder's torturer. The new message said, R u OK?

Sukhvinder put the mobile back into her pocket. She might walk toward Yarvil and catch a bus outside town, where nobody would see her. Her parents would not miss her until five thirty, when they expected her home from the café.

A desperate plan formed as she walked, hot and tired: if she could find a place to stay that cost less than fifty pounds...all she wanted was to be alone and ply her razor blade.

She was on the river road with the Orr flowing beside her. If she crossed the bridge, she would be able to take a backstreet all the way round to the start of the bypass.

"Robbie! *Robbie!* Where are you?"

It was Krystal Weedon, running up and down the riverbank. Fats Wall was smoking, with one hand in his pocket, watching Krystal run.

Sukhvinder took a sharp right onto the bridge, terrified that one of them might notice her. Krystal's yells were echoing off the rushing water.

Sukhvinder caught sight of something in the river below.

Her hands were already on the hot stone ledge before she had thought about what she was doing, and then she had hoisted herself onto the edge of the bridge; she yelled, *"He's in the river, Krys!"* and dropped, feetfirst, into the water. Her leg was sliced open by a broken computer monitor as she was pulled under by the current.

XIV

When Shirley opened the bedroom door, she saw nothing but two empty beds. Justice required a sleeping Howard; she would have to advise him to return to bed.

But there was no sound from either the kitchen or the bathroom. Shirley was worried that, by taking the river road home, she had missed him. He must have got dressed and set off for work; he might already be with Maureen in the back room, discussing Shirley; planning, perhaps, to divorce her and marry Maureen instead, now that the game was up, and pretense was ended.

She half ran into the sitting room, intending to telephone the Copper Kettle. Howard was lying on the carpet in his pajamas.

His face was purple and his eyes were popping. A faint wheezing noise came from his lips. One hand was clutching feebly at his chest. His pajama top had ridden up. Shirley could see the very patch of scabbed raw skin where she had planned to plunge the needle.

Howard's eyes met hers in mute appeal.

Shirley stared at him, terrified, then darted out of the room. At first she hid the EpiPen in the biscuit barrel; then she retrieved it and shoved it down the back of the cookery books.

She ran back into the sitting room, seized the telephone receiver and dialed 999.

"Pagford? This is for Orrbank Cottage, is it? There's one on the way."

"Oh, thank you, thank God," said Shirley, and she had almost hung up when she realized what she had said and screamed, "no, no, not Orrbank Cottage…"

But the operator had gone and she had to dial again. She was panicking so much that she dropped the receiver. On the carpet beside her, Howard's wheezing was becoming fainter and fainter.

"Not Orrbank Cottage," she shouted. "Thirty-six Evertree Crescent, Pagford—my husband's having a heart attack…"

XV

In Church Row, Miles Mollison came tearing out of his house in bedroom slippers and sprinted down the steep sloping pavement to the Old Vicarage on the corner. He banged on the thick oak door with his left hand, while trying to dial his wife's number with his right.

"Yes?" said Parminder, opening the door.

"My dad," gasped Miles "…another heart attack…Mum's called an ambulance…will you come? Please, will you come?"

Parminder made a swift move back into the house, mentally seizing her doctor's bag, but checked.

"I can't. I'm suspended from work, Miles. I can't."

"You're joking…please…the ambulance won't be here for—"

"I can't, Miles," she said.

He turned and ran away from her through the open gate. Ahead, he saw Samantha, walking up their garden path. He called to her, his voice breaking, and she turned in surprise. At first, she thought that his panic was on her account.

"Dad…collapsed…there's an ambulance coming…bloody Parminder Jawanda won't come…"

"My God," said Samantha. "Oh my God."

They dashed to the car and drove up the road, Miles in his slippers, Samantha in the clogs that had blistered her feet.

"Miles, listen, there's a siren—it's here already…"

But when they turned into Evertree Crescent, there was nothing there, and the siren was already gone.

On a lawn a mile away, Sukhvinder Jawanda was vomiting river water beneath a willow tree, while an old lady pressed blankets around her that were already as sodden as Sukhvinder's clothes. A short distance away, the dog-walker who had dragged Sukhvinder from the river by her hair and her sweatshirt was bent over a small, limp body.

Sukhvinder had thought she felt Robbie struggling in her arms, but had that been the cruel tug of the river, trying to rip him from her? She was a strong swimmer, but the Orr had dragged her under, pulled her helplessly wherever it chose. She had been swept around the bend, and it had thrown her in towards land, and she had managed a scream, and seen the man with his dog, running towards her along the bank...

"No good," said the man, who had worked on Robbie's little body for twenty minutes. "He's gone."

Sukhvinder wailed, and slumped to the cold wet ground, shaking furiously as the sound of the siren reached them, too late.

Back in Evertree Crescent, the paramedics were having enormous difficulty getting Howard onto the stretcher; Miles and Samantha had to help.

"We'll follow in the car, you go with Dad," Miles shouted at Shirley, who seemed bewildered, and unwilling to get into the ambulance.

Maureen, who had just shown her last customer out of the Copper Kettle, stood on the doorstep, listening.

"Lots of sirens," she said over her shoulder to an exhausted Andrew, who was mopping tables. "Something must have happened."

And she took a deep breath, as though she hoped to taste the tang of disaster on the warm afternoon air.

Part Six

Weaknesses of Voluntary Bodies

22.23 …The main weaknesses of such bodies
are that they are hard to launch, liable to
disintegrate…

Charles Arnold-Baker
Local Council Administration,
Seventh Edition

I

Many, many times had Colin Wall imagined the police coming to his door. They arrived, at last, at dusk on Sunday evening: a woman and a man, not to arrest Colin, but to look for his son.

A fatal accident and "Stuart, is it?" was a witness. "Is he at home?"

"No," said Tessa, "oh, dear God…Robbie Weedon…but he lives in the Fields…why was he here?"

The policewoman explained, kindly, what they believed to have happened. "The teenagers took their eye off him" was the phrase she used.

Tessa thought she might faint.

"You don't know where Stuart is?" asked the policeman.

"No," said Colin, gaunt and shadow-eyed. "Where was he last seen?"

"When our colleague pulled up, Stuart seems to have, ah, run away."

"Oh, dear God," said Tessa again.

"He's not answering," said Colin calmly; he had already dialed Fats on his mobile. "We'll need to go and look for him."

Colin had rehearsed for calamity all his life. He was ready. He took down his coat.

"I'll try Arf," said Tessa, running to the telephone.

Isolated above the little town, no news of the calamities had yet reached Hilltop House. Andrew's mobile rang in the kitchen.

"'Lo," he said, his mouth full of toast.

"Andy, it's Tessa Wall. Is Stu with you?"

"No," he said. "Sorry."

But he was not at all sorry that Fats was not with him.

"Something's happened, Andy. Stu was down at the river with Krystal Weedon, and she had her little brother with her, and the boy's drowned. Stu's run—run off somewhere. Can you think where he might be?"

"No," said Andrew automatically, because that was his and Fats' code. Never tell the parents.

But the horror of what she had just told him crept through the phone like a clammy fog. Everything was suddenly less clear, less certain. She was about to hang up.

"Wait, Mrs. Wall," he said. "I might know…there's a place down by the river…"

"I don't think he'd go near the river now," said Tessa.

Seconds flicked by, and Andrew was more and more convinced that Fats was in the Cubby Hole.

"It's the only place I can think of," he said.

"Tell me where—"

"I'd have to show you."

"I'll be there in ten minutes," she shouted.

Colin was already patrolling the streets of Pagford on foot. Tessa drove the Nissan up the winding hill road, and found Andrew waiting for her on the corner, where he usually caught the bus. He directed her down through the town. The streetlights were feeble by twilight.

They parked by the trees where Andrew usually threw down Simon's racing bike. Tessa got out of the car and followed Andrew to the edge of the water, puzzled and frightened.

"He's not here," she said.

"It's along there," said Andrew, pointing at the sheer dark face of Pargetter Hill, running straight down to the river with barely a lip of bank before the rushing water.

"What do you mean?" asked Tessa, horrified.

Andrew had known from the first that she would not be able to come with him, short and dumpy as she was.

"I'll go and see," he said. "If you wait here."

"But it's too dangerous!" she cried over the roar of the powerful river.

Ignoring her, he reached for the familiar hand- and footholds. As he inched away along the tiny ledge, the same thought came to both of them; that Fats might have fallen, or jumped, into the river thundering so close to Andrew's feet.

Tessa remained at the water's edge until she could not make Andrew out any longer, then turned away, trying not to cry in case Stuart was there, and she needed to talk to him calmly. For the first time, she wondered where Krystal was. The police had not said, and her terror for Fats had obliterated every other concern...

Please God, let me find Stuart, she prayed. *Let me find Stuart, please, God.*

Then she pulled her mobile from her cardigan pocket and called Kay Bawden.

"I don't know whether you've heard," she shouted, over the rushing water, and she told Kay the story.

"But I'm not her social worker anymore," said Kay.

Twenty feet away, Andrew had reached the Cubby Hole. It was pitch black; he had never been here this late. He swung himself inside.

"Fats?"

He heard something move at the back of the hole.

"Fats? You there?"

"Got a light, Arf?" said an unrecognizable voice. "I dropped my bloody matches."

Andrew thought of shouting out to Tessa, but she did not know how long it took to reach the Cubby Hole. She could wait a few more moments.

He passed over his lighter. By its flickering flame, Andrew saw that his friend's appearance was almost as changed as his voice. Fats' eyes were swollen; his whole face looked puffy.

The flame went out. Fats' cigarette tip glowed bright in the darkness.

"Is he dead? Her brother?"

Andrew had not realized that Fats did not know.

"Yeah," he said, and then he added, "I think so. That's what I — what I heard."

There was a silence, and then a soft, piglet-like squeal reached him through the darkness.

"Mrs. Wall," yelled Andrew, sticking his head out of the hole as far as it would go, so that he could not hear Fats' sobs over the sound of the river. "Mrs. Wall, he's here!"

II

The policewoman had been gentle and kind, in the cluttered cottage by the river, where dank water now covered blankets, chintzy chairs and worn rugs. The old lady who owned the place had brought a hot-water bottle and a cup of boiling tea, which Sukhvinder could not lift because she was shaking like a drill. She had disgorged chunks of information: her own name, and Krystal's name, and the name of the dead little boy that they were loading onto an ambulance. The dog walker who had pulled her from the river was rather deaf; he gave a statement to the police in the next room, and Sukhvinder hated the sound of his bellowed account. He had tethered his dog to a tree outside the window, and it whined persistently.

Then the police had called her parents and they had come, Parminder knocking over a table and smashing one of the old lady's ornaments as she crossed the room with clean clothes in her arms. In the tiny bathroom, the deep dirty gash on Sukhvinder's leg was revealed, peppering the fluffy bath mat with black spots, and when Parminder saw the wound she shrieked at Vikram, who was thanking everyone loudly in the hall, that they must take Sukhvinder to the hospital.

She had vomited again in the car, and her mother, who was beside her in the backseat, had mopped her up, and all the way there Parminder and Vikram had kept up a flow of loud talk; her father kept repeating himself, saying things like "She'll need a sedative" and "That cut will definitely need stitches"; and Parminder, who was in the backseat with the shaking and retching Sukhvinder, kept saying, "You might have died. You might have died."

It was as if she was still underwater. Sukhvinder was somewhere she could not breathe. She tried to cut through it all, to be heard.

"Does Krystal know he's dead?" she asked through chattering teeth, and Parminder had to ask her to repeat the question several times.

"I don't know," she answered at last. "You might have died, Jolly."

At the hospital, they made her undress again, but this time her mother was with her in the curtained cubicle, and she realized her mistake too late when she saw the expression of horror on Parminder's face.

"My God," she said, grabbing Sukhvinder's forearm. "My God. What have you done to yourself?"

Sukhvinder had no words, so she allowed herself to subside into tears and uncontrollable shaking, and Vikram shouted at everyone, including Parminder, to leave her alone, but also to damn well hurry up, and that her cut needed cleaning and she needed stitches and sedatives and X-rays...

Later, they put her in a bed with a parent on each side of her, and both of them stroked her hands. She was warm and numb, and there was no pain in her leg anymore. The sky beyond the windows was dark.

"Howard Mollison's had another heart attack," she heard her mother tell her father. "Miles wanted me to go to him."

"Bloody nerve," said Vikram.

To Sukhvinder's drowsy surprise, they talked no more about Howard Mollison. They merely continued to stroke her hands until, shortly afterwards, she fell asleep.

On the far side of the building, in a shabby blue room with plastic chairs and a fish tank in the corner, Miles and Samantha were sitting on either side of Shirley, waiting for news from theater. Miles was still wearing his slippers.

"I can't believe Parminder Jawanda wouldn't come," he said for the umpteenth time, his voice cracking. Samantha got up, moved past Shirley, and put her arms around Miles, kissing his thick hair, speckled with gray, breathing in his familiar smell.

Shirley said, in a high, strangled voice, "I'm not surprised she wouldn't come. I'm not surprised. Absolutely appalling."

All she had left of her old life and her old certainties was attacking familiar targets. Shock had taken almost everything from her: she no longer knew what to believe, or even what to hope. The man in theater was not the man she had thought she had married. If she could have returned to that happy place of certainty, before she had read that awful post...

Perhaps she ought to shut down the whole website. Take away the message boards in their entirety. She was afraid that the Ghost might come back, that he might say the awful thing again...

She wanted to go home, right now, and disable the website; and while there, she could destroy the EpiPen once and for all...

He saw it...I know he saw it...

But I'd never have done it, really. I wouldn't have done it. I was upset. I'd never have done it...

What if Howard survived, and his first words were: "She ran out of the room when she saw me. She didn't call an ambulance straightaway. She was holding a big needle..."

Then I'll say his brain's been affected, Shirley thought defiantly.

And if he died...

Beside her, Samantha was hugging Miles. Shirley did not like it; *she* ought to be the center of attention; it was *her* husband who was lying upstairs, fighting for his life. She had wanted to be like Mary Fairbrother, cosseted and admired, a tragic heroine. This was not how she had imagined it—

"Shirley?"

Ruth Price, in her nurse's uniform, had come hurrying into the room, her thin face forlorn with sympathy.

"I just heard—I had to come—Shirley, how awful, I'm so sorry."

"Ruth, dear," said Shirley, getting up, and allowing herself to be embraced. "That's so kind. So kind."

Shirley liked introducing her medical friend to Miles and Samantha, and receiving her pity and her kindness in front of them. It was a tiny taste of how she had imagined widowhood…

But then Ruth had to go back to work, and Shirley returned to her plastic chair and her uncomfortable thoughts.

"He'll be OK," Samantha was murmuring to Miles, as he rested his head on her shoulder. "I know he'll pull through. He did last time."

Shirley watched little neon-bright fish darting hither and thither in their tank. It was the past that she wished she could change; the future was a blank.

"Has anyone phoned Mo?" Miles asked after a while, wiping his eyes on the back of one hand, while the other gripped Samantha's leg. "Mum, d'you want me to—?"

"No," said Shirley sharply. "We'll wait…until we know."

In the theater upstairs, Howard Mollison's body overflowed the edges of the operating table. His chest was wide open, revealing the ruins of Vikram Jawanda's handiwork. Nineteen people labored to repair the damage, while the machines to which Howard was connected made soft implacable noises, confirming that he continued to live.

And far below, in the bowels of the hospital, Robbie Weedon's body lay frozen and white in the morgue. Nobody had accompanied him to the hospital, and nobody had visited him in his metal drawer.

III

Andrew had refused a lift back to Hilltop House, so it was only Tessa and Fats in the car together, and Fats said, "I don't want to go home."

"All right," Tessa replied, and she drove, while talking to Colin on the telephone. "I've got him...Andy found him. We'll be back in a bit...Yes...Yes, I will..."

Tears were spattering down Fats' face; his body was betraying him; it was exactly like the time when hot urine had spilled down his leg into his sock, when Simon Price had made him piss himself. The hot saltiness leaked over his chin and onto his chest, pattering like drops of rain.

He kept imagining the funeral. A tiny little coffin.

He had not wanted to do it with the boy so near.

Would the weight of the dead child ever lift from him?

"So you ran away," said Tessa coldly, over his tears.

She had prayed that she would find him alive, but her strongest emotion was disgust. His tears did not soften her. She was used to men's tears. Part of her was ashamed that he had not, after all, thrown himself into the river.

"Krystal told the police that you and she were in the bushes. You just left him to his own devices, did you?"

Fats was speechless. He could not believe her cruelty. Did she not understand the desolation roaring inside him, the horror, the sense of contagion?

"Well, I hope you *have* got her pregnant," said Tessa. "It'll give her something to live for."

Every time they turned a corner, he thought that she was taking him home. He had feared Cubby most, but now there was nothing to choose between his parents. He wanted to get out of the car, but she had locked all the doors.

Without warning, she swerved and braked. Fats, clutching the sides of his seat, saw that they were in a lay-by on the Yarvil bypass. Frightened that she would order him out of the car, he turned his swollen face to her.

"Your birth mother," she said, looking at him as she had never done before, without pity or kindness, "was fourteen years old. We had the impression, from what we were told, that she was middle class, quite a bright girl. She absolutely refused to say who your father was. Nobody knew whether she was trying to protect an underage boyfriend or something worse. We were told all of this, in case you had any mental or physical difficulties. In case," she said clearly, like a teacher trying to emphasize a point sure to come up in a test, "you had been the result of incest."

He cowered away from her. He would have preferred to be shot.

"I was desperate to adopt you," she said. "Desperate. But Dad was very ill. He said to me, 'I can't do it. I'm scared I'll hurt a baby. I need to get better before we do this, and I can't do that and cope with a new baby as well.'

"But I was so determined to have you," said Tessa, "That I pressured him into lying, and telling the social workers that he was fine, and pretending to be happy and normal. We brought you home, and you were tiny and premature, and on the fifth night we had you, Dad slipped out of bed and went to the garage, put a hosepipe on the exhaust of the car and tried to kill himself, because he was convinced he'd smothered you. And he almost died.

"So you can blame me," said Tessa, "for your and Dad's bad start, and maybe you can blame me for everything that's come since. But I'll tell you this, Stuart. Your father's spent his life facing up to things he never did. I don't expect you to understand his kind of courage. But," her voice broke at last, and he heard the mother he knew, "he loves you, Stuart."

She added the lie because she could not help herself. Tonight, for the first time, Tessa was convinced that it *was* a lie, and also that everything she had done in her life, telling herself that it was for the best, had been no more than blind selfishness, generating confusion and mess all around. *But who could bear to know which stars were already dead,* she thought, blinking up at the night sky, *could anybody stand to know that they all were?*

She turned the key in the ignition, crashed the gears and they pulled out again onto the bypass.

"I don't want to go to the Fields," said Fats in terror.

"We're not going to the Fields," she said. "I'm taking you home."

IV

The police had picked up Krystal Weedon at last as she ran hopelessly along the riverbank on the very edge of Pagford, still calling her brother in a cracked voice. The policewoman who approached her addressed her by name, and tried to break the news to her gently, but she still tried to beat the woman away from her, and in the end the policewoman had almost to wrestle her into the car. Krystal had not noticed Fats melting away into the trees; he did not exist to her anymore.

The police drove Krystal home, but when they knocked on the front door Terri refused to answer. She had glimpsed them through an upstairs window, and thought that Krystal had done the one unthinkable and unforgivable thing, and told the pigs about the holdalls full of Obbo's hash. She dragged the heavy bags upstairs while the police hammered at the door, and only opened up when she considered that it had become unavoidable.

"Whatcha wan'?" she shouted, through an inch-wide gap in the door.

The policewoman asked to come in three times and Terri refused, still demanding to know what they wanted. A few neighbors had begun to peer through windows. Even when the policewoman said, "It's about your son, Robbie," Terri did not realize.

"'E's fine. There's nuthin' wrong with 'im. Krystal's got 'im."

But then she saw Krystal, who had refused to stay in the car, and had walked halfway up the garden path. Terri's gaze trickled down her daughter's body to the place where Robbie should have been clinging to her, frightened by the strange men.

Terri flew from her house like a fury, with her hands outstretched like claws, and the policewoman had to catch her round the middle and swing her away from Krystal, whose face she was trying to lacerate.

"Yeh little bitch, yeh little bitch, what've yeh done ter Robbie?"

Krystal dodged the struggling pair, darted into the house and slammed the front door behind her.

"For fuck's sake," muttered the policeman under his breath.

Miles away in Hope Street, Kay and Gaia Bawden faced each other in the dark hallway. Neither of them was tall enough to replace the lightbulb that had been dead for days, and they had no ladder. All day long, they had argued and almost made up, then argued again. Finally, at the moment when reconciliation seemed within touching distance, when Kay had agreed that she too hated Pagford, that it had all been a mistake, and that she would try and get them both back to London, her mobile had rung.

"Krystal Weedon's brother's drowned," whispered Kay, as she cut Tessa's call.

"Oh," said Gaia. Knowing that she ought to express pity, but frightened to let discussion of London drop before she had her mother's firm commitment, she added, in a tight little voice, "That's sad."

"It happened here in Pagford," said Kay. "Along the road. Krystal was with Tessa Wall's son."

Gaia felt even more ashamed of letting Fats Wall kiss her. He had tasted horrible, of lager and cigarettes, and he had tried to feel her up. She was worth much more than Fats Wall, she knew that. If it had even been Andy Price, she would have felt better about it. Sukhvinder had not returned one of her calls, all day long.

"She'll be absolutely broken up," said Kay, her eyes unfocused.

"But there's nothing *you* can do," said Gaia. "Is there?"

"Well…" said Kay.

"Not again!" cried Gaia. "It's always, always the same! You're not her social worker anymore! *What,*" she shouted, stamping her foot as she had done when she was a little girl, "about *me?*"

The police officer in Foley Road had already called a duty social worker. Terri was writhing and screaming and trying to beat at the front door, while from behind it came the sounds of furniture being dragged to form a barricade. Neighbors were coming out onto their doorsteps, a fascinated audience to Terri's meltdown. Somehow the cause of it was transmitted through the watchers, from Terri's incoherent shouts and the attitudes of the ominous police.

"The boy's dead," they told each other. Nobody stepped forward to comfort or calm. Terri Weedon had no friends.

479

"Come with me," Kay begged her mutinous daughter. "I'll go to the house and see if I can do anything. I got on with Krystal. She's got nobody."

"I bet she was shagging Fats Wall when it happened!" shouted Gaia; but it was her final protest, and a few minutes later she was buckling herself into Kay's old Vauxhall, glad, in spite of everything, that Kay had asked her along.

But by the time they had reached the bypass, Krystal had found what she was looking for: a bag of heroin concealed in the airing cupboard; the second of two that Obbo had given Terri in payment for Tessa Wall's watch. She took it, with Terri's works, into the bathroom, the only room that had a lock on the door.

Her aunt Cheryl must have heard what had happened, because Krystal could hear her distinctive raucous yell, added to Terri's screams, even through the two doors.

"You little bitch, open the door! Letcha mother see ya!"

And the police shouting, trying to shut the two women up.

Krystal had never shot up before, but she had watched it happen many times. She knew about longboats, and how to make a model volcano, and she knew how to heat the spoon, and about the tiny little ball of cotton wool you used to soak up the dissolved smack, and act as a filter when you were filling the syringe. She knew that the crook of the arm was the best place to find a vein, and she knew to lay the needle as flat as possible against the skin. She knew, because she had heard it said, many times, that first-timers could not take what addicts could manage, and that was good, because she did not want to take it.

Robbie was dead, and it was her fault. In trying to save him, she had killed him. Flickering images filled her mind as her fingers worked to achieve what must be done. Mr. Fairbrother, running alongside the canal bank in his tracksuit as the crew rowed. Nana Cath's face, fierce with pain and love. Robbie, waiting for her at the window of his foster home, unnaturally clean, jumping up and down with excitement as she approached the front door…

She could hear the policeman calling to her through the letter box not to be a silly girl, and the policewoman trying to quieten Terri and Cheryl.

The needle slid easily into Krystal's vein. She pressed the plunger down hard, in hope and without regret.

By the time Kay and Gaia arrived, and the police decided to force their way in, Krystal Weedon had achieved her only ambition: she had joined her brother where nobody could part them.

Part Seven

Relief of Poverty…

13.5   Gifts to benefit the poor…are charitable,
and a gift for the poor is charitable even if it
happens incidentally to benefit the rich…

Charles Arnold-Baker
Local Council Administration,
Seventh Edition

Nearly three weeks after the sirens had wailed through sleepy Pagford, on a sunny morning in April, Shirley Mollison stood alone in her bedroom, squinting at her reflection in the mirrored wardrobe. She was making final adjustments to her dress before her now-daily drive to South West General. The belt buckle slid up a hole tighter than it had done a fortnight ago, her silver hair was in need of a trim and her grimace against the sunshine blazing into the room could have been a simple expression of her mood.

Shirley had walked up and down the wards for a year, wheeling the library trolley, carrying clipboards and flowers, and never once had it occurred to her that she might become one of those poor crumpled women who sat beside beds, their lives derailed, their husbands defeated and weak. Howard had not made the speedy recovery of seven years previously. He was still connected to bleeping machines, withdrawn and feeble, a nasty color, querulously dependent. Sometimes she pretended to need the bathroom to escape his baleful gaze.

When Miles accompanied her to the hospital, she could let him do all the talking to Howard, which he did, keeping up a steady monologue of Pagford news. She felt so much better—both more visible and more protected—with tall Miles walking beside her down the chilly corridors. He chatted genially to the nurses, and handed her in and out of the car, and restored to her the sense of being a rare creature, worthy of care and protection. But Miles could not come every day, and to Shirley's profound irritation he kept deputizing Samantha to accompany her. This was not the same thing at all, even though Samantha was one of the few who managed to bring a smile to Howard's purple vacant face.

Nobody seemed to realize how dreadful the silence was at home either. When the doctors had told the family that recuperation would take months, Shirley had hoped that Miles would ask her to move into the spare room of the big house in Church Row, or that he might stay over, from time to time, in the bungalow. But no: she had been left alone, quite alone, except for a painful three-day period when she had played hostess to Pat and Melly.

I'd never have done it, she reassured herself, automatically, in the silent night, when she could not sleep. *I never really meant to. I was just upset. I'd never have done it.*

She had buried Andrew's EpiPen in the soft earth beneath the bird table in the garden, like a tiny corpse. She did not like knowing it was there. Some dark evening soon, the night before refuse-collection day, she would dig it up again and slip it into a neighbor's bin.

Howard had not mentioned the needle to her or to anyone. He had not asked her why she had run away when she saw him.

Shirley found relief in long rattling streams of invective, directed at the people who had, in her stated opinion, caused the catastrophe that had fallen on her family. Parminder Jawanda was the first of these, naturally, for her callous refusal to attend Howard. Then there were the two teenagers who, through their vile irresponsibility, had diverted the ambulance that might have reached Howard sooner.

The latter argument was perhaps a little weak, but it was the enjoyable fashion to denigrate Stuart Wall and Krystal Weedon, and Shirley found plenty of willing listeners in her immediate circle. What was more, it had transpired that the Wall boy had been the Ghost of Barry Fairbrother all along. He had confessed to his parents, and they had personally telephoned the victims of the boy's spite to apologize. The Ghost's identity had leaked swiftly into the wider community, and this, coupled with the knowledge that he had been jointly responsible for the drowning of a three-year-old child, made abuse of Stuart both a duty and a pleasure.

Shirley was more vehement in her comments than anybody. There was a savagery in her denunciations, each of them a little exorcism of the kinship and admiration she had felt for the Ghost, and a repudiation of that awful last post which nobody else, as yet, had admitted to seeing. The Walls had not telephoned Shirley to apologize, but she was constantly primed, in case the boy should mention it to his parents, or in case anybody should bring it up, to deliver a final crushing blow to Stuart's reputation.

"Oh yes, Howard and I know all about it," she planned to say, with icy dignity, "and it's my belief that the shock caused his heart attack."

She had actually practiced saying this aloud in the kitchen.

The question of whether Stuart Wall had really known something about her husband and Maureen was less urgent now, because Howard was patently incapable of shaming her in that way again, and perhaps never would be, and nobody seemed to be gossiping. And if the silence she offered Howard, when she was unavoidably alone with him, was tinged with a sense of grievance on both sides, she was able to face the prospect of his protracted incapacitation and absence from the house with more equanimity than she might have thought possible three weeks previously.

The doorbell rang and Shirley hurried to open it. Maureen was there, hobbling on ill-advised high heels, garish in bright aquamarine.

"Hello, dear, come in," said Shirley. "I'll get my bag."

It was better to take even Maureen to the hospital than to go alone. Maureen was not fazed by Howard's dumbness; her croaky voice ground on and on, and Shirley could sit in peace, smile a pussycat smile and relax. In any case, as Shirley had taken temporary control of Howard's share in the business, she was finding plenty of ways to work off her lingering suspicions by administering sharp little slaps in the form of disagreement with Maureen's every decision.

"You know what's happening down the road?" Maureen asked. "At St. Michael's? *The Weedon kids' funerals.*"

"*Here?*" said Shirley, horrified.

"They're saying people got up a collection," said Maureen, brimful of gossip that Shirley had somehow missed, in her endless back and forward trips to the hospital. "Don't ask me who. Anyway, I wouldn't have thought the family would want it right by the river, would you?"

(The dirty and foul-mouthed little boy, of whose existence few had been aware, and of whom nobody but his mother and sister had been especially fond, had undergone such a transformation in Pagford's collective mind by his drowning, that he was spoken of everywhere as a water baby, a cherub, a pure and gentle angel whom all would have embraced with love and compassion, if only they could have saved him.

But the needle and the flame had had no transformative effect upon Krystal's reputation; on the contrary, they had fixed her permanently in the mind of Old Pagford as a soulless creature whose pursuit of what the elderly liked to call kicks had led to the death of an innocent child.)

Shirley was pulling on her coat.

"You realize, I actually saw them that day?" she said, her cheeks turning pink. "The boy bawling by one clump of bushes, and Krystal Weedon and Stuart Wall in another—"

"*Did you?* And were they really...?" asked Maureen avidly.

"Oh yes," said Shirley. "Broad daylight. Open air. And the boy was right by the river when I saw him. A couple of steps and he'd have been in."

Something in Maureen's expression stung her.

"I was hurrying," said Shirley with asperity, "because Howard had said he was feeling poorly and I was worried sick. I didn't want to go out at all, but Miles and Samantha had sent Lexie over—I think, if you want my honest opinion, they'd had a row—and then Lexie wanted to visit the café—I was absolutely distracted, and all I could think was, *I must get back to Howard*...I didn't actually *realize* what I'd seen until much later...and the dreadful thing," said Shirley, her color higher than ever, and returning again to her favorite refrain, "is that if Krystal Weedon hadn't let that child wander off while she was having her fun in the bushes, the ambulance would have reached Howard so much more quickly. Because, you know, with two of them coming...things got confu—"

"That's right," said Maureen, interrupting as they moved out towards the car, because she had heard all this before. "You know, I can't *think* why they're having the service here in Pagford..."

She longed to suggest that they drive past the church on the way to the hospital—she had a craving to see what the Weedon family looked like en masse, and to glimpse, perhaps, that degenerate junkie mother—but could think of no way to frame the request.

"You know, there's one comfort, Shirley," she said, as they set off for the bypass. "The Fields are as good as gone. That must be a comfort to Howard. Even if he can't attend council for a while, he got that done."

Andrew Price was speeding down the steep hill from Hilltop House, with the sun hot on his back and the wind in his hair. His week-old shiner had turned yellow and green, and looked, if possible, even worse than it had when he had turned up at school with his eye almost closed. Andrew had told the teachers who inquired that he had fallen off his bike.

It was now the Easter holidays, and Gaia had texted Andrew the previous evening to ask whether he would be going to Krystal's funeral the next day. He had sent an immediate "yes," and was now dressed, after much deliberation, in his cleanest jeans and a dark gray shirt, because he did not own a suit.

He was not very clear why Gaia was going to the funeral, unless it was to be with Sukhvinder Jawanda, to whom she seemed to cling more fondly than ever, now that she was moving back to London with her mother.

"Mum says she should never have come to Pagford," Gaia had told Andrew and Sukhvinder happily, as the three of them sat on the low wall beside the newsagent's at lunchtime. "She knows Gavin's a total twat."

She had given Andrew her mobile number and told him that they would go out together when she came to Reading to see her father, and even mentioned, casually, taking him to see some of her favorite places in London, if he visited. She was showering benefits around her in the manner of a demob-happy soldier, and these promises, made so lightly, gilded the prospect of Andrew's own move. He had greeted the news that his parents had had an offer on Hilltop House with at least as much excitement as pain.

The sweeping turn into Church Row, usually made with an uplift of spirits, dampened them. He could see people moving around in the graveyard, and he wondered what this funeral was going to be like, and for the first time that morning thought of Krystal Weedon in more than the abstract.

A memory, long buried in the deepest recesses of his mind, came back to him, of that time in the playground at St. Thomas's, when Fats, in a spirit of disinterested investigation, had handed him a peanut hidden inside a marshmallow…he could still feel his burning throat closing inexorably. He remembered trying to yell, and his knees giving way, and the children all around him, watching with a strange, bloodless interest, and then Krystal Weedon's raucous scream.

"Andiprice iz 'avin' a 'lurgycacshun!"

She had run, on her stocky little legs, all the way to the staff room, and the headmaster had snatched Andrew up and sprinted with him to the nearby surgery, where Dr. Crawford had administered Adrenalin. She was the only one who had remembered the talk that their teacher had given the class, explaining Andrew's life-threatening condition; the only one to recognize his symptoms.

Krystal ought to have been given a gold merit star, and perhaps a certificate at assembly as Pupil of the Week, but the very next day (Andrew remembered it as clearly as his own collapse) she had hit Lexie Mollison so hard in the mouth that she had knocked out two of Lexie's teeth.

He wheeled Simon's bike carefully into the Walls' garage, then rang the doorbell with a reluctance that had never been there before. Tessa Wall answered, dressed in her best gray coat. Andrew was annoyed with her; it was down to her that he had a black eye.

"Come in, Andy," said Tessa, and her expression was tense. "We'll just be a minute."

He waited in the hallway, where the colored glass over the door cast its paintboxy glow on the floorboards. Tessa marched into the kitchen, and Andrew glimpsed Fats in his black suit, crumpled up in a kitchen chair like a crushed spider, with one arm over his head, as if he were fending off blows.

Andrew turned his back. The two boys had had no communication since Andrew had led Tessa to the Cubby Hole. Fats had not been to school for a fortnight. Andrew had sent a couple of texts, but Fats had not replied. His Facebook page remained frozen as it had been on the day of Howard Mollison's party.

A week ago, without warning, Tessa had telephoned the Prices, told them that Fats had admitted to having posted the messages under the name The_Ghost_of_Barry_Fairbrother, and offered her deepest apologies for the consequences they had suffered.

"So how did he know I had that computer?" Simon had roared, advancing on Andrew. "How did fucking Fats Wall know I did jobs after hours at the printworks?"

Andrew's only consolation was that if his father had known the truth, he might have ignored Ruth's protests and continued to pummel Andrew until he was unconscious.

Why Fats had decided to pretend he had authored all the posts, Andrew did not know. Perhaps it was Fats' ego at work, his determination to be the mastermind, the most destructive, the baddest of them all. Perhaps he had thought he was doing something noble, taking the fall for both of them. Either way, Fats had caused much more trouble than he knew; he had never realized, thought Andrew, waiting in the hall, what it was like to live with a father like Simon Price, safe in his attic room, with his reasonable, civilized parents.

Andrew could hear the adult Walls talking in quiet voices; they had not closed the kitchen door.

"We need to leave *now*," Tessa was saying. "He's got a moral obligation and he's going."

"He's had enough punishment," said Cubby's voice.

"I'm not asking him to go as a—"

"Aren't you?" said Cubby sharply. "For God's sake, Tessa. D'you think they'll want him there? You go. Stu can stay here with me."

A minute later Tessa emerged from the kitchen, closing the door firmly behind her.

"Stu isn't coming, Andy," she said, and he could tell that she was furious about it. "I'm sorry about that."

"No problem," he muttered. He was glad. He could not imagine what they had left to talk about. This way he could sit with Gaia.

A little way down Church Row, Samantha Mollison was standing at her sitting-room window, holding a coffee and watching mourners pass her house on their way to St. Michael and All Saints. When she saw Tessa Wall, and what she thought was Fats, she let out a little gasp.

"Oh my God, he's going," she said out loud, to nobody.

Then she recognized Andrew, turned red, and backed hastily away from the glass.

Samantha was supposed to be working from home. Her laptop lay open behind her on the sofa, but that morning she had put on an old black dress, half wondering whether she would attend Krystal and Robbie Weedon's funeral. She supposed that she had only a few more minutes in which to make up her mind.

She had never spoken a kind word about Krystal Weedon, so surely it would be hypocritical to attend her funeral, purely because she had wept over the account of her death in the *Yarvil and District Gazette,* and because Krystal's chubby face grinned out of every one of the class photographs that Lexie had brought home from St. Thomas's?

Samantha set down her coffee, hurried to the telephone and rang Miles at work.

"Hello, babe," he said.

(She had held him while he sobbed with relief beside the hospital bed, where Howard lay connected to machines, but alive.)

"Hi," she said. "How are you?"

"Not bad. Busy morning. Lovely to hear from you," he said. "Are you all right?"

(They had made love the previous night, and she had not pretended that he was anybody else.)

"The funeral's about to start," said Samantha. "People going by…"

She had suppressed what she wanted to say for nearly three weeks, because of Howard, and the hospital, and not wanting to remind Miles of their awful row, but she could not hold it back any longer.

"…Miles, *I saw that boy*. Robbie Weedon. *I saw him, Miles*." She was panicky, pleading. "He was in the St. Thomas's playing field when I walked across it that morning."

"In the playing field?"

"He must have been wandering around, while they were—he was all alone," she said, remembering the sight of him, dirty and unkempt. She kept asking herself whether, if he had looked cleaner, she might have been more concerned; whether, on some subliminal level, she had confused his obvious signs of neglect with street-smartness, toughness and resilience. "I thought he'd come in there to play, but there was nobody with him. *He was only three and a half, Miles*. Why didn't I ask him who he was with?"

"Hey, hey," said Miles, in a "whoa there" voice, and she knew instant relief: he was taking charge, and her eyes pricked with tears. "You're not to blame. You couldn't have known. You probably thought his mother was somewhere out of sight."

(So he did not hate her; he did not think her evil. Samantha had been humbled, lately, by her husband's capacity to forgive.)

"I'm not sure I did," she said weakly. "Miles, if I'd spoken to him…"

"He was nowhere near the river when you saw him."

But he was near the road, thought Samantha.

In the last three weeks, a desire to be absorbed in something bigger than herself had grown in Samantha. Day by day she had waited for the strange new need to subside (*this is how people go religious,* she thought, trying to laugh herself out of it), but it had, if anything, intensified.

"Miles," she said, "you know the council…with your dad—and Parminder Jawanda resigning too—you'll want to co-opt a couple of people, won't you?" She knew all the terminology; she had listened to it for years. "I mean, you won't want another election, after all this?"

"Bloody hell, no."

"So Colin Wall could fill one seat," she rushed on, "and I was thinking, I've got time—now the business is all online—I could do the other one."

"You?" said Miles, astonished.

"I'd like to get involved," said Samantha.

Krystal Weedon, dead at sixteen, barricaded inside the squalid little house on Foley Road...Samantha had not drunk a glass of wine in two weeks. She thought that she might like to hear the arguments for Bellchapel Addiction Clinic.

The telephone was ringing in number Ten Hope Street. Kay and Gaia were already late leaving for Krystal's funeral. When Gaia asked who was speaking, her lovely face hardened: she seemed much older.

"It's Gavin," she told her mother.

"I didn't call him!" whispered Kay, like a nervous schoolgirl as she took the phone.

"Hi," said Gavin. "How are you?"

"On my way out to a funeral," said Kay, with her eyes locked on her daughter's. "The Weedon children's. So, not fabulous."

"Oh," said Gavin. "Christ, yeah. Sorry. I didn't realize."

He had spotted the familiar surname in a *Yarvil and District Gazette* headline, and, vaguely interested at last, bought a copy. It had occurred to him that he might have walked close by the place where the teenagers and the boy had been, but he had no actual memory of seeing Robbie Weedon.

Gavin had had an odd couple of weeks. He was missing Barry badly. He did not understand himself: when he should have been mired in misery that Mary had turned him down, all he wanted was a beer with the man whose wife he had hoped to take as his own...

(Muttering aloud as he had walked away from her house, he had said to himself, "That's what you get for trying to steal your best friend's life," and failed to notice the slip of the tongue.)

"Listen," he said, "I was wondering whether you fancied a drink later?"

Kay almost laughed.

"Turn you down, did she?"

She handed Gaia the phone to hang up. They hurried out of the house and half jogged to the end of the street and up through the Square. For ten strides, as they passed the Black Canon, Gaia held her mother's hand.

They arrived as the hearses appeared at the top of the road, and hurried into the graveyard while the pallbearers were shuffling out onto the pavement.

("Get away from the window," Colin Wall commanded his son.

But Fats, who had to live henceforth with the knowledge of his own cowardice, moved forward, trying to prove that he could, at least, take this...

The coffins glided past in the big black-windowed cars: the first was bright pink, and the sight robbed him of breath, and the second was tiny and shiny white...

Colin placed himself in front of Fats too late to protect him, but he drew the curtains anyway. In the gloomy, familiar sitting room, where Fats had confessed to his parents that he had exposed his father's illness to the world; where he had confessed to as much as he could think of, in the hope that they would conclude him to be mad and ill; where he had tried to heap upon himself so much blame that they would beat him or stab him or do to him all those things that he knew he deserved, Colin put a hand gently on his son's back and steered him away, towards the sunlit kitchen.)

Outside St. Michael and All Saints, the pallbearers were readying themselves to take the coffins up the church path. Dane Tully was among them, with his earring and a self-inked tattoo of a spider's web on his neck, in a heavy black overcoat.

The Jawandas waited with the Bawdens in the shade of the yew tree. Andrew Price hovered near them, and Tessa Wall stood at some distance, pale and stony-faced. The other mourners formed a separate phalanx around the church doors. Some had a pinched and defiant air; others looked resigned and defeated; a few wore cheap black clothes, but most were in jeans or tracksuits, and one girl was sporting a cut-off T-shirt and a belly-ring that caught the sun when she moved. The coffins moved up the path, gleaming in the bright light.

It was Sukhvinder Jawanda who had chosen the bright pink coffin for Krystal, as she was sure she would have wanted. It was Sukhvinder who had done nearly everything; organizing, choosing and persuading. Parminder kept looking sideways at her daughter, and finding excuses to touch her: brushing her hair out of her eyes, smoothing her collar.

Just as Robbie had come out of the river purified and regretted by Pagford, so Sukhvinder Jawanda, who had risked her life to try and save the boy, had emerged a heroine. From the article about her in the *Yarvil and District Gazette* to Maureen Lowe's loud proclamations that she was recommending the girl for a special police award to the speech her headmistress made about her from the lectern in assembly, Sukhvinder knew, for the first time, what it was to eclipse her brother and sister.

She had hated every minute of it. At night, she felt again the dead boy's weight in her arms, dragging her towards the deep; she remembered the temptation to let go and save herself, and asked herself how long she would have resisted it. The deep scar on her leg itched and ached, whether moving or stationary. The news of Krystal Weedon's death had had such an alarming effect on her that her parents had arranged a counselor, but she had not cut herself once since being pulled from the river; her near drowning seemed to have purged her of the need.

Then, on her first day back at school, with Fats Wall still absent, and admiring stares following her down the corridors, she had heard the rumor that Terri Weedon had no money to bury her children; that there would be no stone marker, and the cheapest coffins.

"That's very sad, Jolly," her mother had said that evening, as the family sat eating dinner together under the wall of family photographs. Her tone was as gentle as the policewoman's had been; there was no snap in Parminder's voice anymore when she spoke to her daughter.

"I want to try and get people to give money," said Sukhvinder.

Parminder and Vikram glanced at each other across the kitchen table. Both were instinctively opposed to the idea of asking people in Pagford to donate to such a cause, but neither of them said so. They were a little afraid, now that they had seen her forearms, of upsetting Sukhvinder, and the shadow of the as-yet-unknown counselor seemed to be hovering over all their interactions.

"And," Sukhvinder went on, with a feverish energy like

Parminder's own, "I think the funeral service should be here, at St. Michael's. Like Mr. Fairbrother's. Krys used to go to all the services here when we were at St. Thomas's. I bet she was never in another church in her life."

The light of God shines from every soul, thought Parminder, and to Vikram's surprise she said abruptly, "Yes, all right. We'll have to see what we can do."

The bulk of the expense had been met by the Jawandas and the Walls, but Kay Bawden, Samantha Mollison and a couple of the mothers of girls on the rowing team had donated money too. Sukhvinder then insisted on going into the Fields in person, to explain to Terri what they had done, and why; all about the rowing team, and why Krystal and Robbie should have a service at St. Michael's.

Parminder had been exceptionally worried about Sukhvinder going into the Fields, let alone that filthy house, by herself, but Sukhvinder had known that it would be all right. The Weedons and the Tullys knew that she had tried to save Robbie's life. Dane Tully had stopped grunting at her in English, and had stopped his mates from doing it too.

Terri agreed to everything that Sukhvinder suggested. She was emaciated, dirty, monosyllabic and entirely passive. Sukhvinder had been frightened of her, with her pockmarked arms and her missing teeth; it was like talking to a corpse.

Inside the church, the mourners divided cleanly, with the people from the Fields taking the left-hand pews, and those from Pagford, the right. Shane and Cheryl Tully marched Terri along between them to the front row; Terri, in a coat two sizes too large, seemed scarcely aware of where she was.

The coffins lay side by side on biers at the front of the church. A bronze chrysanthemum oar lay on Krystal's, and a white chrysanthemum teddy bear on Robbie's.

Kay Bawden remembered Robbie's bedroom, with its few grimy plastic toys, and her fingers trembled on the order of service. Naturally, there was to be an inquiry at work, because the local paper was clamoring for one, and had written a front-page piece suggesting that the small boy had been left in the care of a pair of junkies and that his death could have been avoided, if only he had been removed to safety by negligent social workers. Mattie had been signed off with stress again, and Kay's handling of the case review was being assessed. Kay wondered what effect it would have on her chances of getting another job in London, when every local authority was cutting numbers of social workers, and how Gaia would react if they had to stay in Pagford...she had not dared discuss it with her yet.

Andrew glanced sideways at Gaia and they exchanged small smiles. Up in Hilltop House, Ruth was already sorting things for the move. Andrew could tell that his mother hoped, in her perennially optimistic way, that by sacrificing their house and the beauty of the hills, they would be rewarded with a rebirth. Wedded forever to an idea of Simon that took no account of his rages or his crookedness, she was hoping that these would be left behind, like boxes forgotten in the move...But at least, Andrew thought, he would be one step nearer London when they went, and he had Gaia's assurance that she had been too drunk to know what she was doing with Fats, and perhaps she might invite him and Sukhvinder back to her house for coffee after the funeral was over...

Gaia, who had never been inside St. Michael's before, was half listening to the vicar's singsong delivery, letting her eyes travel over the high starry ceiling and the jewel-colored windows. There was a prettiness about Pagford that, now she knew that she was leaving, she thought she might quite miss...

Tessa Wall had chosen to sit behind everyone else, on her own. This brought her directly under the calm gaze of St. Michael, whose foot rested eternally on that writhing devil with its horns and tail. Tessa had been in tears ever since her first glimpse of the two glossy coffins and, as much as she tried to stifle them, her soft gurglings were still audible to those near her. She had half expected somebody on the Weedon side of the church to recognize her as Fats' mother and attack her, but nothing had happened.

(Her family life had turned inside out. Colin was furious with her.

"You told him what?"

498

"He wanted a taste of real life," she had sobbed, "he wanted to see the seamy underside — don't you understand what all that slumming it was about?"

"So you told him that he might be the result of incest, and that I tried to kill myself because he came into the family?"

Years of trying to reconcile them, and it had taken a dead child, and Colin's profound understanding of guilt, to do it. She had heard the two of them talking in Fats' attic room the previous evening, and paused to eavesdrop at the foot of the stairs.

"...you can put that — that thing that Mum suggested out of your head completely," Colin was saying gruffly. "You've got no physical or mental abnormalities, have you? Well then...don't worry about it anymore. But your counselor will help you with all of this...")

Tessa gurgled and snorted into her sodden tissue, and thought how little she had done for Krystal, dead on the bathroom floor... it would have been a relief if St. Michael had stepped down from his glowing window and enacted judgment on them all, decreeing exactly how much fault was hers, for the deaths, for the broken lives, for the mess...A fidgeting young Tully boy on the other side of the aisle hopped out of his pew, and a tattooed woman reached out a powerful arm, grabbed him and pulled him back. Tessa's sobs were punctuated by a little gasp of surprise. She was sure that she had recognized her own lost watch on the thick wrist.

Sukhvinder, who was listening to Tessa's sobs, felt sorry for her, but did not dare turn around. Parminder was furious with Tessa. There had been no way for Sukhvinder to explain the scars on her arms without mentioning Fats Wall. She had begged her mother not to call the Walls, but then Tessa had telephoned Parminder to tell them that Fats had taken full responsibility for The_Ghost_of_Barry_Fairbrother's posts on the council website, and Parminder had been so vitriolic on the telephone that they had not spoken since.

It had been such a strange thing for Fats to do, to take the blame for her post too; Sukhvinder thought of it almost as an apology. He had always seemed to read her mind: did he know that she had attacked her own mother? Sukhvinder wondered whether she would be able to confess the truth to this new counselor in whom her parents seemed to place so much faith, and whether she would ever be able to tell the newly kind and contrite Parminder...

She was trying to follow the service, but it was not helping her in the way that she had hoped. She was glad about the chrysanthemum oar and the teddy bear, which Lauren's mum had made; she was glad that Gaia and Andy had come, and the girls from the rowing team, but she wished that the Fairbrother twins had not refused.

("It'd upset Mum," Siobhan had told Sukhvinder. "See, she thinks Dad spent too much time on Krystal."

"Oh," said Sukhvinder, taken aback.

"And," said Niamh, "Mum doesn't like the idea that she'll have to see Krystal's grave every time we visit Dad's. They'll probably be really near each other."

Sukhvinder thought these objections small and mean, but it seemed sacrilegious to apply such terms to Mrs. Fairbrother. The twins walked away, wrapped up in each other as they always were these days, and treating Sukhvinder with coolness for her defection to the outsider, Gaia Bawden.)

Sukhvinder kept waiting for somebody to stand up and talk about who Krystal really was, and what she had done in her life, the way that Niamh and Siobhan's uncle had done for Mr. Fairbrother, but apart from the vicar's brief reference to "tragically short lives" and "local family with deep roots in Pagford," he seemed determined to skirt the facts.

So Sukhvinder focused her thoughts on the day that their crew had competed in the regional finals. Mr. Fairbrother had driven them in the minibus to face the girls from St. Anne's. The canal ran right through the private school's grounds, and it had been decided that they were to change in the St. Anne's sports hall, and start the race there.

"Unsporting, course it is," Mr. Fairbrother had told them on the way. "Home-ground advantage. I tried to get it changed, but they wouldn't. Just don't be intimidated, all right?"

"I ain' fuck—"

"Krys—"

"I ain' scared."

But when they turned into the grounds, Sukhvinder was scared. Long stretches of soft green lawn, and a big symmetrical golden-stoned building with spires and a hundred windows: she had never seen anything like it, except on picture postcards.

"It's like Buckingham Palace!" Lauren shrieked from the back, and Krystal's mouth had formed a round O; she had been as unaffected as a child sometimes.

All of their parents, and Krystal's great-grandmother, were waiting at the finishing line, wherever that was. Sukhvinder was sure that she was not the only one who felt small, scared and inferior as they approached the entrance of the beautiful building.

A woman in academic dress came swooping out to greet Mr. Fairbrother, in his tracksuit.

"You must be Winterdown!"

"Course 'e's not, does 'e look like a fuckin' buildin'?" said Krystal loudly.

They were sure that the teacher from St. Anne's had heard, and Mr. Fairbrother turned and tried to scowl at Krystal, but they could tell that he thought it was funny, really. The whole team started to giggle, and they were still snorting and cackling when Mr. Fairbrother saw them off at the entrance to the changing rooms.

"Stretch!" he shouted after them.

The team from St. Anne's was inside with their own coach. The two sets of girls eyed each other across the benches. Sukhvinder was struck by the other team's hair. All of them wore it long, natural and shiny: they could have starred in shampoo adverts. On their own team, Siobhan and Niamh had bobs, Lauren's hair was short; Krystal always wore hers in a tight, high ponytail, and Sukhvinder's was rough, thick and unruly as a horse's mane.

She thought she saw two of the St. Anne's girls exchange whispers and smirks, and was sure of it when Krystal suddenly stood tall, glaring at them, and said, "s'pose your shit smells of roses, does it?"

"I *beg* your pardon?" said their coach.

"Jus' askin'," said Krystal sweetly, turning her back to pull off her tracksuit bottoms.

The urge to giggle had been too powerful to resist; the Winterdown team snorted with laughter as they changed. Krystal clowned away, and as the St. Anne's crew filed out she mooned them.

"Charming," said the last girl to leave.

"Thanks a lot," Krystal called after her. "I'll let yer 'ave another look later, if yeh want. I know yeh're all lezzers," she yelled, "stuck in 'ere together with no boys!"

Holly had laughed so much that she had doubled over and banged her head on the locker door.

"Fuckin' watch it, Hol," Krystal had said, delighted with the effect she was having on them all. "Yeh'll need yer 'ead."

As they had trooped down to the canal, Sukhvinder could see why Mr. Fairbrother had wanted the venue changed. There was nobody but him here to support them at the start, whereas the St. Anne's crew had lots of friends shrieking and applauding and jumping up and down on the spot, all with the same kind of glossy long hair.

"Look!" shouted Krystal, pointing into this group as they passed. "It's Lexie Mollison! Remember when I knocked yer teeth out, Lex?"

Sukhvinder had a pain from laughing. She was glad and proud to be walking along behind Krystal, and she could tell that the others were too. Something about how Krystal faced the world was protecting them from the effect of the staring eyes and the fluttering bunting, and the building like a palace in the background.

But she could tell that even Krystal was feeling the pressure as they climbed into their boat. Krystal turned to Sukhvinder, who always sat behind her. She was holding something in her hand.

"Good-luck charm," she said, showing her.

It was a red plastic heart on a key ring, with a picture of her little brother in it.

"I've told 'im I'm gonna bring 'im back a medal," said Krystal.

"Yeah," said Sukhvinder, with a rush of faith and fear. "We will."

"Yeah," said Krystal, facing front again, and tucking the key ring back inside her bra. "No competition, this lot," she said loudly, so the whole crew could hear. "Bunch o' muff munchers. Le's do 'em!"

Sukhvinder remembered the starting gun and the crowd's cheers and her muscles screaming. She remembered her elation at their perfect rhythm, and the pleasure of their deadly seriousness after laughter. Krystal had won it for them. Krystal had taken away the home-ground advantage. Sukhvinder wished that she could be like Krystal: funny and tough; impossible to intimidate; always coming out fighting.

She had asked Terri Weedon for two things, and they had been granted, because Terri agreed with everyone, always. The medal that Krystal had won that day was around her neck for her burial. The other request came, at the very end of the service, and this time, as he announced it, the vicar sounded resigned.

Good girl gone bad —
Take three —
Action.
No clouds in my storms…
Let it rain, I hydroplane into fame
Comin' down with the Dow Jones…

Her family half carried Terri Weedon back down the royal blue carpet, and the congregation averted its eyes.

J.K. ROWLING is the author of the bestselling Harry Potter series of seven books, published between 1997 and 2007, which have sold over 450 million copies worldwide, are distributed in more than 200 territories, have been translated into 73 languages, and have been turned into 8 blockbuster films.

As well as an Order of the British Empire for services to children's literature, J.K. Rowling is the recipient of numerous awards and honorary degrees, including the Prince of Asturias Award for Concord, France's Légion d'honneur, and the Hans Christian Andersen Award, and she has been a commencement speaker at Harvard University. She supports a wide number of causes and is the founder of Lumos, which works to transform the lives of disadvantaged children.